INFLUENCER

INFLUENCER

ADAM CESARE

**UNION
SQUARE
& CO.**

NEW YORK

UNION
SQUARE
& CO.
NEW YORK

UNION SQUARE & CO. and the distinctive Union Square & Co. logo
are trademarks of Sterling Publishing Co., Inc.

Union Square & Co., LLC, is a subsidiary of Sterling Publishing Co., Inc.

Text © 2024 Temple Hill Publishing
Cover illustration © 2024 Union Square & Co., LLC

ISBN 978-1-4549-5424-8
ISBN 978-1-4549-5425-5 (e-book)

Library of Congress Cataloging-in-Publication Data

Names: Cesare, Adam, author.
Title: Influencer / Adam Cesare.
Description: New York : Union Square & Co., 2024. | Audience: Ages 14 and
up. | Audience: Grades 10-12. | Summary: Told in alternating voices,
teenage Crystal discovers Aaron, the charismatic new boy in school, has
a dark and violent secret.
Identifiers: LCCN 2023055178 (print) | LCCN 2023055179 (ebook) | ISBN
9781454954248 (trade paperback) | ISBN 9781454954255 (epub)
Subjects: CYAC; Interpersonal relations--Fiction. | Social media--Fiction.
| Psychopaths--Fiction. | High schools--Fiction. | Schools--Fiction. |
Horror stories. | BISAC: YOUNG ADULT FICTION / Thrillers & Suspense /
Psychological | YOUNG ADULT FICTION / Horror | LCGFT: Horror fiction. |
Thrillers (Fiction) | Novels.
Classification: LCC PZ7.1.C46498 In 2024 (print) | LCC PZ7.1.C46498
(ebook) | DDC [Fic]--dc23
LC record available at https://lccn.loc.gov/2023055178
LC ebook record available at https://lccn.loc.gov/2023055179

For information about custom editions, special sales, and premium purchases,
please contact specialsales@unionsquareandco.com.

Printed in Canada

2 4 6 8 10 9 7 5 3

unionsquareandco.com

Cover and interior design by Liam Donnelly
Cover illustration by Tomasz Majewski

For MQ. My newest, biggest influence.

CONTENT WARNING

Please note: This novel contains themes of graphic violence, sexual assault, animal death, and drug addiction. Reader discretion is advised.

NIGHTTIME IN ARIZONA

LARISSA

I wake to a loud noise, and then the baby kicks.

Or maybe the baby kicked first.

I'm disoriented.

Back when I had cheerleading practice in the afternoons, I used to be able to catnap. I'd sleep for forty-five minutes exactly, didn't need to set an alarm, and would wake refreshed.

But now I nap all the time. And the naps aren't restful. They *disorient* me.

I roll over, off my left side, and stare at the ceiling. Above me are half-peeled-away superhero stickers and glow-in-the-dark plastic stars.

This isn't my room. This is Todd's room.

These last few weeks I've been napping in here. I do this knowing that after Mom and Dad make him sit for dinner, Todd will run up to his room. He'll evict me so he can play video games, and I won't mistakenly sleep through the night. A little-brother alarm clock. With no snooze button because I'm not allowed to punch him.

But tonight is different.

What *was* that sound that woke me?

There are some more noises, downstairs in the den, and the fogginess in my head clears a bit as I realize why my heart's racing.

There are people in my house.

What does that mean, though? "People." This could be a pregnancy-brain nap dream; I've had them before. Anxiety is turning into a heaviness in my belly, the weight of the baby pinning me down to the bed.

It's possible that I'm safe and my baby is safe and the loud sound that's woken us both was in my head, part of a dream.

But still, I lie here in my partial sleep paralysis and strain to listen.

There are always people in the house, Larissa, I try reasoning with myself.

They're called your family.

But the sounds downstairs aren't *family* sounds.

I can hear them, unfamiliar voices and heavy footsteps.

It's not Mom's knitting circle. Those are on the weekends. Todd doesn't have any friends, so it's not like he has people over. If it were Dad's buddies, the neighborhood's low-stakes poker brigade, they'd be in the garage and—

"She's not in her room!" a voice yells. Whoever it is, they're down the hall. They're on the second floor with me.

Who *is* that? It's not an adult voice. It's a boy's voice. A boy my age. I don't recognize who, though. It's not one of my friends or any of Brendan's friends I can remember.

"She has to be here," another voice answers him from downstairs. A girl's voice. "We would have seen her leave!"

There are young people in my house, young people who I don't know . . . I try to quickly think of a plausible reason they could be here.

I haven't been to school in weeks. I'm not going back until the baby's here, maybe never. I get all my assignments via Google Drive.

Is this the senior prank?

No. It's not that. And it's not Brendan coming over, insisting to see me when my parents won't allow it.

I hear a floorboard creak in the hallway.

There's somebody headed this way.

The tendrils of sleep that have been holding me to Todd's twin bed release, and moving is no longer a problem.

I rise from the bed the best I can, feeling heavy, my sore back and swollen belly slowing me down.

I used to be in good shape. No, not good shape; I used to be in *great* shape. Better shape than most of the athletes we cheer alongside.

I love the baby already, even though we haven't met, but I hate the way the baby makes my body feel.

Downstairs, there's the shuffle-thud of somebody moving furniture. This is serious. I think we're being robbed.

Angling my head over, I look out Todd's bedroom window to see if there's another car in the driveway. But I can't see much with the blinds closed. I can tell that it's dark outside and the streetlights are on. Maybe Todd never came upstairs after dinner. Maybe he was watching TV in the den and fell asleep. Maybe it's the middle of the night, 3:00 a.m. or something. That would make more sense; you'd wait until the dead of night to rob a house.

I look around Todd's room.

There's a lot of crap in here, and if I start digging through sock drawers, I'm afraid I'll make a lot of noise, set off a toy that beeps or talks or lights up.

I can't let them hear me.

Then I see it: the baseball bat.

I move toward it, arm outstretched, fingers moving, shaking, in a way I can't control.

At least the carpet of Todd's room silences my footsteps, even if there are crumbs and Legos and—

"Please! Just stop this," my mom says from downstairs. "Tell us what you want."

The house is so quiet, I have no problem hearing her. She doesn't yell; instead, she talks clearly and calmly.

But I can hear in her voice that my mom's scared.

And that terrifies me.

But what the girl, the female intruder, says in response makes it even worse:

"We're here for your daughter."

The playfulness in the girl's voice causes the bat in my hand, already slick with my sleep sweat, to tremble.

I can hear Mom, but where's Dad? Have they done something to him? Where's Todd? What could these two teenagers have possibly done to make my mom plead with them like that? What was the sound that woke me? The sound that caused the baby to—

"Come out, chicky," the voice down the hall says, and I firm up my grip. Did I make a noise? Does he know I'm in here, or is he just guessing?

It's not a full-size bat. Todd is *not* a baseball kid. He's small for his age, a twelve-year-old who looks like he's nine or ten. I call him a small, big nerd. This miniature souvenir bat was a giveaway from a Diamondbacks game dad took us to . . .

The footsteps creep toward my brother's bedroom. But then they stop, step into my parent's room for a moment, and then continue to the second-floor bathroom.

The guy searching for me doesn't know where I am.

But he's one door away.

I need to hide. I take two big steps and get behind the bedroom door, trying to make myself as flat as I can, thirty-two weeks pregnant.

"Hurry up, Chuck," the girl downstairs yells.

Upchuck? Chuck? I know a Chuck. Kind of. Or at least there was a Chuck in some of my classes, when I had classes. Charles during roll call, Chuck to his friends. I wasn't one of his friends. We didn't talk much. He was one of those "put your head down on the desk halfway through the test and take the zero"–type kids.

"Just keep going without me," Chuck says to her. "I'll be down in a second."

"Ooooh-kay," the girl yells, in the same tone she had before. Sadistic. Cartoon sadistic. Theater-kid theatricality.

"Wait, don't!" my mom yells.

Then there are the sounds of fists and muffled grunting. Someone who's been gagged trying to cry out from behind fabric.

My mom starts crying and screaming, no more words, but she's loud enough that she drowns out the other sounds.

The baby kicks again, and I'm not properly braced for it. My bladder almost lets go. Then it does a little, just a few drips.

I'm listening so intently to Mom's screams, trying not to cry, that I don't even see Chuck push through the doorway and his shadow slip into Todd's room.

"There you are," the figure says. He finds me easily in the low light slanting through the windows.

I had the element of surprise, and I let myself get distracted.

This person in my house is wearing a black long-sleeved shirt and some kind of black hood over his head. A canvas mask or . . . maybe a pillowcase. There are eyeholes cut in the sheet and something securing the hood around his neck, a belt or a dog collar.

"I got her, Kells," the guy yells, angling his face toward the other side of the door. "Kill the rest of them."

Kells? Kill?

The words hit me like a blast of arctic air. Wake me even further.

Seeing Chuck here, in the orange of the streetlight and the green glow of the stickers on the ceiling, I'm no longer afraid.

I'm angry. Because whoever this is—whether he's the Chuck from school or a strange Chuck who's wandered in off the street—they look ridiculous. And they're hurting my family.

I rage forward, not noticing until I'm almost on top of him that he's got a weapon in his hand. It's an old-timey revolver, looks like a prop from a movie about the Wild West but smells like extinguished birthday candles as I get closer.

Gunpowder.

He begins to level the gun.

"Wait, we—" Chuck says to me, but I don't let him finish. And I don't let him pull the trigger.

I try to remember what we learned in elementary-school gym class. I try to swing *through* the ball.

Wait, is that baseball, or is it golf?

In cheer we didn't do baton routines; the competitions have been phasing them out, too old-fashioned. The emphasis now is on tumbling.

On how high you can toss your flyers. But we should have used batons in our routines. I would have been good at it.

Chuck's head bounces once where I hit him across the temple. Or maybe I hit him in the cheek and chin. It's hard to tell with the sheet covering his face.

Then his head bounces a second time as it connects with the corner of Todd's desk.

Todd's computer monitor is jostled out of sleep mode, and the whole room is cast in a blue light. I breathe for a second, the video-game-character desktop background staring at me as I look down at Chuck.

"What was that?" the girl asks from downstairs.

Kells. Short for Kelly? A friend of Chuck? The girlfriend of Chuck? The two of them always making out in the hallways? Yes, that sounds familiar, but try as I might, I can't picture either of their faces. I used to care about these things. Used to keep tabs on everyone, even the seat-fillers, the untouchables, but things change. I've grown a lot in the last few months. As my body's grown and transformed, so has my thinking. I can't be bothered worrying about and judging other people.

In the light of the monitor, I readjust my stance so I'm standing over Chuck's head. He's been knocked unconscious, his eyelids fluttering under the holes in his mask.

Downstairs, Mom's screams have turned to ragged sobs.

I hit Chuck again.

Whack.

And I don't stop hitting him until the sheet is concave and my back hurts the worst it has in weeks.

"Get away from him!" The girl is not downstairs anymore. She's climbed the stairs and is in the room with me, an inch from my ear.

She's dressed just like her boyfriend is. *Was?*

7

I'm trembling and crying, and I just want to see my mom and know she's all right.

"What did you do?" the girl screams at me, the fabric of her own pillowcase mask sucking in so I can see the outline of her mouth.

I run at her, too tired and frantic to aim correctly, so I just collide into her. I have both hands holding the end of the bat out like a blunt javelin, so as we clash, I hear aluminum running across the top of the girl's teeth.

She tries to scream but can't with her mouth full.

That's when the pain blooms. There's no gunshot, because the girl—"Kells"—doesn't have a gun. She's armed with a knife, and she's stabbed me in the side. It hurts. But realizing *where* it hurts is worse than the pain itself.

I look down, see a dark spot spreading along the pleats in my maternity top.

No. They won't take this from me. Not after everything with Brendan and the arguments and the decisions and finishing school remotely and my dad looking at me like . . .

I roar, drop my shoulder, and flatten the girl into the door to Todd's bedroom. The doorknob jabs her in the spine, and she hisses in my ear.

I ram into her again with my shoulder.

Something drops away into the shadows.

But it's not the knife. I catch the blue-white glint of a phone's screen as it falls, face up, onto the carpet.

Kells is . . . filming this? Whatever she's been doing downstairs with my mom, coming up here to stab me? She's had her phone's camera recording?

But there's no time to consider what that could mean, who the video could be for. I readjust my elbows, trying to keep the knife away. I can't let her stab me—stab *us*—again.

I flip the end of the bat over, clip her in the chin with the hard metal bulb at the end, then lay the skinny part of the bat, the grip, across her neck.

I hold it there.

The girl tries to swear at me but can't manage more than a few syllables as I press down, hard, all the muscles in my back and shoulders that I've let go slack over the last few months called back into action.

You know how much upper-body strength it takes to throw someone into the air? High enough to win a championship?

Kells does now.

Spittle starts to stain the pillowcase over her mouth, turning the black fabric even darker. She drops the knife, and I count to ten before I let the pressure off, her not moving, neck bent, held against the door.

I look at my little brother's room, the two bodies that I've made, and I want to do a lot of things. I want to freak out. I want to find where my phone's tangled up in Todd's sheets and call the cops. I want to say something cool like "You picked the wrong house," like I would if this were a TV show. Because if it were a TV show, it wouldn't be real.

I want to sit down, because I don't know if I've ever been in this much pain, holding my side where the knife went in. Which isn't near the baby. At least I don't think it is. I pray it's not.

But I can't do any of those things because the first thing I want to do is to make sure my family is okay.

I don't move out of Todd's room. First, I listen. I can't hear any more footsteps or yelling between home invaders and decide that there's nobody else in the house who's not supposed to be. That it was just these two.

I limp out of the room, my side hurting, and listen again at the top-floor landing. No more voices. No more heavy footsteps . . . but also no more sounds from my mom.

I lean against the banister, taking the stairs down into the den, and I don't even get all the way to the bottom of the stairwell before I see the worst thing I've ever seen.

There are harsh shadows; the floor lamp and end-table lamps are tipped over, lampshades angled up.

Todd, small for his age, has been stuffed into some kind of sack, possibly carried in it to where he lies now. There's blood leaking through the fabric, and his legs stick out the mouth of the bag, pale and still.

My dad—I can tell it's him from his work shirt—is lying face down beside the coffee table. The tabletop's shattered, and there's glass underneath him.

His hands are tied behind his back, his knees bent and feet behind them. One of the throw pillows from the couch has been placed over the back of his head, and there's a quarter-size hole in the pillow, black singe marks around the hole.

That was the sound that woke me. The baby and I heard the gunshot that killed my dad.

I need to descend the bottom two steps and go farther into the den to find my mom.

She's been stabbed. She's always warm in the house, so she never wears sleeves. There are puckered slash marks all down her arms, dark splotches across the front of her blouse.

They've killed them. These two nobodies, literal nobody loser NPCs from a school I don't even go to anymore. They've killed my whole family.

And then my mom breathes, the suddenness of it like she's startled herself awake.

She's alive!

"Mom!" I say, my voice cracking even on the small word. I'm so ashamed we ever fought. That there was ever a gap in understanding between us, that there was ever a Brendan to get in the way and make me forget that I love my mom and I love my dad and I even love Todd. Just as much as I love the baby that I so badly want to see.

I need to call for help. My mom probably has her phone in her pocket, but I can't risk moving her; some of the cuts on her arms and chest look really deep. There's the handset in the kitchen. I can go grab that and . . .

"You've made a real mess of this whole night, you know that?" the voice behind me says. It's flat. The tone of it not even angry, more disappointed. And unlike the other two intruders, I can't tell if this is an adult or someone my own age.

He's been waiting down here for me. Moving quietly, not yelling and stomping around like the other two.

I turn.

And he's not wearing a black outfit like a cat burglar or a hood or anything else stupid like that.

And I know him.

Then he raises something, another gun, and there's a spark, and I don't even hear the sound of the shot that kills me.

The last thing I feel is the baby kick.

ONE

AARON

Olivia's tongue pushes forward, and I have to open my mouth wider to accommodate.

I'm not enjoying this.

To pass the time while we kiss, I try to think of whether I've *ever* enjoyed it.

But I can't remember an instance. Especially not with the other thoughts fighting for my attention.

Normally I'm quite the multitasker. I've never been tested, but I imagine I'd score somewhere on the spectrum of genius with my ability to hold simultaneous pieces of information in my mind.

But even I'm not enough of a prodigy to separate the sensation of Olivia's teeth clicking against mine from the image of Chuck last night, a yawning hole in the side of his face when I lifted his mask.

Larissa Coates had done that with a baseball bat shorter than my forearm.

She'd knocked half his teeth out. Which will mean it'll be harder to identify Chuck from his dental records. If Charles Lang had ever gone to the dentist, that is. He seemed to *lack* in the personal-hygiene department.

Just as I'm starting to get comfortable with the shape of Olivia's tongue, the thin veins of its underside, she exhales through her nose and pulls its mass back into her own mouth.

Olivia wipes her lips on the back of her sleeve as she moans—a sound more anatomical than orgasmic—and lies back.

"You okay?" she asks.

She's missed a spot. There's a string of spittle on her chin.

"Yes," I say.

She smiles at me, pops the dimple on the left side of her face, trying her best to act cute.

She's not cute.

"Are you thinking about snow?" she asks.

I'm thinking about arson and ritual murder.

We've been together nearly a year, but Olivia doesn't know much about me. On the surface we have enough in common: parents with money, private school, and that's enough for her. Olivia Stewart is uninquisitive. And that is why I've chosen her.

She doesn't know who I am. Not who I am in person, at school, and certainly not who I am online.

Which mean she doesn't know anything about last night, other than what she needs to know to be an alibi. As far as Olivia's aware, we've been together since she arrived home from school yesterday afternoon. Might have even had sex a time or two, but between the Smirnoff and the powders, who can remember?

I didn't sleep here, and we didn't have sex, but I've left some condom wrappers at the foot of the bed to sell the illusion.

And to get her in trouble with her parents. Because I find that sort of thing mildly amusing. Her parents are tech people, both employed by separate start-ups. Real go-getters, spending all day and night at their respective companies' "campuses" but still taking time to be in their daughter's life, snoop in her room.

"By the time it gets cold, you'll be wishing you were back home with me," Olivia says, then she fakes a shiver, for emphasis. "I hate snow. Even when my parents go skiing. I like skiing, but I hate the snow."

These are the kind of quality conversations I have with Olivia.

"I'll get used to it, I guess," I say, forcing myself to engage with her. What is she even talking about? Snow? Does she think I'm moving to Alaska? There won't be snow in New York until months and months from now. But I don't ask any follow-up questions. I try my best to smile at her, let her keep talking to herself.

Usually, it doesn't take me this much effort to feign intimacy. Social cues aren't hard to mimic once you understand where other people are looking, the expressions they expect to see. And I understand everything I put my mind to studying. Which means I'm a better-than-average conversationalist. In fact, most people who meet me genuinely enjoy my company.

I take her chin in my hand, use my thumb to wipe away the spot of drool she missed.

She takes the gesture as I intend: like I love her and that I want to touch her.

"I won't miss the weather as much as I'll miss your face," I say.

"Oh, that's so sweet. I've been thinking about us and how we can make long distance work, and I . . ."

I stop listening. Once Olivia Stewart begins a sentence with "I've been thinking . . . ," the conversation becomes one-sided for the next few minutes.

It took me only two hours to clean up at the Coates residence. Which should make me proud. Especially because so much of the process needed to be improvised. But much like Olivia's kisses, the thought that I've gotten away with multiple murders—or as an accomplice to multiple murders, one committed by myself—does nothing for me.

A year ago, things might have been different. I might have felt satisfied, powerful. But now? Nothing—my emotions are a void.

Well. Not nothing. I can still *feel* things; I just don't feel them as strongly. It's as if there's a thin layer of spun cotton covering my rage and joy.

Have I broken something in myself? I've crossed lines before last night, done criminal things, but not murder. Not myself.

Seeing a dead body, in person, used to be a rarity.

Now I've seen six in one night and . . .

Nothing.

Not even when the pin hit the shell for Larissa, with me pulling the trigger myself for the first time.

The Coates family: Papa Bear, Mama Bear, Baby Bear, and . . . Pregnant Daughter Bear. Then two high-school thrill killers, Chuck and Kelly. The six of them, murderers and murder victims, lined shoulder to feet, shoulder to feet in the living room . . .

Looking at them, I didn't feel anything but a slight frustration at Chuck and Kelly for bungling the plan.

I had expected their deaths to be a transformational experience. Something that would take me to the next level. If not in my consciousness and philosophy, then at least outwardly. It might have been able to do that, in a public-relations sense. But because of how things played out . . . instead of basking in the afterglow, I was moving around the house, starting a fire.

There was no way to spin what had happened last night into a success. So I needed to hit the reset button. I had to make a tactical retreat, to allow myself to try again another day.

In her bed beside me, Olivia is weighing the pros and cons of Zoom, Skype, or FaceTime for the phone dates she imagines we'll be having.

I ignore her, replay the events of last night one more time.

My parents hadn't given me much warning. Less than a month's notice that we're moving. Moving again. And this time to somewhere— as Olivia points out—that has snow. Which meant that every plan I had for the Coates family, an event I've been working toward for nearly a year, had needed to be accelerated.

Larissa Coates needed to die before the last moving box was packed and the trucks arrived.

And as much as I'd like to blame Chuck and Kelly, I shouldn't. Their sloppiness was my sloppiness, in a way.

But also, *really?* Days of spying and prep and rehearsal and you *lose her?* You lose her in her own house? How the fuck does that happen?

And, on my own end, how could I have anticipated that the disgraced captain of the cheer squad would be capable of physically destroying two delinquents in a matter of minutes, armed only with a souvenir baseball bat?

I couldn't have known that. It's just one of those things, really. Fate taking a few freak bounces, ruining everyone's plans.

Chuck and Kelly *were* destined to die, of course. But not *that* way. They were supposed to end it themselves. Double suicide, right there in the house, after I'd directed them to set-dress the home invasion to include a few Easter eggs.

Yes, Easter eggs. Kind of a greatest-hits collection. Homages. Not to be too cute about it, but taken as a whole, these nods to the past would have worked to hide motive, not broadcast it.

Larissa, she's the obvious one. Our tribute to Sharon Tate.

The murder weapons, a mix of knives and guns, also very reminiscent of 1969.

But it wasn't all supposed to be Manson-inspired. It was more of a collage. There would be other touches, more subtle. Deeper cuts for a more discerning audience.

For instance, Chuck and Kelly had been filming with their phones. Home movies. And I'd directed them to film a few more in the weeks before. Once investigators found the videos, along with the series of text messages on their phones, the total picture would imply a kind of Paul Bernardo and Karla Homolka—the Barbie and Ken Killers—situation.

There was also the killing of the boy, the bag thrown over him before his execution. A visual echo of *Funny Games*. The remake or the original, it doesn't matter; they're both Haneke. Yes, it's a fiction film, but at least he's a foreign director. Adds a layer of class.

And there were a few more small details I had planned on including. But things had to change. The murder scene couldn't *look* like a murder scene. Not if I was going to cover my tracks long enough to be hundreds of miles away, a ghost before any formal investigation was opened.

The deaths needed to look like the result of a fast-moving fire. At least at first glance.

After gathering the bodies in the living room, I went around the house pulling up carpets and moving furniture until I found what I was looking for. There are no basements in Arizona, but luckily there are crawl spaces.

It was itchy, strenuous work, but I was able to get Chuck and Kelly entombed in the flame-proof fiberglass insulation under the house. Then I collected the weapons, used kitchen gloves and bleach-based sprays to try and eliminate obvious signs of struggle.

It wouldn't be perfect, of course. There were stab wounds, ligature contusions, and bullet holes. But I researched a few tricks.

For example, I looked up where in a house a fire needs to start to burn hottest. Whether windows and interior doors should be open or closed in order to create a cross draft like you'd find in a kiln.

Of course, I used Larissa's phone to do that research. To add some extra confusion if anyone were somehow able to check.

With a little luck and underwhelming investigative work, the fire would be marked down as a tragic accident. And if two extra, confusing bodies were discovered in the house's foundation? Well . . . nobody would be able to put it together. At least not to trace it to me, and that's all that matters.

Kelly and Charles? I don't know those kids. They didn't even attend my school. They were Larissa's classmates, not mine. I hung out with them a few times, keeping our sessions short and private, and any text communications we'd had were through WhatsApp . . . on a burner phone, purchased at a gas station with cash.

"I mean. New York," Olivia says, finishing up whatever speech she's been making. "Life's going to be different. But I think we can get through it together."

Even Larissa Coates I'd only talked to a couple of times. More to get a few details about her life and school than anything else. I think she might have liked me. She'd begun to show at that point, was clearly going through some problems at home and with her boyfriend—Brandon? Brendan? What does it matter?

Larissa had been selected because she was the right type. It was nothing personal. She would look good in newsprint. And she was popular, the type of girl my followers would love to see taken down a few . . .

In bed beside me, Olivia's voice goes up like a question. Then she blinks at me.

Shit. What did she ask?

"Aaron?" she asks. "Are you listening to me?"

Oh well. No use prolonging this.

"Olivia," I say back. I move my hand to cover hers. She should really clean these sheets. We're lying in sweat and crust from weeks ago.

"Yes?" she asks.

I look her in the eyes. There had been more life in Larissa Coates's gaze, even after, when she had a dime-size hole at the corner of her forehead. Why had I stayed with Olivia for so long? Why had I kept her around? Could *she* be the reason I'm starting to lose connection to the human world? The dead numbness inside of me stemming from our make-out sessions and brief, clinical sexual encounters?

No. That's not fair to Olivia. I've done this to myself.

I've kept Olivia because she's normal. Not too pretty. Not too plain. Eager to please but wrapped up enough in her own internal life and storyline that she's done no real thinking about mine. Like I said, she's incurious. She's never once attempted to see behind the mask, to glimpse the real me.

She's not even that active on socials. I don't think she's ever even *heard* my other name.

I look Olivia deep in the eyes, and now her dreamy expression is starting to waiver. Maybe she's more perceptive than I've given her credit for.

"I've been thinking too," I say.

"Yes?"

"And I think we should break up."

"What?" she asks, and starts to cry.

I'd like to say I feel relief. That the clean break makes me feel unencumbered, hopeful for this next phase in my life and career.

But I don't feel anything at all.

TWO

CRYSTAL

I tell myself to take a deep breath.

And I do. I bring in a big gulp of air.

But then I have to remind myself to let it out.

And I can't.

I hold the breath in, my lungs full, lips sealed together.

I lock eyes with myself, the version of myself on-screen. As I watch, a vein starts pulsing at my temple, my face getting moist and splotchy.

Well . . . moister and splotchier.

You're making it worse! You've got to breathe! I yell at myself.

Finally, I close my eyes so I'm not looking at my phone—or the tripod or the ring light. Without the pressure of seeing my own face, I can begin to breathe normally.

I wait a few seconds like this, eyes closed. I wait for the sting in my cheeks to dissipate, my eyelids feeling numb, and then I try again.

I don't have much time.

They'll be here soon.

"Hey, guys—" I say.

I try my best to ignore my own image and to keep my eye contact locked on the phone's camera. But I keep getting distracted by the screen, by how uncomfortable I look. How the muscles in my neck seem to bulge when I speak.

I've done this a hundred times, but some days, if I build it up in my head too much, then it becomes as difficult as the first time.

I clear my throat.

Let's try that again.

Now.

Say something.

"Hey, guys."

Good. That's better. Keep going.

"Uh. Today I wanted to talk about . . ."

I pause. What *did* I want to talk about?

My mental health? How classes are going? My friends?

All those topics make me upset to think about. I mean, I talk about them all the time, but they still upset me.

"Shit, forget it," I say, and it's as real as I've ever gotten in one of these. I stop recording, navigate to my photos, and delete the video to save space.

I look away from the setup, and there's a black circle taking up most of my vision, the glare of the ring light burned into my retinas. Am I sitting too close to the light? This can't be how the professionals do it. I think about professionals. Those girls who stream all day, their hair and skin pristine, the guys who bite their lips and always have the light perfectly centered around their pupils so their blue or green eyes don't lose their color.

I'm not one of those girls who's had her brain completely melted by unrealistic beauty standards. Really. I'm not. I don't want to be perfect. I just want to be able to record a video without stammering or sweating or rage-quitting midsentence.

Sometimes I can. And I offload that footage from my ancient 6S, then edit those clips in iMovie to take out all the *ums* and *likes* and *y'knows* so that I'm able to watch the videos back and feel good about myself for a second. To feel like, even if these are just for me, I'm able to talk to a camera like I talk to a friend. Better than I talk to my friends, actually.

But this morning is not going to be one of those successful recording sessions. It's Wednesday, a school day, and my ride will be here soon.

I reach over and pull the ring light's USB from the wall adapter. The light's been on for ten minutes, and the metal connector is already hot to the touch. One day I'm sure I'll leave it plugged in and burn the house down. That'd be just my luck.

Without removing my phone from the tripod, I exit the camera app and check the time. It's already 7:30. I don't know what I was thinking even *attempting* to make a video this morning. And what *was* I going to talk about? Something about how I couldn't sleep? Maybe the six and a half volumes of manga scans I stayed up reading instead?

I keep them on a private YouTube account. Not because I ever intend on turning them public. But because it's free storage; my phone's got no memory. If I'm being honest, I like watching the videos back that way, with that red and white around the edges of the frame.

But this morning, not even I'm interested in hearing about my own insomnia.

I'm sure I've talked about worse, though. I *want* my vlogs to be an honest accounting of my thoughts and emotions. But these days, as high school winds down, I have less and less to share about my life. With no news—social, romantic, or *anything*—my recording sessions have become a collection of nerdy tangents. The last few months, my account is pages and pages of videos with titles like *Thoughts about the New Sriracha Doritos* or *Why I Prefer Wario to Waluigi* or *Sometimes I'm So Sad that My Stomach Hurts.*

Not that I don't have friends I can talk to. I do.

I have friends.

I still have friends. Still have a *best* friend. Even if Gayle and I don't see each other as much as we used to.

Lifting the spring-loaded clasp on the tripod, I free my phone and navigate over to texts.

I read that at 7:26 a.m.: Trevor Seye has shared his location.

Trevor does this every morning, texting each of us separately, not letting the notification get lost in our group text. Like he's our Uber. Like he's not just going to honk once he's outside anyway.

I click the link next to Trevor's text and it opens Maps. He's four blocks away. I watch in real time as the van turns onto my street.

I stand, the plushie I use as a lower-back pillow to improve my posture rolling off the seat and onto the floor. I look behind me. The sliver of room that the camera can see is dusted and well curated: some Pops, book spines organized by color so they form a loose neon rainbow, and a *Phantom of the Opera* poster I got on a school trip in eighth grade. I don't have a lot of space to work with.

This used to be the nursery; I got kicked out of my own bedroom a few years ago when Ant needed the space. The rest of the room is my bed (half of it heaped with laundry), piles of three-ring binders, a window that doesn't let in much natural light, a stack of dishes that I should bring out to the kitchen, and some anime merch that I shouldn't bring with me to college . . .

Hello, I'm your roommate, Crystal Giordano, and yes, this under my arm is a body pillow of two cartoon boys about to kiss.

I hitch my school bag out of one of the piles of laundry and leave the bedroom without checking myself in the mirror hanging over the door.

If I check the mirror, I'll scrutinize, and if I take the time to scrutinize, I'll be late.

Gayle can touch up my makeup in the van.

My family is awake and eating breakfast. I try to hug the corner as I cross through the hall and kitchen.

It's like I've stumbled into a commercial for orange juice. They look so normal. They're not. But they *look* normal in this moment.

"No, it's next Thursday," Dad says. "*This* Thursday we don't have anything." He's standing next to the fridge, tightening his belt and looking at the calendar. My parents aren't old. They could learn how to use the calendars in their phones, but they don't seem to want to learn. They aren't *old* but like things *old-school.*

My brother, Ant, has picked all the marshmallows out of his cereal and is putting them back into the box. Ant is currently being tested by the elementary-school counselors. They're not sure what's up with him.

"Hey, baby," Mom says as I try and sneak past. I don't slow for her. "Breakfast. Eat breakfast, please."

"I will at school," I lie.

Last week I read an interesting thread about time-restricted eating and I'm giving it a try.

A van honks outside.

Trevor's here.

"I'm sure the neighbors love that," my dad says, leaning around the corner, watching me go. He still doesn't have his belt cinched quite right; his shirt's too wrinkled. He hates the way his job at the dealership makes him dress.

"Love you all," I yell as I reach for the doorknob.

"I don't love anyone!" I hear Ant yell in response, but I'm out the door before I can hear my mom gasp and tell him something like: "Don't say that, Anthony. Take it back!"

Trevor's van is idling at the end of our driveway, the bumper very close but not touching the back of my dad's truck. The van has an ugly chipped reddish-purple paint job that Trevor insists is "mahogany." It also has a stripe of fake wood paneling, the grain on the wood decal mostly rubbed off. I have no idea how Trevor's parents are okay with his choice of car, especially considering how strict they are with every other aspect of their son's life. Strict with his grades. His curfew. How he dresses. That he's home to pray with them and his sister. My parents aren't nearly as controlling, but anytime my dad sees the van around town, he mutters something like: "I'm glad it's only a ten-minute drive to school."

I'm halfway down the lawn when the van's side door rolls open.

"Come on, we're skipping today," Gayle says, voiced raised like she's hoping my parents or neighbors will hear. "We're going to go drink forties and sell our bodies behind the gas station."

Gayle says something like this every morning. Gayle is short with a round face and pronounced cheeks. It's a soft, kind face. People would call her bubbly if she didn't dress all in black with heavy combat boots and a leather jacket with more silver studs than leather. Gayle Byrne looks like a Cabbage Patch Kid doll who, somewhere along the line, has gotten really into *The Crow* and collecting bootleg Misfits concerts.

I climb over Gayle's legs and take the seat behind Trevor. My house is the last stop before school, so the others are all here. Paul and Gayle live three houses over from each other and are picked up at the same time. That's why I like to be punctual in the mornings. I don't want to hold them up. They're my friends now, but who's to say that'll *stay* the case if I start making everyone late to school?

Paul rides shotgun. He has his AirPods in and is watching something on his phone. Harmony is alone, behind us in the van's third row, lying on the bench seat with no safety belt and also watching something on her phone.

Gayle slides the door closed. "Package secure, driver," she says to Trevor.

"Yeah, yeah," Trevor says, checking his mirrors as we pull back into the street. His van may be a shitbox, but at least he's a careful driver.

Sometimes the others make fun of him for how carefully he drives, but he'll just reply, "Always be prepared."

Trevor Seye is a Boy Scout. Literally. Well, he's an Eagle Scout, actually, since we're all getting older.

And Trevor might not "always be prepared" to deal with the foolishness of his friends, but he keeps his short hi-top impeccably neat and is the only one of us responsible enough to be trusted to drive the carpool. Trevor's Black. And most people in East Bay, New York, are . . . not. We don't talk about it much, hardly ever, but I think that's because we all don't want it to matter. I made a video about this once, how I think for Trevor it matters. How, to Trevor, I think it matters *a lot*. And how he tries to project a level of control in every area of his life because of it.

We drive for two blocks, and nobody speaks.

And then Gayle does.

"Wow. Nobody say 'good morning' to your friend or anything."

Paul and Harmony don't respond. They're both still staring at their phones. It must be good, whatever it is they're watching, because these drives aren't usually like this.

"I'm driving," Trevor says. His hands are at ten and two, even though we're the only car on the block—it's early, slight mist in the air, morning dew still clinging to the grass because the sun's behind thick cloud cover. It'd been a cold March, but it's April now. Spring is here. For the most part, we all know where we're going to college. High school is almost over. Things *have* to warm up soon.

"It's fine," I say, turning my face to Gayle so she can assess my makeup situation. "How do I look?"

The tinted windows of Trevor's van make it hard to see, so Gayle flicks on the small light above us, then leans over the gap separating our second-row seats. She stares at my face for a moment, uses the back of one hand to tilt my chin toward the light. I know there are blackheads there, but they've been resistant to everything I've tried: exfoliants, tweezers, wipes . . .

The spots of concealer I applied this morning feel ashy and hot under both the light and Gayle's inspection.

"Hmmm," Gayle says, ready to deliver her verdict. "You look gorgeous. Spectacular. A goddess. Wonder—"

"Stop," I say, giggling.

"I'm not finished! Wonderful. A godsend. Would fall on a grenade for you."

Gayle says this kind of thing whenever I ask, but it's still nice to hear. That's the thing: even though we're spending less and less time just the two of us, over at each other's houses, at the movies, getting food—in interactions like this, nothing has changed. And it makes me even more confused why we've stopped seeing each other.

"Girl," Gayle keeps going, making it sexual. Which is also something she does. "I would make out, right now, if you wanted. I'd toss my heteronorms to the wind and—"

"I *mean*," I say, interrupting, "is my makeup running? Do I need to reapply?"

"What makeup?" Gayle asks. And I frown at that, because it's the one thing she said that feels like an outright lie. As smooth as I can blend, no matter how many tutorials I watch, I'm still prone to breakouts and use a lot of makeup, just to maintain. My complexion is neither my father's tannable olive nor my mother's year-round island glow but an uneven mix of both, and as a result, I try to hide the darkness under my eyes.

"I mean it looks good," Gayle says, realizing that I want her to be serious for a second, give me a real opinion. "I don't think you need anything. But . . . I could always draw some cat eyes on for you. I think they'd look hot."

"No. No cat eyes. I don't want to copy your style."

"Corpse paint, maybe?"

"I'm . . . still not goth," I say. And I'm not. I'm not anything. I don't want the attention of being part of a group, because if I *were* sorted into any one group at our high school, I'd have to sit at the lunch table with the kids who speak in mispronounced Japanese and get asked to remove their plush cat ears in gym class.

"Eh. We'll get you on our team one of these days," Gayle says, switching off the overhead light, settling back into her seat, and checking her safety belt.

"Hey, Harm," Paul says, turning to face us, shouting without realizing he's shouting. He's still got his AirPods in.

Gayle reaches a hand behind her and pats Harmony on the top of her head to get her attention.

"Huh?" Harmony says, sitting up and taking one of her own—wired—earbuds out.

Neither Paul nor Harmony has looked in my direction; neither has acknowledged I've gotten into the van with so much as a "Hey, Crystal."

But that's okay. Of the four of them, no matter how much we see each other, Gayle is the one I love the most, my *real* friend.

"Yeah," Harmony says back to Paul. She lets the earpiece drop, the plastic bulb of it bouncing against her neck.

It's a pretty neck, a neck that's attached to a brain that . . . How do I describe Harmony's brain? Extremely Online? Not in a bad way. In fact, I found it amazing how Harmony Phillips, she of the slightly upturned nose, delicate amber ringlets, and C-plus attitude, was able to predict the next trending topic or find the new big meme for the rest of the group text to use.

None of us want to be that person, but we all benefit from her sacrifice.

"He says a new post will go up after this stream!" Paul says, still talking too loudly, AirPods in. Whatever the two of them are watching, it's got Paul excited. Giddy, even.

"I know; I'm watching too," Harmony says.

Maybe her attitude's more of a C-minus.

"Oh," Paul says. "He never streams this early."

"Is this some internet thing?" Trevor asks, looking ready to pull over. "Is this what you're doing in my van instead of socializing?"

Internet thing.

Trevor's parents don't let him have socials, so he leans into it, makes being offline into a part of his personality. Hip in being square. Even though we all know he keeps secret accounts on Paul's phone.

Paul doesn't answer. Trevor looks into the rearview at Gayle and me. "Do you two have your seat belts on? I might mess around and crash into a tree to teach them a lesson."

"Oh, hush," Gayle says. "Let people enjoy things. They can watch their sadboy Instagram poet if they want."

"The Speaker?" I hear myself ask. I know enough about Harmony and Paul's recent obsession to know his name, but not enough that I don't still feel left behind from their fandom. The two of them aren't the only people at school following the account. But Harmony was the first. If you ask *her*, she's brought the Speaker into East Bay's "collective consciousness." I've scrolled the account a few times. Angry poems and cryptic images. Not for me. I don't follow. It seems like the type of stuff that would make me anxious if I had it served to me every day. And I have enough anxiety as it is.

"He's not a sadboy," Harmony says, maybe not hearing me but responding to Gayle.

"A fuckboy, then," Gayle mutters.

"I heard that," Paul says. "He's not a fuckboy."

"Like you even know what that is," Trevor says, reaching over to scoot Paul's knees off where he's rested them against the dashboard. Trevor and Paul used to date; they've tried a few times, actually. But it never works. They're too different. Trevor is into the great outdoors. Paul is all about the mediocre indoors. Paul is hoodies to hide his coppery red hair and three monitors on his gaming PC. Trevor is secondhand-store Timberlands and archery tutorials. Not to mention how Trevor's parents would react . . .

Not that I've ever asked specifics about Trevor's religion and family. Trevor and I aren't close, and I don't ask questions like that. But I know his family's conservative enough that Trevor's not out to them yet. That he's only out to the people in this van because he fears word getting back to his troop and his parents.

"Really, though, Paul's right," Harmony says. She leans forward, into the space between the second row's two seats. She holds her phone so Gayle and I can watch what's on her screen. She doesn't take her headphones out, so we still can't hear.

Harmony smells like something sweet, and for a moment, my eyes on her curls, I have a hard time focusing on what she's saying.

". . . not usually, he doesn't stream this early *ever*," Harmony explains. "If I want to see his morning streams, I have to get a pass to the bathroom."

On Harmony's phone, I watch the Speaker.

He doesn't look like a typical streamer. At least not the ones I watch. The screen pixilates a bit, and I get the impression that this is a stream of a stream, another app's watermark shifting between Instagram's own reaction and comment bars. Maybe the trends are different on this, whatever new corner of the internet Harmony likes to frequent.

There's a microphone, but the Speaker doesn't have a big obnoxious sound guard pressed up against his face. He isn't awash with neon LEDs and seated in an expensive gaming chair. Instead of fill lights and a well-defined background—which is what all the tutorials tell you to use to make videos—the Speaker is barely lit at all. He sits in harsh shadows, Harmony's phone running off cell data, making the blacks in the image crush together into an unfocused fuzz.

Oddest of all, the Speaker is wearing a mask. It's kind of a cross between a bandana and surgical mask. Which doesn't sound that odd . . . but it *is* odd to see on a stream, where the whole point—I thought—is getting people to recognize you.

33

But maybe I'm wrong. The mask is distinctive. It's branding. And it isn't *completely* obscuring his features. More like it's accenting the ones we can see.

It's hard to tell, the image so small, the fidelity spotty, but it looks like the Speaker's our age, maybe a little older. He has thick but well-manicured brows sitting over light-colored eyes. In the low light, it's impossible to tell if the eyes are blue, green, or gray. They seem to be a combination, shift between all three colors as the Speaker gesticulates. The effect's so striking that I think maybe he's got some kind of filter running, a really subtle one, or maybe they're contact lenses.

Even without knowing what he's saying, I can see how, if I were watching this alone, headphones on, I might be intrigued. Maybe even intoxicated. I watch the fabric of his mask work, much tighter over his mouth than you'd wear a regular face mask.

Because this mask's worn for style, I think, *not to keep germs out.*

The Speaker moves his hands the way my dad does. Italian story-telling, Mom calls it. Without the sound, it should look silly, but it doesn't. And maybe it's the smell of Harmony wafting over, combined with the intensity of the Speaker's eyes, but . . . I feel something. I feel goose bumps start at the base of my neck. And suddenly I'm embarrassed.

But nobody's noticed.

Nobody's paying attention to me at all.

"See? He's great," Harmony says. "Gayle, how do *you of all people* not like the Speaker? He's spooky and . . . and . . ."

"Deep!" Paul says, trying to help her out.

"Yes. Not usually my type at all," Harmony says. "But Paul's right. The Speaker's got a lot to say about life. And I know he's got to be cute under that mask."

"Sure," Gayle says, crossing her arms. She's not buying it. "Real deep. Real cute."

Gayle's pissed. I can never quite tell what my other friends are feeling, but Gayle I can read. I can even anticipate what she's about to say.

"This"—Gayle motions down at her outfit, skirt, stockings, hands gliding down to the soles of her boots—"I don't wear this to be 'spooky.' It's not *for* anybody else. It's my style, my philosophy. I wear it *for me*. This guy"—she points at the phone—"and all the fuckers like him, they have no philosophy. They have an image. And that image exists to be monetized."

"Oh, come on," Harmony starts, but Gayle keeps going.

"*Influencers.*" She says the word like a slur. "Give me a break. They're built in a lab. I bet Disney or some shit owns the rights to the Speaker. How many followers does he have?"

"Half a mil," Paul answers.

"See? Not huge," Harmony says, nodding. "It's not like he's *corporate* or anything."

Gayle ignores them, sitting forward, pulling her seat belt tight. "Half a million's enough. Do you know how much people like this get paid? Not just for views; that's never where all the money comes from. Harm, you know this. It's all brand deals. They can make thousands of dollars for something small, like having a can of Red Bull sitting on their desk while they stream."

"Gross," Harmony says. "The Speaker doesn't drink Red Bull."

Beside me, Harmony takes her eyes off the screen, but I keep watching.

"Yeah, he can't, with the mask," Paul adds.

"Not what I meant, and you know it," Gayle says. "Guy's a fucking carpetbagger. Fake goth. Stolen valor. I renounce him and his kind."

There's quiet for a moment. I'd speak up, but I'm not sure whose side I'd be on. I love Gayle, but she's being . . . pretty mean about this.

"Gayle," Trevor says from the driver's seat, "whatever happened to letting people enjoy things?"

At this, Gayle seems to realize what she's done, that Harmony's slowly putting her earbud back in, slinking back into her seat behind us.

"I mean," Paul says, "we'll see how his content is today, after the stream, but he really hasn't been as good lately. Since he got popular."

I stare straight forward, looking into the rearview mirror at Harmony, ready to look away if she glances up at me.

Harmony points a finger at Paul. "Don't you try switching teams now, Paul. You like the Speaker just as much as I do. And don't act like you're so fucking original. So bleeding-edge underground. Because *I* was the one who told you about him."

Paul shushes her, points at his AirPods. "Quiet. He's wrapping up; here it comes."

Harmony leans forward again, phone turned away from Gayle, showing her screen to me and only me.

It's nice. I rarely get to share moments with Harmony.

"See," she says to me. Her breath smells good, and I don't see gum, so it must be the still-fresh scent of mouthwash. "At the end of every stream, he posts a poem on his socials. Or sometimes it's a picture, or a piece of art."

"Sometimes all three, and sometimes he posts randomly, without a stream," Paul says, but I don't look up, I keep looking at the phone, nodding at what Harmony's explained to me.

Harmony and I are watching together as she navigates to the Speaker's feed. We see his follower and following counts (he follows zero accounts, at least on IG). Then the top of his grid, six recent posts.

Harmony's left thumb, a holographic star sticker on her nail, pulls down and refreshes the page.

The grid doesn't change.

She waits a second, then pulls down again.

It's like I'm watching a slot machine. Unsure what we'll win.

"Here comes," she whispers in my ear.

I get a slight, queasy ASMR tingle. I don't care about the Speaker, but suddenly I care that *she* cares.

With Gayle in the same van, this feels like I'm being caught committing some kind of friend-infidelity. Not that Gayle probably cares.

"Here comes," Harmony repeats, sounding less sure.

There's still nothing new on the grid, but we stay hunched, waiting.

And then Harmony clicks and drags one final time and the page refreshes. The images in the grid change position, and Harmony makes a happy little noise in her throat.

She taps on the new tile.

On the phone in front of us is a white square, a few lines printed on what looks like a napkin in neat, blocky handwriting:

**These changes
I'm told they're for the best
But they make me
Feel.**

. . .

And I hate to feel.

I read the poem, then wait for her to scroll to the post description, so maybe we can read more, get an explanation, but there is nothing else. That's it. That's the entire post.

My friends just had a relationship-straining argument over an Instagram poet? And the payoff is a six-line poem that I don't even think is very good?

"Hmmm," Harmony says beside me. "This is a short one. 'Changes.' What do you think it means, Paul?"

I can practically hear the blood begin to flow, Gayle biting her cheek, not wanting to say any more to get herself in trouble. If she explodes, reiterates how she thinks the Speaker is a fraud, I might change sides and agree with her.

"Holy shit," Paul says, looking away from his own phone screen, back at us from the passenger seat. "Who cares what it means, Harm?!"

"Excuse you?" Harmony asks.

"Look at the post. It's location tagged!"

Harmony touches the photo again, holds her thumb to toggle the post info on and off, and there it is. . . .

I look away from the words, then to Harmony. There's a glimmer in her eyes that might be the start of tears. She's so happy. And so pretty.

"Why, what's it say?" Gayle asks. Her arms are uncrossed, her interest is piqued.

"East Bay, New York."

The Speaker has posted this poem from our town.

THREE

AARON

"Don't just speak, act," I say.

Then I end the stream and remove my mask.

The fabric is starting to smell.

I need to sew another one. I've tried machine washing them before, but the material can never withstand the spin cycle.

Last month I was approached by a company that wants to sell the Speaker merchandise. T-shirts, phone cases, even replica masks. Their message was patronizing, said that they wanted to "get in on the ground floor, to support a small creator." Which annoyed me, but it was the way the DM had called it "merch" that really turned me off, so I didn't answer.

Merch.

Get out of my fucking face with "merch."

That's small thinking. And only small minds do small thinking.

Yes, it's true, "merch" could make me a few dollars. But the company would need personal information, bank routing numbers, at the very least a mailing address. And I could probably find a way to fake all of that, to avoid the paper trail, maybe by setting up a PO box, but *why* would I? For a tiny percentage on the Speaker–branded hot/cold travel mugs?

No. What I'm trying to build here—what I've built—is more important than money. More impactful.

Just ask the Coates family of Scottsdale, Arizona.

I have to write the poem.

There's a napkin on the desk in front of me. My father has this thing with his American Express card, because he travels so much, where we get to go through airport security and straight into a "concierge lounge" with free food and drinks.

I took this napkin from that lounge, in PHX.

I consider the softness of the napkin's paper, how a regular pen will not photograph well.

I look through my desk organizer, then decide to write the poem on the napkin in fine-tip Sharpie.

It takes fifteen seconds to draft.

Took me longer to decide on the pen.

Not my best work, but I doubt there are many poetry scholars in my audience.

My followers don't want art. They want *content*.

Content they can search for meaning in.

I open the camera app, quickly experiment with different focal points, then tap the shutter.

It's a nicer photo than it is a poem.

The whole poem is built around "changes." . . . There are so many possible interpretations of that single word.

Consider just the one cultural allusion someone in the comments will probably point to: David Bowie. Which makes it an investigative skip and a jump to Wikipedia, where someone finds the nickname Thin White Duke, then comes back to the comments to begin to unpack *those* esoteric implications. And from one six-letter word, we have a ton of fan engagement.

Engagement, good or bad, leads to more visibility, which leads to more followers, which means . . . I can put even *less* effort into the next poem.

I upload the photo with no hashtags or description. I used to use tags when I started out. I would spend hours selecting the phrases that would get me singled out by the algorithm, avoiding anything that would get my content shadow banned.

But now I don't have to do any of that. I'm not looking for an audience. I've already found one. They'll take care of the rest, disseminate my work. I have several fan accounts who repost my photos, minimal overlay or branding of their own, just spreading the message. Then, of course, there are the fans who are actually me in disguise, sock-puppet accounts I switch between so I can comment on my original posts and drive speculation, argue with assholes . . . alter the direction of the discourse.

Is tagging the photo with East Bay, New York, too much . . . autobiography?

Maybe.

But actually. No. I don't think so.

I don't take geotagged photos, but I *have* posted to socials once or twice from Arizona, with location services turned on, and I've done the same thing while on family trips. And, more than that, I sometimes use VPNs that allow me to spoof locations I've never been to.

The Speaker spent last Christmas in Paris.

Romantic.

The streams are trickier, could reveal more about myself than I want if I'm not careful. I try to pay close attention to my language, mixing and deliberately confusing the localisms I say. Misdirection is part of the fun, but it's even more satisfying when I can throw a kernel of truth into my posts, then watch in the comments as, say, something like tagging East Bay gets disregarded as "too obvious."

There's something so satisfying about—

There's a knock.

"Good luck today," my father says, not opening the basement door. "Don't be late."

I don't need luck, and I'm never late if I don't intend to be.

"Thanks," I say, standing from my desk, tilting my head so I can be heard from where he's standing at the top of the stairs. "You too."

My father doesn't say anything else. I hear his footsteps retreat from the basement door and then a few moments later hear my mother starting the car outside.

The specifics of today have been agreed upon. My mother and father will drive to the train station together. They will then take the Long Island Rail Road into Pennsylvania Station.

Ick.

I'm not used to the thought of my parents taking public transportation, and I don't like it. Aside from the . . . *class* implications, it's difficult to have members of the household at the mercy of a train's scheduling changes and delays. When my parents were commuting to work in Phoenix, they took separate cars. I could calculate, within a few minutes, when and who would be home at any one time. Taking a train . . . it will take some getting used to the new schedule.

My parents are rich. But if both want to playact at middle-class living and ride the train, so be it.

My mother and father are workaholics. Which is a cute way of saying "distant and borderline neglectful." It's fine. I like it that way. It means that, at least for the next few weeks while they're both trying to impress, they will work late in their offices and be home even later.

Which means I'll have time to plan.

I cross the room and switch on the lights. The basement is transformed from the Speaker's shadowy realm of make-believe, the camera seeing what I want it to see, to something much closer to a bedroom.

Not a regular bedroom, of course, but the kind of bedroom young men my age dream about. There's not much to see now; most of my belongings are still packed away in moving boxes, but there's so much . . . potential down here, in my new room. I've already got my bed and desk set up, and they take up hardly a quarter of the floor space.

This weekend a large sectional couch will be delivered. By suspending a projector from the ceiling, I could ditch my old TV. I don't like adornment, would be a complete minimalist if I had the choice, but I have to play the role, be a teen boy. Which means I need to turn this basement room into a great spot for entertaining.

I think back on Chuck and Kelly, the problems they'd cause, all the planning they'd ruined, and remind myself to find a better social circle this time.

And then there's my ex, Olivia Stewart . . . She hasn't stopped texting. Mostly it's about wanting to "try again" and "get back together" and how I should "come out for a visit," but she's also tried to goad me into small talk. She's shared news stories with me about the Coates family, how sad, how weird the fire was. I respond only with emojis, leave our conversation on mute so her constant buzzing doesn't cloud my focus.

I raise my phone, unlock it, and check the likes on the poem. Not something I do compulsively, because minute-to-minute engagement tells you very little, but I am curious what my numbers are, since today's stream was *much* earlier than normal.

The poem is performing well.

I don't spend much time reading the comments.

Or my DMs.

If I read too much about myself, my work, I'll begin to tailor my content to what my fans want. But they don't know what they want, not really, so I try to keep my creative process pure.

I bring up Maps and check again how long it will take me to drive to school. I've already exercised, showered, and moisturized before hopping on stream. The last few days of packing and travel have disrupted my routine. Clogged my pores and challenged my diet. I may have rushed things with Larissa Coates, but I will not set aside my plans for my mind and body just because my parents have moved us to . . . Long Island. It's not that my power lies in my abdominal muscles or my taut, lithe arms. Or my clear skin and manicured brows and hair. No, my power is derived from *recognizing* that I possess those features, then maintaining them and leveraging them to further the brand.

The only worthwhile private academy in the area is a Catholic school. And I am *not* going to spend the day wearing a clip-on tie and studying the catechism.

Which is why I wanted to try public school, for once. My parents were mortified by the idea at first, but I knew they would be, and I prepared a rebuttal:

I will get into most of the colleges I've applied to; the letters have already started to arrive while we're having this argument.

It will be a drastically abbreviated school year, starting in April, and won't those final grades look that much more impressive when we consider that I achieved them while braving the culture shock of a middling public school?

Academics aside, won't I learn much more about the world, its people, by attending a public school?

In the end, my parents took the money they would have spent on a semester of private school and bought me a car instead.

I know a bribe when I see one.

It's not often I feel guilt, but I can recognize the emotion in other people. I understand that, as distant as my parents are, they felt guilty for uprooting the life I'd built in Arizona. Like they'd felt guilty moving us from Oregon before that, and California before that, back before I can remember much of anything.

The Acura is a very nice car.

The car senses me approach, and the headlights click on before I can reach for the driver's-side door handle.

I look down the street—the sky is gray, and the visibility is low. Because I am a realist, I don't see foreboding in the gloom and fog. I may play a poet on the internet, but I don't see whimsy and figurative language when I look at the world. All I see are wide lawns and large houses bending away down to the intersection, our new neighbors with their trash and recycling cans set out in the gutters.

We didn't have mornings like this in Arizona. Moisture. I feel it in my hair, weighing me down. I will need to check myself before getting out of the car, possibly comb. I keep my hair slightly forward, messier, when I stream as the Speaker. When I'm Aaron, I push it back over my ears, more orderly. It helps me keep the characters I play separate.

Like the headlights, the Acura's door locks, engine, and seat warmers are all automatic.

I lower myself into the seat, gears whirring gently as it conforms to my presets, then I press a single button and I'm ready to drive.

As nice as the car is, I do find aspects of the Acura . . . inconvenient.

Back in Arizona, I may have attended a private school, but within that environment I'd taken great pains to appear normal, middle-of-the-road, unassuming.

I want attention as the Speaker. I do *not* want it as Aaron Fortin.

Here in New York, with this car, with this house, attending *this* school, maintaining my former persona will be . . . more difficult. I don't imagine any of my new classmates will be driving sixty-thousand-dollar cars to school. At least not *this year's* model of sixty-thousand-dollar car.

I'm going to stand out.

I'll find a way to deal with the car, incorporate it into my story. Build it into the character of whatever new version of Aaron I'll be playing here. And that's part of the fun, isn't it? Seeing who the Aaron that attends East Bay High will reveal himself to be.

The drive to school is a little less than fifteen minutes, and, thankfully, the scenery isn't strictly morning mist, suburban homes, and strip malls.

For the last mile, after I turn off the highway, the road to school is bordered on both sides by lush greenery.

Zooming out on the Acura's nav system, I can see that I'm only a couple miles south of a large body of water. The Long Island Sound. I zoom out a bit more, ignore the warning that pops up telling the driver not to work the display while the car's in motion.

I don't need a warning. I can multitask.

I wasn't aware we'd moved so close to the beach. Or so close to Connecticut, for that matter, with a thin line of salt water separating us from the state. I wonder if Connecticut would have been better or worse than here.

I hover my finger over the park to my side, looking for its name. The John Campbell Arboretum, nothing but deciduous trees and—

There's a robotic chirp, and the Acura begins to brake on its own. I look up to see the back of a van approaching rapidly. I stomp on the brake, even though the automated system already has the pedal most of the way to the floor. Tires screech. The center console display changes to the view from the front camera, shows me that I've skidded to a stop less than half an inch from a fender bender.

I breathe. Nothing's broken. There's been no accident.

I'm not angry. But I'm not *calm*. My blood hums, a physiological reaction to the almost-crash.

The van's ugly, its paint job the color of old blood. There's a rectangle of wood paneling on one back door and four steps of chrome ladder on the other. The van looks like it belongs in an antique store.

A face peeks out at me from the circular rear window. I wave two fingers at the girl there, big hair and her features blurred by dirty, tinted automotive glass.

I crane my neck to see around the idling van.

There's a long line of cars and buses waiting outside the school.

The van creeps forward one car length, and I realize I don't need to be in this line. This must be the line of poor kids, public schoolers, being dropped off by their parents.

There's a parking lot on the opposite side of the street, and I can see a few open spots.

I put on my turn signal, look behind me, then back into the oncoming lane, and pull forward, crossing into the lot.

I take a lap in the lot, trying to judge the roomiest spot. The Acura's quite wide, and I'm still getting used to how it corners, how best to park.

I find my spot, then back in.

I let the car's parking assist help, keeping my hands above the wheel, then cut the engine and exit the car.

Not bad.

"Hey!" someone yells.

They can't mean me. Nobody knows me here. Not yet.

"Hey, you!" Or maybe they *do* mean me. "You can't park here!"

I turn to them.

"Excuse me?" I ask. I keep my voice neutral. I'm not sure who this woman is, what this interaction is about to be. But I don't like the way she's looking at me, her hair unkempt, face red as she closes her own car door and crosses the distance to me.

"Don't play smart, wiseass," she says. "Move your car."

Yes. She is mistaken.

I don't *play* smart.

"Am I not supposed to—" I start.

"N-n-no you're not," she says, mimicking a stutter I don't have. What a charming woman.

I look at her shoes—scuffed flats, possibly purchased online, in bulk, coming in a package of three pairs. Then I look back up at the woman, then glimpse her car. There are fifteen years' worth of presidential campaign stickers on the bumper, the losers peeled off but not all the way.

This is a teacher. I'm sure of it.

I estimate she's in her late thirties or early forties, but that on some days, in some lights, she looks older. She used to be pretty. Not a knockout, but maybe a popular girl, at one time, when she was my age. An ancillary figure in her class's yearbook.

From there I infer that she's an alumnus of East Bay High and that a teaching career was her plan B, she probably wanted to be . . . hmmm. What did she want to be? I look into her tired eyes, and the only thing that fits is that she wanted to be a writer. A novelist or essayist. Literary stuff. But she's not interesting enough, didn't have the connections or the ambition to stick with it. So she's now a teacher.

In the two or three seconds I'm thinking this, sizing her up, I also gather that I've made the mistake of parking in the faculty lot, but *why* has that made her this upset?

Because this is one of the few things in her pathetic life that is hers, that she feels she has control over.

"I'm sorry," I start.

I'm not sorry.

"But I don't know what I did wrong," I finish.

I do know and I don't care.

"This is the staff parking lot," the teacher says. "Don't pretend like you don't know that. We've had letters sent home. We've been hearing about it on morning announcements for months."

I hold up my hands, palms out. I try and make myself look anguished, flustered, even though I am none of those things. This is an opportunity. It's an invitation for me to stretch my acting muscles a bit. The New Aaron, maybe he'd feel guilty about something like this.

"It's my first day!" I say. "Honest! I just moved to town."

Saying "honest" like that feels like too much, but we'll see if it lands.

"Oh," the woman says, her face going slack.

Underpaid, overworked, and with a white streak of deodorant across the hem of her blouse, the teacher stares back at me for a moment.

"I *really* didn't know," I say. "I'm really sorry. Can you tell me where the student lot is?"

She scrutinizes my face, like she's got some kind of lie-detector test built into her DNA. And maybe she does, having dealt with teens for so long.

But I'm good at this.

I'm better than good.

I'm the best.

And as she's squinting at me, I ask, "Please?" one more time, and that seals it. She thinks I'm telling the truth, that it was an honest mistake. Which I am and it was, but who cares?

She sighs.

"There is no student lot," she says. "There's a *guest* lot. Stickers are given out at the beginning of the year to seniors who apply. But . . ." She turns, then points. "It's around the back of the school. You better move your . . ." She looks over to the Acura.

My car's almost more expensive than her house. *If* she owns a house.

"Better move your car. They'll tow it if you don't have a sticker."

"I'll do it right now," I say, flipping the key fob over in my hand. I don't need it. The doors are automatic, but it makes a nice prop, makes my motions look urgent.

"I . . ." The teacher starts to say something. I look back, and she smiles at me, meekly, trying to be chummy, but I can tell she's worried I'm going to get her in trouble with an administrator. "I hope you have a good first day. I'm really not usually *that* kind of teacher. Just not a morning person, ya know? I . . . I'm sorry I yelled."

She's not sorry yet.

But she will be.

"It's no problem," I say, then move the car.

FOUR
CRYSTAL

"Good hustle!" Coach Pat yells.

I make the mistake of looking over to the sidelines at her.

"No. Not you, Giordano."

Having second-period gym sucks. And this week our alternating schedule means I have second-period gym *three* times.

Three days of working up a sweat in the morning, then not feeling clean for the rest of my classes.

But at least Gayle's here with me.

We return to the line. Coach Pat blows her whistle, and the ball's tipped. The other team, wearing blue pinnies to our no pinnies, take possession, and Gayle and I try our best to look like we're playing defense.

She's slightly more athletic than me. But only slightly.

"What do you think it means?" Gayle swats her hand, black nail polish becoming a line in the air.

"What *what* means?" I ask, then inhale, juke to the side as Tina Russell passes to a teammate.

Oh shit, this girl's going to blow right by if I don't do something. I squat, put my hands out, but before I have to worry about my lack of coordination, the ball is stripped away by one of the girls on our team who's really playing.

It's Ava Roberts. Ava's an all-star, unconcerned with getting sweaty during second period. She's so comfortable playing sports that she uses the locker-room showers, even when nobody else does. I admire her bravery.

"Their guy," Gayle says, jogging over to me. "What do you think of the Speaker posting from East Bay?" She straightens up, rubbing her lower back as we stop running at half-court and watch our team score. Gayle's wearing black exercise shorts and a faded black T-shirt for the band Cattle Decapitation. Earlier in the semester Coach Pat tried to get her to wear something else. Gayle swapped her usual gym shirt to one that said "Pro-Death" in block letters, and the coach's position on Cattle Decapitation softened.

"I guess I hadn't really thought about it," I say. "Just a cool thing for them, I guess."

I'm lying.

I thought about the Speaker all through Ms. Leigh's calc class.

Not in a starstruck way, like I'm sure Harmony and Paul have been thinking about it. They're no doubt, right now, filling the group text with speculation we'll have to wade through when we get our phones out of our gym lockers.

I've been thinking about the Speaker in the way that . . .

I mean, what are the odds?

It wasn't like he'd tagged the photo somewhere in Nassau County, closer to the city, like he could have been traveling to Manhattan or Brooklyn or wherever social-media people went on vacation.

We were watching his stream. Everyone in Trevor's van was talking about the Speaker, *thinking* about him, and a minute later he posts that he's in our town.

Not Bethpage or Massapequa or Commack or any of the Islips. He said he was in East Bay. He said he was *right here.*

An astronomical coincidence.

It must be a trick. I think about how the IG live looked a little off, a stream of a stream. Maybe the Speaker isn't even a social-media influencer; maybe he's fiction. Some kind of location-based alternate reality game thing that Paul and Harmony have opted in to without realizing. A game they don't know they're playing.

So in first period I brought up the Speaker's account. But it was just a regular Instagram account. And yes. His latest photo *was* tagged East Bay, New York.

Looking at his page and his older posts, I was unsettled.

And there was something even more unsettling in the way that Harmony and Paul had been discussing the post and poem afterward. As Trevor found parking, Harmony and Paul spent the rest of our time together on the walk into school debating what it could *mean* with each other.

They kept using that exact word.

"What does it mean?"

"I think it means . . ."

"Remember last week, when we were talking about the meaning *of . . ."*

It wasn't like they were trying to track a celebrity's movements, or even solve a mystery, it was more like they were having some kind of spiritual discussion.

Or maybe I just don't understand. One of those conversations you can't overhear, if you lack the context to—

Shit, there's been another tip-off. Before I know it, there's an elbow in my side, Catherine Doyle jostling me out of the way.

"Play or don't," she hisses at me, "but don't just fucking stand around."

Honestly . . . she's right. I look for Gayle, but she's not there.

I rub the spot on my stomach. Catherine didn't hit me hard, more tapped me awake than anything else. Then Gayle runs by, following the ball. She laughs, shakes her head at me, then continues playing crappy defense.

I head to the sideline and Coach Pat calls one of the subs in. The PE teacher doesn't give me shit about taking myself out of the game, *not* something we're supposed to do. Maybe she sees on my face that I'm spaced out, has decided to be kind to me.

I look up at the gym's clock, old and dusty, a metal cage to protect it. There are fifteen minutes left in the period. I don't talk to any of the girls on the sidelines with me, and Gayle doesn't sub out, so I just lean against the bleachers, pretending to watch the game while I think more about what it all *means*.

Six minutes before the bell—barely time to change, never mind shower (which nobody but Ava Roberts does anyway)—Coach Pat declares the blue pinnies the winners and sends us to the locker room.

I wait until most of the other girls are done changing, the girls with boyfriends, the girls who take their bags into the hallway to wait for the bell by the soda machines, before I start to undress.

Gayle waits too, in solidarity.

"You doing anything different?" Gayle asks, not speaking until I have my shirt pulled over my head, most of my body angled in toward the locker door.

"Huh?" I say, hurrying to get my sweatshirt on before I turn around. "You look good. Toned. I know you have the exercise bike, but anything else?" Gayle says. She has her own shirt off, the paleness and curves of her like a challenge to the handful of other girls still changing with us.

She's confident and she does this sometimes, tries to get me to join her in that confidence, boost me up. I could tell her about the time-restricted eating. But I'm not feeling like having this conversation here, with this audience, or having it at all today, audience or not. Anyway, this is only the second day I'm attempting it, lunch is an hour away, and my body's already regretting that I skipped breakfast. So maybe I'll give up on this experiment and never share with her that I tried in the first place. Not that we have all that many heart-to-hearts these days.

"No, just the bike," I say, lying, because last time I looked, the bike's got a thin layer of dust over the seat. Then I change the subject: "What happens in the chapters, for Hobbes?"

Gayle blinks at me, then shakes away her exaggerated cartoon daze.

"Crystal Diaz Giordano!" She says my whole name, like my mom does sometimes. "Did . . ." She points a finger at me, lets it mock shiver. Gayle looms so large in my mind, I sometimes forget she's about a foot shorter than me. "Did you not do the reading?"

I did the reading. I just don't want to talk about my body. At least not in the way Gayle wants to, somewhere between denial and toxic positivity.

"Can you stop and just tell me what happens in the chapters?" I swipe away all the group text notifications and show her my phone. We have two minutes to the bell. I have English next period. Gayle doesn't have Ms. Hobbes until the end of the day.

"The monster kills Victor's father," Gayle says. But she doesn't look sure of herself. "Or his fiancée. Or both. Or maybe it's his cousin. As revenge."

She didn't do the reading. Or if she did, she skimmed and didn't understand what she read.

"Wait. What?" I ask.

"I don't know. I want to like the book." Gayle motions down at her skirt, black fabric with neon-green stitching. "Obviously. Seems like it'd be my kind of thing. But there's just . . . a lot of talking. And so much of it is the monster talking. I like in the movies how the monster's not chasing anyone around, shouting, 'Debate me!'"

I giggle, slip my shoes on, and explain to her that it's Victor Frankenstein's brother, William, who gets strangled by the monster. Then, to make matters worse, his family's young female ward, Justine, gets blamed for the murder. I don't remember how far we were supposed to read last night, I've already finished the book, but spoiler alert: Justine's then *executed*, all because Victor doesn't want to speak up to clear her name, which might require telling the world about his monster.

Gayle listens, seeming to be digesting in case there's a reading quiz.

"What a dick," Gayle says, working the clasp on her third and final belt. "Wait. Then why'd *you* ask *me* what happened?"

The bell rings, and I tell her I'll see her at lunch and scurry away in the crowd, up to the second floor.

"Good morning," Ms. Hobbes says, not looking up from her computer. Then says it again as each student after me enters the room.

I'm the only one to wish her a good morning back.

Ms. Hobbes is an acquired taste, but *I* think she's cool. I enjoy the books she picks, that she goes outside the state-required syllabus. And she's one of the few teachers who treats us like adults. Which is what some of my classmates don't like. That Ms. Hobbes isn't afraid to get a little sarcastic or call BS on a kid.

I get the impression that Ms. Hobbes teaches this way because she's a little burnt-out, but something about her teaching style works. She counteracts our senioritis by implying that she, the teacher, has had senioritis for years now.

It's well after winter break, most of the school year is done, major grades are sealed and off to colleges, so we've already spent a lot of time with Ms. Hobbes. There's a comfort to the class that's almost boredom, probably *is* boredom for my classmates.

In all these months, even through the change of seasons, I've only ever seen Ms. Hobbes dress in four or five outfits. And none of them are nice. Currently she's wearing the salmon blouse and gray corduroy pants, a combination that doesn't work at all. It's made worse by the deodorant stain.

But still, I want to be her.

A few months ago, around Christmas, I saw Ms. Hobbes at the mall. It's always odd, seeing a teacher in the wild, but this was different.

She was hard to recognize. She wasn't wearing any of her normal looks. It wasn't that she was dressed *nice* or anything, she was in jeans and a sweater, but it made all the difference. And it wasn't just the jeans, she was wearing her hair differently: slight curls, where for school she straightens it. She was smiling. She looked fantastic, happy. I didn't say hi. She was with her husband. Or fiancé. I don't know, she wears a ring but never talks about him in class. He looked happy too.

I watched them for a little while as they shopped, Ms. Hobbes stopping to look in a display case.

I liked that. Seeing Ms. Hobbes that way. We haven't talked much, inside or outside of class, but seeing her outside of school gave me a better understanding of who she is. I want what she has; if not her job, then at least her attitude toward it. I want to stop caring about what people think of me while I'm at school. And I want to be able to be happy when I'm out of school.

"Okay," Ms. Hobbes says, standing from her computer, "clear your desks. Reading quiz time."

The class groans.

Good thing I told Gayle what happened in the chapters.

"I'm serious," she says. "Half sheet of paper. Put a proper heading on it. Name, date, and period. And not just your *first* name, Cody."

She watches as loose-leaf paper is torn in half, slips passed around to kids who didn't bring their binders today, who've stopped carrying books at all from class to class.

"Ah, I'm just kidding, I'm not grading that shit," Ms. Hobbes says, taking the remote for the Smartboard off her desk, angling it up at the projector. "But sounds like you all would have failed."

The class laughs uncomfortably, relieved. On the board, the projector bulb warms, showing us the attendance grid.

Ms. Hobbes looks around the room, checking off students. "No Burke again?" she asks. One of Tommy Burke's friends, Ekon Smith, shakes his head.

Ms. Hobbes gives a slight tsk, then says to the room but also to herself: "So close but so far. You figure he'd try and show up the last couple months, if not to graduate, then at least so he can go to prom."

She's not joking; she seems genuinely melancholy that Tommy Burke, an asshole who made fun of me all of middle school, is going to low-level drug-deal his way out of graduating.

I envy that about Ms. Hobbes, though. Her empathy. Because, even trying, and I *do* try, I couldn't care less about Tommy's diploma. I understand that he's probably had a hard life to make him act the way he does. But still: screw him.

"Oh," Ms. Hobbes says, looking to a student in the back. "You."

I follow her gaze.

As a rule, I don't talk to my classmates, not during this period. I only talk in school when Harmony, Paul, Trevor, or Gayle is in a class with me. Not that I *only* talk to my friends, but I tend to need at least one of them around to ease my social anxiety enough to want to talk with a casual acquaintance. And none of my friends are in this period, so English is usually just me and Ms. Hobbes. Which sounds sad, but it's actually a quiet, relaxing part of my day. English class is a little vacation from worrying about what everyone else is doing.

I've been with half of these kids since elementary school, the rest since middle school. Even if I don't speak to most of them, I know their faces.

And it's a new face back there where Ms. Hobbes is looking.

Ms. Hobbes clicks the board with the stylus; I don't see what name she's checking off, but I hear the plastic on plastic.

"Class," she says, talking like a kindergarten teacher for a second, "we've got a new student today. Everyone give a big senior-English welcome to Aaron Fortin."

There's a group mumble, slightly happier than the sound they made for the fake quiz, but nobody says any real words.

Aaron nods at everyone.

"Actually," the boy says, looking back up at Ms. Hobbes with a smirk at the corner of his mouth, "it's pronounced Four-teen. Like the number but with a little accent to it."

"Apologies," Ms. Hobbes says. "Aaron Four-teen."

"I think it's French," the boy says back to her. He seems to anticipate the eye rolls he's already starting to get, mainly from the other boys. The row to my left is all boys, a spot left for the missing Tommy Burke.

"But don't hold that against me," Aaron Fortin says, waving at them.

Half the class, Ms. Hobbes included, seems to instantly like the boy; the other half looks like they want to punch his teeth in.

I like him.

It's early to tell, but it seems like he's got nice-guy class-clown delivery. As opposed to dickhead class-clown delivery, which is a very different vibe.

And there's something about his hair, slightly damp looking, and those eyes, half-lidded as he smiles, that I find familiar. He looks like any number of skinny boy-next-door types that Harmony and Gayle crush on. Singers and actors who get fancams made of them. And he seems aware of how he looks, but not conceited. Which is a weird thing to think, only looking at him for ten seconds, but somehow I know it, that this guy's not a narcissist.

I like to think I'm pretty observant, can see things about people most would miss. Probably comes from how quiet I am most of the time. I pay attention. To the little details.

"Well, Aaron," Ms. Hobbes says, "I hope that you won't hold how I yelled at you this morning against *me*." She lifts the travel mug from the edge of her desk. It's not a Yeti, but it does have a sticker of Bigfoot on it.

"I didn't have my coffee yet. Or my booze."

Some of my classmates laugh; some do not.

"It's cool," Aaron says, beginning to get uncomfortable, all of us watching him, Ms. Hobbes having turned this into a comedy bit.

I turn forward in my seat, not wanting to be part of adding to his embarrassment.

"I'd ask you to share where you're coming to us from, what's one fun fact about yourself, but I'm, uh," Ms. Hobbes says, "I'm sure you want me to stop talking to you. So I'll just say that this unit we're talking about Mary Shelley's *Frankenstein*."

Ms. Hobbes crosses to a bookshelf full of classroom sets, grabs a paperback, then tosses it underhand toward the back of the class at Aaron.

"Catch," she says.

I don't turn to see whether Aaron catches the book or not.

But I imagine he does.

After a few minutes, the excitement of a new addition to the class has faded, and we all listen while, phones occasionally buzzing, Ms. Hobbes recounts last night's reading.

She knows nobody around me has read, probably assumes that *I* haven't read, since I don't raise my hand and she's not one of those teachers who will cold call on you to make a point. She tells us all about Victor's poor brother, William, his and Justine's deaths, then asks us what those deaths *mean* for the book and its themes.

I find it hard to focus on the follow-up questions Ms. Hobbes asks, or the answers she herself provides when nobody volunteers. I'm trying to think whether or not I'll be good and opt for the healthier salad option at lunch or go for the pizza slice that I really want.

"Actually," a voice says from the back row. I turn again—most of us who are awake do. It's Aaron Fortin. "And it's been a while since I read this, at my last school, but I always thought about it the other way around."

Aaron *isn't* from around here. His accent, I don't know, it's slightly surfer dude-ish? Just slightly; he still sounds intelligent.

"The other way around?" Ms. Hobbes asks.

"That the book's not saying science or even Victor's ambitions are necessarily a bad thing. Like, I don't think Shelley wants him to be *judged* for that part of himself."

Ms. Hobbes puts a hand on her hip. She's not insulted to be contradicted; she's just . . . taken aback. She's not used to students interrupting her, at least not to talk about the books, to try to have an actual discussion on our discussion days.

"Go on . . . ," she says.

"It says right here." Aaron holds up the book, flips open the cover, points to the title page, then reads aloud: "*The Modern Prometheus.* That's the subtitle of the book."

"Go . . . on." Ms. Hobbes smiles. She's charmed by whatever's happening here, Aaron's thoughts about literary theory. Charmed like I am, like Donna Collins, one desk over from me, is also charmed.

"Prometheus gave humans fire, right?" Aaron continues. "And fire enables all kinds of technological advances."

"And art and culture," Ms. Hobbes says as he pauses, motioning for him to continue.

"So maybe Victor makes a lot of mistakes, regrets a lot of what he's done, but his science has the ability to change the world. Like, not the application of making the monster, but just the innovations he's made. And ultimately, it's the fact that he's kept this knowledge a secret that causes actual harm. It's not the science or even the monster itself that gets Justine killed, but Victor keeping the monster a secret. It's a *moral* failing. Not a scientific failing."

The class is silent, including Ms. Hobbes, who's no longer smiling but has instead crossed her arms, started to nod silently while she tries to untangle what he's just said.

I guess I *kinda* follow what Aaron's saying.

But I'm not sure that's what *I* got out of reading this part of the book . . .

There's a moment here where I could raise my hand. Where I could join this discussion and share why I think Aaron's slightly misreading the text.

But I don't do it.

Of course I don't.

"So, what you're saying is, Victor should . . ." Ms. Hobbes sounds like she's trying to form her own follow-up to this thesis. "Victor should be . . . more Prometheus-like, not *less* Prometheus-like? That he should share his knowledge?"

"I guess. Sort of," Aaron says. But it doesn't sound like he agrees with that conclusion.

"So, for the rest of the class, the ones that are awake, Aaron's saying Victor Frankenstein's like a Victorian-era Elon Musk."

Ms. Hobbes laughs, and as she does, I see an expression cross Aaron's face. It's very quick, a nanosecond, and it's gone.

But in that nanosecond: Aaron's disgusted.

By both Ms. Hobbes and by her turning his idea into a punch line. He was trying to make a real point, is brave enough to try talking about the book on his first day in class, and she's treated it like a joke.

Even though I don't agree with what he said, I actually . . . don't blame him.

I'd be pissed too.

But Ms. Hobbes doesn't seem to notice the flash of disgust; she walks up the center aisle of desks, tapping her knuckles against desktops to get students to put their phones away. And she keeps talking:

"I don't know where Mr. Fortin *was* going to school, but we should see if we can get an exchange program going. That was great, Aaron. Thank you for sharing. But also, for the rest of you because I know how you think: that's not going to be on the test."

Aaron looks around at the faces of our classmates, most turned to him, then seems to get uncomfortable again.

I go through my day making sure to never have this many eyes on me. But a lot of times my anxiety makes it *feel* like I do, so I can sympathize with him.

"But I'd love to hear more about that idea," Ms. Hobbes says, "if you want to write about it in the open-essay section of the test, Aaron."

"Cool," he says. "Will do."

Then there are a few seconds of awkward silence. The bell rings.

Oh, thank god.

Time to go to lunch.

FIVE

AARON

I've never read *Frankenstein*.

I don't read much fiction. Don't have the time.

It's pretty easy to make it sound like I've read *Frankenstein*, though.

My second period is a "study hall." Whatever that is. We didn't have these periods at my previous schools. But this morning I quickly learn that study hall is less about studying, more about students asking a bored-looking teacher if they can have the bathroom pass.

Public school. I love it already.

I lean over to the two girls in front of me, one with her desk turned around to face the other, and ask them who they have for English.

One girl has freckles, and the other has clear braces. Both are fine-looking, but neither has what it takes, surface-level, to be the new Olivia.

The one with the freckles is a junior, so can't help me, but the one with the braces is a senior and has Hobbes.

Hobbes. I check the school's website. That's her, the teacher who chased me out of the parking lot. The picture on the school's directory has her looking ten years younger, but that's her.

Victoria Hobbes.

I tip my schedule toward the two girls.

I have Hobbes too. Third period? Me too. How is she? As a teacher? Oh. She's one of those. Well, what's the class reading right now? Frankenstein, *cool.*

Yeah. I've read that. Yes. Donna, was it? Yes. The book is . . . *confusing. I guess.*

It sure has been nice talking with you two.

I turn away from Donna and friend and spend the rest of study hall actually studying.

I read everything I need to know about *Frankenstein*. I mean, clearly, I know the story. Everyone does. It's part of the collective unconscious. But there's more . . . *thematic meat* in the original novel than I thought there'd be.

First, I read the summary on the Wikipedia page. Then I click through, check with one or two of the linked sources so I can sprinkle in some information that I couldn't have gotten from *just* the Wiki.

Then I go to the second page of Google results and pick an article at random. I form what I find during *that* search into my thesis.

The trick to sounding like you've read a book you haven't read is to let the person who *has* read it speak first.

Then you disagree with them.

Not to the point you tell them they're wrong. You tell them you see where they're coming from, but you have a slightly different interpretation of the text.

Before the bell, I read as much as I can, which is everything I need to.

Then I head to English class.

I'll give Victoria Hobbes this much: she's the first person at this school I've seen even *attempt* to teach.

Hobbes is . . . well, she looks better than she did in the parking lot. Her cheeks are less pink. Her eyes are prettier without the crimp of anger at the edges. But she's still kind of pathetic.

She tries, though, engaging me in banter during attendance.

In interacting with her, I get a firmer grasp on the type of person I'm going to be in this town, in this school.

I get a glimpse of the new Aaron Fortin.

I tend to match energies. Or I can when I want to. It's part of being a good mimic. And I match Victoria Hobbes's energy to help shape the new Aaron.

New Aaron smiles more. He's a bit of a dweeb. But—I look over at Donna from study hall—the girls here seem to like him. The competition in this class for female attention . . . most of the guys here smell like pot smoke and are scabbed with razor acne. I'll have to be careful of these burn-out boys and their slightly more handsome jersey-clad counterparts, the lacrosse team or whoever. Most of them have a look I'd describe as "working class." They won't be charmed by New Aaron, and they'll probably be less charmed when I start taking their women. But otherwise: finding a new Olivia here at East Bay High shouldn't be a problem. Or do I even need a new Olivia? Do I even need that kind of liability, that much responsibility? It's like adopting a stray. Even if having a puppy or kitten disarms people.

Victoria Hobbes paces the front of the class, makes sound effects with her mouth as she talks about the book, then does a terrible English accent when she's quoting Victor or the monster.

I still think teaching was her plan B, but I was mistaken in thinking she wanted to be a writer. I now think she wanted to be an actor. Or a comedian. A performer of some kind. Because she's putting on a show for her class, telling jokes, acting a fool. It's both admirable and, like a lot of aspects of Victoria Hobbes, pathetic. Have I used that word yet to describe her? I have. It's the least attractive quality in a person, I think. That even when they try, they can't help but be less-than, that their failures are grand enough to cause others to feel pity for them.

"Actually," I say, interrupting her lesson.

Then I go on to make the point I prepared in study hall.

Hobbes looks a little confused at first, but eventually she loves what I have to say about Mary Shelley's 1818 trailblazing masterpiece of science fiction.

There's a rocky moment, before her praise comes, where she gets flip with me. Victorian Elon Musk, really? I don't like it. She'll pay for that quip eventually.

Seated low in my desk, looking up at her, I can see in her eyes . . . a glimmer of hope. That she's marked me down as her new star pupil.

I can also see that my intelligence excites her. Maybe even turns her on. I think about how there are multiple ways I could destroy this woman's life. So many options. If I wanted to, I could make her front-page news without any kind of violence.

The bell rings.

✗

The cafeteria is simultaneously huge and cramped. High ceilings with fluorescent light fixtures that look like they haven't been dusted since the nineties. Resin flooring that's been recently polished, but not well, so it still carries a full school years' worth of sneaker skids across its shiny surface.

It's very different from where we used to eat, back in Arizona. But it's not all that different from the lunchroom in Oregon, which had been larger.

What *is* different, here in East Bay, are the students.

My first three classes, if study hall can be called a class, offered glimpses of what the school culture must be like, but here in the lunchroom, where lowerclassmen and upperclassmen are mixing, I get a fuller picture of what East Bay High has to offer.

And it's not offering much.

No. I shouldn't be that dismissive. *I* am above this lunchroom. But the *New* Aaron's not. Detached and snobbish is not how I'm going to play this. Not who I'm going to be.

Standing by an empty table, I notice that I'm catching a few glances. It's a largish school, several hundred students per grade, but even with all those faces, the student body recognizes fresh blood.

I'm being watched, and I have to make sure I project New Aaron energy.

Students enter the lunchroom from the three sets of double doors, some stopping off at lunch tables to set down binders and backpacks but most opting to hold their bags and head straight for the lunch lines. The *growing* lunch lines. I watch hungry students bottleneck at the counter, those behind them taking trays.

Some students ignore the food, ignore the tables, and head to a small booth set up against one wall. At the booth, two students, a girl and a girlish-looking boy, sit beneath a sign that says *Prom Voting! King, Queen, and Theme!*

I've been to dances. Winter formals. A junior prom, with Olivia as my date. But something about reading the word *prom* in bubble letters. It strikes me as much *realer* than all of those.

Something inside me, not necessarily an emotion, warms at the idea of prom. An honest-to-god prom, attended by—I look back out over the seething mass of the student body—*these* people.

But which of *these* people will be *my* people? Which of these students, with their discordant styles, cliques, and ages . . . which of them will I choose? It's not a question of them choosing *me*; I could *make* myself fit with any of them.

But that won't be necessary.

I've already decided, generally, who the New Aaron is.

Now I have to find him a table that fits.

The lines are getting shorter. Students have begun finding their seats, their choice of milk or chocolate milk made, their lunches paid for.

Tables are filling in.

I walk to the far wall, gray brick, and lower my head to the water fountain there, pretend to take a drink.

I can't look like I'm observing. No, New Aaron is full of good-natured, go-with-the-flow confidence. He gets along with *anyone*, just needs an empty seat to eat his lunch, man.

I shift my body, scan the lunchroom.

The table nearest me is a group of girls with highlighted hair and pastel nail polish. One of them might be the next Olivia, but it's not like I'm going to sit down now, try to socialize with them. That's not who the New Aaron is. He's nice, but he's not an only-has-female-friends kind of nice. He's quirky, a handsome guy with a sense of humor, not an athlete but friends with a few athletes, because he's friends with everyone.

I move on.

There's a table of nerds next. Not that the social structure of East Bay seems rigid, cleanly delineated like it would be in a teen movie, but there's a pecking order to the world, and to ignore that would be naive. The nerds, they're a mix of boys and girls, and they've got a small game system set up. They're eating bagged lunches—potato chips on their sandwiches and processed, prepackaged foods—while they take turns, four of them at a time, playing their game.

They're not who the New Aaron would gravitate toward. I'm no good at video games. I'm sure I could learn, but why do that, just to fit in with . . . *these nerds?*

Next there's a table of all boys. All boys, not usually an issue, but on closer inspection: no. There's not a baseball cap or jersey between them. None of them are athletes.

Not that I'm a fan of athletes, but that many unathletic boys together . . . that's a red flag. Bunch of incels. I'd bet at least one or two of them follows the Speaker.

I stand from the water fountain, mime wiping my chin. I'm beginning to get worried. I have to make a choice soon.

And then I see them.

Yes. Them.

Let's try *them* out.

They're lived in. Slightly discordant. I could sort each to another table, from their look and dress, without disrupting the order and hierarchy of the room. But why would I? They look so good grouped together. So natural.

They're a motley crew—but, no, that's not the right term either. Because even if it's not literally the definition, calling a group a "motley crew" brings to mind a louder group of individuals than the ones I'm looking at. They're colorful, but they aren't conspicuous.

And joining a group like that . . . I like the challenge of it. To mold myself into a New Aaron who can fit with them, preserve their pH balance.

If it doesn't work, I can move to a different table tomorrow.

But I think it's going to work . . .

I take a step toward them.

"Can I . . . ," I say, pausing, faking a tiny bit of nervousness. The New Aaron's confident, but not *that* confident. "Mind if I sit here?" I ask the girl. The normal one, not Wednesday Addams next to her.

The girl looks over at the rest of them, like *What should she do?* The boy on his phone looks up, barely seems to see me, he's so absorbed in what he's watching, but it's the other guy, the Black one, who speaks first:

"Sure." He gestures to the seat beside him. "Nobody's sitting there."

I sit, open the front pouch of my bag, remove an apple, and set that on the table in front of me. I'll take a bite in a moment. But for now it's just a prop to show that I'm eating something during lunch.

They watch me, none of them speaking.

The girl, the normal one, Girl Classic. She's pretty, with nice hair, not flat-chested, manicured nails, and a charm bracelet on one wrist. She has the school lunch in front of her, fries and a meatball sandwich, but she hasn't touched it yet.

Next to her is a short goth girl in a skirt it's too cold for outside. As I watch, the goth sneaks a fry off Girl Classic's lunch tray and eats it.

Skipping over an empty seat, kept there as boy-buffer or something, we move on to the white guy.

He has fair stubble and clean ginger hair pushed up in bedhead . . . bedhead that's nearly made it to noon, so I guess it's a deliberate choice. He's still watching his phone, one AirPod in. He's eating a Lunchables pizza, which is something I don't think I've seen a person do *ever*. I'm surprised he's not at the table with the nerds, but maybe he's slightly too aloof for that; it's hard to tell why he's here, why *any* of them are here. Maybe it's his shoes, which I clocked on my way over: Air Force 1s. Customs. And they're spotless. Which implies that he has more in other colors. The shoes combined with the AirPods . . . that means money. Not *my* level of money, but rich for this lunchroom.

The Black guy, he's smiling at me. Unlike his well-to-do friend, he's shaved this morning, but he's missed one or two hairs under his chin. He may not have the money, but he's dressed better, is better kempt than his buddy.

Hmm. Buddy or boyfriend? I tilt my head, note the slight closeness of their bodies. They hold themselves differently than the girls, with regard to the other.

The Black guy's brought his lunch from home in a Tupperware container, probably last night's family meal. The leftovers are some kind of rice or couscous, chunks of protein that's probably chicken. Yes. Definitely chicken. I lean a bit in, catch a whiff of the oils he's wearing, distinctive and earthy, not hard to discern from the pretty girl's perfume, and not a typical cologne. No, it may not be chicken in his lunch, but I'm *certain* it's not pork. This guy's Muslim. Or at least his family is; who knows what he believes?

Each aspect of these people, what they're wearing, what they're eating, how they smell . . . each tells me a story, and then, taken as a whole, the four of them tell an even bigger story, one I hadn't clocked on first glance but one that delights me regardless.

Nobody at East Bay High thinks about these four. Or doesn't think about them much.

They aren't complete loners.

They aren't the popular kids, but they aren't problem children or suicide-prevention outreach cases either.

They *could* overlap with the other lunch tables, but they don't. They prefer each other's company.

They are a microcosm, a world unto themselves, here at East Bay High.

They're not just gathered here to have a place to sit. They're friends. True friends.

Let's see if they've got room for one more.

"I'm Aaron," I say, picking up the apple, cleaning it on my sleeve. Which isn't really cleaning it, not after it's been on this filthy table hastily wiped down by some derelict work-release janitor. But the New Aaron wouldn't have a problem with a few germs, so I will push through, eat the damn apple.

We go around the table, and they introduce themselves.

Trevor.

Harmony.

Gayle—Gayle with a *y*, she says, and I wonder if that's even her real name . . . Well, at least it's not Raven or Hecate or something.

Then, finally, needing to be poked in his ribs by Trevor, the boy on his phone lets me know he's Paul.

It's nice to meet all of you.

I just moved here.

Nobody asks me from where, and I don't tell them. I think New Aaron's from California, at least from the voice I'm using, but I'd rather not be put on the spot and made to commit right now. It'd be easier to say Arizona, just tell the truth, but that's flying too close to the sun. It can't all be autobiography. For New Aaron to stand on his own, I have to invent *some* parts of him. Not that I think I'll be recognized without my mask. Or at least I'm not planning on it, not anytime soon. It hasn't happened yet, but . . . I gain hundreds of new followers every day. Probably twenty or twenty-five since the lunch bell. It's not impossible I'll be recognized. Just improbable.

I'm about to bring up my schedule, ask the table if they have any opinions about my social studies teacher, because that seems like the kind of icebreaker that gets kids like this talking, when a *fifth* friend appears.

I've misjudged. I thought these four looked like a complete unit on their own. But I guess not. The girl's carrying a lunch tray and sits down across from me, completing the circuit and joining the half circle of the two boys and the two girls.

Now there are three boys and three girls sitting here, and the symmetry . . . it makes things feel off.

Before she sat down, I had liked being the gender tiebreaker. Her being here, it dampens my enthusiasm for this whole endeavor, makes me think I should just choose a new table tomorrow.

I'm not sure why she makes me feel that way, but I do.

"Hi," I say to her. "I'm—"

"Aaron," the new girl finishes for me, then looks down at her food. Chicken tenders, the breading looking soggy, and a slice of square, dry pizza. I wonder if she had to pay extra for these two delicious dishes, or whether the lunch counter is one-price-fits-all.

I don't like the way she says my name. It's the Long Island accent, holding the *A*'s too long.

Ehhh-ron.

"Have we met?" I ask. The New Aaron would be surprised someone's remembered his name, kind of flattered.

I can't remember which class I share with this girl.

But why would I?

She's got dark hair, slight undeliberate grease to it. Her skin is tan, but not in a way some of the girls in the lunchroom have darker skin, the ones at the all-girls table who probably have standing appointments at tanning salons. This girl's tan is uneven, possibly due to slight vitiligo or a birthmark that's faded over time.

She's probably only a size or two bigger than her friend Gayle, but she's much less comfortable in her skin; she speaks softly enough that I can tell she rarely speaks at all.

"We have Ms. Hobbes together," the girl says. "Last period."

Oh, *Ms.* Hobbes, she says. So respectful. Someone's an academic, maybe a teacher's pet. I think back on the class. I remember her now, kind of. She was some of the human white noise that'd been sitting toward the front of the class, one of the girls and boys eye-fucking me while Victoria Hobbes and I had our exchanges.

"This is Crystal," Gayle finally says, her friend's and my awkwardness taking too long, making Gayle impatient.

I agree; we were all in such a nice rhythm before Crystal showed up.

I tell Crystal that it's nice to meet her, and she nods and begins to eat.

Maybe she won't upset our group dynamic.

I'll probably never even notice she's here.

"I watched the stream again," Paul says, looking over to Harmony. "Someone put it on YouTube and . . ."

Trevor slices his hand down between Paul and Harmony, like he's calling a foul. "We've got someone new here. You're just going to ignore him and start talking about your internet thing?"

Paul starts to say something, but Trevor's not finished.

"A thing that *we*"—he indicates himself, Gayle, and Crystal— "already had to listen to this morning and made it clear that we are not interested in."

"Oh, come on," Paul says. "Do I look like I'm on the yearbook committee?" Then he points at me. "Look at him. He's fine. He's got his apple. We're having lunch. It's a lunch table. We can have multiple conversations."

No, I realize, Paul and Trevor are not boyfriends. They're ex-boyfriends. And probably lifelong friends before that, because why else would they still be sitting next to each other?

Interesting.

I can work with that . . . New Aaron can work with that. New Aaron is open-minded.

"Really, don't mind me," I say.

"I won't," Paul says. Then, to Harmony, "He said this really interesting thing at the beginning. He said . . ."

"Shush, Paul," Harmony says, then turns to me. She likes me. I can tell. She's unbuttoned her sweater, and in the process, her shirt's slipped open a bit. It's something she's maybe even done subconsciously, but now I can see she has a mole at the base of her neck. "Paul and I follow the Speaker? Do you know him?"

I'm so dazzled by Harmony's mole, it takes me a moment to realize what she's asked.

Do *I* follow the Speaker?

Six hundred thousand followers, a third of those gained in the last two months, but the real world's a big place. The Speaker is *not* famous. He's not even internet famous, not yet, but he'll be there before the end of the year.

I've never *once* heard somebody say the Speaker's name aloud. Well, with two notable exceptions. But Chuck and Kelly don't count. And they weren't like this, stumbled upon in the wild. I had to go looking for them.

Hearing Harmony ask me about the Speaker, it staggers me for a second. But only a second.

"Please say you know what I'm talking about," Harmony says. "It'll drive Trevor crazy if we had a third fan at the table."

I smile.

I know how the New Aaron would play this.

"I . . . Yes," I say to her, then wink, an exaggerated enough movement so they all see it. "I *totally* know what that is you're talking about."

"Ha. Stop it. No you don't," Harmony says.

"Sure I do . . . ," I say. "It's a . . . Paul said 'stream,' so it's one of those video-game guys, right?"

"Nooo," Harmony says, swatting me lightly with one hand.

"So not, uh, a Twitch person? A streamer?"

My words don't sound 100 percent convincing to my ears. But I'm my own worst critic; the people at this table seem to be buying it. Harmony would buy whatever I'm selling.

"God," Trevor says, "I wish it were a video-game guy. Then he wouldn't have anyone else to talk about it with."

"Where did you move here from, Aaron?" Gayle asks. From the tone of her voice, it sounds like she wants to change the subject. She's not a fan of the Speaker; that's good.

"California, actually," I say, committing, not worried about the decision.

I left California when I was eleven. I can't remember much of it, certainly have no frame of reference for what high school there might be like. But neither do these five. I can make it up, sprinkle in details from all the nonfiction books I've read. Lots of serial-killer stories take place in California.

"Cool, what part?" Gayle's warming up to me. Despite the dark lipstick and cat-eye makeup, she's actually got quite an outgoing personality.

"Southern California," I say. "Mountains with sun, not mountains with snow."

They all seem interested; even Paul's angled his phone screen down at the table.

All except one.

I look across from me, and Crystal's done with her pizza, has left the crust, but hasn't started her tenders. She's staring at me.

If the New Aaron were different, if he were a tough guy, more standoffish, I'd ask her what the fuck she's looking at.

But, my character solidified, I ask, "What is it, Crystal? Is there something on my face?"

Then I smile, the closest approximation I can get to kindness, and wipe at one side of my face and then the other.

I can feel the slight stick of apple juice at the corners of my lips. I hate to be dirty, will wash my face the first chance I get.

"You're lying," Crystal says.

It takes a lot to surprise me. And it's now happened twice in five minutes. Having Harmony ask me about the Speaker. That was kind of a mild surprise, novel, gratifying, even.

To be called a liar . . . that surprise I find *less* amusing.

"Whoa, Crystal," Gayle says. That's it, these two are friends. Maybe best friends. The rest of them . . . they can take or leave Crystal.

"I . . . I'm sorry," Crystal says, embarrassed, tan skin not really blushing, just going mottled and unappealing under her too-much foundation. "I didn't mean to say it like that."

"I assure you, Crystal," I say, slipping out of character a bit, losing the slight surfer-dude lilt I've been trying to affect, "I'm really from California."

Paul's fully got his phone away now, is tweezing out the AirPod from his ear.

Harmony smiles at me, her smile concealing an anger at her friend. She's embarrassed. Her eyes are trying to meet mine, trying to tell me, *I don't know her.* But I don't meet her gaze.

I keep looking at Crystal.

"I don't mean California. I just . . . I know where I recognize you from," Crystal says. Then she swallows. I can hear how thick her saliva is, how unaccustomed she is to speaking, like this, to strangers. Then she finishes:

"You're the Speaker."

I feel the blood leave my face, and I want to throw up.

I take a bite of the apple.

Fuck.

I chew, trying to masque my surprise by scrunching up my face.

I didn't think I'd have to deal with a problem like this. Not this soon. It pushes things forward. It's not some insurmountable roadblock, it doesn't mean I have to scrap anything and go again, but it's like those moving boxes in Arizona—it puts a timer on things.

But maybe there's a simpler way out . . .

"Are you kidding?" I ask, keeping eye contact with Crystal. "You really think I'm this, um, not-video-game guy?"

Crystal breaks first, looking down at fingernails that she's bitten to unattractive nubs.

I think I might have cowed her into silence, but then she speaks again:

"If it's a secret, I understand," she says, her voice getting lower with every word. The hush of her voice, like she's talking to herself, should be swallowed up by the bustle of the lunchroom, but I'm too focused, too intent on reading her lips. "But you're him," she finishes.

I begin to cough, purposefully inhaling a bit of apple, hoping I don't mistakenly aspirate it and kill myself.

I need time to think. I can think while I cough.

"Are you okay?" Harmony reaches her hand over, touches my wrist, then rubs my back as I continue to cough.

Fuck. What do I do?

I cough a few more times, lower, getting myself under control.

Okay.

No. This isn't all that different from what I thought I'd have to do, moving here.

I know how to play this. Crystal's a dog. An ugly little terrier, after a rat.

And she's pushed me into a bold new era. We're past establishing New Aaron, feeling out the school. We're well beyond all that.

These five, they aren't a trial lunch table. They can't be *casual* friends. Not now.

We are all bound together now.

I wipe my chin, point at Crystal, who still hasn't looked up from her hands. If she really was this mousy, this quiet, she wouldn't have said what she said. She should stop fucking pretending.

I *knew* she was a problem. I knew it the second she sat, interrupted the conversation we had going.

"Everyone," I say, coming back to New Aaron's voice and confidence. I look around the cafeteria, less because I'm worried someone's going to overhear, but more to impress upon them that what I'm about to say is a secret.

I lean in.

They lean in.

Crystal too, who looks somehow worse than I feel.

I look at them. Can they keep a secret?

Maybe. Yes. The ones who matter can. At least for a little while.

Crystal's made it clear denial's not an option, that she *knows*.

And I don't know why I attempted to deny in the first place.

I *am* the Speaker.

This simpering nothing of a girl. Two lunches on her tray and not an ounce of charisma in her body. My new personal project. Not someone to be extinguished, like Larissa Coates. Not a candle in the wind, someone people will lay out flowers and hold vigils for, not someone they'll remember. No, Crystal is someone to be studied, a curiosity of science, and then . . . obliterated. Like she was never here.

I clear my throat one final time, not because of the apple, but because I want everyone's absolute attention.

"Crystal, you're—" I start to say.

No.

Don't do this.

It's a mistake.

But this voice telling me not to do it, not to admit who I am, it's neither New Aaron or Old Aaron's voice, but some naysaying interloper. And that small, insecure voice inside that I've been trying to squash since

I was a child, since I was weak and felt emotions more keenly. That weak, cowardly voice strengthens my resolve.

I *don't make mistakes*, I tell it.

This is the way forward. The only way forward.

"You're right," I continue. Then I lean in and whisper to my new friends, "I am the Speaker. But you can't tell anyone, okay? You have to swear it."

SIX

CRYSTAL

In sixth period, US History, I see, but don't talk to, Harmony and Paul. They text—I assume with each other—the whole class, barely looking in my direction. Then, last period of the day, Gayle's with me in Film, an elective, but it's a screening block, so the lights are out and we can't talk.

None of my friends say anything to indicate they're mad at me, but I think they are.

In my anxiety, I even consider calling my dad to come pick me up from school. His hours at the dealership aren't that flexible. But he would do it, no questions asked.

But I shouldn't call him.

No. I have to take the carpool home. I need to face the friends I've embarrassed.

I play the words over and over.

You're lying. You're the Speaker. You're the Speaker. You're the Speaker.

And so fucking what? Why did I say that? Why was I so intent on saying it?

I've never said anything like that before. Never said those words, called someone a liar like that. They're very assertive, aggressive words.

But it was the way he'd talked with his hands. The shape of his eyebrows. His eyes, the way the color seemed to change.

Sure, without the mask his hair's a little different. But how could I be the only one to notice? Not Harmony, not Paul—after they'd been thinking and talking about him all day?

Because they, all of them, don't pay attention like I pay attention. Not that it's a good thing. Not that I'm proud of it. Paying attention's why I've always got a sour stomach, why I think the worst, because I notice the worst, the little things that add up to give away how people *really* feel, who they are.

Between periods, in a bathroom stall, I watch a few seconds of a stream, prerecorded, and hear the Speaker's voice for the first time. It's completely different than how Aaron Fortin speaks. He either puts on an accent while he streams or digitally disguises his voice, or both. Maybe that's how Harmony and Paul could be speaking with their hero and not know it. Or maybe *not* being familiar with the Speaker's voice is how I was able to recognize him.

I'm the first to arrive at the van. The lock to the driver's side rear door doesn't work, though, so I'm able to sit in my normal seat, in the quiet, and wait for Trevor and the rest.

I take a moment to consider *why* Aaron was lying. The reasoning he gave us.

That the Speaker was an artistic outlet. And that the identity of the account needed to remain secret for Aaron to be able to benefit from it, artistically and—what was the word he used?—*therapeutically.*

Who am I to argue with that logic, the girl with the dozens of hours of rambling stored on a private YouTube account? At least Aaron is brave enough to let people in, let them see his weirdness.

He then went around the table, got us all to agree we won't reveal his secret.

Paul and Harmony, they swear it, want him to know that they'll never tell. Trevor's not as emphatic, but Trevor's also a man of his word, someone who knows how to keep a secret, is the best of all of us at it.

Gayle nods, taking it seriously in a way that surprises me.

And then their eyes fall on me.

Harmony and Paul glare. If they could have kicked me under the table without anyone noticing, they would've.

Don't ruin this for us. Don't you dare blab this secret.

Gayle too, who doesn't even like the Speaker, she looks at me a similar way. But there wasn't a threat in her eyes, there was pity, an "Oh honey, the mess you've made" kind of embarrassment.

I sink lower into the van's back seat.

I don't see Trevor cross the parking lot. He unlocks the driver's-side door, gets behind the wheel, checks his mirror, and then finally . . . sees me there behind him.

"Shit!" Trevor yells, looking back at me. "You have to stop it with creeping like that!"

I've done this a few times, mostly on days it's raining, to stay dry.

I'm one of the first seniors to leave the building because . . . I have no reason to linger.

"Sorry," I say, smiling.

He's not angry. In fact, I think he likes when his heart rate's up, the jump scare in a horror movie he and Paul are watching, the thrill of rock climbing with his troop.

In a few seconds Trevor's drumming his fingers lightly against the wheel. Impatient.

To break the awkwardness, so he can talk but not really *to* me, he says: "No rush, everyone. Just your friendly Lyft driver, waiting outside for you." He smiles back at me in the mirror, then adds, "And his sidekick."

Trevor and I aren't close, but he's always kind. He might be the most genuinely nice person of all of us.

I talked about that in a video once. In that same video I sorted my friends into the Dungeons & Dragons alignment chart. I've never played D&D, but I've seen the chart online enough.

Trevor was Lawful Good.

Gayle was Chaotic Good.

I had Paul down as, I think, at the time, Chaotic Neutral. Not sure I would still say that, with how he's been this year—snarkier, more argumentative.

And then Harmony's alignment was—

I'm startled out of the memory by Paul and Harmony crashing against the passenger door. They're fighting for shotgun. Not play-fighting; it may have started that way, but now they're *actually* fighting.

Harmony slaps Paul, catching him on the side of the face with her bracelet, close to his eye.

"Fuck, that hurts," I hear him say, muffled, through the glass.

In the driver's seat, Trevor shakes his head.

I try not to react at all. I stare forward, preparing for whatever weird vibes this ride is going to have.

Gayle rolls open the side door. "Looks like you lost, Pauly. Into the back with us."

Harmony rides shotgun, Paul steps up and back, into the third row, and Gayle fastens her safety belt in the second-row seat beside me.

"Everyone clicked?" Trevor asks, turning over the engine but not taking us out of park.

"Yes," everyone says. Everyone except Gayle, who crosses her eyes, sticks her tongue out like an e-girl, drools a little, and says, "Yes, Daddy."

Trevor shakes his head again. But he likes it, this kind of comical inappropriateness. Gayle, Harmony, and Paul . . . they all give him something he can't get at home, something a little forbidden but still wholesome, since they're all good friends.

I wonder what *I* give Trevor, if anything. I guess I'm someone for him to drive around, feel like he's helping out. A charity case.

We're quiet for a moment, Harmony scanning through the radio presets as Trevor begins to maneuver the van out of the space. It's a slow process, him stopping three times to let cars pass, other kids who drive more carelessly than he does and in way nicer cars.

I should be the first to speak.

I should acknowledge what happened at lunch head-on. Take ownership over what I did.

But even I have trouble understanding what happened. The odds were astronomical that the Speaker would move to our town, but they're a hundredfold crazier that he would choose to sit down at our lunch table.

So in the surprise, I reacted, I was shocked, I—

"There he is!" Harmony says.

She's only been messing with the radio to look like she's doing something. I can see now that she's been watching cars in the parking lot. She points out the window, the radio stuck between stations, tuned to static. "What a fucking babe!" she says.

Paul looks. Gayle looks.

Trevor . . . keeps his eyes on his mirrors as he backs out, a careful driver.

I look too, but I can't see yet.

"Wow," Paul says. "An Audi."

"An Acura, dipshit," Harmony says. "That *A* stands for Acura. Audi's the four rings."

They're so mean to each other, you'd almost think they were hooking up, if you didn't know the history.

Then Trevor turns the van enough, is finally out of the spot now, so that I can see what we're looking at.

I don't think Aaron can see me through the van's tinted windows.

But he's looking right at me.

I called him a liar, but as he follows behind us, I'm watching the slight concentration on his face as he drives. I don't know why, but I get the sense that Aaron Fortin's a good guy.

I think about how I may have screwed up Harmony and Paul's chances to get to know him.

"I'm sorry," I say.

I say it out loud. Not to Aaron, but to my friends.

But nobody hears me. Or they pretend like they don't.

Then I see it.

"Arizona," I say, reading.

Aaron's license plate. It says Arizona.

"He told us he moved here from California."

"What the fuck do you have against this guy, Crystal?" Harmony asks. It's a fair question—why am I being this way? Why am I noticing these things? Why am I *paying attention* like this?

I start to apologize, but then Harmony points out the windshield and says, "New Jersey," indicating the car ahead of us.

"Huh?" Paul says.

"Arizona borders California," Harmony says.

"It does?" Paul asks.

"It does," Gayle confirms.

"I'm sure there's plenty of Arizona plates in Cali," Harmony finishes, not directing her words at me. "Shit. He's turning," she says as Aaron's car moves out of sight, headed toward the highway. "I wonder where he lives."

"An Acura?" Trevor says, hands at ten and two. "You *know* he lives on the circle."

"We're in *dense* suburbia, Trev. Don't act like there's *one* place in town that all the rich kids live," Harmony says. "Paul doesn't live there."

"I'm not rich, but . . . thanks?" Paul says. I can tell he takes what she's said as half insult, half compliment. Nobody in our school wants to be called rich, but we'd of course all like to *be* rich. And Paul's rich.

"Is anyone listening? I said I'm sorry!" I yell it this time.

Everyone blinks at me. Even Trevor is looking back, and I can feel the van decelerate slightly, pull into the shoulder a bit.

"Cris . . . ," Gayle says. I can't tell if she's worried for me or embarrassed of me for the second time today. Either way, I feel like today's driven a wedge further between us. I'm not even sure why or how, but my anxiety tells me that if Gayle and I had been drifting apart before right now, that I just gave us a *push*.

Then Harmony speaks.

"Sorry?" she asks, then strains against her seat belt, reaching back to brush a strand of hair out of my face. "What are you *sorry* about, Crystal?"

"Uh . . ." Despite the patter of butterfly wings in my stomach, I'm unsure if a trap's about to snap closed around me. Harmony is unpleasant to Paul most days, but, at one time or another, she's taken turns being cruel to us all individually.

I watch as Harmony unbuckles her seat belt.

"Hey!" Trevor says.

But she ignores him. She leans back from the front seat, her hand covering mine, bracelet cool on my wrist. They aren't Pandora charms. Harmony can't spend much, but she wouldn't be caught accessorizing at the mall. The charms come from a small jewelry shop in Sayville.

"Do you really think we're mad at you?" Harmony asks, her body laid over the center console into the back of the van.

I can't remember the last time Harmony's touched my hand.

I can't even remember the last time Harmony's said my name.

"Yes?" I say.

"Crystal. This is the best thing you've ever done."

"What?"

"We're friends with the Speaker now."

"We?" I ask, but she doesn't seem to hear.

"I didn't recognize him without his mask. Like, not at all," Harmony says, "but the second you said it, I could see it."

"I actually . . . ," Paul says. "I got a feeling when we first—"

"No, you didn't, Paul. Shut the fuck up."

I'm so dizzy with the warmth of her hand on mine, the prolonged eye contact I'm not used to making with anyone, that I have to think back over the words she's just said.

Wait.

Friends with the Speaker? The last thing Aaron said to us at lunch, conversation stalling out after we'd been sworn to secrecy, was an awkward "I'll see you around, I guess."

I figured that was the end of it. That tomorrow during lunch he'd find a new place to sit.

Harmony, still leaning over, still touching my hand, must see the confusion on my face.

"He AirDropped me his contact." She reaches back with her other hand, digs out her phone, holds it up. "I've been texting with him all day!"

Harmony makes a face, expecting me to respond with something.

"Cool!" I say. Somehow I feel better *and* worse.

"Wait," Paul says from behind me. "*That's* who you've been texting with? He sent me his number too. I thought he might like me . . ."

Now it's Trevor's turn to say "Cool!" but he doesn't hide the contempt in his voice.

Harmony squeezes my hand one last time, then says, lower, just for us, "Really, thank you, Crystal." And then she wiggles back into the passenger seat.

"Well, *I'm* not flirting with him," Gayle says. She enjoys attention, and it makes me feel good, the idea that she felt the need to speak up after Harmony and I shared a moment. That she might be a little jealous.

That she needs me how I need her. "He didn't send *me* his number," Gayle continues.

"Me either," Trevor says. "And after I was very welcoming. I'm the one who told him he could sit in the first place."

It's odd; I can't tell if they're kidding.

Because it sounds like they aren't. That they envy Harmony and Paul getting to text with a minor internet celebrity all day.

Why do either of them *want* that?

"Not sure why that'd be," Harmony says, "both of you saying how you don't follow the Speaker. Telling Paul and I we couldn't talk about it during lunch."

"Hey," Gayle says, "I thought we weren't supposed to bring up the Speaker. I thought we were getting to know the *real* Aaron first." She curls one hand into a loose fist and makes the jerk-off sign.

For all Gayle's sexual jokes, she insists—the few times I've worked up the courage to ask—she's never done more with a guy than kiss. And those kisses only happened a few times, early in high school. I don't know for sure why she's stopped. But I think something scary happened, around that time, and that she couldn't get herself back into being with guys once that fear set in.

I worry for her.

And I spend a lot of time thinking about what that scary thing could have been and whether it's still going on.

I have a theory, pieced together through years of paying attention. But it's too terrible to ask her about it without her bringing it up first.

There's silence in the van. I glance back to the shadows of the third row. Paul's phone is out. Then I see that Harmony's got hers out too.

"So," Gayle says. "Not that I care, of course. But . . . what are you two talking about with Aaron?"

"Nothing," Harmony and Paul say at the same time.

"That's not suspicious at all." Gayle pulls her knees up, sitting weird in her seat so that she can pick at her laces. I watch her do this, then watch her take a tissue from floor of the van, dab the paper on her tongue, then use it to wipe away some of the dirt smudges on her boots.

And then, before I realize we've driven so far, we're pulling into my driveway and I'm going to have to get out.

I'm the last to be picked up and the first to be dropped off.

I look up at the house.

Neither of my parents are home. Ant might be; he's old enough that they'll leave him by himself in the hour or so when he's out of school and I'm not home. But he could also be at therapy. That's a new thing, and I can't remember his schedule.

The house might be empty.

And I don't want to be alone.

"Hey," I say, Gayle already shifting in her seat, moving back to let me out onto the correct side of the driveway. "Want to come hang out?"

It's worth a try.

These days, when we *do* spend time together after school, it happens because Gayle invites herself in. And it's almost always at my house. It *used* to be at her house, but we haven't done that in a long time. Since even before this recent . . . drifting.

I have a hard time even remembering what Gayle's house looks like.

"Sure," Gayle says, pulling the door open, the sound of metal rollers loud.

It's a surprise, but she must sense how much I need her. I'm so thankful to have this one good friend in my life.

Then, the cool air flooding into the van, Gayle sucks her teeth, makes a noise that she knows I hate. "Oh shit," she says. "I can't. My stepdad's doing this thing tonight."

Gayle's stepdad works from home, doesn't ever really leave the house, so I have trouble imagining what kind of "thing" he has to do and why he needs his stepdaughter for it, a stepdaughter who he's not close with, to hear her tell it.

But I don't push back.

I never do when she makes an excuse like this.

"It's okay," I say.

The house is empty. I look out the living room blinds, watch as Trevor slowly backs onto a completely empty street.

Through the windshield, not tinted like the rest of the windows, I watch Harmony laugh. She's saying something to the rest of the van.

I sometimes wonder what the drive home is like once I've left the van. Are they more comfortable? Can they be more themselves? Do they talk about me? Probably not.

Trevor shakes his head at whatever it is Harmony's said and they pull away down the street, disappear around the corner.

It's dark outside by the time my family gets home, and I spend most of that time watching old the Speaker streams and feeling even worse about myself.

And it's not so much what he says, but *how* he says it, because the more I watch, the more I pay attention, the more anxious and afraid I become.

Excerpt from a private message conversation
between Suspect in the Tacoma, WA, attack and
Unnamed Person of Interest

10:30 P.M.

Him: Hey.

Her: Hey.

Him: I hear you like the Speaker . . .

Her: Yup.

[two-minute pause]

Her: Who is this? ur account's private.

Him: What do you like about him?

Her: Just a guy. I follow a lot of guys. Who
is this?

Him: Not that many guys. Def not that
many poets.

Her: I mean. He's not really a poet. Just an
interesting guy.

Him: Fair enough.

[an extra minute passes]

Her: y. are you jealous, Jeremy? ;)

Him: Who's Jeremy?

Her: cute

Him: This is taking too long: you've liked
every one of the Speaker's posts for the
last six weeks. Most of these daily posts,
no more than an hour elapsed between upload
and interaction.

Her: Jeremy. Ur being a real fucking stalker
right now. Go to bed and if you see me tomorrow,
first thing you say better be sorry.

Him: This isn't Jeremy. And if you really are
a fan of the Speaker, you'll want to be nicer
to me.

[long pause, five minutes]

Her: Why?

Him: Because I can get you on the phone with
him. Tonight. And one day you'll maybe even get

to meet him.

[two-minute pause]

Him: Would you like that?

[two-minute pause]

Him: You would, wouldn't you?

[two-minute pause]

Her: Prove it.

SEVEN

AARON

Charlie used to call it "creepy crawling."

Manson, I correct myself.

Charles Manson.

I don't know why I sometimes think of him by his first name. And not even as Charles, but as the more informal "Charlie." That's a bad habit. One I've picked up while listening to too many podcasts and audiobooks. Nonfiction where the authors like to blur the line between journalism and *fandom*.

Losers.

I have more contempt for serial-killer "fans" than I do for actual serial killers. Not that Charles Manson's a serial killer. He never killed anyone himself, that we know of. He only shot that one guy, not even fatally. But I digress.

I'm *not* a fan.

I try and keep a level of . . . professional detachment when I'm researching these men. And women. Can't forget the women. Aileen Wuornos. The weight of seven dead bodies—confirmed—bursting through the glass ceiling.

Yes. *Manson. You have to think of him as his last name,* I tell myself.

It's not like I respect the guy. He was a racist, for one thing. Not to mention stupid, borderline illiterate, and too impetuous for his own good. An abused child who grew up to abuse others. *I* come from a happy home—happy enough. I'm educated. I shower every day.

And, most important, I am capable of exhibiting patience. I'm capable of planning. And I'm flexible, adaptable, if one of my plans goes slightly astray. Even when some fucking whisper-voiced, spotty-faced b—

No, let's not think about her.

Let's remember that I've got that handled. That I'm not Charles Manson. That I don't do lame-brained shit like leave mountains of physical evidence at a crime scene *on purpose.*

But we all have shortcomings. We all make mistakes.

In a way I'm already more successful than Charles Manson. I've already had my own Cielo Drive, and I was able to walk away from it. A Cielo Drive that nobody even knows about yet, because I didn't *want* them to know.

Hiccups and all, that's planning. That's control. That's the difference between us.

Nobody knows about the Coates murders. I'm positive of that. Even if investigators have a suspicion, they don't *know.* And they certainly don't know *me.* I check local Phoenix and Scottsdale news once a day, and the police blotters, keeping an eye on things through those trusty VPNs I mentioned.

Anyway. Credit where credit's due. Charles Manson had *some* good ideas.

Like creepy crawling.

For those unfamiliar, creepy crawling is the act of walking around a new neighborhood and then breaking into houses that seem unoccupied. The goal is to go unseen and leave no trace.

Manson specifically directed his followers—all dirt-poor, remember, getting most of their camp's shared food out of grocery-store dumpsters—he told them *not* to steal anything. Later he scrapped the "leave no trace" stuff and told his followers to rearrange furniture. The goal, Manson said, was to mess with the homeowners' minds, rich little piggies needing to inventory every item to find that nothing had been stolen during the break-in.

Manson's followers treated creepy crawling like a game.

And for them it was. But not for Charli—

Not for Manson.

For him, it was a multipurpose tool. Manson was sending family members out on creepy crawls for both conditioning and escalation. A training exercise that he disguised as a game.

Brilliant, really.

Because when he decided that the Family *really* needed the money? He changed the rules, said they should start taking valuables, and turned creepy crawling into burglary with a cuter name. And his followers needed no convincing to cross that extra line. It was just a game, after all.

Like they'd needed no convincing when he *again* escalated things. When Charles Manson thought he needed to speed up helter-skelter, the race war he convinced his followers was coming, he made the game's rules more extreme, upgraded burglary into "go to this address and kill everyone you find in the house."

And, of course, they did it.

Where Manson fucked up, in my opinion, is that he didn't creepy crawl himself.

Oh, he did plenty of criminal trespassing, just not in the structured way he was directing his followers to do it.

If you do any reading about business leadership or entrepreneurship, you'll find that the first rule of effective management is that you *never* instruct an employee to do anything that you yourself have not done first.

To delegate, a good manager needs to understand the demands of the task he's assigning.

You can't hope to properly manage dishwashers if you've never washed a dish.

You can't get perfect results asking people to stand outside the house of a new enemy, either for reconnaissance or intimidation, searching for a way into their home, if you *yourself* have not stood outside that same house and peered into its windows.

Which is all a long way of saying that . . .

I'm creepy crawling right now.

I'm in a backyard. Looking up, trying to tell if the rooms with lights on also have people in them.

It's late. Nobody should be awake. But I see a shadow and pause, stand completely still.

Creepy crawling these days is a lot more difficult than when the Family did it.

For example in the 1960s, homes in affluent neighborhoods didn't have video doorbells. Well, *no* homes in the 1960s had electronic surveillance of any kind.

Not that I'm in an affluent neighborhood right now. But I needed to walk through one to get here—parking the car at the nearest LIRR stop, then cutting through yards, avoiding motion-detecting porch lights, stumbling through the dark, trying not to fall into covered pools, which I guess is a thing here on the East Coast: aboveground pools disguised as in-ground pools by building porch decks around them.

I'm sure getting here I wasn't perfect. I'm sure someone saw me, that I was caught on some Ring doorbell or security system. And my car will be on the train station's cameras. But even with all that, I'm not taking a huge risk.

I have no weapon on me. I'm not looking to steal anything. And I'm dressed as inconspicuously as possible. Dark jeans, a black hoodie, clothes that I only ever wear when I come out like this. Which means I'm not wearing anything that's recognizably Aaron Fortin. I keep the hood on the sweatshirt down—nothing attracts scrutiny like a raised hood—but I have my knit cap pulled low over my hair and ears. I *want* people to be able to see my face if they're looking, so they can see that I'm just a high-school kid out late, clean-shaven and healthy-looking.

The shadow in the window above me resolves itself into a figure.

Ah. There she is.

She's up late. I can't check my watch, not going to chance the glare, but I know it's well after midnight, maybe after one at this point.

I angle my head down, try my best to blow my exhalation into the neck of the hoodie so the white cloud of my breath doesn't give me away in the moonlight.

Her shadow leaves the window and I crouch low, then carefully start to make my way to the side of the house.

Are there kids here? Why are there all these broken toys? And this swing set? I can't imagine Victoria Hobbes with kids. She doesn't seem like a mom to me.

There's nothing to see on the side of the house, the drapes are drawn, but when I get to the front, I understand:

This is a two-family household. There are two front doors, one that leads to the first floor and one that leads up to the second floor, a separate living space.

I was right. *Ms.* Hobbes doesn't own property. At least, I don't think she does. I bet she rents this second floor from whoever lives on the first floor.

I lean a little further out, stepping onto the walkway beside the drive. It's an ugly house. More poured concrete than lawn, which wouldn't be that strange if this were Arizona, but it's not Arizona. And every house in *my* new neighborhood, Connetquot Circle, has an expansive lawn.

If Hobbes is awake—which I think she is, I'm almost certain that was her shadow that I saw from the backyard—then there's not much more I can do tonight.

I can't risk going into the house, that's for sure.

Using the walkway, treading lightly, trying not to scuff the soles of my shoes, I step to the front of the house and to the two iron mailboxes beside the two doors.

The first box, for the first floor, has a single name on it, etched onto a brass plate welded to the iron mailbox:

The Shanes.

I imagine an older Irish couple. A pair of grandparents who need their property to make extra income, to supplement their retirement. The couple who rents to Hobbes.

I check the mailbox next to the second door.

Patterson/Hobbes.

The names are not etched in brass but instead written in faded marker on a length of masking tape that's been stuck over the previous tenant's name.

Yes, they definitely rent.

But who is Patterson? A roommate? No, not even Hobbes seems *that* pathetic. Maybe a boyfriend? Could even be a husband if Hobbes didn't want to take his name. I think of Victoria Hobbes refusing to let go of that winner of a last name, too much of a feminist.

Carefully, I lift the lid on the mailbox. The hinges are rusted, and the noise they make is unavoidable, but I doubt anyone's coming to check on the sound.

Inside, there's some junk mail. I begin to flip through; none of the mail is addressed to Patterson *or* Hobbes—the closest is a supermarket circular marked for "Current Resident"—and then, last in this folded stack of unchecked mail: the heavy cardstock and silken envelope of a wedding invitation.

Ms. Victoria Hobbes and Mr. Adam Patterson.

I imagine it's *her* friends getting married if they're putting her name first. College friends? Likely. This was sent from Illinois.

Not a wealth of information here on this invitation, but it's enough to do some digging. I take a picture of the envelope with my phone, just in case there's anything I can puzzle out using the return address.

I restack the mail the way it was, put it back in the mailbox, but don't close the lid yet.

There's one more thing I have to do while I'm here tonight.

I take the Ziploc from my hoodie pocket, unzip the plastic, and turn the baggie inside out.

The dead bird plops into the box.

I had been hoping for something more substantial. Roadkill, a racoon or opossum, something I could mutilate, cut the head or the tail off, but there's not much traffic on these streets. The best I could do is the waterlogged sparrow. Which might have died some months ago, been frozen in a snow drift, only in the last weeks thawed and floated down into the gutter where I found it.

Its feet are pale, and its eyes are empty rotted sockets.

I close the lid.

I wonder how long it'll take Victoria to find the bird. The bird corpse could be writhing with maggots, flies buzzing, bodies colliding with the sides of the iron box by the time she checks the mail.

Or maybe Adam Patterson will find it. If that happens, it's possible he doesn't even tell his maybe-wife about it.

Oh well. It's not meant to be a *big* gesture.

Just a little hint.

A teaser of things to come.

I head around the side of the house again, following the way I came in. I pass through yards, then once I'm off Victoria and Adam's block, I keep to the sidewalks and streetlights, where I'm less conspicuous, for the rest of the way.

I have nothing to hide now; my creepy crawl has ended for the night.

I check my texts. Doesn't anyone sleep?

No. Paul and Harmony are too excited to sleep.

I was forceful enough in the lunchroom that I've scared them off asking me specifics about my life as the Speaker, but as the afternoon's turned to evening and the evening into night, they've begun to test boundaries.

I keep having to redirect the conversations.

I want to know about *them*, I tell them.

I'm genuinely interested.

And it's true. I am.

And, luckily, Harmony and Paul are Harmony and Paul's favorite subjects.

I'm learning so much. About each of them, and their friends. But mostly about them.

Harmony, she loves animals. She has a cat named Madame Tabitha—Tab for short. Her grades are strong enough that she's gotten into veterinary tech school, but she isn't sure her financial-aid package is strong enough. Her mom works two jobs, which means that she's alone a lot—winky emoji—and when I dig deeper, ask her for something more real, she tells me that her dad killed himself when she was eleven.

It was Harmony who found the body.

He hadn't known she'd been home sick from school that day. Otherwise, one imagines, he wouldn't have done it. At least not there in the kitchen.

Interesting.

I'm fascinated by the little tragedies you can find anywhere, in the most normal of people, if you poke around inside for any length of time.

Paul is almost as interesting, though not to me, since there's not much death in his story.

I was right, Paul's family does have money. Relatively. Paul's actually Paul Witkowski III. A name that he has more for marketing reasons than because his parents love the name Paul or want to honor a family line. His father, Paul Jr., owns a bakery in Yaphank, which, Googling, is a few towns over from here. His mother runs the business, which was started by Paul's grandfather—Paul Prime—when the family left Staten Island in "like the 1920s or something" (Paul's not sure of the exact timeline, but, doing the math, I'm guessing it was more like the fifties or sixties).

Paul's mother and father hate each other. But neither can leave, because of the business. They hate each other but love Paul.

And that love manifests itself as nice shoes and AirPods.

But material goods don't really make up for the fact that Paul's disturbed by his father's constant infidelity. Some of which—and Paul's not sure of this either, but he strongly suspects—might be with guys.

Which isn't wrong, Paul knows that. Paul himself is gay. But it's the extra level of lying that *gets* to Paul.

It fucks him up if he thinks about it for too long. And that's a paraphrase, but it's pretty close to an exact quote.

This topic, this stuff about his family, I had to drag it out of Paul, but now he's using it to try to find out about me. He thinks that because he was open with me, that I owe him something.

He wants to know whether I'm gay. Or bi.

I don't think I am.

But never shut a door completely, I tell him.

Then—borrowing from Harmony—I add a winky emoji.

While I've been working on each of them, whenever things get too intense, I give them a break, time out of the hot seat where I ask them easy questions. I ask them about the town of East Bay. About school. About their friends.

I ask Harmony about Gayle, and I ask Paul about Trevor, because those seem to be the configurations where I'll learn the most.

Gayle Byrne. The goth thing, according to Harmony, started slowly: hair dye in sixth grade, a choker in middle school. But it ramped up really quickly sophomore year of high school. Harmony thinks something specific happened to cause it. Interesting. But also, considering the source, possibly false. Could just be Harmony being catty, wanting to pathologize her friend's fashion choices, poison the well and keep *me* for herself. Warrants further investigation, I guess.

Gayle's parents separated when she was young. Her mother works at a chain hotel by MacArthur Airport. Managerial position. Stepfather does something with remote tech support, works from home, is kind of weird. According to Harmony, who's heard it from Crystal, the man never comes out of his office.

Interesting.

There are daddy issues up and down this group.

Trevor Seye, well, with him, I've guessed pretty much his whole life story.

Muslim. One sister, younger. Closeted to his family. Tries to get along with everyone. Works hard. Thinks he's the leader of the group while both Paul and Harmony, separately, think *they* are.

Trevor's parents are from West Africa. Paul thinks that he may have even been born there, come over when he was a baby. I ask *which* country in West Africa, and Paul is unaware that "West Africa" isn't a country.

I ask whether Trevor's his real name or is it an American name. Similar to the country thing, Paul's never even thought of that. His mind's actually blown by that idea, he tells me, that his friend's name may not even *be* Trevor.

What I didn't guess about Trevor—couldn't have, really, I'm not Sherlock Holmes, I wasn't at lunch scrutinizing the clay dust on his inseam—is his scouting. As Paul tells me about it, it does make a certain amount of sense, jives with all the other efforts Trevor makes toward assimilation.

Interesting.

I don't know that much about the Boy Scouts of America, but I have to assume if one makes it to Eagle Scout that they've demonstrated some baseline level of competency. At least where tying knots, first aid, and CPR are concerned. It also means Trevor's the most physically fit among them.

Not that I have to worry about getting in a fistfight with anyone. But something to consider, when approaching Trevor. Someone I have special plans for, I think, as what I want to do in this town, with these people, begins to resolve itself into a clearer vision.

I've learned all these gems, and yet the one subject that neither Paul nor Harmony seems to know much about is Crystal.

Do they not know about her because she's new to the group?

No, Paul says that she's "always been there."

Paul doesn't even know Crystal's last name, which seems like something you'd have to go out of your way *not* to learn about a person you went through grade school with. I decide I don't believe him. That he does know her full name, is just pretending he doesn't to indicate to me he's only friends with the girl by association.

I *could* reassure him, tell him I'm not angry at the girl for outing me.

But why lie?

Harmony's attitude toward Crystal is a bit different; she seems to have warmer feelings. At least she knows the girl's last name. Crystal Giordano.

But, Harmony tells me in a tone that seems to border on xenophobic, Crystal's not as Italian as that name sounds. She's half. She's also . . . Latinx, is that the term? Crystal's mom is . . . Harmony doesn't want to name a country and end up being wrong, sounding racist.

No, never that, Harm.

That's what she goes by, to her closest friends. "Harmony" shortened to "Harm."

I like it.

But now that Harmony's given me something to go on, I dig in, ready to find out all about my new little buddy Crystal.

I Google housing deeds, search for any Giordanos in East Bay. There are four listings, but only two that have two names on the deed. Between the two, I look at the second name on the listing and take an educated guess which house is Crystal's.

Ana Diaz. Must be Crystal's mother. From there I check Facebook—older people put *far* too much information on their public Facebook pages. There are a few Ana Diazes in the area, but it doesn't take long to find the right one. "Puerto Rican American" is the term Harmony was searching for. Crystal's mom is kind of attractive. And prettier when you look back to her photos from ten years ago, before the second kid. Her second kid, Crystal's little brother, is named Anthony.

Anthony. Wow. Dad is winning when it comes to the Italian American names, I guess.

Harmony says one other thing about Crystal.

She describes Crystal as Gayle's "security blanket." She speculates that it's Crystal's constant, calming presence that allows Gayle to be so outgoing. Of the two, Gayle's much more fun to hang out with, has more of a personality, but you really need both of them around to add up to a complete person.

And not that Harmony doesn't love her friends, but . . .

This is bad to say, but Harmony wonders if next year when she's off to school, even if she stays local for an eighteen-month program, if she'll ever talk to—ever even think about—Crystal Giordano again. Or Gayle, for that matter, who's already started cutting the cord with her best friend. That's the phrase Harmony uses: "best friend."

This is all good information. But frankly, I don't give much of a shit about what Harmony Phillips sees as her future, what she *thinks* she's doing *next* year.

Because I'm starting to get an idea of what she and her friends are going to be doing *this* year.

And as much as I can find about Crystal's family, there's almost nothing online about the girl herself. Which means I'll need to get to know Gayle.

Gayle didn't seem to love me, in our first brief interaction, but I have a way of growing on people.

Once I arrive back at the car, I take my phone from my jacket pocket and put it in the glove box.

It's good to get away from it, if only for a few moments.

I drive in silence, windows down, even though there's a chill in the air.

I have too many thoughts. Today has been information overload.

The quiet of the tires rolling over asphalt calms me. In a few months, once spring turns into summer, there will be cricket and cicada sounds buzzing through these streets.

But right now there's the absolute quiet of sleeping suburbia.

I get back to Connetquot Circle, my new home, a little after two.

My parents are asleep.

Before I went on this midnight excursion, we ate a meal together. Neither said much about how their days went. Not that I care. But they did bring home takeout. Supposedly the best fried-chicken sandwich on the island of Manhattan. Very expensive. A celebrity chef makes it.

The sandwich may have been award-winning at one point, but by the time we eat, it's steamed in the bag, can't be resuscitated by our new convection oven.

I lie in bed, in the basement, too awake to sleep and too bored with Harmony and Paul to continue those conversations.

I have an early start, an alarm already set, so I have time to drive where I need to before school.

I open up Instagram and log into one of my alternate accounts. Then I find a girl who loves the Speaker—it doesn't matter who she is, where she is, or what she looks like. Just needs to be a girl who comments on his posts all the time. I find one quickly, then I begin to DM her.

After a few moments of that kind of conversation, my eyes are heavy, and I finally sleep.

EIGHT

CRYSTAL

I was able to go to bed early last night.

A little after 11:30, my phone started doing this thing where it got really slow, then the metal got really hot, then the screen shut off.

Which sounds bad, but my phone's done this before. It just needs some quiet time, so I plug it in to recharge, peeled out of its case so it can cool.

Actually, after a few minutes staring at the ceiling, I'm glad I have a shitty phone.

Because with no phone, I'm not tempted to cycle through the same three apps. I don't compulsively check a group text that never updates, and I'm tired enough that I don't think about my anxiety and "are they talking about me" FOMO. I'm able to sleep for the first time in a week.

But there's a trade-off.

When I sleep too well, I dream. And if I stay in a dream long enough, it tends to turn into a nightmare.

Sometime before dawn, my room still dark, I wake up crying.

Not because I've had a sad dream, but because I imagine someone is standing over my bed, that they have their hands on my throat, that they press down with all their weight until my vision is nothing but growing black spots.

There might have been more to the dream, buildup to who the person is and why they're in my bedroom, but the choking is the only part I can remember.

I don't know what time this happened. In my sputtering, teary half-dream state I tried to check, but my phone's screen is still the red blinking low-battery indicator.

Now, the room lighter, I roll onto my side and stare at the wall. My upper lip is salt-crusty with dried tears.

Which also sounds like a bad way to wake up, but it's not really.

I feel better than I did yesterday, having slept.

I feel . . . hopeful? I can remember the worries of yesterday, wondering if my friends have moved into a new group text without me, but those worries don't seem as sharp. They've been placed in bubble wrap by a good night's sleep.

I check my phone. I touch the metal backing, and it's only as warm as my hand. I hold the button on the side, and the device boots up . . . fairly quickly, actually.

There's still life in the old guy.

It's 6:00 a.m. There's a hazy green glow behind the blinds, which means it's going to be a sunny day—early-morning light hitting the overgrown shrubs that cover my room's lone window.

It's 6:00 a.m. There's plenty of time to film a video.

I apply makeup and while I do, I begin rehearsing. Actually, what I'm doing can't really be considered rehearsing; it's more like vocal warm-ups.

"Hey, guys," I say, repeating the phrase as I lay on foundation.

"Hello, friends," I try a few times, moving to concealer and then my eyes and lips.

My makeup job is . . . I look as good as I need to for an audience of zero and for a school day spent blending into the crowd.

I check my phone's temperature one more time and place it into the tripod, more careful than usual because I haven't slid the case back on.

I hit record.

No false starts, no rambling. I'm able to pick a topic and stay on it. I use the video like a diary. Not just a mood journal. And I don't feel the urge to deflect, veer into harmless opinions about weird junk food or my ranking for the Five Nights at Freddy's games. Which is what I usually do when a video gets too personal.

I talk for ten minutes uninterrupted.

Recording goes so smoothly. I look back over the footage, and for maybe the first time ever, I don't feel the need to edit out pauses or blank stares. Not that I'm talking all ten minutes, or even that I'm that articulate, just that my pauses and my furrowed brow or even wiping my nose with the back of my hand: It all feels like it belongs. It feels authentic.

It's such an improvement from how things went when I tried this same thing yesterday morning.

I chalk the difference up to good sleep. But that's probably not it.

I type out a title for this video.

I'm usually bad at titles. But today I don't have to think about what to call this one.

I name the video *A Special Guest Comes to Lunch.*

Then, because Trevor's going to text soon and I want to get things moving, my finger hovers over the UPLOAD button.

I hesitate.

I remember that I swore to keep Aaron's secret.

But this isn't really revealing his secret, is it? Sure, the video goes *somewhere* when I put it online for storage, a server farm or something, but nobody can watch it.

But what if I make a mistake somehow?

I double-check my upload settings. Yes, I'm still set to private, like I have been for years' worth of videos.

But what if someday I left my computer or phone somewhere, logged in? And somebody then navigates to my private accounts, watches enough of my videos to stumble on this one and find out who the Speaker is?

There's a lot of *ifs* in those scenarios, I tell myself.

No, I'm safe to do this. Nobody even knows I make these videos. Besides Gayle, but I doubt she . . .

But then my train of thought switches tracks; what would happen if I posted this video as public?

Not as a mistake.

What if I did it *on purpose*?

It's the same way, sometimes, when we're all together and I'm feeling really sad or angry, when my friends are acting like I'm not there, talking and joking among themselves. I'll look around at them and think, *What would Harmony say?* Then I'll come up with the worst, most judgmental things I can think about each of them. I would never say any of what I think out loud. In fact, most times I feel guilty even *thinking* what I think.

But sometimes I enjoy playing the what-if game.

What if I ruined everyone's fun?

And now I play that game.

What if I tell the world that Aaron Fortin is the Speaker?

It would be easy. Two clicks: a toggle switch in settings to change my privacy options, then another to start the upload.

Whoops, my finger slipped.

Oh, who am I kidding? I'm not only being dramatic, but I'm being unrealistic.

For "the world" to see one of my videos, I would first need an audience. Uploads from a previously private years-old account can't go viral. It's a good video, as far as my videos go. But it's not exactly viral content. Even if I renamed it something like *The Speaker's Secret Identity Revealed!*, who knows if it'd get picked up in search. Nobody would want to watch me mumble, making uneasy eye contact with the camera, not saying the important part of the story until around two and a half minutes in.

No, if I tried to share the secret like that, the only person I'd hurt is myself.

And my friends. Who are excited to know him and don't want me ruining things.

I don't change the settings. I hesitate to even upload the video at all, like speaking the words on a completely locked account could get me in trouble. Like somehow Aaron would know.

But that's just as silly as the idea that I'd unmask him in front of the whole world.

He can't know something like that. And he wouldn't go looking. Because he doesn't know me, doesn't *want* to know me. Nobody wants to know me, not really, but some people are stuck with me.

So I hit the UPLOAD button, watch the progress bar begin its slow crawl, get the usual warnings not to leave this screen or I'll create an error.

And that's it. It took less than a half hour, and I've got a video done.

I'm proud of myself.

I'm feeling *so* good this morning that instead of running out the door like I do most mornings, I go into the dining room and hug my parents.

"Good morning," Dad says. He seems surprised, but he hugs me back with one arm, his phone in the other hand, angled away. He looks up at me from the kitchen table, then says, "I love you very much, but you can't have any money."

"I'm not looking for money," I say. Then I go to the stove and scoop myself out a bowl of breakfast hash.

My mom stands over Ant, pulling the back of his shirt down, tucking it into the elastic waistband of his pants. I wait a second to make sure she's watching, then take a forkful of eggs and meat, blow on it, then pop it into my mouth.

"Talk to your daughter," Mom says. "She's eating your cooking. She definitely wants money."

She uses a tone that's almost unbearably hokey. She's worried I'll think she's serious and use that as an excuse to stop eating.

I take another bite, smaller this time, then watch as my mom leaves the room, headed to the hall closet. Today must be a performance review or something. Mom's got her skirt and blazer on when she usually just wears pants. She's recently been given a new title at the bank, but we still drink Stop & Shop store-brand soda.

My phone buzzes. Trevor's sent his GPS location. The van's arriving soon. While I have the phone out, I see a notification that the upload is complete and the video has begun processing. That was fast. Our house's discount Wi-Fi hookup must be having a good day.

Typically, I wait a while to revisit my uploads, wait for the *cringe* of having spoken on camera to subside. But I'm excited to watch this video back. I'll probably watch it in bed tonight. Maybe I'll even record an update if anything new happens. I feel almost giddy. And I recognize it as the feeling I used to get when Gayle would come over more. When, before her mom would drop her off at my house, I'd make little lists of conversation topics, news and gossip from the last time we saw each other that I didn't want to forget.

It's fine that Gayle didn't want to hang out last night. Fine too that Paul and Harmony seem to have a new friend they like better than the rest of us.

Because their excitement has become my excitement. Even if we're not all sharing it together. I still get to live it, talk about it, even if it's just with myself.

"*Delicioso*, papa," I say, putting the bowl into the sink.

I make sure my pronunciation is extra appalling to distract from ditching the mostly uneaten breakfast.

"Why didn't you take Spanish like I asked?" Mom says, stepping back into the kitchen. While she's been gone, Ant has stripped off his shirt, is sitting at the table bare-chested.

I pat Ant on the head, then kiss my father on the cheek and tell him to sell a whole fleet today. Which is something I haven't told him to do in a while.

"Tell your friend to stop by," he says. "I'll even take the van for trade-in credit. Five or ten whole dollars for that piece of . . ."

But I'm already out the door before I can hear any more about the age and safety of Trevor's van.

Trevor's down the block.

I don't immediately detect what's different about the van this morning as Trevor pulls into the driveway, stopping a few inches from my dad's back bumper.

I walk down the grass, mud soggy under my feet; this morning is the warmest it's been in forever. Nearly halfway through April. Finals are a joke this year, so the biggest and most stressful event left on the calendar is prom. And I may not even go to prom if Gayle skips it, which she's been saying she might.

I tip my face up to the sky. The warmer weather is a reminder that high school's basically over, another reason to feel hopeful.

I'm close to the van. Close enough to reach out and touch it, but . . .

The side door still hasn't slid open.

Is Gayle asleep in there? Why hasn't she opened the door to hurry me along? Why hasn't she yelled something embarrassing that I'm worried my parents and neighbors will hear?

I stare at the door, the tinted window, and it still doesn't open.

I reach out, pull the handle, let the door slide open to reveal . . .

An empty van.

There's nobody in Gayle's seat. Nobody in the third row, no Harmony or Paul.

Trevor leans back in the driver's seat. I'm still standing on the driveway, so he needs to crane his head back to look me in the face.

"Hey, I texted you," he says. He sounds a little annoyed. "It's just you and me today. Come sit up front."

"What?" I ask. I hate the way my voice sounds, like he's a stranger who's just pulled into my driveway.

"I'm driving you to school. Get in."

I slide the back door closed; it takes some effort, the casters sticky on this side, then I climb into the passenger seat.

Riding shotgun feels strange.

I don't think I've *ever* been up here.

I think of this as Paul's spot, even though he sometimes shares it with Harmony. Missing both of them wouldn't feel so strange if I wasn't up here, if I'd just hopped into my normal seat. This isn't my place.

"Buckle up," Trevor says. But it doesn't sound, not to me, how he usually says it. This morning it's a command, not a suggestion.

I pull the shoulder strap down, wiggling the end until I can get it to catch. At the click, Trevor ratchets the van out of park and pulls back out of the driveway. He barely glances in his mirrors.

There's no traffic on my street, of course, but still . . . that's not like him.

He sighs, readjusts his grip on the wheel.

"What's . . . ," I start to ask. Then I decide to rephrase: "Are they—"

"I don't really know," he cuts me off.

I'm not sure how he wants me to respond to that.

This is all so new. The change in surroundings. Being alone with a friend who I'm always in a group with. I'm unsure of the dynamic. And, although I'm riding shotgun, it doesn't feel like I've gotten an upgrade. If anything, I feel like an imposition.

I begin to fidget to calm myself. I put my hand into the compartment beside the door, but there's crumbs or sand or something in there. I panic, pull back my hand, and a used tissue falls into my lap.

It's gross up here. I'd rather be back in my normal seat.

"I'm sorry," Trevor says after a moment. "I don't even know what I'm angry about. Harm texted me last night, told me that she wouldn't need a ride this morning. Which isn't that weird. Whatever. But then Paul texted the same thing an hour ago."

"And Gayle?" I ask.

He looks over at me, then back at the road, then swallows. Now it's his turn to be unsure what to say.

This happens sometimes. The others are always surprised to learn, or be reminded, that Gayle and I aren't in constant contact, not anymore. And maybe it *should* be surprising. For best friends, we don't talk all that much.

"Paul said Gayle was already at his place, that they'd take her to school too," Trevor says after a pause, his eyes on the road.

"They?" But I already know the answer, as weird and improbable as it sounds.

My friends aren't skipping school. They caught another ride.

Why did they do this? And how did Gayle end up invited?

Because Gayle lives close to Paul, was already there to be picked up, I tell myself. I try to imagine how the explanations will sound in Gayle's voice.

It just kind of happened, Crystal. Don't freak out about it or anything.

And we would have invited you, but Trevor was already on the road. And it's not like Aaron's Acura can seat six, not comfortably. Sorry! Don't be clingy. I'll see you later.

"Jeez," I say.

"That," Trevor says. "That's a word you could use. A very mild word." Trevor doesn't swear much, or not as much as Paul, Harmony, or Gayle.

"Is Aaron really driving our . . ." I try to say the word *friends*, but it feels so odd, and I can't. "Is he really driving them to school?"

I know that's what is happening; I just need to hear someone else say it.

"Yeah," Trevor says, then slaps the dashboard with one hand, points at the dials and chipped chrome paint on the radio. "And I bet he doesn't even have a cassette player."

It's the kind of joking you do when you're trying to keep from getting upset. Trevor hits the dash again, harder.

I know how he feels.

But why? Is it really that much of a problem that the three of them got a ride from a new friend? Even if he—

"We talked to this guy for like, what? A half an hour?" Trevor says.

It's like he's reading my mind. But he's not. He's working through the same emotions I am, is asking similar questions.

"I don't even know why I'm pissed. What do I care that I don't have to pick them up? It's more of the feeling of being ditched, you know?"

I nod. I understand him perfectly.

And Paul, specifically, getting a ride from another guy . . . for Trevor, that's got to be more than a break in routine. For Trevor, that's a betrayal.

Because Paul and Trevor have more than what Gayle and I have. They have more than I'd ever have with Harmony if I were a braver version of myself, if secret daydreams counted.

"Screw them," I say. I don't even know I'm going to say it until the words are out. But then I nod, say it again: "Screw them, if they want to drive with the cool new guy."

"Yeah," Trevor says, smiling. "Fuck 'em."

Trevor slows into a turn, takes the opportunity to look over to me. He's still smiling.

It's such a handsome smile, but I can see in the circles under his eyes that he's tired. He has a job he goes to, right? Once he drops us all off in the afternoon? I don't know where he works, but I'm pretty sure he does work. But the exhaustion in his face isn't just school, work, and whatever he does with the Scouts. Trevor, even when he's not doing those things, has to be a lot of things to a lot of people. I don't know him that well, but I know that.

I should try and know him better.

But it's not like we have a lot in common. I don't have a job. I don't have to keep any major secrets from my parents. And, as far as religion goes, my family attends church twice a year—Christmas and Easter.

I remember this morning, how rested I felt. Despite the salt of my tears. How the biggest struggles of my week were trying to work up the courage to make silly videos.

Dammit, I think, searching my memory, *where does Trevor work?*

I used to know this. Is it Ralph's Italian Ice? No, they aren't open for the season yet. Why don't I know these simple facts about Trevor's life? I've speculated, I've speculated plenty, a lot of it on camera, but why have I been so scared to *talk* to these people I think of as my friends?

I want to ask him a million questions. What's his sister's name? What does he want to do after high school? If he's applied to any colleges. Whether he got in. Whether any of them are out of state.

Or even just where the hell he works.

But I don't ask him any of those things.

He stops at a yellow light. This is the first and only major intersection we cross on our way to school. Long Island commuters are crazy. Trevor always stops here on anything but a green.

In front of us cars pass, changing lanes without signaling to each other. Ten minutes ago, these streets would have been empty. Now the world is coming to life.

"You know?" Trevor says. "This ride has been kind of nice. We haven't learned one thing about pop music. Gayle hasn't made one dick joke. And you don't keep trying to put your knees up on the dash."

"Yeah," I say, "it is nice."

"I prefer it. Actually. And you can tell the rest of them that; I don't care if they know."

We drive the rest of the way in silence. Not awkward silence, but silence that says we're both on the same wavelength. We're both a little pissed off, both a little thankful for the quiet, happy to not have our frivolous friends in the van with us. Frivolous friends arguing with each other about frivolous things.

But that peace can't last.

Soon I can see the brake lights up ahead, the line of cars and buses for drop-off, the arboretum on our left.

And then Trevor's eyes flick up to the rearview mirror.

I look into the side mirror and see it.

Aaron's car, the Acura, slides into traffic behind us.

I can feel the mood deflate.

Neither of us says anything.

In the car behind us, Harmony rides shotgun. Paul sits behind Aaron. I can see a bit of Paul's hair, an ear, but Gayle's not blocked at all by Harmony. Gayle has slid into the center seat, leans forward so that her round face appears between the two front headrests.

All three of them are laughing, and while we watch it seems like Gayle is doing all the talking.

They have to have realized that they've pulled up behind Trevor. But none of our friends look up in the van's direction. Not once.

Aaron does, but just to judge the distance to Trevor's bumper. He keeps his eyes lower than the van's back windows, so there's never any eye contact.

"I'm going to say a thing," Trevor says, waiting until we're two car lengths from being able to turn into the lot. "But we're not going to tell the rest of them, okay?"

I nod.

"I hate this guy," Trevor says.

"Yeah," I say. "I get that."

We smile at each other, like it could be a joke, just between us, to bond us. But it's not and we both know that.

Trevor parks. Aaron pulls the Acura in two spaces away from us.

I take a deep breath, so does Trevor, and we both get out of the van.

NINE

AARON

I'm sure the Boy Scouts of America award a merit badge for fishing. After the fish is caught, I imagine the Scoutmaster teaches the kids how to filet and debone their catch.

And it looks like Trevor Seye wants to do that to me right now.

He wants to gut me.

I've taken his man. And the rest of his friends along with him.

I don't have a reason to hate Trevor. I *don't* hate him. This is just the way things go sometimes, how the universe works. If I'm going to turn his friends into my acolytes, I can already tell he's going to have something to say about that.

The trick to discrediting someone's authority, making them look jealous and irrational, is to provoke them into *acting* jealous and irrational.

It's less clear, as she looks at us, what Crystal's thinking . . .

That's if she is thinking, behind those dull eyes. But I don't pay her much mind right now. It's Trevor's response I want to see. With his Scooby-Doo van empty.

Trevor waves at us, keys in hand.

I don't have to say anything.

Harmony, Paul, and Gayle will do the talking for me.

I just smile that New Aaron smile at Trevor and Crystal. I stand behind the open car door, hoping that I look a little dumb, that I exude a dash of Golden Retriever Boy energy.

"Heated seats!" Paul says, climbing out of the Acura. "In the back!"

"Literal new-car smell," Harmony says.

"I hope you guys didn't miss us too much," Gayle adds.

The goth girl doesn't stay beside the car like the others; she crosses the lot to Crystal and puts her arm around the girl in an awkward hug. It will take a lot more conditioning to get Gayle to give up her friend. I can see in her body language, how she's guiding Crystal toward the school building, that she feels guilty for taking the ride with us.

I'll leave the two of them alone for the rest of the day. Mostly. I have so many other irons in the fire, aspects of my new life to figure out.

"Car," Trevor says, waving for Harmony to get out of the way of a car behind her. "Come on," he says, hitching up his bag, locking his shitty van.

I follow after them, leaving a few steps between me and the group, so that I can better observe my little social experiment.

Paul, Harmony, and Gayle ask Trevor and Crystal how they're doing, trying to have the small talk they missed in their carpool. No small talk in my car. We discussed more profound topics.

As we walk the hallways, none of them pay much attention to me lurking back here, moving with the group, carving a path through the other students. The faces we pass—there are a few glances in my direction, a couple of arched eyebrows asking *Who's the new kid?* But nowhere near as many as yesterday. It's like I've already been claimed by this group, the association already sapping away my novelty.

Good.

The schedule has shifted today, which means my elective and half-credit classes will be different. The core subjects I had yesterday don't move.

I've compared schedules with both Paul and Harmony. I don't share a first period with any of them, so it's easy for me to peel off as they stop at each other's lockers.

I turn down a hallway and have to ask someone directions to classroom B01.

Here at East Bay High, *B* doesn't stand for *basement.* No, that'd be too obvious.

It stands for the Bourdain Wing. The wing has four specialized classrooms that would look at home in a trade school: an automotive shop; a test kitchen for cooking classes; an out-of-date TV studio, all the cameras still recording to tape; and a classroom with sawdust and metal filings under the worktables.

I've signed myself up for woodworking, so that's where I'm headed.

It's a nothing class. I've already been emailing with the teacher, a short man named Mr. Duffy with a push-broom mustache. He's made it clear that nothing is expected of me. The class is already working on their end-of-the-year project since it's fairly complex, and he wants everyone to finish before their *real* finals.

The class is building birdhouses; he says I can try and follow along or join a group, if I would like.

Otherwise, Mr. Duffy seems content to let me sit and look at my phone while he talks to the class, reviews proper sawing procedure or whatever.

I'm glad he doesn't care. I've been so busy, first talking with Paul and Harmony, then putting a dead bird into my English teacher's mailbox, then this morning driving everyone around, that I've completely neglected the Speaker's page.

There's not going to be a stream today. My streams may seem improvised and unscripted, but they're not. I put a *lot* more thought into writing them than I do the poems or photos. With the artwork I'm trying to engage an audience, develop a following and a mystery. With the streams, I'm trying to cultivate an entire language.

Much more difficult.

But if I don't have time for a stream, there needs to be *some* content today.

Three or four months ago, you could point to plenty of days I'd gone a day without a post, but now, with the audience I have, it would be foolish not to keep that momentum going.

I look back in my camera roll.

On the socials I use, I have broken through on my two or three verticals and been marked as "head" content. Which means that I don't even have to try very hard to get the algorithms to play ball. And it's not about my followers, not entirely. These platforms will show my content to *most* of my followers, as good a percentage as they'll allow me to reach without paying. The goal is to land on the For You and Discover pages, where accounts who don't follow me can see what I've posted.

I look up. Mr. Duffy is finished talking, and the students around me are shifting into groups, each of them gathering around mismatching pieces of wood, some small piles of lumber looking closer to birdhouses than others.

I keep scrolling through my photos, then sort them by folder, trying to jog my memory of any good pictures I've taken, decent poems I've written, banked content that I haven't gotten around to posting yet that would fit today's vibe.

It's good to keep a backlog of content in case of emergencies, but with the move and the stress of covering up six homicides, I've run through a lot of mine and am down to the dregs.

But no.

I shouldn't rely on stale trunk work.

I should write something new, something that not only the Speaker's wider audience will enjoy, but that Paul, Harmony, and Gayle can read into. Something they can think is *just* for them.

Yes, Gayle too. She's part of the audience now. Sorting through my notifications I can see that Gayle started following the Speaker this morning, on the drive to school.

Welcome aboard, Gayle.

I unzip my backpack, take my Moleskine notebook out of a mesh inner pouch. Then I root around in my bag looking for a pen, not happy until I pull back a felt tip.

Hmmm. Maybe I'll write a prose poem. No white space at all. A lot of words at once, no spaces between them, no punctuation.

Yes. That's great.

There will be a lot of discussion in the comments, arguments about where one sentence ends and the next begins.

I start writing.

My life is like a

No. I strike through, one clean line, start again.

The sky is a . . .

A what?

fire.

The sky is a fire that stretches stretches stretches beyond these borders beyond this good taste and it con—

"Hey."

Mid-word, loving the repetition I've got going, the lack of punctuation I'm employing as a literary device, I am interrupted.

"Hey," a voice says again.

I look up from my notebook. There's a boy. He's uncomfortably close to me. One of his eyelids droops slightly. His chin has both not enough and too much stubble to look like a high-school senior. He's in sweatpants *and* a sweatshirt. This close, I can tell he smells faintly of hard-boiled eggs.

Beside him stands another boy, smaller but looking just as unwashed. Skin so pale and sickly, he looks green, with smooth hands and forearms but hairy knuckles. He's skinny where his friend is rotund. He's also in a sweatshirt. But he wears highwater jeans instead of sweatpants.

I don't want to sound like too much of an asshole, since I think there's something *medically* wrong with these two, but they look like I'd been imagining most of my classmates would look when I thought *public school on Long Island.*

"Hi," I say to the bigger boy, closing my notebook over my pen.

"Want to be in our group?" the smaller one asks.

I look behind them, over at their worktable. Theirs is by far the most fucked-up-looking birdhouse. Which is almost an achievement. And there are only two of them, where most of Mr. Duffy's students are working in groups of three minimum.

"Sure," I say. I take the pen out, point with it. "But I've got something I have to work on first. For another class. Why don't you start without me? Would that be okay, guys?"

The bigger boy's drooped eyelid squints, and I can tell that he's a little—maybe a lot—savvier than I thought at first glance.

And a lot angrier.

"You don't have to be a condescending dick about it," he says.

Oh. *Condescending.* Definitely not a word I was expecting to hear coming out of that wiry mess of blond stubble.

He's right. I *was* being condescending.

But I thought I was going to get away with it.

"Look," I say, putting my hands up into a shrug. Maybe New Aaron can dig his way out of this. Be everyone's buddy. "I won't be much help. I've never taken shop. You'd have to show me. I don't even know how to hold a—"

"No," he says. "It's fine. We were just trying to be nice. Fuck yourself and fuck your gay little notebook."

Wow. That escalated quickly.

And *gay* as a pejorative term. You rarely hear that outside of old movies.

"Grant, stop," the little one says, eyes darting around the specialized classroom. "We can do it ourselves."

These two are friends. Maybe the only friends each has in the world. They've probably built their schedules, both chosen woodshop, so they wouldn't be alone in here.

I stand. None of our classmates have looked over, even though Grant's outburst was more than audible.

Grant's the kind of kid everyone's going to ignore until he's national news for a few days. Back in Arizona, I might have even been interested in using that. But this is a new town. I keep better company here.

"Grant." I say his name. I say it soft, pleading. People like hearing their own names. They want to be *seen*. "There's no reason to be rude. I didn't mean to sound condescending. I want to help."

I point to a section of the birdhouse, then to a clamp, then to a coping saw.

"What should I work on?" I try and keep my voice kind, understanding. New Aaron. He's so empathic. I can see that I'm reaching the boy. He's clearly got emotional problems, anger issues, the way he went from zero to sixty like that, and I reach out to him in understanding. Or New Aaron does.

"I was working on gluing these," he says, voice lowered. He points to two sides of the birdhouse, way too much wood glue joining them at a right angle, then going stringy as the pieces of wood fall away from each other. "You and Tim can measure and cut another side, I guess."

There we go.

Poor bastard. Grant probably thinks he's just made a friend.

He hasn't.

I put on safety goggles, the strap messing up my hair, and the little one, Tim, and I work for a few minutes.

"Everyone, can I have your attention please?" Mr. Duffy says, holding up two fingers, waiting for eyes to turn to him.

I make sure Grant and Tim are listening to Mr. Duffy, then I take a small chisel from the next table over. I score a deep diagonal line in one of the sides of birdhouse Grant has been struggling to fit together. The wood's fairly soft, so it only takes a second, a few quick movements of my hand to shave a gouge.

A minute later, Grant is back to trying to glue the pieces, bearing down with his full strength instead of using a clamp, hammer, and nails like he should be doing.

Nobody even looks my way when the scored side of the birdhouse shatters outward. The booby trap works better than I planned, a long shard of wood coming loose and embedding itself in Grant's palm.

The boy screams, looking at the three-inch splinter, the wound not even bleeding yet, the thick flesh waxy and white.

Then, with everyone turned to watch, he pulls at the splinter, the ragged edge of the wood cutting deeper, and his palm starts to gush—a gout of blood at first, then a steady stream.

Tim accompanies Grant to the nurse's office, and I am left alone for the last twenty minutes of class to work on my poem.

In English class, Hobbes gives no indication that she had a disturbing find in her mailbox this morning. I answer three of the questions she asks the class about last night's reading. I deliberately get one of them wrong.

Crystal doesn't look back my way once.

Before I leave, Hobbes asks me if I'd like to sit out the unit test tomorrow, do a makeup assignment instead, since I haven't been here for class discussion. I tell her no, that I'll take the test and that she should count it.

And then it's lunch. I'm back with them, my little rock stars.

"Tomorrow," I say. "Why don't you all come over? I'd invite you today, but I still have to unpack some things."

And plan my next stream. And then I have some additional research and prep to do, but they don't need to know any of that.

"Yes," Paul, Harmony, and Gayle each say as I look around the table to them. They're eager. Crystal does whatever her friends do, so she smiles and nods, and I count that as a yes.

Trevor stays silent. I raise my eyebrows at him. "Come on, Trevor. I can get beer."

I can get a lot of things. I can get the keys to my dad's extensive collection of antique and rare firearms.

"I'll have to check," Trevor says. "I . . ."

"What?" I say, "You have to do homework? It's Friday. Come on."

I'm well aware what I'm doing to Trevor.

I watch Paul in the corner of my vision, waiting for him to understand why his ex-boyfriend is reluctant to hang out.

On a Friday.

Come on, Paul, you can do it. Trevor may not be observant, might be having a crisis of faith, but he's still a family man, I can tell.

It takes a beat longer than anticipated. Paul's not the brightest, something I'd assumed upon first meeting him, had confirmed by the simplistic language in his texts. And the misspellings.

Paul shakes his head. He was Trevor's boyfriend long enough, cares enough about him, to realize that Friday's no good.

"Yeah," Paul says. "Actually, now that I think about it, I can't do tomorrow either."

Cute. I thought he'd be less subtle about it, tell me that Friday's a holy day for Trevor's people. But he doesn't. He stands by his man.

"Saturday, then," I say. "All of you?" I do the eyebrow-raising trick for the whole table now, sure to make eye contact with each of them as I say their names. People like hearing their names.

Trevor? Yes. What else could he say now that we changed the whole plan around to accommodate him?

Paul? Yes.

Harmony? Yes.

Gayle? Yes.

I need them all. A crack team.

Then I turn to Crystal.

"Crystal? Yeah? You'll come?"

I don't want a head nod. I want to hear her say it.

She looks at Gayle. Then:

"Yes," she says. "Sounds good."

That's great. All of them have agreed to come hang out.

The thing is, by Saturday, Crystal won't want to show her face.

Gayle said something interesting on the drive over here, shared something her good friend keeps secret from most of the world.

Something very interesting. Something that worries me a little. But also something I can use.

TEN

CRYSTAL

I have another dream.

In the dream I'm at school but not at school. Well, the school's kind of my house. Which is typical dream stuff. But I'm running from room to room in my not-house, trying to tell everyone that there's been a carbon-monoxide leak, that the alarms have stopped working but there's definitely a leak, I know it. We all have to get outside.

But because it's a dream and the logic's weird, I can't remember the words *carbon monoxide*, so I'm trying to communicate that idea to my friends and classmates, but none of them are getting it. In my dream, charades aren't good enough. Then, as I plead, as they don't listen, Harmony says that she knows, that she understands, and she gives me a hug and rubs my back.

I've never hugged Harmony in real life. I don't know what it's like, but in the dream it's pretty great. Soft, sweet-smelling.

And that makes me feel better, of course, the scent of her, but as I take a big warm whiff, I remember that I'm *also* breathing in the carbon monoxide.

And that's when I wake up.

This time I don't wake up crying. It's not a traumatic enough dream for that.

I just wake up.

But something's off. It feels too bright in my small room.

I reach for my phone.

It's 8:15!

Shitballs!

I stayed up late, occasionally glancing at my English notes for the unit test while watching anime on shady websites. But I thought I'd set my alarm. No, wait, I never have to "set" my alarm. It's programmed to repeat every weekday.

Goddamn.

Why did Trevor let me sleep? Why didn't he honk or something?

I look. I've got no text notifications on my phone's lock screen.

Weird, but the back of the phone's cool to the touch, so maybe there was some kind of required update installed in the early morning that messed with my alarms.

I unlock the phone, go to navigate over to my texts but get an error message before I can.

MAIL COULD NOT REACH SERVER. CHECK SETTINGS.

Hmmm. That's a new one.

I hit okay to close that prompt. It's strange, probably another sign of my phone's steady decline.

There are no new texts from Trevor. The last thing sent was yesterday's GPS pin drop. Did he even drive today? Or has he completely given up the carpool to Aaron?

But maybe it's not just the email account that's unreachable. Maybe my phone's fried, even with two bars of signal. Because there's nothing new in the group text. No activity in there since yesterday afternoon. That's *really* odd. I have to keep the group thread on silent. There's usually a hundred or so messages a day, accelerating at night, and my phone can't take all the vibrating.

The last message in the group is from Gayle. A picture of her dog's genitals with no caption, which is a running joke that's been going so long, I can't even remember when it started. Or why Gayle finds it funny.

Functioning phone or not, I have to get moving. I'm late for school.

I put on pants, pack my makeup into my bookbag, hoping I can rinse my face in a sink at school, and run out of my bedroom.

If I don't hurry, I'm also going to miss my . . .

"Dad," I say.

Thank god. He's still here.

He turns from the refrigerator, milk carton pulled away from his face, spattering milk onto the magnets holding up Ant's drawings of dinosaurs and feet.

I've surprised him.

"Cris—" He says my name, then chokes for an extra second, looks down at the carton, then says: "Don't tell Mom."

Most times my father's fear of my mother is played like a joke. She's not a scary woman. They're a team, working together to keep the wheels on, financially and otherwise.

But Mom *would* actually get mad at him if she saw him drinking milk straight from the carton, a sleeve of Aldi-brand knockoff Oreos on the counter.

I let him wipe his chin, then smile and say:

"I won't say anything . . . *if* you drive me to school."

"I'm opening today," he says.

I look at the clock on the microwave. Which blinks *12:00*, *12:00*, *12:00*, but it's more for effect then to actually check the time.

"Mom just left, right?" I ask, lifting my phone. "I'll call and see if she wants to turn around and come—"

"Oh stop it, I'll take you," he says, brushing crumbs off his tie, resealing the bag of not-Oreos.

We hurry to his truck. It's clean, like new, kept that way because the dealership insists. My dad's job is the only reason our family can afford to drive two cars . . . and it's because of his discount, not because of the pay.

There's more traffic than normal. We pass a drive-through line at Dunkin' that's backed up into the street. The adult world is scrambling to get where it's going but needs caffeine first.

Phone issues aside, why didn't Trevor honk? Did the carpool even stop at my house?

I don't blame my parents for letting me sleep. Even before the carpool, I'd been in charge of getting myself ready for school and to the bus stop. And I'm never late, never get tardies, so they aren't in the habit of checking to see I'm awake.

My dad's driving too close to the sedan in front of us, making them nervous enough that they put on their blinker and turn. It's a big truck. Intimidating. I've driven it a few times, never without either my mom or dad in the car, mostly in empty parking lots.

"That's right, missy, out of the way," my dad says. He's not a jerk, really. He just likes having the road to himself. "The bigger the car, the safer you are" is something the dealership makes him say to sell trucks, but also something I think he believes.

"How's school?" he asks.

"How's work?" I ask back.

"Touché."

I look down at my phone, begin to comb through the apps I look at most mornings. Or whenever I go on my phone, really. They all work, all update. The browser works. I have service.

Weird. Then I go into the group text, start typing:

> You guys even try and pick me up?
> Or was there not room in Aaron's car?

No. Way too spicy. Too bold. Not something I'd dare send.

I delete that message, then retype:

> No ride? Is all okay?

And send.

I wait for a moment. Don't get an error message or a prompt to resend as a text. So, as far as I can tell, my phone's able to send iMessages.

I move to my email, pull down, try to refresh.

CANNOT REACH INBOX.

I guess the message this morning wasn't a mistake; I really have been logged out of my account.

I need to go back into settings and reenter my password.

Which is easier said than done, because I really can't remember which variation of my normal numbers and words and capitalized letters I used to register for Google. Google's one of those universal log-ins. Whether on the laptop or the phone, it runs a whole bunch of apps and it just *stays* connected to all of them.

I stare at the screen asking me for my password.

These things don't typically give you many guesses before they lock you out, so I think long and hard before typing in what I'm 99 percent sure is the password.

I hit enter.

INCORRECT PASSWORD.

Damn. Well. They have my phone number. I can reset that way. That's probably good to do anyway; I haven't changed it in a while.

"Boy trouble?" my dad asks.

I look at him, trying not to roll my eyes, but definitely still rolling my eyes.

"Oh, sorry—*or* girl trouble?" he says, correcting himself.

He's not making a joke about my identity. He really does try to understand. He just says everything "funny."

"Not boy or girl trouble. Phone trouble," I say.

"Oh, then never mind. You're SOL there. That one's got to last you *at least* two more upgrade periods."

I look up at the road, because otherwise I'll say something that sounds ungrateful. The next phone my mom's able to get through work has already been promised to my dad. If they don't need to sell it back.

Up ahead, I can see the arboretum recede and the front of the school building appear. I'm so late that we don't have to wait behind any buses.

My dad pulls up to the door and stops. I kiss him on the cheek, tweeze a piece of cookie out from under his collar.

"Yeah, I wouldn't buy a truck from me either," he says, but then lapses into seriousness, wishes me good luck, and says that he loves me.

I love him too.

I'm out of the truck, through the vestibule and inside the school as I hear what I'm pretty sure is the second homeroom bell.

My first period is Calc.

Ms. Leigh tends to keep her back turned for most of class, is bad at watching the room as she writes equations on the whiteboard, so for the first few minutes of the do-now, I'm able to keep my phone on my desk to try resetting my password.

A RECOVERY CODE HAS BEEN SENT TO YOUR EMAIL.

Email? Hmmm. I assumed it'd be sent as a text message. But Google must have my school email address too. I can check that account with my school iPad.

With the do-now explained, Ms. Leigh asks us to hand forward our homework. She's one of those teachers who assigns homework every night but only collects it once or twice a week.

Everyone groans. I groan with them. Even though I've actually done it, I'm ready to take it out of my binder and hand it forward.

But there's an odd moment, as I snap open the three rings of my binder, when I look up and suddenly don't feel quite as invisible as I normally do.

Jerry Gasparro, Kristen Tourt, and the entire row behind me—as I turn to collect any homework that's been passed forward, they're all looking at me.

"Hey, guys," someone says. But it's someone all the way in the back, and I can't see who it is. After they say it, though, those faces in class that never look at me, they all smile.

I don't know what to make of it. I think of the cookie crumbs on my dad's face, wonder if I somehow—

"Just you, Crystal?" Ms. Leigh says, snapping my attention back to the front of the classroom. She takes my homework, puts it onto the thin pile she's collected. It's only three problems a night, and you don't even need to get them correct; it's participation credit. I don't know why everyone sitting behind me wouldn't just copy the problems from the book and then write *something* down.

I look back at them, judging them for their minimal effort, but they don't care. Only one of them is still looking up at me. Zach Ross. Who used to make fun of me with Tommy Burke but hasn't gone out of his way to do so in years since they both discovered weed.

"Hey," Zach says, smiling a weird, mocking smile at me. I turn away from him, and he adds, on a long delay: "Guys."

Everyone in the desks around me cracks up. Laughter that grows louder as each of my classmates looks at each other, tries to stop.

Ms. Leigh shushes them but doesn't try too hard. It's a loud enough outburst, so it's best to just let them laugh it out.

She never has been great at classroom management. She—

Oh no, I think.

I finally get it.

I know why they're laughing.

My eyes immediately cloud with tears.

How fucking stupid am I?

How has it taken me so long to put it together?

Fat and stupid and slow, no matter how much homework I do, no matter how much I apply myself.

I can't log into my email because I've been hacked.

And Google . . . Google owns YouTube. They're the *same* log-in.

Oh fuck, oh fuck, oh fuck, oh fuck . . .

I might be saying these "oh fucks" aloud or I could just be frantically thinking them to myself. Either way, I'm breathing heavy.

Ms. Leigh regains control of class, starts threatening class-participation zeros for the next person to say "Hey, guys."

I sit through the remainder of Calc, trying not to cry, trembling but knowing that if I look at my phone, check to see what's going on with my YouTube page—the number of views, the comments—then I'll start screaming and crying and run out of class.

It feels like an eternity, but eventually the bell rings, and I'm the first person out the door.

I have to find a way to fix this.

In the hallway, kids I've never even talked to before say "Hey, guys" as I pass.

Do I really say it that much? Is it *every* video? Isn't that what everyone says when they start talking to their phone camera?

The kids I pass flick their phone screens at me, let me see my own face, horribly lit.

In the five minutes between bells, I stop in the bathroom near the caf and sit in one of the stalls.

It's no use at this point, but I use my iPad to check for the password-reset code. There's nothing in there but some homework reminders. Whoever's in my account, they've gone and changed things so I'll never recover my password, not the normal ways.

I'm breathing so heavy, I'm not sure how I can even stand up from the toilet, never mind figure out a way to get back into my account and fix this.

Then the late bell rings, and I remember:

It's Friday.

I have second-period gym *three* times this week.

Gayle! My class right now is with Gayle!

She'll be able to help me. If not help me, at least none of these fuckers would dare say "Hey, guys" in her presence. She'd put a Hot Topic block-heel boot up their asses.

But by the time I get to the locker room, Gayle's already changed into her shorts and T-shirt and is closing her locker.

"Hey," I say to her, wincing when my mind finishes with *guys*.

She doesn't seem to hear me. I watch her press her combo lock shut and begin to walk the other way out of the room, passing the showers.

"Gayle," I say, jogging a few steps to grab her by the wrist.

She stops, looks at my hand, then looks up at me.

Gayle looks different. She's not wearing her cat eyes today.

Or maybe that's not true, maybe she wiped them away. She's been crying. It's such a change, seeing her natural skin tone, now reddish and swollen where she's usually powder white.

"Get your fucking hand off me," Gayle says. She pulls her wrist away, her nails scratching me as I try to hold on.

She pushes out the swing doors, the girls behind us in the locker room a mix of secondhand embarrassed for me and openly chuckling.

Oh fuck, that's right.

A lot of my videos are about her.

Her and the rest of my friends. Their lives. Their secrets. The secrets I've uncovered when I'm quiet in the carpool, when I listen to their stories, what I piece together when I pay attention.

And there's no more wondering, there's no more questioning whether or not we're drifting apart. It's as simple as this—my best friend is not my best friend anymore.

ELEVEN

AARON

Hacking.

The dark web.

Cryptocurrency.

All of these buzzwords and concepts . . . they're not as sexy as the media wants you to believe. The news presents B-roll of shadowy figures hunched behind keyboards, highly skilled techno-thieves ready to empty grandma's retirement account. But the media only covers "cyber security breaches" to scare people over fifty, to get them to waste money on CreditSecure, antivirus programs, and other services that won't help.

No. Nothing will stop your personal information from being compromised.

Because it's already compromised.

If people understood *how* information is sold on the internet, they'd see that phrases like "the dark web" are *less* sexy, but *more* frightening.

Because finding the password to Crystal Giordano's Google account will cost less than a hundred US dollars and will take about twenty minutes of my Thursday afternoon.

I'll expend more time and effort on the essay section of Ms. Hobbes's unit test tomorrow, I'm sure.

The piece of information I need, the key to cracking into her account, is Crystal's email address. And that's easy enough. In fact, that's already on my phone. My first night texting with Harmony, I asked her to forward me her contacts. I told her it was so I could have "everyone in town I could need to talk to, since you seem to know all the best people." Harmony didn't hesitate to send.

I begin the process of retrieving Crystal's password after I get out of the shower, and I have it and am logged into her account before my hair's dry.

I don't like to stream with wet hair. Yes, I use product to seal in moisture, keep that semi-damp look, but I apply it after my hair air-dries.

But that's not important right now.

Oh. Yes, "cyber security."

Most people's information, *your* information, is on the internet. And it's all available for purchase.

There's not much the average person can do to prevent that. Other than practice good password hygiene, of course. Ugh, too much of a hassle, and who can remember all those different passwords? And remember to change them on a regular basis?

All these sites, apps, and the video games your aunt plays on her phone that are actually foreign data-mining operations: they *all* have security breaches. And these breaches are happening all the time. The general public hears about these hacks when it's a big company, when a bumper on the local news tells them that Apple was hit, they better change their passwords. But it's the small apps you have to worry about. That expensive salad place with the loyalty program that gives you half off every seventh bowl? Yeah, someone's skimmed that password while we were having this conversation.

And for a lot of people, not even particularly stupid people, the password they use for the froufrou salad place and the password they use for their bank account are the same.

Those data breaches, when it's a case of servers being infiltrated and data stolen, those are the only time that *real* "I'm almost through the firewall and into the mainframe!" hacking happens. The kind you see in movies. And the real-life guys aren't wearing leather jackets and sunglasses. No, they've all got bacne and are sharing a single cramped office in the suburbs.

I, personally, can't code for shit. But I know how to access the fruits of their labor.

All I have to do is Boot Camp into Windows, then run a single illicit—but very easy to find—program. Then I dial up a digital wallet I've had since Oregon, pay, and I'm the proud owner of Crystal Giordano's Gmail account.

She doesn't even have two-factor turned on! Come now, Crystal.

We're so close in physical proximity, the same zip code, I doubt Crystal's even going to get a "new device" log-in notification. It's not like I'm accessing her account from Beijing.

I scroll her Gmail for a second. It's sad. Not a single personal email on the first page. Her inbox is warnings that her rewards bucks for Michaels are about to expire, then endless promotional emails from a company called Crunchyroll. Not a fast-food restaurant, as I'd assumed, but instead an anime thing.

But I'm not here to spy on Crystal's email correspondence.

I'm here for her videos.

I open a new tab, go to YouTube.

The new tab doesn't prompt another log-in; instead, it automatically shows me Crystal's personalized front page. On the left side of the screen, I can see the names of all the channels she subscribes to, then in the center, I see the twenty or so videos the algorithm's trying to serve her right now. There are thumbnails for videos like *Lo-Fi Hip-Hop Beats to Study To* and *The History of Mr. Toad's Wild Ride* along with assorted let's-plays and makeup tutorials.

The YouTube algorithm seems to think Crystal needs help with contouring and layering. Which is an impressive bit of computer learning, because she does.

Although I have fans who rip and upload my streams to YouTube, I'm not a YouTuber. Which means that I'm unfamiliar with the site's layout. It takes me a second to find that if I click on Crystal's face in the upper right corner of the page, I'm allowed to select from several options including "Your Channel" and "YouTube Studio."

Okay.

Let's see her channel first, before we dive deeper into settings. During the ride to school, Gayle told us very little about the videos themselves. Partly because she seemed to be embarrassed to tell her friends the videos existed at all, and then because she admitted that she'd never seen any of them. That Crystal is "weird about them" and that Gayle only knew about it because she had seen the tripod in Crystal's room.

Paul and Harmony seemed surprised to hear about the existence of the videos, but not overly interested. They were both too busy trying to flirt with me.

On the channel page, I have to go to the videos tab and sort the listing by clicking "See All."

There are *way* more videos than I assumed there were going to be.

So many, I think, that I should probably put a pin in this right now, go do my own stream before I am consumed by this. I should stop before I dive too deep down the depressing rabbit hole of watching Crystal Giordano's private YouTube videos.

I almost do pause, save this for later.

But then I see it.

The first video on this list was posted yesterday.

And it's called: *A Special Guest Comes to Lunch.*

Oh, you fucking . . . I try to conjure the worst insult, but nothing can come close to expressing what I want to call Crystal fucking Diaz fucking Giordano right now.

I mean.

She couldn't have . . . She wouldn't, right? A mousy girl like that?

I click the video to find out.

Even though *I'm* the subject of the video, it's dreadfully boring, so I scan through, getting the basic gist of a ten-minute video in two minutes of clicking around.

Then I lean back in my chair, sit with this knowledge for a moment.

What's the correct move here?

Back in Arizona, I had begun to suspect that I was going numb, becoming unable to feel normal, unmuted emotions.

Crystal's cured me of that, because I am *angry.*

Furious.

But I had an inkling this might have happened, right? That's why I'm spending this much energy, and digital currency, on Crystal Giordano at all.

As I sit, digesting, letting my hate simmer to a light boil, I realize that Crystal doing this has caused me to respect her a bit more.

I scroll through the rest of the videos. Some are longer; some are shorter. There's none of the polish of a *real* YouTube channel. But that's to be expected; she's not a real YouTube Creator. She's using this more as a video diary? I guess? Maybe pretending she has a YouTube channel makes her feel a little better, a little less awkward in front of the camera? The psychoanalytics would be fascinating if Crystal Giordano weren't the most banal person I can imagine. A composite sketch of a human girl.

The thumbnails are all Crystal's face in the same depressing, poorly lit room, posed midsentence so that her mouth is blurred. If you cursor over to preview the clip, her head moves slightly and her jaw works, but there's never anything compelling, nothing that would get someone to click the video.

The uploads have titles that range from incredibly matter-of-fact (*Three Things I Did This Weekend: Mall, Minecraft, Brother's Birthday*) to more downbeat (*They Went to the Bowling Alley Without Me Today*) to—most intriguingly—gossipy (*I Think My Best Friend's Being Abused and I Don't Know What to Do*).

The videos go back years. It would take me days to watch them all, but I sample some. In the earliest videos I'm surprised to find that Crystal didn't used to look as bad as she does now. In—I do the math using the upload date—eighth grade, she was halfway pretty.

But after a few minutes of these early videos, I see she's always been this neurotic.

Crystal has done all this work. Put in her Malcolm Gladwell ten thousand hours, all for nothing. She's performed for the camera, created all this content, but she's done it without an audience.

Well. I think that's a shame.

I navigate to "YouTube Studio," a dashboard that allows me to see her nonexistent analytics, her zero subscriber count. Then I click on the

"Content" tab and see all her videos in a much more manageable grid system, a checkbox next to each.

I check the box next to her most recent video, the one where she talks about me.

I delete it, needing to click through a prompt asking if I'm sure.

Yes, I'm sure.

Sorry, Crystal. But this is not how the Speaker is unmasked. And you are not the one to do it. This is not how everything I've worked for, all that I've cultivated, comes undone.

I don't care if deleting this video puts my fingerprints on things. Because what I'm about to do next is going to make things a "her word against my word" situation, and nobody's going to think Crystal Giordano's word is worth shit.

I use the "Select All" function to checkbox the rest of the videos. The years and years of videos.

There's no use taking a slow-burn approach to this. This isn't a situation where I blackmail, threaten to release a few at a time to keep the girl in check.

No. If I'm not going to kill Crystal, not for the moment, then I'm going to *erase* her.

In two clicks I set all her videos to public.

Then I change Crystal's Google password. And her preferred method of recovery.

I'm sure she could regain *control* of the account somehow, or at least have it locked for suspicious activity if she picks up an actual phone and calls a helpline.

But by then it'll be too late.

Using Crystal's own linked school email account, I send a link to her channel to every student at East Bay High.

I wonder how long it will take Crystal to figure out her life is ruined?

With that taken care of, reinvigorated, full of feelings, I start to deliver a career-best stream.

In the chat there's a lot of speculation about the new time, whether this is the new normal, then about my relative silence over the last few days. Yes, there's more time to do them after school, so this will, generally, be when I do new streams. But I don't wade into the chat to confirm this. Let them figure it out themselves.

I don't keep my script out while I stream, otherwise I might become over-reliant on it and look like I'm reading.

I do keep my notebook open beside me, in case I need to glance down.

The handwritten outline is like a musician's set list. I check off topics to cover, current events to allude to—only slightly, because I don't want this content to seem dated—then a list of names to drop, research rabbit holes I'd like to send my followers down.

And finally, at the bottom, underlined, are the words *Don't just speak, act.*

That's a reminder to always include my sign-off.

"It's been a pleasure talking with all you out there," I say. "Remember: don't just speak, act."

Actually, it's more than a sign-off. More than a branding slogan or social-media call to action. Yes, it does have part of the Speaker's name in there. But it's more than a saying that some intrepid fans have started putting on shirts and buttons, selling on their Redbubble stores.

It's a mantra.

All the greats use them.

Controlling how your followers greet each other, inserting yourself into their everyday language, altering their lexicon is how you blur the lines between a fandom and a religion.

Don't just speak, act.

They're words to live by.

After the stream, I call it an early Thursday night, ignoring the constant texts from Harmony and Paul. Tomorrow's going to be a big day, and I've been running myself too hard.

I could creepy crawl my way out of bed, stand below Hobbes's window.

But I don't feel like it tonight.

No. Maybe if I wake in the middle of the night and can't sleep, maybe then I'll do something. Maybe I'll take the thirty-minute drive to see the *Amityville Horror* house. Ronald DeFeo Jr. was a family annihilator, not a serial killer or cult leader, so not my *specific* interest, but still: when in Rome. Or maybe, instead of sightseeing the best Long Island has to offer, I'll go for an early-morning jog. Or continue one of the DM conversations I've started on my dummy accounts.

But I should stop thinking about that for now.

I've set everything I can set in motion.

It's time to rest.

✗

"My stepdad doesn't molest me!" Gayle says. "Is she insane? How could she tell everyone that? How could she even *think* it?"

Gayle looks around the lunch table, her shoulders set. She's trying to keep her voice down, but most of the lunchroom is stealing glances over here.

They've never been this interested in this table.

That's the thing about keeping a "low profile" in high school: low profile isn't *no* profile. The kids in your class still know your name. And they all know what your insecurities are when you step out of line. They know who to stare at when a bit player suddenly becomes one of the main characters for the day. For this Friday.

"Look," Trevor says. He reaches over, touches Gayle's forearm. "I'm not saying it's not fu—messed up." He corrects himself. Closer to god every day, old Trevor. "But these are her *private* thoughts. We were never meant to hear them."

"You think I don't know that?" Gayle says, but she doesn't pull her arm away. Her eyes are watery, but they haven't spilled over into tears. Her makeup is gone; she's all cried out for the moment. "It still sucks. It still hurts. She hurt me."

"She hurt all of us," Harmony says, holding up a finger. "Trevor especially. Since he—"

Trevor looks up at her, looking confused, but—and this is my first time seeing Harmony express hesitancy of any kind—she wavers.

"What?" Trevor asks.

"Never mind," Harmony says. "You didn't see the ones about you, I'm guessing."

"No," Trevor says. "I didn't watch any of them. It's not right. Anyway, who has time for that? This morning I had to help my mom with . . ."

But his voice trails off, and I can see his hands begin to tremble.

Because what is it about Trevor Seye that Crystal could have told the world? Something that maybe he's not ready to share with everyone? That only four of the people at this table are supposed to know?

"Wait," Trevor says. "You said *ones*. Plural. She has *multiple* videos about me? Why?"

Harmony picks at a cuticle. There's a coldness to her. When I first saw her, I thought she could do as the new Olivia Stewart. But she's more than that. Harmony's got a few drops of killer instinct in her blood. She thinks like me, or at least has the *capacity* to.

"Yeah, and she—" Harmony starts. But Paul cuts her off.

"She thinks your family is from the Middle East," Paul says. He looks up from his phone, relating this as if he's watching the video right now. Which he may be, but it's probably just for dramatic effect.

"My parents are from Senegal," Trevor corrects.

"Well, *I* know that," Paul says.

"She also thinks that your sister's not allowed to go to school because your family hates women," Harmony says.

Trevor blinks, screws up his face. There's a thin sheen of sweat on his forehead now. I feel like I can read his thoughts spiraling out of his ear like closed captioning.

Okay. This stuff is pretty ignorant. Maybe even racist. But he can deal with it. It's not as bad as he'd thought.

"But Mia *needs* to be homeschooled," Trevor says.

"Yeah. I know," Paul says, then puts his own hand not on Trevor's arm, like how Trevor's still holding Gayle to comfort her, but on his knee.

Then, quickly, like Harmony's pulling off a Band-Aid but maybe enjoying the pain a little too much, she says: "Also one video's all about you being gay."

"I . . . ," Trevor says. One letter, and he makes it sound like his whole world unraveling.

Paul pushes down on his knee. He's not only comforting his friend; he's stopping Trevor from jumping to his feet, preventing him from making more of a scene of the group than they already are.

"Trev. Trev. Calm down. It's going to be okay," Paul says.

Trevor looks around. Yes, now he can see the impact of Crystal's videos on the cafeteria. There's the more innocent attention he's getting: girls cupping smiles behind their hands. But there's also the more dangerous looks. The looks from boys who spend weeknights drinking in their parents' garages, the ones who were in Cub Scouts and Boy Scouts with Trevor but didn't stick with it into high school. The boys who always thought there was something a little *off* about that African kid. The boys who don't care how far society's come, the boys who still call each other homophobic slurs and love-hate the sound of the words, special centers in their brains lighting up whenever they have an occasion to use them. And they *always* find an occasion. The boys who are dangerous on a good day, but a lot more dangerous when they've got three boilermakers in them.

Then Trevor's eyes fall on me.

Like he's trying to figure out if I'm friend or foe. Because he hasn't liked me before now. But that was just a feeling. Now it's more important that he know for sure. Am I a new friend, or am I one more liability?

"It's . . . It's such a violation," I say, shaking my head slightly, like him being outed is the worst thing I've ever heard. Extreme emotions are much trickier for me to pull off. But I think I do a pretty good approximation of sincere, radical empathy. "Trevor, I . . . I know we don't know each other well. But I'm sorry this is happening."

Maybe that last bit was too much. Like I said, extreme emotions are tough for me to mimic; sometimes they come out like sarcasm. Because now Trevor's eyebrows narrow, and he looks ready to tell me to save it, that I'm right, that I *don't* know him *or* his situation and maybe I should go, that they don't need me around.

But Harmony speaks up before Trevor can say anything.

"If it helps you feel any better," Harmony says, "she outs herself too."

"Outs?" Trevor says, turning his attention away from me.

"Yeah. She's obsessed with me. Straight-up lesbionic. Has a whole video about how my hair smells. Which, no bigotry or anything, I'm an *ally*, of course, but . . . it's gross."

Paul nods. "Well. I feel left out. She doesn't say anything at all about me, really. Other than that I'm a prick to her." He's trying to lighten the mood. "Which, ya know, fair."

I want to say something, to all of them, but I don't want to end up striking another false note.

I'm a bit off my game. I expended way more energy on Hobbes's little unit test than I'd imagined I would, spent all last period sharing my genius in short-answer question responses that were long and essays that were longer.

But I can't just be an impassive observer right now. I don't want to overstep, get too familiar in a way that threatens tomorrow's party, but I need to say something.

"Look," I say. I wait for them all to turn to me. I see the flash of distrust in Trevor's expression. But he's not overly concerned with me. He's hurting. I imagine he's playing through scenarios in his mind, trying to figure out how the whole school knowing his sexuality is going to tip over into his parents finding out.

It's Gayle who looks at me with hostility. That's fine. I can still win her over, have plans to. In fact, I've already started. She watched the stream last night. I made sure to check, and she was there, tuned in the whole time.

Paul and Harmony, I can see in their eyes that they *want* me to speak. That they want guidance. So I do.

"It's not my place to say. Because I don't know you all that well," I say. "But these kinds of things"—I wave at the eyes on us—"they seem way worse at the onset. They blow over quickly. It's almost too much scandal, too much going on. People will remember Crystal; they won't really remember or care what they learned about the people at this table. And we're going into the weekend. That'll make people forget faster."

There's a beat. Maybe I've misjudged.

"That's . . . not helpful, Aaron," Gayle says.

I didn't mean it to be helpful. It's the truth. And saying it will make me seem smarter when Monday rolls around and nobody cares or remembers that this happened.

"Maybe it's not," I say. "But have you guys, like, gone to the videos and reported them as harassment and bullying?"

They blink at me.

"Not to be mean," I say, "but she has very few subs, very few views, and a lot of videos. You can probably get the whole channel pulled down right now if you all go to a video about you and report it."

They all exchange "why didn't we think of that?" looks with each other. Even Trevor. And then, except for Paul, who already had his out, they're all on their phones.

By the time lunch is over, Crystal's channel has been suspended, marked for permanent removal, pending review.

I wonder where Crystal is, what she's doing—now that I've read everyone her diary, then struck a match and burned the whole thing to cinders.

I have the strong feeling that I've just removed her from the game entirely until I'm ready to play with her again. That I may see her—a ghost slinking around the hallways of the school, a hollow shell in the far corner of our shared English class—but that she will no longer impact me or my plans.

Yes. I doubt I'll ever have to waste another thought on Crystal Giordano again.

TWELVE
CRYSTAL

Someone did this to me.

Some. One. Did. This. To. Me.

I've entered a different stage of upset. My thoughts are a little slower, my lips have stopped tingling, and I'm angry.

Who . . . who could have done this? I picture every face I've seen laugh at me today, boys and girls, some of whom I've known since we shared cubbies and lay down next to each other for nap time.

All their faces, superimposed over each other until there's no distinguishing features, just an open toothy hole for a laughing mouth.

I wonder how many of my classmates have disliked me for our whole lives, since the days of juice boxes and sticker books.

Not that I've been worried about it for that long. For the last, what, five or six years? Since middle school, basically, I've gotten through the day by telling myself that I'm being *paranoid*. That the people in the hallways who I sometimes catch whispering, hear laughing when I'm not sure what they're laughing at, that they don't notice me at all.

That they're not *all* laughing at me *all* the time.

That they don't hate me; they just don't know me.

But. But maybe they do hate me.

No. This isn't helpful.

Who did this?

I can't let my emotions overwhelm me. I have to approach the question logically. What is it they say on mystery shows? I have to determine who had both motive and opportunity.

I turn the amorphous everyperson in my mind into a rotating image of the four boys who used to torment me. Tommy Burke can't be bothered to come to school anymore, so he's out.

And those remaining boys, maybe they have motive if they suddenly decided to begin bullying me again after years of silence, but how would they have opportunity? They wouldn't be able to get into my account, right? My iPad's been in my backpack, and my phone and laptop were at home.

Or maybe that's faulty thinking. Maybe this was done remotely. Or it had to be done remotely, right?

But, no, it still doesn't feel right to blame four boys who've become complete strangers.

It has to be someone I know. A friend.

I think of Gayle. No, it couldn't be her. Look how upset she is. How much she hates me, how much damage my videos about her have done. She wouldn't do that to herself.

Then I think of Harmony, who can be mean. Very mean.

But that still doesn't fit.

Then Paul, who in some ways can be worse.

And then I think—

"Uh . . . Crystal?" Ms. Hobbes says.

I look up at her.

The classroom is empty except for us. Ms. Hobbes pushes the foil lid back over her now-empty yogurt container, tosses it into the small garbage pail beside her desk.

She adjusts some of the papers in front of her, our tests from today, a stack that's graded and a stack that's untouched by her green pen, and then looks over to the door. Once I pushed inside, crying, Ms. Hobbes let down the paper curtain over the door's small safety-glass window.

I don't think teachers are supposed to put down that curtain. Or close the door with kids in the room. That curtain's supposed to be for shelter-in-place drills only.

Over the last half hour, I've stopped crying. But I haven't touched my lunch. I was one of the first people in line for food. I grabbed my tray and got out of the lunchroom as quickly as possible so I didn't have to face my friends.

Former friends.

"If you're not going to eat that, babe," Ms. Hobbes says, "maybe go throw it out in one of the bins in the hall?" She looks toward the small pail where she just threw her yogurt tub. "It's . . . We can't have meatloaf in here this long. My classroom is going to smell."

I pick up a Tater Tot and push it into my mouth to show that I'm eating.

That seems to be enough. She continues grading. Or maybe she's pretending to work, is not sure how to handle the crying kid she has in her room, because she's been on the same test for at least ten minutes since she opened the yogurt, scribbling notes.

I could tell when I knocked that Ms. Hobbes didn't want to let me in here. She said that this is her protected time to grade and eat her lunch. I understand that. But I had nowhere else to go.

One of the reasons I like Ms. Hobbes is: she's not *that* kind of English teacher. She doesn't run the drama club, only helps with college essays on designated days. She's not going above and beyond. She wants to teach, do lesson prep for tomorrow, and then go home. And she does everything she can to avoid becoming the kind of teacher where students loiter around her classroom. She has a laminated sign washi-taped to her door that lists her "office hours." She says that that's the way it'll be when we get to college, that you have to respect a professor's time.

I stand, take a couple of shaky steps toward her desk.

"Ms. Hobbes," I say. She looks up from the test in front of her. I see a lot of green.

The school says we're not supposed to use red pen because it fosters a "negative mindset," I remember her saying at the beginning of the year, holding up our first essay assignments, *"so imagine all this green is red."*

"Yes, Crystal?" she asks. It's like I've nodded off standing up; I catch myself, almost go face-first into the empty yogurt cup atop the trash.

"Um, I . . ."

"Crystal, are you okay?" Ms. Hobbes asks. "You don't have to tell me all the details, but if it's something I have to report, then . . ." She trails off.

I think about my dad, then my mom, the stress of their jobs, how it permeates. Then about how I probably made my dad late to work by asking him to drive me to school this morning. I think about other ways to get home. About the school bus. But it's been over a year since I've taken the bus. Which bus number am I? And how many times will I have to hear "Hey, guys"?

No. I can't take the bus.

I bite my cheek, look Ms. Hobbes in the eyes, and go for it:

"Ms. Hobbes. You . . . you wouldn't be able to give me a ride home, would you?"

She blinks.

"Oh, I can't," Ms. Hobbes answers, then pauses, like maybe she's considering it, or maybe she's trying to think of an excuse. "There's just no way that's allowed. With administration and all."

"Yeah. That makes sense," I say. "I'm sorry I asked. Thank you for letting me sit in here. It's been a terrible day." I show her that I'm taking all my trash and the uneaten parts of my lunch with me as I leave.

I wedge the tray against my belly, ready to carry it out of the classroom with one hand so I can open the door.

"Crystal, wait," Ms. Hobbes says. "You know what?" I can tell she regrets what she's about to say. "I'll meet you in the teacher's lot at two thirty."

I thank her, and for the first time since I've stepped into the building today, I smile.

"If you're late, I'm leaving without you," she says.

I'm grateful, shuffle up to the desk to throw out the napkins I didn't use, and then do a weird little bow.

And suddenly I'm looking down at the test with all the green on it, the words *See me* in big letters across the top.

Ms. Hobbes moves her hand to try and block the heading, but I've already seen the name written there.

That's it.

The name on the test. That's the only person who could have done it. Or, if not the only person, the one who makes sense to me right now:

Aaron Fortin.

But why? We've said maybe ten words to each other. I feel emotionally charred, hollowed out, so maybe I'm looking for an easy solution.

No.

He did it.

I don't know how or why I'm certain. But I am.

Victorian Elon Musk.

See me.

The flash of disgust I'd seen pass over Aaron Fortin's features that first day in class. When he didn't think anyone was paying attention.

No. He's not a nice guy. He's just very good at playing one.

He fooled me. But he didn't fool Ms. Hobbes. She's tearing his unit test apart and taking way more time than she has to do it, a full ten minutes while she has her lunch, like she's savoring catching him as a phony.

And that last part I don't *know*. It's conjecture, based on a half-second glimpse at a test. Over the last few hours, I should have learned some kind of lesson about the pitfalls of leaping to conclusions.

But this isn't like the theories I've shared about Gayle's or Trevor's home lives. Stuff I know I shouldn't have said but thought I was letting out in the privacy of my own room.

In this case, with Aaron, I *know* I'm right. And it's all because I notice little things. Because I pay attention.

It was him. I noticed his eyes, the way his hands and shoulders moved, right after I called him a liar. I crossed him. I made an enemy.

This is how he's punished me for it.

I toss the Styrofoam tray into one of the hall trash cans, then pull out my phone.

If it is Aaron, what about my latest video? Telling everyone about him?

There are no notifications on my lock screen, and I use the YouTube app to try and take a look at my channel, to see how bad the damage is, how many views I have, if the video about the Speaker is still there.

But there is no channel. Just a blank page with my avatar and a notice that the account I'm looking for has been suspended.

Somehow that makes me feel better.

Other days, losing all that work, all those memories, all the videos that aren't harmful, that are just me being silly, talking to myself—that would crush me. But now, knowing that they're gone is like a boot being lifted off my neck after hours of pressure.

Aaron's boot. The Speaker's boot.

And I'm going to prove it.

But I can't right now. I have class. I have to head to the bathroom, reapply my makeup, and try not to cry any more in my remaining classes.

It seems like I might make it, because fifth period and sixth period are no problem, nothing happens that makes me want to cry. In US History, both Paul and Harmony are absent. Well, not absent, but skipping. I saw each of them separately in the hallways as I was trying to travel the shortest, least-trafficked routes between my classes. If they saw me, they didn't stop me to chat. Or throw rocks at me. Neither of them looked angry, just embarrassed to know me.

But then I walk into the final class of the day, Film Studies, and instantly regret it.

I should have gone to the nurse. Or called my parents. Or just walked out the front door of the building and kept walking until I was home, even if it's miles on foot.

Because in our shared film elective, it's not a screening day or a lecture day, but a discussion day. The desks have been pushed to either side of the classroom, and the chairs are aligned in a circle.

Gayle hasn't skipped. She's forcing me to face her. She's sitting there, in the center of the far end of the circle.

She's wearing her Siouxsie and the Banshees sweatshirt, something she only grabs from her locker when a teacher asks her to cover her shoulders. Or when she's cold. But she's never cold.

There aren't that many open seats, not where I could avoid looking at her, so I have to take one of the chairs closest to the door, where I'll be right across from her, so that we sit facing each other the whole class.

Mr. Nyquist does these discussion days infrequently, after screening days. There's no test, he says, you just have to speak at least twice during the discussion. Asking a question about the movie, even if it's clarifying something small you didn't understand, counts as discussion.

Mr. Nyquist means well. He's a younger teacher with tattoos and bad facial hair. And even students who don't take his classes know him since he's also one of the in-building substitute teachers.

But everyone in *this* class period hates discussion days. He should really read the room and stop trying to make us do them.

He starts our discussion, like he always does, by reading us the Roger Ebert review of the movie we finished watching on Wednesday: *Dr. Strangelove.*

The movie was funny enough, I guess. At least I thought so on Wednesday. Now I couldn't tell you one thing about it. Because all of my energy is being taken up by trying not to look Gayle in the eyes.

Which is hard to do, trying to look nonchalant in a classroom where students are being forced to talk about a movie they didn't like to a teacher who does, for participation credit, all the while Gayle's . . .

I steal a look.

Yes. She's got her arms crossed, is picking at the ratty elbows of her sweatshirt, and is staring right at me.

Fuck.

Once in ninth grade, Gayle got in a fight. I don't remember what started it. I just remember it was early in the school year, warm out, and we were eating lunch in the courtyard between the library and the main building. Someone laughed, and, like always, I was convinced they were laughing at the two of us. Only this time Gayle seemed to agree with me. She marched over to the biggest of the girls, Rebecca Potts, grabbed a handful of her hair, and pulled her off her bench and onto the dirt.

It took a group of three kids and a teacher to pull Gayle off Rebecca.

I think about that now as I try to keep Gayle in my peripheral vision but not look right at her in case that's what'll set her off, make her start throwing fists and pulling clumps of my hair out.

To my knowledge, that fight in ninth grade was the only fight she'd ever been in. At the time, I wondered what she thought Rebecca Potts said to deserve that, but now that I think back on it, I doubt the girl had said anything. Because it wasn't about the girl. It was about Gayle and how she was feeling.

Back in ninth grade, Gayle hadn't gone fully goth yet, or at least hadn't been wearing boots like the ones she has now.

I really don't want to feel those boots against my ribs.

"Crystal?" Mr. Nyquist asks.

"Huh? Sorry, what?" I say.

"Foster said he would have liked the movie better if it were in color. Do you agree?"

Foster Greaves says this about every black-and-white movie. I don't think he believes it. But it counts toward his participation grade.

"Uh. Maybe?" I say.

I can feel Gayle's eyes on me. How long has it been? Please, god, let me look back up at the clock and find that at least thirty minutes have passed.

Mr. Nyquist smiles, lifts his grade book, hovers his pencil over the grid of names there. He's telling me that I haven't said enough to earn a check mark for this discussion. That I should keep going.

"It's . . ." I'm struggling. What was this movie even about? Atom bombs? The stupidity of war and governments? The movie got it wrong. We weren't stupid enough to blow each other up back in the sixties. Or at least we haven't blown ourselves up *yet.* "I, uh . . . It's kind of stereotypical," I say.

"How so?" Mr. Nyquist asks.

"The general. The cowboy guy. The German doctor. They're all, like . . . cartoons."

This isn't a groundbreaking discussion point, it's a very basic description of the movie, but it gets Mr. Nyquist to stroke his chin with the pencil's eraser, then lean back in his seat and give me a check.

"Yeah," Judy Frank says, jumping in on my point. "And the Nazi salute? In a comedy? That's not funny. Something like that is *never* funny."

Mr. Nyquist tilts his head at Judy, looks uneasy, then begins asking the question he's *always* asking the class:

"But *is* depiction endorsement?"

I look up at the classroom clock.

Shit. Not even ten minutes have passed.

I look back, and Gayle's still staring at me. She shifts in her seat. She's tapping her heel, bouncing her foot.

Looking at her, I regret everything I said in my videos. Even if what I said—the big thing, the accusation that I could never quite find the words to ask about because it's too big, too scary—even if that theory's all true.

I can see the hurt fall off her in waves with each bounce of her foot. She's a space heater giving off pain and anxiety. Nobody else is looking at her. And come to think of it, nobody in this class has looked at me or tried to make a joke since I walked in. It's like Gayle and me being in the same room has given them pause.

I slip my phone out of my pocket, try typing out a message, keeping the phone on the left side of my body where Mr. Nyquist can't see.

> I'm sorry. I'm so sorry. I'm sorry.

I type, mostly without looking, relying on autocorrect for the second "I'm sorry." And then send.

But Gayle's phone doesn't buzz. Either she has her phone muted or she's blocked my number.

With five minutes left in class, after I've been called on one more time to get my participation credit, I grab my bag and run out.

I can't face her. And I'm not going to attempt fumbling out a lie to Mr. Nyquist to pretend like I have early dismissal. I simply stand and leave.

It takes me a few minutes to get to the lobby, and the bell rings right as I'm pushing out the school's front doors. I cross the street between parked buses, and Ms. Hobbes is already in the parking lot. I guess she doesn't have a last-period class. Or "office hours" today. Maybe when you're a teacher, some days you're even more eager to leave than the kids are.

Ms. Hobbes's car is newer than Trevor's van, but the interior's way messier.

I open the passenger side and stare down at a bag of laundry. "Here, sorry, it's my husband's. It's clean. Just throw it back there," she says, but I don't have to pick up anything. She leans over, scoops the bag from the seat, and wedges it into the back, the bag's fabric getting caught up in the headrests.

"Where we going?"

I tell Ms. Hobbes my address, and she types it into her phone, then clips the phone into a plastic mount attached to one of the car's air vents.

There's a slight musty odor in the car. Something . . . biological in the air, and I decide it's not the uncapped Diet Coke in the cup holder, not the paint cans and mixing sticks I can see in the back seat, or even her husband's laundry, which Ms. Hobbes claims is clean.

I'd like to tell Ms. Hobbes everything about what happened today. She doesn't know me well. Doesn't know me at all, really. But I want to have a heart-to-heart. All I need is for her to get me started. I just need her to ask me, one more time, what's wrong.

This time I'll answer.

But as soon as she turns over the engine, she brings up Spotify and starts playing music.

"You like Cardi?" she asks, and we spend the first half of the ride not talking but listening to a few bars of a song, then skipping, then skipping, and finally settling on a tune. It's not all Cardi on the playlist, but it's mostly rap, songs that are fully school-inappropriate. I think Ms. Hobbes likes sharing this playlist me, that these songs are closer to the *real* her.

Ms. Hobbes drives and mouths the lyrics to a song. I don't recognize the artist. But the words are *very* angry and very explicit.

"Sorry," she says, noticing that I'm watching her. She turns the music down slightly. "You're there. You know how it is. Teaching . . .

I hold in a lot dealing with you guys. Actually, your period isn't bad, but . . . seventh period? Woof."

"No, I get it," I say.

She motions at the road in front of us, then the sky. It's sunny today.

"Getting warm out, huh?" Ms. Hobbes says, then hits a button on the dash, turning on the air-conditioning.

The mustiness is dialed up a hundredfold as she turns on the fan and a wave of rank air smacks me in the face.

I'm not squeamish. I get pimple-popping TikToks on my FYP. And, like I assume everyone else does: I watch them, but this smell is so strong that I instantly feel my gorge rise.

Ms. Hobbes coughs, the car lurching to the side.

"Oh Jesus," she says, struggling to breathe. She shuts off the air, but that just stops more of the smell from pouring in; it does nothing to dissipate the cloud of stink that's already riding in the car with us. "Your window, lower your window," she yells, pawing at the side of her own door to get the power window down.

The smell. It is biological, but it's *not* rot. It's more like . . . burning hair? Cooked meat?

We ride the rest of the way to my house with the windows down, but it barely helps. I can feel the smell clinging to my nose hairs, soaked into my clothes.

I start to spill out of the car before it's fully in park, thanking Ms. Hobbes for the ride. But then she shuts down the engine, stops the car in a crooked parking job against the curb in front of my house.

For a moment, my heart does an irrational jump. Is Ms. Hobbes going to ask to talk to my parents? Does she feel obligated to do some kind of wellness check? Because I was crying so much in her classroom?

But no, she can't. My parents aren't home.

I keep walking toward my house, glancing over my shoulder when she doesn't follow. She knocks on the hood of her car.

"Don't you want to see what it is?" she asks me, standing over her car at the curb.

"What?"

"The smell!"

No, I don't really want to. But I get the sense that Ms. Hobbes wants me to see it so that, whatever it is, she doesn't have to face it alone.

I look down my street to see if any neighbors are watching us. Nobody's outside. Then I walk back to stand beside her in front of the car.

She puts her hand under the hood, finding the latch, then looks at me. "Okay. Let's just see it in . . . three, two, one," she counts quickly, lifting the hood, a fresh burst of stink mushroom-clouding out at us.

My eyes tear, and I look over and see—hazily—that hers seem to be too.

Then we both look down.

The cat's very recognizably a cat, but in its stillness and exaggerated features, it also looks like bad taxidermy of a wild animal. Its mouth is open, like it's snarling. Maybe it's a bobcat or a lynx or something. But we don't have those on Long Island. The pads of its paws are bloody and raw, and it's missing fur in patches. The cat's been scalded by the heat of the engine.

"First Tweety," Ms. Hobbes says to herself, upper lip pulled back in disgust, "now Sylvester."

I don't know what she's talking about, and I don't ask.

She averts her eyes, but I keep looking at the poor animal.

"Must have curled up there for heat," Ms. Hobbes says, fanning herself, then coughing. "They say they do that in wheel wells, but, god. It's cooked itself. How did it even get up in there?"

I don't know what to say, but spending all this time with Ms. Hobbes, I feel like I have a better sense of who she is, how cool she is outside of school. So I ask myself: What would she say?

"And I thought *I* had a bad day," I say, looking at the cat.

Ms. Hobbes chuckles, then frowns to show she doesn't really think the situation is funny. "Go," she says, waving me back toward my house. "Have a good weekend. And stop pretending like you haven't done the reading when I ask questions in class."

I don't say anything to that, just nod, then steal one last look at the cat.

If I didn't know better . . . or if its skin hadn't gone all melty, if it had more fur, were more alive . . . I would have thought it was Madame Tabitha.

Harmony's cat.

A cat I've never met, but a cat I feel like I know because of Instagram.

But it can't be. I don't think Ms. Hobbes lives anywhere near Harmony, and Madame Tabitha's an indoor cat.

Back inside, I wait for Mom and Ant to get home, and the adventure with Ms. Hobbes is enough to make me forget, for a few minutes, about how this day has gone. About how my life is ruined.

But then I remember what I wanted to do tonight. I have to find out why Aaron Fortin's done this to me. And who he is. And why he wants my friends.

Then I remember: Arizona plates.

It's not much, but it's somewhere to start.

Afternoon becomes night, and Ant sits cross-legged on the floor of my room while I sit on my bed, laptop screen angled away from him, a bunch of different search windows open.

I'm going to get you, I think. *You motherfucker.*

That's when the messages start. Or that's when I notice them. My phone doesn't give me notifications for them, and there's already dozens by the time I check my messages. They've been filtered into my "Requests" folder on Instagram.

I can't tell if my phone's hot in my hand because it's overheating or because my palms are getting sweaty.

Instagram's right to filter the messages. I don't know these people. The accounts have blank slabs of color as their avatars. The screen names are also generic. Short first names—"Amber" or "Robert" or "Sue"—and then a string of letters and numbers. Which makes me wonder, is it all one person using some kind of bot, or multiple accounts, or a click farm or something?

The messages are all the same: *Keep your mouth shut about Him.* The *H* in *Him* capitalized.

And then, as I watch, screenshotting a few of the messages, reporting some for abuse, I thumb back into the main folder and notice that the oldest messages have already started to disappear.

I squeeze my phone, taking screenshot after screenshot, but as the final message disappears, I'm not even sure why.

Yes, it's Him. But who am I going to tell?

Excerpt from message log between Bakersfield, CA, suspect and sock-puppet account belonging to *Unnamed Person of Interest*

Caligirl213: You're running right?

_____: Running?

Caligirl213: For Prom King.

_____: I think you have the wrong account.

Caligirl213: [suspect name redacted], right? Senior at Oaks?

_____: Yeah but.

_____: nvm

_____: I don't know why I'm talking to a bot.

Caligirl213: Not a bot. Just a follower.

_____: No you're not. I have like ten followers.

Caligirl213: 48. And I'm one of them. Have been here for months. I like your stories.

_____: No you don't.

Caligirl213: Not technically. Not like I double-tap and "like" them. But I enjoy them.

[15 minute pause, according to time stamp]

Caligirl213: You're more handsome than you know.

_____: Nice try, Connie.

Caligirl213: Not Connie. But not Caligirl either.

Caligirl213: You should run.

_____: For Prom King? Why the hell would I do that?

Caligirl213: Your school lets all the nominees up onstage so that even the losers feel special while they read the results.

_____: So?

Caligirl213: If you were on the stage, you'd have the high ground.

_____: The high ground?

Caligirl213: To act.

THIRTEEN

AARON

When I'm in the middle of a massive project, like I am now, I have to be sure to remind myself to take a moment to destress. Hell, my focus is so acute that I often need to remind myself to eat.

It's hard to describe to someone who doesn't have my work ethic. Between tasks I have to actively *stop* making preparations for what's next and just *be* for a moment.

And not just for my "mental health." When I've been in character too long, I start to get frazzled and make mistakes. Not that I'm not great at multitasking. I am. I'm usually pretty good at turning my performances off at the end of the day, segregating my time spent on the Speaker from the rest of my life and pursuits.

But ever since . . . Crystal *fucking* Giordano told four strangers my business the second I rolled into town . . . I've been all in, full-time.

For *days* now, I've either been the Speaker or New Aaron, sometimes the roles overlapping. I've slept only a few hours each night, waking with ideas that I tell myself *have* to be implemented *now*, even if it means grass stains on my shoes or talking to fans online.

It's been *exhausting*.

And on top of that, while keeping an eye on Arizona news alerts, I see that Charles and Kelly have been found. Their bodies have been exhumed from the crawl space. I'd begun to feel too safe, like it'd never happen. That words like *suspicious* and *foul play* would never grace the Scottsdale wires.

But here we are.

It's okay, though. There's nothing to tie me to the bodies.

But how did they get down there? Who put them there? Within the week, armchair detectives in Facebook groups will probably have working theories to these questions and more. But their theories will be wrong. At best, they'll sensationalize the mysterious corpses into an Elisa Lam–type news item. And my name won't be part of any of their theories. So it's fine.

But what if I left something in the crawl space of the Coates house? Some piece of evidence to connect me to them?

No. I didn't. It's fine. I just need to . . .

Focus.

Relax.

I just have to relax.

Thankfully, there are few things that help destress me like a party.

I enjoy the unstructured *structure* of a party. I like preparing refreshments. I like brainstorming entertainment options and laying out a few possible outfits.

Many would argue that five people is not a party. But I disagree.

Five is the perfect size. It's manageable. Time to give each guest a little face time, make them feel special, but enough bodies that mingling is possible.

I like to enter a party having a social goal for myself with each guest. And I'll have time and space to complete those goals, because we have the place to ourselves.

Right now, my parents are having a kind of second honeymoon. They're in Manhattan, staying three nights at the Ritz-Carlton. Good for them. Those crazy kids, keeping the spark alive, rewarding themselves after a difficult move. Never mind the boy. He'll be fine by himself.

They were out of the house last night too, which afforded me uninterrupted time to get things ready.

The basement is looking great. The couch has been out of the plastic and the basement windows open long enough that the noxious foam smell has aired out. The projector works perfectly, and even though the screen hasn't yet arrived, I'm able to project directly onto the basement's white walls. I've curated a playlist of music and videos to set the mood. Images that will get subtly more extreme as the night moves on.

I've ordered food and drinks through an app. Yes. Alcoholic drinks. Something I learned in Arizona: if you lead with a big enough tip, nobody asks to see ID. Then I hit up one of the contacts from the list Harmony sent me to secure additional . . . party favors.

The doorbell and the knock on the front door are simultaneous, one person knocking and another ringing.

I already know they've arrived—a few moments ago I got a motion alert on my phone, the security cameras picking them up.

I open the door and reveal Harmony, Paul, and Gayle.

Then I frown. A big frown, a show for them. Emotion. Everyone likes emotion. It's a party.

"Trevor didn't come?" I ask.

But then he appears out of the darkness. I knew he had to be out there. Who else drove the three of them? But I wanted Trevor to *hear* that I'd have been disappointed if he hadn't come. I want him to feel included. He is, in some ways, the guest of honor.

We walk in, past the vestibule, their hands in pockets, arms crossed, that awkward body language of teenage socialization. Like we're all supposed to pretend we're not here to have a good time.

But they warm up quickly. And they're all impressed by the house.

I walk them to the kitchen. Open concept. Lots of polished stone and brass. All custom, my parents are obsessive, only use certain brands of fixtures in every house we move into. Which means, in some way, our houses have all been the same.

I don't know much about snack foods, since I don't eat junk—maybe I should have watched some of Crystal's reviews before they were taken down—but I've ordered dozens of bags of potato chips and puffed corn, all artificial flavors and colors, and piled them on the kitchen table.

Nearby, across the marble countertops, I've laid out the beer, hard seltzers, and a few bottles from the liquor cabinet that I'm sure won't be missed. No mixers, though. Nothing soft. If any of them decide not to drink tonight, I want them to have to *ask* me for a glass of water.

I even bought red plastic cups, which nobody in this house will use once our guests are gone, but I bought them because I thought they might make everyone feel more comfortable.

The cups are meant to make things look like parties they've been to. Parties that were never in a house this nice.

The food and drinks are like a test.

I view them the same way an amateur ornithologist might watch their new bird feeder, making note of how long it takes certain species of wild birds to get comfortable enough to peck at the seed.

Paul and Harmony aren't shy. They don't even wait for me to offer. Paul takes a lime-flavored hard seltzer.

Harmony then takes a Bud Light. She's still got cat scratches up and down her arms. But they're faint, a mix of makeup and antibacterial lotion, maybe?

Paul then crosses to the table, fishing a "fun-size" bag of chips out of the large cardboard variety pack I've purchased.

"Wow," Paul says, opening the bag. "I haven't had Funyuns since elementary school."

I've never had Funyuns, ever, but I nod and laugh like I have.

Gayle's approach to the refreshments is different.

She looks first, then runs her hands over the array of cans and bottles.

Then stops.

Gayle, for all her bluster and humor, is still polite enough she wants to be given permission.

I tweeze a red plastic cup from the stack, offer it to her.

"Really," I say, "it's cool."

Gayle says thanks, then fills the bottom inch of the red cup with some of my father's whiskey. Bottom shelf for him, but a bottle more expensive than most TVs.

Trevor doesn't approach the table or the countertop.

I knew this would happen.

He's looking out of the kitchen, into the den, has an expression on his face like he's about to ask me something about the fireplace. Which is also custom, a modern wrought-iron monstrosity that my father had the house rebuilt around.

I've looked on Zillow. It *is* expensive to live on Connetquot Circle. Which would make you think our neighbors would have bought themselves a certain amount of class, but no. Too many mirrors, curved archways, and white leather couches. All of which must be the Long Island aesthetic.

"Drink?" I ask Trevor, then punctuate the question by popping the top on my own can of Bud Light.

Look at me, a man of the people. Drinking Bud Light.

"No, I'm good," Trevor says. "Thank you."

"Come on," I say. "Look how much we've got. This could get dangerous if you don't chip in and help us."

I'm being playful with him, and I watch as Paul slurps his drink, then furrows his brow at me. I can't tell if it's jealousy or if Paul wants me to stop asking Trevor to drink, since Trevor *never* drinks.

Trevor joins the rest of us as we move to stand around the table. He then opens a bag of pretzels, like that will seem like he's indulging in my hospitality, maybe get me off his back.

It won't.

I sip my own can. Then pick up a napkin from the table to soak up the condensation. I just have a tiny sip. I won't drink much tonight. I have to keep my wits about me.

It tastes . . . pretty good, actually. I was expecting to hate it, but there's something simple and clean about the flavor. Like mineral water. At the parties back in Arizona that Olivia dragged me to, the drinks were craft beers stolen from parents' second fridges, Grey Goose body shots, and Fiji water and ecstasy.

Nothing so working class as Bud Light.

"Really," Trevor says, seeing the question in my eyes. "I can't drink tonight. I'm the designated driver."

I knew that's what he'd say. It's a good excuse because there's a seed of truth in it. I respect the way Trevor has architected his double life. I even recognize myself a bit in his struggle to balance his two halves.

He's not not drinking because his religion forbids it. He's not drinking because his friends need him to drive them home. Yeah. That's it.

Both Harmony and Paul have their driver's licenses, and Paul has his own car. But neither planned on driving, because each told me they wanted to "get fucked up" tonight.

We'll see if Trevor's van is full by the end of the night, but okay. I believe I've been temporarily checkmated; I'll stop for now.

"This house is insane," Harmony says, setting her can down. There's an aluminum ping, the can already empty. This is going to be a fun night.

My phone buzzes. I have most notifications silenced, so I know the message might be important. I make sure none of them can see my screen while they eat their snacks and drink their drinks.

Hmmm. I thought this was *possible*, but I didn't think it would actually happen.

Inside the security camera app, I can see her there.

She's standing on the lawn, hands on the straps of her backpack.

Crystal's out there.

She hasn't pressed the doorbell, is nowhere close to it, but I've turned the security camera's motion sensitivity up to max.

She's just looking up at my house and . . . staring.

Well, to be fair, I never *un*invited her to tonight's little soiree.

But she's not dressed for a party.

I thought she'd become a ghost, especially after the warnings, but I didn't think she'd become one so . . . literally. Because that's what she looks like now, standing on the far outskirts of where the camera's night vision can pick her up. A ghost.

A ghost I can disperse with the sprinkler system if I wanted to.

How did she even get here? Does she drive? Did she borrow a parent's car? I switch to a different camera. I don't see a car. She must have walked. I can't remember where her house was, but I doubt it's close to Connetquot Circle or the pricey surrounding streets. A lot of the roads around here, the ones that separate the different neighborhoods in East Bay, they don't even have sidewalks.

I watch her in the black and white of the lowlight glare of the camera. She's blocky and desaturated.

And she doesn't walk any closer to the house. She just stares.

She's come here to see her friends, maybe even to confront me. But now that she's here, she's chickening out.

"Whatcha looking at?" Harmony asks.

"Ah, nothing. Dumb phone game," I say, putting my phone back in my pocket. If Crystal is going to ring the bell, then she's going to ring the bell.

There's not much I can do to stop her.

But I don't think she has it in her.

I think she's going to walk home after a few more minutes of lurking. And if she doesn't . . . well, I'll deal with it then.

"Want to see something really cool?" I ask the group, then lead them all into my father's home office, making a show of unlocking the door.

I did this same tour back in Arizona with Charles and Kelly. That was later in our relationship, of course, but things with these four are moving so fast and going so well.

Not to mention that we've got a deadline to hit.

So I want to see their reactions.

"My dad collects them," I say, sweeping my hand across the office.

There's a moment of stunned silence.

"It's like a museum!" Paul says. He's getting Funyun crumbs everywhere, and I offer him the napkin from around my beer.

I like parties but dislike the mess they leave. And I especially can't be leaving a mess in here.

Gayle approaches one of the display cases which is only half full since my father's been taking his time unpacking.

"Is he like . . . Billy the Kid or something?" she asks. The last time I saw her, Friday, her makeup had been cried away. I can tell—from the way she holds herself, the low energy she's been exhibiting so far—that she's still not over the shock of hearing her best friend spread terrible rumors about her. But at least the makeup is back: shiny black lipstick, eye makeup more elaborate than what she wears in school. A design approaching the Egyptian Eye of Ra, swirling out from her lashes onto her cheeks.

"No," I say, motioning to the weapons. "My dad doesn't even go to the gun range. Most of these can't fire."

But *some* of them can. The more modern revolvers and rifles don't even require special ammunition. They'll fire rounds you can find at most sporting-goods stores.

There's a store ten minutes from Trevor's house, actually, that sells the correct rounds. It's in a strip mall. A place an old maroon van might be seen parked from time to time.

"This one's pretty dope," Paul says, pointing with an onion-salted finger at a pistol too old to fire. I nod.

Scanning the various displays behind my father's desk, I don't see the two pieces I took to the Coates residence. They must still be in one of the boxes stacked behind the door. Good. That's about as far away from an Arizona ballistics lab as they can get.

"Hey, Trev," Paul says, pointing to the knife my father has cradled in a pedestal on his desk. I think my dad uses it as a letter opener.

No, I don't know why my father collects weapons. He's a numbers guy, has never gone hunting, never been in a fight. But maybe something about owning deadly weapons connects him to his ancestors, the people who actually *did* things. Maybe it makes him feel more like a man.

Trevor turns away from admiring a flintlock pistol and bag flask.

"Whose is bigger?" Paul says, pointing at the blade. I want to take the napkin away, wipe that finger for him.

But then my attention leaves Paul as Trevor switches his bag of pretzels to his other hand, lifts his shirt, and produces a long hunting knife, needing to undo the button on its leather sheath.

Huh. Interesting.

It's not a threatening motion. Trevor's not "pulling a knife" on us; he's simply allowing Paul to compare its size.

Another trick they taught him in the Eagle Scouts? Maybe, but Paul's right: there's a little more . . . girth to the blade than your typical Swiss Army knife.

Gayle laughs. "Sorry, I think Aaron's dad's got you by an inch or two."

Trevor shrugs, puts the knife away, and continues eating his pretzels.

I'm glad I was here to witness this exchange.

Trevor's armed. I'm sure he doesn't bring that to school, but it's good to know he'd bring it here.

I'd expected a slightly different response to the guns from Harmony and Paul, but I'm happy with the one I've got. They're one drink in and totally comfortable around the weapons. But it's not an overeager sort of comfort. Chuck and Kelly had the cases open by now, were leaving greasy fingerprints on the polished wood and iron of the guns. Cleaning up after them was a nightmare.

Harmony and Paul are well mannered: they look with their eyes, not with their hands.

Harmony turns to me, asks me where our recycling is, and that's my cue. They've seen enough, and it's time to move the party downstairs. While I lead the way, I check the camera again. Like I thought: Crystal's gone. If she skulks back, regains her nerve, my phone will buzz with another motion-detection notification.

If the group was impressed with the rest of the house, they're more so by my room.

I use my phone to switch on the basement lights, change the colors of the LED accent strips against the floor and ceiling.

"Nice trick," Gayle says, while I can see that Paul and Harmony are much more impressed. They're practically vibrating, Harmony dribbling her second drink down her chin.

"You want spookier colors?" I ask Gayle.

I turn off the overhead lights, then dial the colored LEDs to red and dark purple.

I make sure to smile so she knows I'm trying to be a good sport, not making too much fun of her.

The basement room looks like something out of an Italian horror movie.

She chuckles. I'm making inroads. She's loosening up.

"Do you—" I start to ask Gayle if she needs another drink, but I'm interrupted.

Trevor gets between us. Is he protecting Gayle from me?

"Hey, where's your bathroom?" he asks, pointing upstairs.

I get the feeling that Trevor wants to wander my house, that he's uncomfortable down here. I don't blame him—being in such an intimate five-person party, the only one of us committed to sobriety. Or so he thinks. I'm only making it look like I drink my Bud Light, taking tiny sips and letting them evaporate on my lips.

"Oh, there's actually one down here," I say, pointing to the half bath behind me. I reach my hand inside the door, flick on the light switch for him.

"Thanks," Trevor says, clearly disappointed that he can't get away from the party.

I dial up the music to give him a better sense of privacy while he tinkles. Or discomfort, if he doesn't like my choice of soundtrack.

"Holy shit!" Harmony screams, and for a moment I think either she or Paul has spilled their drink on my new couch, and I flush with anger.

But no. They're over in the corner. By the desk.

They've found the mask.

I wanted them to see it eventually, but I didn't think they'd find it in our first two minutes down here.

"Sorry," Harmony says, pointing at the desk. "I know we're not supposed to ask you about the Sp—" She stops herself, doesn't even want to say the name. "Ask you about internet stuff, but can I *please* try it on?"

Who could deny her? She's so enthusiastic.

This has been difficult, socializing with people who know who I am, but there is something about it that's nice, that scratches an itch. They love me.

"Don't take any pictures," I say, firmer than I mean to. Then I soften and smile: "But, yeah, go for it. Try it on."

I watch as Harmony picks up the mask, one ear loop of it draped over the end of my mic stand.

Paul's next to her, shifting from one foot to the other. He pumps his arms, wants her to hurry up so that he can try it on.

All this excitement to put a somewhat-soiled piece of cloth against their mouths.

I showed them a house of wonders. Tasteful architecture. An entire armory of very expensive guns. But it's a simple cloth mask that really gets Paul and Harmony riled up.

Behind me, I hear Gayle's voice: "You love that."

I turn to her, needing to angle my head down a bit. I've never noticed how short she is until standing this close; is she in different shoes? Do the combat boots add *that* much height? She's finished her drink. I can smell the warm astringent stink on her breath.

"You love that they're your fans," she continues.

We're alone here, in the center of the room.

I smile down at her. "Yeah, of course I do. But maybe not as much as you think."

She nods. I'm not sure if she believes me or not. But that's fine, she doesn't have to, she simply has to think that my relationship with internet microcelebrity is a healthy one.

People want to be seen.

They also think that you think more highly of them if you show some vulnerability, question yourself in front of them.

"Can I get you another drink?" I ask her. "I have a fridge down here or . . ." I make a show of looking over to Paul and Harmony, checking that the coast is clear for us to have a *real* conversation, one-on-one.

This was on the agenda tonight, to get Gayle alone, but I thought I'd have to work a little harder at it. I've still not heard the flush of the toilet. And Trevor seems like the type to always wash his hands, so even after the flush, I'll have a moment as he lathers and rinses.

I touch Gayle on the elbow and move her aside so that we're standing in the projector light and both have to squint.

"Yesterday . . . ," I say, trying to sound unsure of myself even though I've thought this all out ahead of time. "Yesterday was—" I pause. "Was not a great day for you."

"That's a bit of an understatement. Crystal—"

"Said all those things," I say, feeling like we need to speed this up.

"That's not what I was going to say." She pouts down at her empty red cup, a little angry. I shouldn't have rushed. She was about to open up.

"I'm sorry, what were you going to say?"

She takes a moment, then continues: "Well, of course I'm fucked up by what she said, how she speculated about my—I don't know, trauma?—like that. But . . ."

I halve my attention for a moment. Is Trevor okay in there? Did he fall in? Maybe he's even more uncomfortable in my home than I thought. Maybe he has IBS.

Paul and Harmony I don't have to worry about; if I let them, they'd spend all night pawing over my desktop and some of the rejected poems I've left out for them to find.

I didn't think I'd be getting this far in this conversation with Gayle. It's meant to be a nightlong dance culminating in giving her what's in my shirt pocket. But if we can get it all done now, why not?

"It's just . . . ," Gayle continues. I can see that the corners of her Eyes of Ra are starting to run. "If she thought *that* was going on, with my stepdad. And, really, it didn't . . ."

I don't interrupt her. This is fascinating, that she feels comfortable enough to share this with me. I am attractive. And it *is* good whiskey.

"But the crazy thing is some messed-up shit *was* happening to me around the time she made that video." She pauses. It's hard to tell with the music, but I think she's choking back a sob. "If she thought something was wrong, why wouldn't she ask me about it? Why wouldn't she see if she could help? I thought she was my friend. My best friend. Why wouldn't she just *talk* to me? It's been so bad, it's been so bad that I haven't even tried to . . ." She trails off.

"Well," I say. And I don't have to pretend to be taken aback, because I really am. I didn't think we'd ever have a conversation like this. But this is good. We're bonding. "I don't really know the situation, but I just want to say I'm sorry that happened. And that if you . . . you seem anxious, if you ever *need* anything for that, I can help."

She looks up at me, a little confused. Have I misjudged? Is she offended?

"Need anything?" she asks.

I slip the small pill case out of my shirt pocket.

"My parents, they think therapy is a substitute for love," I tell her. This is not true. I've never been to therapy. My therapy is listening to jailhouse interviews with people like Ed Kemper or Jeffrey Dahmer. "I'm prescribed all kinds of stuff. Benzos." Also not true. I don't even take ibuprofen if I can avoid it. I bought these from one of Harmony's contacts. But people love to think they've learned something about you, that you've confided in them.

"Benzos?" Gayle asks. "Is that the heroin-y one?"

I laugh. Again, I don't need to act. This friend group, so insular and naive since there's not a druggie among them.

"No, that's opioids," I explain. "These are much milder. I take them for stress. Just to even out."

I flip open the pill box, then pour the two pills I've prepared into my palm. I use my pinkie to push one toward her. She looks at the pill, its small roundness casting a long shadow in the brightness of the projector light, and needs to shade her eyes.

"It's Klonopin," I say. "If you want to look it up online before you take some, to make sure that you—"

But I don't get to finish. Gayle plucks the pill from my hand, then dry-swallows it.

Wow. She didn't take much convincing.

I cup my hand over my mouth to show her that, yeah: we've both taken Klonopin.

But *she's* taken Klonopin.

It's not hard to mime taking the pill here in the darkness of the basement. Rolling my hand down the front of my jeans, I secret the other Klonopin back into my—

"What did you just take from him?"

I turn, and Trevor's standing right over my shoulder, the bathroom door open and the light off inside. No toilet flush? Did he even go? I'm angry at him. He comes to my house, then sits in my bathroom to get away from me and my party? That's pretty fucking rude.

"Gayle, what did you take?" Trevor asks again.

I don't like his tone. He's not her dad. He's not even her stepdad. And I can see from how she crinkles up her nose that she's thinking the same thing.

"Trevor," Gayle says. "I took one pill, please calm down."

Harmony and Paul are looking in this direction now. Paul's got the Speaker's mask on. A ginger-haired Speaker. That'd never work.

"Well, are you supposed to be drinking with whatever drug you just took?" Trevor asks. He's doubling down on that tone of voice.

I lower the music so everyone in the basement can better hear the fight that's in the process of breaking out.

A shouting match, I think, but who knows? Gayle's unpredictable tonight. She's set her drink down and has both fists clenched.

She might hit him.

This isn't what I planned, but it's somehow better.

I try not to look like I'm smiling. But it's difficult.

"Trevor," she says, "just because you don't drink doesn't make you better than us. And no matter how many campfires you build, you're not our fucking den mother."

She didn't hit him physically.

But there's still a slapped silence from Trevor. From all of us.

Den mother. That's both mean *and* funny. So pointed, I feel like Gayle's had it in her back pocket for a while.

Paul has the mask off now, has returned it to its place on the mic stand. I watch him mouth "Yikes" to Harmony, both of them looking close to bursting into uncomfortable laughter.

Trevor turns to me. And I see it: the real problem he has.

Trevor's problem isn't with the drinking or the pills—his problem is with me.

"What did you give her?" he asks.

"I gave her," I say, speaking in the kind of even voice that angry people hate to hear spoken back at them, "a pill from my own prescription. It is an anti-anxiety medication called Klonopin. She took less than the recommended first dose. You can look it up—"

"Should she be drinking with it? Are there side effects?" he asks.

This guy's such a square, I'm amazed that he and Paul made as many attempts at a relationship as they did.

I decide to get a little dickish with him. "The side effect is she might, uh, feel better?"

Which is true. True enough.

But also one of the side effects, especially for the first few doses, will be marked drowsiness within the next hour—but I'm not going to tell him that.

Trevor looks at his friends, his hands trembling. He's on the verge of tears. He hates it here; he hates me. He hates how much longer it's taken to get Paul to respond to a text since I've moved to town. He hates what the whole school now knows. He hates the lack of control he feels. The control *I've* taken from him, not that he knows it was me.

Behind us, partially on us, the images from the projector beam shift to nature-documentary footage of great white sharks hunting for seals.

I love these clips, watch them all the time. The momentum of the sharks is so great as they lift their prey out of the water that sometimes the seals' necks snap before the first bite.

"I'm going home," Trevor finally says. He dabs at one eye with his sleeve. "I can either drive people or . . ."

Paul steps forward, his hands out, ready for a hug, but he seems to rethink whatever he's about to do. Because comforting Trevor, it'd mean he has to leave the party. And Paul doesn't want to leave the party. He doesn't want to leave me.

"Or you all have Uber," Trevor says. "You can get yourselves home for once." Then he stomps upstairs.

A moment later, we listen to the front door slam.

We all look at each other. Nobody speaks.

My phone alerts me that the motion sensors have picked up Trevor's van pulling away.

"I am so sorry about him," Harmony says.

I give it a beat, look at each of them, making sure to hold that bonding eye contact, then I smile.

I lift my phone, turn up the music, and they all seem to agree that we shouldn't let one sour note ruin the night.

Everyone gets another drink. And after about an hour, a few song requests from Harmony and Paul that extend my playlist slightly, a demonstration of the VR headset I've gotten for Christmas and never used, an explanation of my computer and streaming setup—a typical rich-kid hangout that's also kind of a flex—I look over to the couch and see that Gayle's fallen asleep.

Good.

I go over to Gayle, kneel beside the couch, and wake her gently. I ask her if I can get her a glass of water.

I make sure that Harmony and Paul see me do it.

Then I ask if she wants us to call her a ride or if she wants to sleep here on the couch or in the guest bedroom upstairs.

It's really no problem either way, I say.

She smiles at me, says that I'm right, that she feels great after the pill, that she feels like there's a warm blanket all over her. I laugh and say that's good, then I tell her she'll be more comfortable upstairs.

Paul takes one arm and I take the other, and we walk her up and tuck her in.

"She's okay," I say. "She barely drank. It's been a long couple days for her."

Paul nods in agreement. We say that we'll check on her later.

I can tell Paul likes this, being alone upstairs with me, but then I say, "We should go back to the basement. I think Harmony might put on the mask and try starting a stream if we leave her alone too long."

Now we can get the real party started.

We return to the basement, and I waste no time.

I walk straight over to where Harmony's sitting on the edge of my bed, scrolling her phone.

I take her hand in mine and give her palm a quick kiss.

Paul watches this. I kiss with my eyes open so that I can keep him in the corner of my vision.

Then I move my lips up, can feel the hairline scabs of cat scratches, the small, perfumed hairs of Harmony's forearms.

And I keep watching Paul as I kiss my way up to Harmony's chin, then finally arrive at her mouth.

Different emotions play on Paul's face: disappointment, sadness, betrayal.

Good.

I stop kissing Harmony, pull her mouth away from mine, needing to work to disengage. She's hungry for someone. But I knew that already. She wants both a lover and a father figure. A father figure who hasn't stretched out his neck with a length of extension cord, voided his bowels in their kitchen.

And I can be that for her.

I look over at Paul, and he starts patting at his pockets, then grabs his jacket from over the back of the couch, finds his phone there; blue light shows on his face as he starts shifting through the icons on his home screen.

"Where you going?" I ask him.

"Oh. It's late," he says, "I should call a—"

I shake my head, then I hold my hand out, get him to take it, pull him in.

"Don't just speak," I say.

"Act," he finishes.

I kiss Paul.

I'm performing. Yes. I've clearly never kissed a boy before. But it's not as much of a stretch as I thought it'd be. Maybe it's because of my time kissing Olivia Stewart well after the attraction had dulled, past the point where I could conceive of her as anything more than a mask, something to distract the world from who I really am.

Kissing Paul, I wouldn't say there's an attraction, but at least it's new.

I look over to Harmony, her elbow resting on my desk, catching her breath.

I haven't been sure how this is going to go, and it's Harmony's reaction that's still the biggest question mark.

You can predict people's behavior *to a degree*. And I'm better at predicting than most. But there's still some mystery to exactly how it'll all play out when I'm doing my thing, when I'm trying to work the Speaker's tricks in real life.

Harmony is selfish. They both are, but I get the impression that Paul will take what he can get and that Harmony would rather take all.

The look in her eyes is surprised but not necessarily upset.

"We don't have to all be together," I say, "all at once."

Then Harmony repeats the Speaker's mantra—"Don't just speak, act"—and the three of us fall back onto the bed.

Even with a night of curveballs that weren't on my agenda, I've still timed my playlist just right.

The last track, which isn't a song at all, begins to play.

If either Paul or Harmony recognizes what we're listening to, the infamous Jim Jones "death tape," neither says anything.

In bed we listen to nearly a thousand people in Guyana in 1978 reckon with their impending deaths.

When it's over, I listen to the quiet of the room. I listen to the sounds of Paul's and Harmony's bodies as they try to get comfortable in my bedsheets.

They didn't touch each other during. Each touched only me, but now they're huddled together for warmth.

This is another of my purposeful designs. I turned the basement's air-conditioning up via an app on my phone as soon as Paul and I put Gayle to bed upstairs.

To break the quiet, I ask them, "You ever want to just . . . kill a bunch of people?"

There are uncomfortable giggles from both of them.

"Sure, all the time," Paul says.

We laugh together.

"Why?" Harmony asks. "Who do you have in mind?"

I don't tell them. Not now. I play it off like I was joking. Some unconventional pillow talk.

They're not ready. Harmony's close; she's already given up so much. But they're not ready.

What I'm doing, it's not a switch you can turn on or off in people. It doesn't work like that. Really. "Brainwashing" isn't a thing. At least, not like it is in popular culture.

It's a more nuanced process. I'm unfolding layers within individuals as I get to know them.

Hey, I'm an influencer, right? Think of it that way. I'm *influencing* them. Like what just happened in bed. I didn't force them to do anything that they didn't already have it inside them to do.

And I find it more challenging to *influence* in person, as Aaron.

As the Speaker, I keep my posts and streams vague as to what exactly he's *speaking* to, for any one follower. Could be rage, sadness, alienation . . . their sense of fashion. The Speaker's a moody inkblot, one that keeps you coming back for his content even if you don't know why. But in person it's tricker. It's not a photo being served to thousands of people. It's a conversation. It takes time. There's got to be conditioning. There's got to be love.

It's easier with these two than it was with Chuck and Kelly, though. They're primed for it. I've only known them since Wednesday, but they've known the Speaker for much longer. I only have to puzzle out *why* they follow.

And once I know that, it's easier to *be* that, for both of them.

And I know what each of them want.

They'll be ready soon.

FOURTEEN
CRYSTAL

My insomnia's back.

Well, it kinda doesn't feel like *my* insomnia anymore.

It feels like a new insomnia I found, preowned insomnia.

For the first few nights, the insomnia felt helpful. I liked that I didn't *need* to sleep, that I wasn't tired. Because those first few nights, I was learning all I could. One search leading me to another small kernel of information, to another, to another, to then cross-reference any new data against everything the Speaker has ever posted.

I'm a B student.

If I ever studied this hard for a test, I'd be an A-minus student, minimum.

But even so, I don't *know* much. Well, technically I *know* plenty. I just can't *prove* what I know. All I've got for sure is speculation, paranoia, and a throbbing pain in my lower back from sitting funny over my computer.

That was the first half of the week. As the nights without sleep have compounded, I feel like anything I've learned is curdling, liquefying, and running out my nostrils as I cry in the shower, trying to wake myself up enough to attend school.

School. What have I been doing this week at school?

It's a blur.

On Monday a few boys try to keep the "hey, guys" thing going, but it doesn't work. They get eye rolls from our classmates. Their friends telling them it's overplayed, that they killed it.

By Wednesday the stares stop altogether, and things are back to normal. I'm invisible. Again. But this time, *truly* invisible. My friends never look my way, even by mistake, when I pass them in the hallway.

Even Gayle, who seems more exhausted, looks more run-down than I feel, whose chin dips in film class so that she needs to be woken up by Mr. Nyquist. Even she never looks my way.

Aaron looks at me, though. Well, I never *catch* him looking. But I know while I sit in English class that his eyes are on me. That he's smiling. I should have knocked on that door last Saturday. I should have told him then that I won't be threatened. That I can't be silenced. But I couldn't do it.

It hurts to think of all the practice I've had at being silent. Years of silence. Unable to talk to my friends about the things in their lives that mattered.

Saturday, walking out of my house in an old sweatshirt and pajama bottoms, wearing my backpack in case anyone asked where I was going, my cuffs wet with dew, that was the strongest my resolve has been. And I wasted it.

But turns out maybe that was a good thing. Because back then, I'd known so little. I had the screenshots of how he threatened me, sicked his mob of anonymous trolls on my DMs. But I know more now. A lot more.

This week I've been watching everything he does, in school and online.

I've been paying attention.

And I have some *theories*.

I haven't taken my lunch tray to Ms. Hobbes's classroom again. I know she doesn't want me in there, that our adventure with the dead cat was a one-time thing. But in class, she does seem to notice me more. She'll look up from her desk when I say good morning now; she'll say it back.

No, this week I eat my lunch in the cafeteria like everyone else. I sit at one half of a folding rectangular table located in the far back corner of the lunchroom, two near-empty tables on either side of it. No-man's-land.

Across from me, on the other half of the table, Grant Milligan and Tim Moody eat their weird bag lunches and occasionally whisper at each other.

I went to elementary school with both of them.

In fourth grade Grant bit a teacher's aide, his teeth severing the webbing between her thumb and forefinger. Socially, he never recovered from being the kid who bit an adult. But I admire the way he was able to turn the incident into his *thing*. He leaned into the notoriety, let his behavior become wild and unpredictable so he wouldn't get picked on.

I try not to pay much attention to either of them, but I do notice that Grant's hand is bandaged. He's got a wrist brace, and he uses the handle of a plastic knife to scratch at the skin underneath. I wonder, in my sleep-deprived state, if that teacher's aide had finally tracked him down after all these years and gotten her revenge by biting *his* hand.

At first, with the way I'm able to watch Aaron and my old friends from my invisible lunch table, my theories are . . . sexual? Like, they're all having sex or something?

Aaron's never *explicitly* affectionate with either Harmony or Paul, but he's constantly invading their personal space. Sometimes he even has a hand on each of them at the same time. As I watch, I can tell that Trevor doesn't like that. Gayle ignores it. Doesn't seem to be making her usual jokes at all, even when it seems like she'd be shooting fish in a barrel, when we can all see the back of Aaron's hand brushing Harmony's thigh.

Gayle looks different. It might be she's wearing less makeup? No, that's not it. Or not entirely it. She stares straight forward and doesn't talk as much as the others, only picks at what's on her tray. I wonder if it's because she knows I'm in the lunchroom. Knows I'm watching.

If Harmony knows I'm watching, she doesn't care. She maybe even likes it.

I used to get jealous seeing Harmony with guys, but my crush seems like such a small, faraway thing now. Now that I don't think any of them are ever going to look in my direction again.

But I'm still looking at them, still paying attention, and every night I take what I see and color it with what I can interpret from the Speaker's streams and posts.

As I do, my theories grow darker.

I Google "Arizona" plus Aaron's name. Then his name with some of the geotags he's posted on old pictures before arriving in East Bay.

I get back nothing.

I combine "Arizona" with the make and model of the Acura, the license-plate number. Nothing.

I search the names of Aaron's parents and his old address, which I'm able to find on a real-estate listing.

Still nothing.

But then, late one night, at a dead end, watching one of the Speaker's recorded streams posted by a fan on YouTube and scrolling his poems at the same time, a word begins to jump out at me. A word I don't think he's aware he's repeated. Or started repeating in both his speech and poems over the last few weeks.

Fire.

I take Aaron's name out of the equation. I search the terms "Scottsdale + fire" then filter by "News."

And there you have it.

Ever since searching that combination of words, I've been fixating on pictures of Charles Lang and Kelly Closterman. Their social-media pages have been taken down, but I'm still able to find plenty of pictures to fixate on. True-crime Reddit threads and community groups have screenshotted and archived everything.

When I look at Charles and Kelly, two dead kids I never met, what I see are Harmony and Paul.

I can't really explain why. Physically, they look nothing alike. And from the sound of it, they acted nothing alike. There are conflicting theories, and no charges have been filed. But Charles and Kelly were, by all accounts, burnouts. Runaways at best, lovesick thrill killers at worst.

Harmony and Paul aren't that.

But maybe they are something close to it.

Because the more I watch Aaron with them, the more I creep on Harmony's and Paul's accounts, tracing their movements, the surer I become.

What the armchair detectives and the news press don't have is motive. Or if not motive, then at least a catalyst.

Why were Charles's and Kelly's bodies in that crawl space? Who put them there? What role did they play in the deaths of the Coates family?

The answer I come back to, even when it doesn't make sense, is Aaron Fortin.

I check school rolls. They didn't go to the same school as Aaron. But they did live near Aaron and go to school with Larissa Coates, the pregnant daughter who died in the fire.

I comb pages and pages of screengrabs of Chuck's and Kelly's social media.

I know what I'll find, but it takes an hour to go through the accounts they both follow because there's no way to control-F to search in the screenshots I find on Reddit. Eventually, I have confirmation. Yes, of course Chuck and Kelly both followed the Speaker.

But there's more than that. I see *more* parallels, so many tabs open in Chrome that my laptop fan runs continuously, that I'm wondering if I should sneak out of my room at 3:00 a.m. and grab an ice pack from the freezer.

The parallels I find make me feel crazy.

I haven't said anything to anyone because . . . well, (a) who am I going to tell?

And (b) if I *feel* this crazy, I'll *sound* crazier.

The only realistic option is calling the cops, but which cops? Do I call Arizona police and tell them about my *hunches*? The best-case scenario there would be a cop taking me seriously enough to *question* Aaron, someone I feel might be a murderer. Or an accessory, at least. I'm not really sure.

But I doubt I have the communication skills to make that happen. Never mind the risk of retribution when he figures out it's me who's told.

No. No one can help me.

I've read every piece I can on the Coates fire, later articles modifying their coverage to call it the "Coates investigation." Unlike Charles and Kelly, who I can stare at all day, it's difficult to look at pictures of the Coates family. When I watch clips from local news affiliates, broadcasting from outside the charred skeleton of the house, images of the Coates flash up without warning as B-roll—and I see my own family.

Father, mother, a grade-school son, a daughter who's a senior in high school.

That's our family. That's me and Ant and Mom and Dad.

The only thing missing is the unborn baby.

In one clip, a fire chief, flustered, has to admit that the bodies of "the two youths" are "cause to reevaluate a fire that was initially deemed unusual but not suspicious."

On Wednesday the details of *the state* the bodies were found in—their causes of death, autopsy reports—are leaked to the press and the headlines become "Bizarre Deaths Baffle Investigators" and "Coates Fire Murder Scene?"

And these are the headlines I print—late at night, once everyone in the house is asleep and I can use the printer in Mom's office without anyone asking questions.

I keep it all in my US History binder. I haven't been taking great notes this year, so it's easy enough to push twenty or thirty pages of loose-leaf notes to the back. I get out my three-hole punch and put the printed headlines, some pictures, and some of the handwritten notes I've taken, trying to parse the oblique references and allusions the Speaker drops into his streams and posts, into the binder.

It feels stupid, scrapbooking like this, but at this point I'm tired enough that it makes a certain kind of sense. Like I'm an investigator, a junior detective with a plastic badge and an FBI lanyard from a Halloween costume. I'm *paying attention*. But instead of ruining people's lives with my theories and hunches, I try to turn my theories into hard evidence by making them a physical object. Something I can touch, something I can point to and say, look, this isn't like what I thought about Gayle. I'm not just *making it up.*

Also, it's not evidence, but while I'm using the printer, I screenshot and print what might be the last text message one of my friends ever sends me.

The group text is dead. Gayle has me blocked, I think, but . . .

Last Saturday, on my long walk back from Connetquot Circle, I got a text from Trevor. A few texts, but I didn't respond to them, so it's not a dialogue, it's a monologue.

Hey Crystal, he wrote. Starting his texts off like a letter, which is something my mom does.

> That thing I said on the way to school, about that guy I hate? Still true.

> I'm actually in his bathroom right now. He's got towels over the sink with his initials on them. Corny.

He sends that as two texts. Then keeps typing. The iMessage dots bounce, my phone feeling hot, battery indicator skipping from halfway full to red. I pray it holds on just a little longer. I need to know what else Trevor's thinking. Live from inside Aaron's house.

> It's weird here. I think you would hate it like I hate it. Maybe even more because you're so

He doesn't finish that thought. Doesn't even put punctuation on the end of the text, which makes me think he didn't mean to hit send.

Trevor doesn't send sentence fragments. He usually uses proper English in all his communications, even texts.

At this point in receiving these messages, I'd stopped walking and stepped onto someone's curb so I wouldn't get hit by a car.

The next text is a long one. It reads:

> Look. I know things are bad now and that everyone's angry at you. I'm angry at you. But you should take time, think about things, and then you should apologize. I'm not saying I promise it's going to work, but . . . take a week. Then try and get back with Gayle. She needs you. Her new friend sucks.

I almost type out a response to that. Not a serious one, not an apology to Trevor, because he *just* told me I should wait on apologizing, but I'm drawn to acknowledge that he's making an attempt at humor by saying her new friend sucks. Not a very Trevor thing to say.

But I don't respond, because he sends another message:

> Okay. I have to get back to this party. Don't worry, I'll keep an eye on everyone.

He sends that but, as I watch, keeps typing for a quick second.

> By the way: I love my sister.

This last text hits me like a gut punch. And, as if to put a final point on the communication, my phone clicks off, the battery dead.

Last Friday, the day of the hack, as I'd been cataloging all the embarrassing shit I've said online, I hadn't even remembered *that* video.

By the way: I love my sister.

Oh no. I've been so hung up about what I'd said about Trevor and Paul, I hadn't even remembered that. But now I do as I think back on the context. Whenever I'd recorded that video, I'd watched a documentary about Malala Yousafzai the same day. And it had gotten me thinking about Trevor's family, how I've only glimpsed his sister a few times, in her hijab. And, like an idiot, I'd decided to record a video about it. I wanted to sound like I knew what I was talking about, to voice to myself, by making the video, that I was a concerned proponent of a girl's inherent right to education.

I'm so fucking embarrassed.

I . . . I may have made some unfair speculations about Trevor's parents keeping his sister out of school.

I made that video over a year ago, maybe two. I'm not the same person now!

It was never meant to be seen! None of them were! I know that doesn't make it right. I know that doesn't *unsay* the things I said about Harmony's cruelty. Or how I think Paul wastes all his time and potential. Or the horrible things I said about Gayle's stepdad, about how I think I'm the only one who's noticed that she's stopped kissing boys but still jokes about penises all the time.

But Trevor's always been the best of us, the bigger man when he and Paul break up, the kind one when one of us needs it. His texts have shaken me, as I'm sure they're meant to, but they've done it gently.

The next morning when my phone's charged, and all through the week, actually, I consider responding to Trevor, trying to start up another conversation. But like with Ms. Hobbes giving me a ride home, it feels, as I read the texts back over, that Trevor is choosing to communicate this to me as a one-time thing. And every time I open the conversation, I'm forced to read those final words:

I love my sister.

I print out Trevor's texts and keep them in the binder's inside cover.

Now, a week after those texts, I hold the binder out in front of me.

I don't say goodbye to my family. My dad is watching a Mets game. My mom is sitting on the den floor beside the coffee table, playing a board game with Ant. She doesn't see me pass because she's too busy trying to remind Ant of the rules as he rerolls the dice, unhappy with what he got.

And when I leave the front step of our house, realizing that today, Saturday, is the first truly nice day we've had all year, I'm not even sure where I'm going.

My feet kick out in front of me, the sun shining so brightly that it hurts to look at anything but the asphalt.

But, in my sleep-deprived fugue state, I can tell that I'm holding my evidence binder, and I'm walking somewhere with purpose.

Eventually, my legs stop pumping, the ragged plastic bits on the ends of my shoelaces stop dragging against the road, and I've arrived somewhere.

I look up, squint into the glare of a cloudless blue late-April sky.

Where has guilt and my stupor brought me?

The police station? The school's administrative offices?

No. This is Gayle's house.

FIFTEEN

AARON

See me.

Two words that have disturbed me. Disturbed me—steely, unflappable me—on an *emotional* level over this last week. A week when I need to be focused, coordinating important work.

See. Me.

This infuriating message, delivered Monday, scrawled across the front of my unit exam in green ballpoint pen, was only the beginning.

"Before you say anything, Aaron, this test is going in as a D. Yes, I have your transcripts. Yes, I see that your English grades average in the mid-nineties, and I have no doubt that you've gotten teachers to change grades in the past, but . . ."

Ms. Hobbes leafs through my exam, then looks at the empty seats of her classroom, the laminated posters beside her desk, then back up at me.

She's faking her confidence, I tell myself. She's rehearsed this. It doesn't matter.

"But I'm not like those teachers. I don't reward bullshit."

"I-I-I'm sure I don't know what you mean."

Or something like that. I can't remember *exactly* what I said. But I remember every word that came out of Victoria Hobbes's mouth while I was . . .

See me.

"Look, Aaron." She keeps repeating my name. That's my bit. She's stolen my bit. "I'm not *that* old. Haven't been doing this for *that* long. But I've been doing it long enough that I've had students like you before." She seems just as angry as I am. Or maybe *indignant* is a better descriptor. "And I bet this conversation won't be the end of it. I'm sure I'll get a call or email from a concerned parent in the next few days. They may even try going over my head to talk to an administrator first. But I promise you: I'm not changing your grade. And I won't be giving you an extra-credit assignment to bring your overall grade up, because that's just more work for me. You'll get a D on this and have to live with it. It's too late in the year to ding your final GPA. You'll go to the same college you'll be going to anyway. Private, I'm sure. And I'll be able to sleep better at night, knowing that I didn't reward"—she holds the test up—"this bullshit. The second page of Google results? Really? With all the time you put in to make it look like you've read *Frankenstein*, you probably could have just read the book."

"But . . . I *did* read the book." I hate that, that she elicited a whine out of me. Not New Aaron. She got the real me to whimper out an excuse.

"And I'm sure there have been teachers who've believed that. But I'm not one of them. And I'm sure I could get in trouble for saying this, but I doubt you're a rat, on top of everything else, so I'll say it again: I've had students like you in class before. You think you're unique, Aaron. But you're a type. Friendly, to a point. Polite, to a point. But always with that smirk. A smirk that says you're smarter than everyone else in class. Me included. But you're not. You're not *that* smart."

I keep my fingernails trimmed, and it's a good thing, because if I didn't, I'd break skin as I clenched my fists.

"Oh, I'm not putting you down, Aaron. You *are* smart. Above average, for sure. And if you applied those smarts, you'd be top of the class, a ninety-eight on this exam, without question. But you never will. Because you're convinced you're *the* smartest. And you're not. You'll do just fine in life. You'll do great for yourself, probably. But this D? I'm sticking to it. Regurgitated ideas, rewritten just enough that I can't claim plagiarism and prove it beyond a doubt to an admin. Which is why I'm not giving you an F. The F you deserve. So take the D. Do better next time." She sighs. "Or don't. It's the end of the year. I don't care."

She hands me back the test, and I leave, and I don't raise my hand in English class anymore.

✘

Maybe what Hobbes said struck such a chord because *some* of it is correct. Well, a lot of it is correct. But I'm not going to sic my parents on her, although I'm sure that will happen anyway if they are ever sent grades.

She's right.

I do smirk. Often.

I have bullshitted. I constantly bullshit.

But there's one place Victoria Hobbes is mistaken.

She's *never* had a student like me before.

But I have more important things to worry about now.

Care and feeding of new friends is a tricky thing.

Trial and error.

And always gradual.

A frog not *dropped* in boiling water, but instead the water brought to a boil around that frog. Frogs with a slight Long Island accent.

Harmony giving Madame Tabitha over to me like that couldn't be called gradual, of course. But I did help things along there. It was a ritual sacrifice, or at least a symbolic one, but I wanted to add shades of gray to the exchange in case she wasn't ready.

"You're studying to become a vet, right?" I say, the cat meowing, half-blind and with a stomach full of poisoned Friskies Harmony doesn't know Madame Tabitha has eaten.

"How old is Tab? She's lived a good life, right?" I say. "The best life. She's in pain. And it would really help me, help the Speaker out, actually, to have this kind of inspiration. To watch."

And I have some other talking points prepared.

Some paternalistic buzzwords to help Harmony think she's found a new daddy in me.

But surprisingly, before I get to use any of those talking points, Harmony's got two thumbs pressing against Madame Tabitha's windpipe. Harmony only cries when the cat finds the strength to fight back and scratches her a bit.

Harmony didn't kill the cat. Not all the way. Old Tab's still breathing when I remove her from my backpack and wedge her under the hood.

And to think, I did that *before* Victoria Hobbes made her little speech.

But no, if she was capable of that so early in our relationship, then out of my new friends, Harmony requires the least maintenance.

Which means I'm able to focus on Paul and Gayle. Not that I'm forgetting Trevor, but my strategy with him is easier. I simply ignore Trevor the best I can, even when we're sitting right across from each other at lunch.

There's no winning with Trevor. No turning him on to my way of thinking. But there's also no need to threaten him in any of the ways I've daydreamed, creepy crawling my way into his sister's bedroom window and leaving bullet casings on her pillow like turn-down-service chocolates. No, that would be too much. If I did something that extreme, it would force Trevor into acting erratically. All I need is to keep Trevor afraid of being outed and to keep a tight enough grip on his true love.

And this week I *grip* Paul often.

Paul and I have a lot in common.

Not really in any deep way, but superficially we have enough in common that I can fake the rest.

I focus on our parents.

We're latchkey kids. That's the term, right? Both of us bought off.

"Sometimes I think . . . not that they can buy love," Paul says.

"But that the shit they buy us, material things, they think that *is* the love," I finish for him, staring up at his bedroom ceiling.

"Exactly."

Then, fingering an AirPod he adds: "Not that it's that big a deal. Not that I care."

But we *do* care, I say. And Paul tears up, agreeing with me.

And I wipe his tears away, first with my thumbs, then with my mouth.

Then, when we're really close, my lips to his ear, I say, putting a little tremor in my voice: "Sometimes it makes me so fucking angry."

And he agrees with me, his agreement pulling a long sob out of him that I have to shush away. Then I say:

"Sometimes I'm so angry that I want to show them. I want to make them pay."

And then, before he can disagree, I kiss him again.

Paul's almost ready. But I can't push him too hard. I don't want him thumbing through a PDF of *The Anarchist Cookbook* and blowing up his parents' bakery. Or running Trevor's van straight through the glass display cases full of cakes and cookies.

No, I don't want Paul Witkowski III acting alone. His is a good name for it, too. Has a real Berkowitz flare. The name of a lone wolf.

But that's not how things are going to go down.

Which leaves the last of them . . . Gayle.

Gayle's nearly as tough to crack as Trevor, almost not worth trying. My initial instinct is to just alienate her from her friends, dig deeper with Harmony or Paul to get something over her I can use to keep her quiet.

But then, at the party, the Klonopin has an unexpected effect.

She not only wakes up paranoid, asking Paul and Harmony again and again if they think something *happened* after she was placed in the strange bed, but once they've convinced her that no, nothing *happened*, Gayle's in my texts.

She wants more pills.

Hasn't felt that way maybe ever. Or not since middle school, she says.

So I have her come over Monday after school. Harmony and Paul are hanging out while I go about my business on the Speaker's pages.

This work is mostly innocuous, but my monitors are double-frosted with privacy screens, just in case any of them tries to watch over my shoulders..

Gayle takes a pill the first day. Same dose, same sleepy Gayle.

And then again the next day, so conked out that she doesn't wake up when I have Harmony and Paul wrestle on the carpet for my amusement.

On Thursday, with her pills, I compliment her on how pretty she is without makeup. And how I like short girls, that her boots are a bit much.

By Friday, she's no longer falling asleep as hard, and I switch her Klonopin to Halcion. She sleeps again, and while she does, I make sure Harmony and Paul have cleared their weekend schedules.

We have something to do this Saturday.

Something big.

SIXTEEN

CRYSTAL

I look up at Gayle's house.

It's time to do what Trevor suggested.

I have to apologize. Or I have to try.

Easier said than done. But I'm *just* incapacitated enough by my fatigue and brain fog while standing here looking up at the two-story house, the white siding green and brown with lichen, that I think: What the hell? Why not?

I ring the doorbell and flinch at the sound. Gayle's doorbell is a harsh electronic buzz, not a chime or music, and it always frightened me as a kid. A kid who didn't like loud noises, a sensitive kid who cried in class way further into elementary school than was normal.

I wait. At first it seems like there's nobody home. I look over. There's no car in the driveway.

But then I hear movement behind the door.

I hear a shuffle, step, shuffle, step.

The jingle of a dog collar. It's Fizzgig.

Someone mumbles at the dog.

Doesn't sound like Gayle, I think as the door opens inward and . . .

No. It's not Gayle.

Or Gayle's mother, Layla. The only mom I've ever called by her first name.

Instead, standing there in the doorway with his knees trembling under his partially tied robe is Gayle's stepdad.

I blink up at him. I wonder if I'm going to pass out because I'm so exhausted.

"Crystal," he says, a frog in his throat that he coughs to try and pass but doesn't seem to be able to.

I don't know why it surprises me—and sketches me out—that he knows my name. But it does. Of course he knows. Gayle's stepdad is someone I don't have a clear mental picture of, a bald spot Gayle and I giggle at on the way to her room as preteens, a crooked smile directed at me from the end of the table the one or two times he's been around when Gayle, Layla, and I had pizza dinners. But he's still someone who knows me. I'm a girl who's been in his house a lot. Or used to be in his house a lot.

"I . . . Hi," I say. I'm surprised by the sound of my own voice. I don't think I've spoken in days. I've eaten dinner with my family, grunting through those meals, but I haven't needed to say actual words. I'm lucky there hasn't been another discussion session in film class this week, because I would have failed on participation.

"If you're looking for Gayle," he says, pointing at the empty driveway, "she's in Bayshore with her mom."

"Oh," I say, then look back down the road the way I came. The walk between our houses is not an impossible walk. But it's not a walk either of us grew up making either. For playdates in elementary school, someone would drive us, either my mom, my dad, or Layla. For playdates now . . . well.

"You're welcome to come in and wait inside, though," Gayle's stepdad says. "Layla and I have an appointment at three. They should be back soon."

I wonder what time it is now. It looks like it could be afternoon, judging by the sun. If I say yes, how long will I have to wait inside?

Alone. With a man I've accused of something horrible.

But before I can figure out the time, I notice two things about Gayle's stepdad I've never noticed before.

First, I notice that his knees are trembling because he's supporting himself with a cane. The type of cane you get at a medical-supplies store, the kind senior citizens use, an aluminum shaft that ends with four plastic feet instead of one. Is that new? Who knows, he might have been using it for years.

Second, I realize that I don't know his name. I've never once thought of him as anything other than "Gayle's stepdad." I don't even know his last name, since it's different than Gayle's and I'm on a first-name basis with Layla.

He turns slowly, with effort, and moves back into the house, away from the door, his shoulders uneven as he leans his weight onto the cane.

This man I've built up in my mind, thought was a pervert because I didn't like the way his thick glasses made his eyes look small, or the tone of Gayle's voice when she talked about him: he's not scary.

I think back on all the little things I've "paid attention" to. On how much I missed. Never mind how long he's had the cane: It's possible I've never seen Gayle's stepdad standing. I can only seem to remember him in the living room as we move to Gayle's bedroom, or already installed at the kitchen table, or as a glint of glasses glare as I scurry to the bathroom, him looking out at me from the first-floor room he uses as an office.

I step inside the house to wait for my friend . . . and am all alone with Gayle's stepdad.

He looks awkward as he crosses to the recliner, a recliner I've never noticed without him in it, so now I'm able to see how the chair's been covered over with towels, pillows, and blankets to better support his lower back.

Fizzgig, a shih tzu with matted gray-and-white fur, gets up from his dog bed in the corner of the room and stands below Gayle's stepdad, who shoos the dog away.

Aiming his butt over the recliner, Gayle's stepdad lets go of his cane and makes a controlled fall into the seat.

I scratch my nose, then under my chin, trying to subtly pinch myself alert. I probably should have given him my arm to help him sit, but it's too late now; he's already in the chair.

Fizzgig crosses to me as I enter the living room, go to sit. I haven't seen the dog in a long time. Well, not completely true, since I often see his balls in the group text.

"I'd offer you a drink or something to eat," Gayle's stepdad says, smiling, "but you'd have to get it yourself." He's winded. The trip to the door has taken a toll on him. And as he holds the smile, I can see that his teeth are yellowed. But it's not the same impression I got as a thirteen-year-old, looking at his face, the gray scruff down his neck.

This man isn't a comic-book villain salivating over little girls, his beady eyes moving over their bodies.

He's sick.

Maybe dying.

I can see now from where I'm sitting—facing the inside of the house, Fizzgig's shaggy head on one of my sneakers—that the office door is half-open.

Inside, the room doesn't look much like an office.

I can see the corner of a bed and an oxygen tank.

How long has Gayle's stepdad been sick? Has she been hiding this from me? Because she's embarrassed? Because it hurts? Because I'm . . . I'm not as good a friend as I should be?

And then a voice inside me tells me what some part of me knew just from looking at him before I stepped over that threshold: he's been sick the whole time. Maybe it's gotten worse in recent years, but he's been like this *for as long as I've been coming over*, and I've been invited over less and less as he's gotten worse.

I think about Gayle needing to "help her stepdad" with something, an excuse she's used as recently as a week ago.

My god.

How had I never noticed all this? How did I instead connect this to Gayle's style and how she talks about boys and to . . .

My imagination is how. Because I sit in the back of the van, spend all my time worrying that my friends aren't my friends, thinking the worst about every situation. And inventing fiction to fill in all the human interaction I'm too scared to have.

I want to scream at myself. Want to slap my face until I get a black eye. Scream in my own ear: *Wake up! You live in a world that continues to exist even when you're not watching.*

I grip my binder, feel the plastic and cardboard bend.

"Crystal, um . . . ," Gayle's stepdad says, looking down at the binder, then up at my face. His eyes are small, sunken in his glasses, but they're kind eyes. "You don't look so good."

I don't look so good! I think, have to stop myself from yelling. *You should get a load of* you.

"Do you need me to call anyone for you?" he asks, pushing up with his elbows to sit closer to the edge of his chair. It takes him some effort, but as he does, we both turn our heads to the sound of tires on concrete, Layla's car pulling into the driveway.

Fizzgig's tags dance and tinkle, his tail starts to wave. He hears it too.

Gayle's stepdad melts back down into his seat. Interacting with me has exerted him.

I hear the key in the lock, then see the knob turn. It's Layla, the shopping bags looped around her wrists crinkling as she falls into the living room. "Who left this unlocked? Gayle, your father—"

Layla looks up into the room, sees me on the love seat.

"Crystal!" she says. She's surprised, but not as surprised as Gayle, who steps in behind her.

"What the hell are you doing here?" Gayle asks.

"Gayle Byrne!" her mom gasps.

"Don't, Mom," Gayle says, not looking at her mom but looking at me. I lift my binder, like it can shield me from the blast of Gayle's vision. "She's not my friend. She . . . she shouldn't be here."

I stand. And that's when I notice it.

Gayle shovels away Fizzgig with her foot.

She's not wearing her boots.

I crane up from Gayle's flats, shoes I've never seen her wear. Not only is she missing her boots, but she's missing her stockings, her suspenders, her skirts, her chains and belts, her choker, 70 percent of her piercings, and all her makeup.

Gayle does not look like herself.

Gayle is wearing a sundress.

There's no time to comment on any of this. I just have to get out of here. The world has gone insane. Or, I correct myself, the world is exactly as sane as it's ever been and it's me who's lost it. Either way, I need to leave.

"This was a mistake, I'm sorry," I say. "I'll go."

I look to Gayle's stepdad, unable to look his stepdaughter in the eyes, not now that she's glaring at me and ready to yell.

"I'm sorry to have bothered you," I tell him. Then, more of an apology for anything else I might have done to him and his family, I repeat, "I really am sorry."

I start to leave.

But Layla will not let me.

"Oh no you don't," she says, laying her arm across the doorway to block it.

"Mom, don't."

Layla shushes Gayle. It's a sharp sound, more than a shush really. I've never heard another mom make a sound like it. It's a Layla-original, that sound.

"You girls go to Gayle's room. Now." She points in the direction of the stairs, then turns to her daughter. "If not, you're grounded."

In the silence, while Gayle thinks, her non-cat-eyed eyelids squinting, I hear her stepdad cough.

"Mom, what the hell are you even saying? We don't *have* 'grounded.' You've never *grounded* me once."

"Then I tear up your prom ticket," Layla says. "Try me. See if I can't be Mean Mom. I'll do it."

"Mom!" Gayle says, but her protestations are losing conviction. She must want to go to prom.

"You two are friends," Layla says, arms crossed. "And I don't see Crystal anymore. On top of that, you're getting worse. Something's been up with you all week. You act different. You dress different."

"Yes. Because I'm pissed at her!" Gayle says, waving at me.

"Horseshit. You look like the daughter I thought I was getting," Layla says, pointing to the sundress, then the shopping bags at her wrist. "And I *don't* like it," she adds. "Now, go to your room, and you and Crystal talk whatever this is out."

Gayle stomps off, up the home's carpeted steps. When she's out of sight, I look up at Layla, and she pulls me into a quick, mentholated-cigarette-scented hug, her acrylics clicking together behind my head. I nod at her, whisper thank you, and go upstairs to Gayle's room.

I close the door behind me.

Gayle may be dressed differently. But her room, which I haven't seen in a while, is as goth as ever. More so than the last time I was in it, actually.

There are black candles partly burned down, their wax collected on paper plates. There are posters and tapestries of bands I only know from shirts Gayle wears. There's a cross-stitched pentagram over her bed, and everything smells like sage.

In the center of all this gothic excess is Gayle, no makeup covering the freckles she never used to let anyone see.

I've noticed the lack of makeup from afar as I've tried to figure out what her spaced-out looks mean, but how long has she been dressing like this? It couldn't have been more than a day, right? I'd had to have noticed . . .

"Do you have a test in US History?" Gayle asks.

"What?"

"Green binder," she says. "In middle school they had us buy binders that were color coded. You've never stopped using the system. Green is social studies."

I look down. Wow, I hadn't even noticed I was doing that. But, yes: red for math, black for English, blue for science, green for history. I've kept the same color coding. I'm such a baby. And Gayle's noticed I've been doing it. She pays better attention than I do.

"I'm sorry," I say. "Those videos. You were never meant . . ." Then I stop. I don't want to offer excuses. Don't want to tell her how she wasn't meant to hear me say those things. Because she's heard them. And I'm the dumbass who uploaded them to the internet.

"I'm just sorry," I say again.

"Yeah," Gayle says. "Me too."

I'm not sure for what, but I don't like the way she says it.

"It's not homework," I say, holding up the binder: "I want to show you something."

Gayle raises a hand. "Stop."

I walk toward her bed, half tripping over a black plush goat. I start to open the binder, saying, "It's Aaron."

"Cris," she says, the short version of my name I've only ever heard her use affectionately, when she's complimenting my bad skin or flattering my fat body. It's not just her voice and her clothes and that she's pissed at me: Gayle seems like a different person than she was a week ago. "Your apology is accepted," she says.

Then she moves toward me and covers my hand with hers.

"But do not do this," she says, glancing down at the first pages of the binder. The printouts from the *Scottsdale Independent*.

"Gayle, I know I've messed things up, but you've got to listen to me. He's . . ."

"He's bad for me. He's bad for us," Gayle says, then she applies pressure, pushing down on my hand and closing up the binder.

"Yes!" I say. "But not just bad, he—"

"Cris. Crystal. Listen to me," Gayle says, moving her hand up to my shoulder. It's a closeness that reminds me of how we used to be. I'd let her draw cat eyes on me now. I'd let her give me a complete and total goth makeover if we could just go back to the way things were. "I'm only going to say this once. And I shouldn't even be saying it once. But I've got a headache, I'm not feeling as good as I have been feeling, I think I'm . . . ," she says.

"You think you're what?" I ask, but she ignores me, doesn't elaborate.

"You have to forget you know his name. You have to forget that you know he's the Speaker. You have to stay away from him and stay away from *them*." She says *them* like I'm supposed to know who she means, but somehow I do. "You have to go home tonight. Be with your family. Don't ask me anything else about what I mean because I don't know. I just know it's bad. And I just know I'm going to try and keep you safe."

Keep *me* safe? What is she talking about?

"He thinks he controls me. And maybe he does, to some extent." She holds up her phone as she says this, takes her hand from my shoulder, then dives to the bed and buries the phone under the pillow.

She can't be serious. He can't be controlling her phone, listening in. Can he? But somehow she is serious. And it's way scarier because Gayle, for all of our lives, has never been the serious one of the two of us.

She gets so close, I feel her breath better than I can hear her whisper, the words coming out in a slurred hurry: "He's planning something. And I can't be your friend. Not for now. Not if I'm going to stay close enough to figure out what it is. You just have to trust me. You—"

"Planning something?" I ask. I don't even try to match her whisper. "Gayle, you have to—"

While I speak, she pinches the bridge of her nose, bares her teeth like she has a migraine, then interrupts.

"No, Crystal. *I* don't have to do anything. *You* need to listen to me. *You* need to get out of here," she snaps. Then, softer: "Go home, like I said."

"Be with my family." I repeat her instructions back.

And she nods, the pain in her expression subsiding.

"Yes. Apology accepted. Now leave."

I rush down the stairs, out the front door, past Layla as she's helping get her husband loaded into the passenger side of the car.

Layla yells something to me, but I don't fully hear it and can't respond anyway.

I'm too busy thinking over what the hell just happened.

That I'm supposed to go home to my family.

My family. I think the words, try to conjure an image of Mom, Dad, and Ant. But I don't see my family.

I see the Coates family: father, mother, son, and teenage daughter.

SEVENTEEN

AARON

I've spread myself too thin.

Each of my East Bay friends is like a newborn, hungry for attention. Which would be fine, but they aren't the only people I need to keep tabs on. There's also everyone in my DMs. I've started a spreadsheet to keep them all straight. Then add school, exercise, the general maintenance that keeps New Aaron's life on track.

But I take comfort in the fact that the activity and stress will soon cease. There's a terminus. There is an end to this plan, a moment after which I'll be able to rest. Deadlines are helpful. A deadline is something to strive toward. Two sets of twelve, and then you can put your arms down, so keep at it.

It's been hard work, of course. But it's paying off. My follower counts are rising faster than they ever have.

My Social Blade analytics charts are showing close to exponential growth. Is it possible to sustain that rate? Probably not, and the strange thing is . . . it's not like I've been posting *that* much content. But what little I've put out there has reached a bigger audience than usual. Is this what people mean when they say "critical mass"? Maybe the algorithm is pushing my posts harder, maybe it's word of mouth, maybe it's both. I could figure out the root cause if I had time to audit my analytics, but I *don't* have time.

At this rate, I'll hit a million followers before we're done here tonight.

Not cumulative followers, spread across all accounts. That's a million on Instagram. I surpassed a million total weeks ago.

Something occurred to me over this last week of recon and training. I wasn't following my own advice back in Arizona. I entered the Coates house to observe Chuck and Kelly. I wasn't there to participate. But I was right: a manager shouldn't assign a task he hasn't, at least once, performed himself.

"Okay, let's do it," I say.

We're in Trevor's van, but we're not with Trevor.

Trevor won't ever be one of us, but he serves a purpose. He handed over his keys when I sent Paul, batting those coppery eyelashes of his and asking to borrow the van.

We park under a NO THRU TRAFFIC sign, one street over from the house, on a block that's residences on one side, trees on the other. I researched these woods; they're not the arboretum that borders the school, but some other state park with an impossible-to-pronounce American Indian name like every third thing on this island has an unpronounceable American Indian name.

Paul and Harmony have followed my directions. They're dressed in all black.

I unzip the backpack and give each the items they'll be working with tonight.

Paul gets a bundle of rope, tied at the center. I tell him to put it in his sweatshirt pocket so the white nylon will be less visible. Then I give him the pruning shears he'll need to cut the rope to size.

Harmony is given plastic zip ties, the thickest that Home Depot sells, meant for securing fence posts and machinery for transport. Overkill for joining together wrists. And then I hand her a butcher's knife. The knife's not some cheap, shitty Amazon special. It's a Wüsthof. Recently sharpened, even though it's rarely seen use. My parents don't cook much.

Harmony smiles, seeming to marvel at the knife's weight—heavy but well balanced. But she doesn't talk.

Good girl.

We have a strict no-talking rule in place. Only I can speak.

Then I distribute the socks. Thin tube socks with a blue racquetball tied into the center. Harmony and Paul each put one in their pockets.

Then I show them what I'm taking from the bag.

The dead-blow hammer weighs forty-five ounces. That's nearly three pounds. Which doesn't sound heavy but sure *feels* heavy when you swing it. It looks a lot like a rubber mallet and kind of *is* a rubber mallet, since it has a soft plastic coating, not just on the head but on the shaft as well. To diminish recoil and reverb to near zero, the head of the hammer is filled with tiny granules of lead that shift inside like sand.

I demonstrate for Paul and Harmony. The hammer sounds like a rain stick.

Then I show them the gun.

The Colt's one of the more contemporary, if not *the* newest, pieces in my father's collection. Which means, forensically, it won't look like the gun originated from an antique collection. Shots fired from the revolver will be virtually identical to shots fired from any number of handguns used for home robberies and violent crimes.

I told Paul and Harmony yesterday, with Gayle snoozing her junkie's snooze on my bed, that this is an operation designed to instill fear. That they won't be required to hurt anyone. That, if it helps, they should think about it as a—somewhat extreme—senior prank.

I tell them that the gun's not loaded. Which I can see from their expressions that neither of them believes, but I can also see they both like having plausible deniability.

It calms their nerves.

Well, it calms Paul's nerves. Harmony seems ready for whatever, and by the end of the night, I'm fairly certain there'll be no stopping her.

We leave the van, me keeping the mallet held against my leg and facing the woods.

The trip takes two minutes, and we're walking at a nice leisurely pace, not running. When we arrive, I look up, take in the house in front of us. There are a few lights on.

That's fine. It's late.

I look over at the neighbors on either side, then the houses behind us.

There are very few signs of life. The flicker of a TV behind closed blinds, a porch light that probably stays on year-round until the bulb needs to be replaced.

Saturday night and most everyone on the street is turned in for bed. Good.

We pull on our masks. Not homemade pillowcase masks like I had Chuck and Kelly wear. No, that had been a mistake. Another element of homage, wanting my mad lovers to look like high-school versions of the Zodiac killer. Stupid. They couldn't see in those things.

Tonight we're wearing ski masks bought at a 7-Eleven. And blue surgical gloves. Even though I don't think fingerprints will end up being our undoing.

I point up to the door.

Paul goes ahead of me, Harmony behind. Like we planned. This last week, getting things ready with these two has drawn into starker contrast how lucky I was to make it out of Arizona at all. Chuck and Kelly were morons. I'd made the mistake of assuming that the weaker the mind, the easier it would be to mold and shape. But how much can you really sculpt, only starting with a teaspoon of clay? Harmony and Paul are a better class of acolyte. They listen when I speak and, more important, remember what they've been told.

Paul's first to the top step, pulling the screen door open so I have a clear shot at the doorknob.

I lift the hammer back, lead filings shifting inside so I have to strain to control the head, get it facing back in the right direction for my swing.

The hammer works as advertised, rubberized shock absorption: I barely feel the impact. But there's a loud metal crack and the knob on our side of the door drops away, taking screws and wood with it.

The homeowners haven't thrown a dead bolt or a chain, and without the knob, Paul's able to put his finger in the lock mechanism, then shoulder his way in the front door.

Harmony giggles behind me.

I purse my lips, soundlessly shush her.

None of us enter the house. We listen at the door for a full five seconds.

Nobody in the house has stirred.

Good.

Now, tonight, I'm going to make her pay.

EIGHTEEN

CRYSTAL

Be with your family.

I think about Gayle's words and . . .

Well, here I am; I'm with my family. And I have no idea what I'm supposed to do now. Whether she was warning me of some evil she didn't want to speak out loud or . . .

"Chugga-chugga . . ."

Ant pushes marbles around inside his toy, making train sounds. On the couch, my mom snuggles against my dad, both of them falling asleep. Dad's fighting it, though, eyes closing, then opening anytime there's an explosion or a gunshot on TV.

I thought an action movie would be loud enough to keep everyone awake. I even petitioned on Ant's behalf for an R-rated one. Look, I said to my parents, it's just blood and language; there's no sex or nudity.

But after the third gun battle, Ant's tuned the movie out and gone back to playing with his marble-run set. I don't blame him. I haven't been paying attention to the movie either. I've been sitting and worrying, watching Ant construct and reroute his toy's metal bars and troughs until none of them connect, then feeding in marbles and watching them fall out and bury themselves in the carpet.

I can't do this anymore.

I can't be this tired.

I can't be sitting here, the four of us, waiting in the living room on a Saturday night for . . .

What? What *are* we waiting for? For death? For fire? For our bones to be wrapped in the pink cotton candy of foam insulation? For nothing. For all of us falling asleep, waking up to Netflix, still on, playing the preview for a romantic comedy on repeat?

"I can't do this anymore!"

I don't think it. I actually shout the words in our living room, standing up from the floor beside Ant.

My dad startles awake. My mom mumbles, then realizes she's left a puddle of drool on the pocket of my dad's work shirt, begins to wipe at it with the palm of her hand.

Ant doesn't even flinch, he's too involved with his marbles.

"What the fuck, Crystal?" Dad asks.

Mom jabs him in the ribs.

"What?" he says. "Talk to your daughter, she's the one screaming."

"Look at us," I say, grabbing the remote to pause the TV. "We can't waste another Saturday night like this!" My voice sounds manic. Because it is, of course. I don't know what I'm saying. It's almost ten o'clock. If my parents were stricter about enforcing bedtimes, they'd notice Ant has missed his by an hour.

But if I'm not going to go full paranoiac, call the cops, and tell them every rambling detail from my binder, I at least have to try to get my family out of this house.

Investigators believe that the fire at the Coates residence broke out— or was set—sometime between midnight and one. Which means the murders that I *think* happened happened in the hours shortly before then.

That's not *that* late.

If, like I think might be happening, history is repeating itself, I just have to get my family out of the house for a couple of hours. And I have to do it now. They could be here any second.

Outside of starting a fire myself, *this* is the only plan I can think of right now.

"Waste a Saturday night?" my mom asks. "You picked the movie!" Then she points over at the bag of microwave kettle corn. "And the snack!"

"My film teacher, Mr. Nyquist, you met him," I say. "He's always talking about the theatrical experience. Why can't we go *out* to a movie? Look, there's . . ." I hold out the search I've pulled up on my phone. "The AMC's got a . . ." I read. I can't make sense of any of these posters. "A Marvel thing, I think. A Disney thing. Something in subtitles. If Ant can read fast enough—I bet he can. I mean, doesn't really matter what it is, right? Have it be a surprise. Let's go by what starts when we get there. Looking at the times, there's a . . . a ten and a ten thirty."

As I ramble, my mom stands from the couch. She holds the bottom of her sleep shirt out, pooling popcorn kernels there, then funneling them into her empty tea mug.

Then she looks up at me, puts a hand on my arm.

"Crystal Diaz Giordano . . . I don't know what your deal is. But we've got enough to worry about with . . ." She flicks her eyes down at Ant. His therapy. His tics. I'm supposed to be the set-her-and-forget-her kid. My mother's eyes soften, imploring me to get it together, be normal. "Now, if you need professional help, we will get it for you, and if you're experimenting with weed, stop—it's making you act goofy. But for right now, please get your ass to bed."

"Mom," I say. But I'm not sure how to argue with her. Especially because everything she's saying is right. "It's just really hard right now." I hear my voice crack, feel the tear run down the side of my nose into one nostril as I breathe in.

My mom frowns, hugs me so that I can feel the mug against my back through my T-shirt, the string of the tea bag getting caught up in my hair. "Do you want a Benadryl?" she asks into my ear. "Don't think we haven't noticed that you don't sleep."

She lets me go. I've held back most of my tears.

I look at my dad. He shrugs.

"Movies are really expensive, babe. But somebody's got a birthday coming up, right?" he says, even though my birthday's over a month away. "Maybe we'll do the movies then."

I . . .

I'm not sure how I thought that would work.

I nod okay, yes, some other time, then watch as my parents do their best to separate the hyper-focused Ant from his toy, my dad stepping with his full weight on a marble not once, but twice.

"We should just throw this thing out," he says, rubbing the meat of his heel, to which Ant responds with a tantrum.

While my parents take my brother into his room, begin the process of deescalating him, I bring popcorn bowls and the rest of the mugs—hot chocolate for myself, orange juice for Ant—into the kitchen.

Then I search the utensil drawer for the sharpest knife we have and take it with me into my room.

When everyone in the house is asleep and the night is finally quiet, I sneak out of my room and switch between watching out the front window, onto the lawn, and the backyard through the kitchen window.

I pace our small house, trying to step lightly so my parents don't hear me over their white-noise machine.

In one hand I have my cell phone, two-thirds of the way dialed to 9-1-1, and in the other hand I have the knife.

Gayle said she's going to try to keep me safe. But what does that mean? Does that mean she's going to the cops herself? Does that mean I'm getting a five-minute heads-up before my family's going to be murdered in their beds?

Eventually, my legs are tired enough that I have to sit. I pick a seat at the halfway point, in the shadows between the front door and the sliding glass door that leads to our small back deck.

Then, head no longer swiveling between the front and the back of the house, knowing that I might be in danger but unable to stop myself . . .

I fall asleep.

NINETEEN

AARON

I take the lead, moving into the house. The stairs are carpeted, but they still creak under my weight.

I put my gloved hand up, the gesture telling Harmony and Paul not to follow until I wave them forward.

As Harmony and Paul climb the stairs, I point where they should step.

I'm trying this hard to be quiet because there's one very annoying variable tonight. The old couple that lives on the first floor, rents to Hobbes and her husband, are a problem.

Not the kind of thing you can easily recon: whether the Shanes are light sleepers or not, how nosy they are, both as neighbors and landlords. If they hear a group of people's footsteps on the stairs this late on a Saturday night, they might think their millennial tenants are throwing a party. That could be an issue for us.

The Shanes' bedroom light is out. If we tread lightly, they probably won't wake up. These are acceptable risks. And believe me, I've weighed them, considered whether there isn't something we could do to the Shanes first to remove them from the equation. But, no, as it is, we're starting far enough into the deep end.

The living room stinks like cooking grease and unrinsed dishes from the kitchenette. Hobbes and her husband have cooked some kind of fish, pan-fried it, and haven't cleaned up or even opened a window to let the smell out.

"Gross," Paul whispers.

I narrow my eyes behind my mask, drag the hammer across my neck to let him know that's his one warning. He nods that he understands, his body language prostrated in apology.

We don't carry lights. There's a small amber hood light under the microwave in the kitchenette. Between that and the ambient light coming in the windows from the streetlamps, moon, and stars, there's enough to see by, if we stand here, be still, let our eyes adjust.

There's one other source of light, down the hallway that leads to their bedroom. And I'm fairly certain we all know what it is.

We have to be quiet; we're doing all of this while the Shanes sleep downstairs, but one advantage we have is we know the exact layout of this floor of the house.

Because we've seen it.

Victoria Hobbes doesn't have an Instagram account under her own name. But she's a thirty-six-year-old woman; she *has* Instagram. And it didn't take very long to find her account. Because Adam Patterson doesn't work with teenagers and has no reason not to use his real name online. His wife likes each of his dopey posts using her unlisted account.

@VHobbesgoblin.

She probably thinks that's a clever name. An indecipherable pseudonym.

Combing through both of their accounts, Harmony and I build a fairly accurate floorplan of the house. We know each room and how they all connect. Living room, kitchenette and breakfast nook, bedroom, and the couple's shared home office, which has a futon and doubles as a guest room when their college friends visit.

The bedroom's in the northeast corner of the house, which, helpfully, is as far away from the Shanes' first-floor, southwest-corner bedroom as can be.

The light at the end of the hallway is not coming from the bedroom, though, but instead from under the office door.

Adam Patterson . . . he's one of those guys. He's got a custom-built computer, a coolant system with more lights than fans. And the couple doesn't have any kids, so he's up late, playing a video game.

Well. He's about to lose this round.

I lead, again, down the hallway. There's a carpet runner here, over hardwood, and the floorboards creak, so I tread as lightly as possible. As I approach the office door, the clack of keystrokes and click of the mouse grow louder. But he must be wearing headphones, because there's no other sound but the occasional grunt of frustration from Adam.

The door opens quickly as I turn the knob, too much paint in the doorframe making the hinges practically spring-loaded.

But Adam Patterson doesn't notice the door open behind him. Harmony and Paul approach from the rear, and I motion for Harmony to watch the bedroom door opposite the office. Paul follows me.

Last night we drilled for this, putting a medicine ball and several dumbbells in pillowcases, testing our combined upper-body strength. And it looks like our assumptions, based on what we saw online, are correct. Adam Patterson weighs 150, maybe 160 pounds. The man's average height but with a slight build, someone who was skinny his whole life but now, in his thirties, has been surprised to see parts of himself—his neck, his waist—filling out.

Still, Adam's not a heavy person.

Paul and I can carry him, no problem.

Adam's headphones have a microphone attachment, but it doesn't seem like he's speaking to any teammates. He hasn't said anything while we've been standing here, maybe doesn't want to wake his sleeping wife.

I take two more steps into the room. And then, suddenly, Adam Patterson turns.

I don't know what gave me away. I didn't make a sound; he shouldn't have been able to hear me coming. But maybe he spotted my reflection in one of the aluminum cans or empty pieces of glassware stacked on his desk. Or maybe he just sensed us there, in that eerie way that sometimes you can sense someone's near simply by the displaced air around their body.

Whatever the case, I don't give Adam Patterson time to alert his wife.

The lead shavings rattle.

I bring the hammer down, as clean and well placed a hit as I delivered to the doorknob moments ago.

I don't smack Adam Patterson across the face; that would be too noisy.

I aim for the top of his head, trying to maximize surface-level contact between the head of the hammer and his skull, aiming for the area where babies have their soft spot, their fontanel.

It's a funny association, because I thought, studying pictures of Adam Patterson online, that he looks a bit like a baby. I wonder if his soft spot ever fully hardened in his thirty-five years on this planet.

Adam's shoulders go up, his neck seeming to collapse inside the trunk of his body, absorbing the shock of the blow like this is Whac-A-Mole. The motion's only funny for a moment, though, because then he collapses forward onto his keyboard, his hands and feet beginning to shake, clear, foamy liquid leaking from the corners of his mouth.

I look back to Paul.

Paul's eyes are wide, more white than pupil in the glare of the dual-monitor gaming setup.

I suspected I might have to talk at this point. But I try to keep my voice as low as possible.

"Hey," I say to Paul. "Hey, look at me. It's your turn now. He's fine. He's just unconscious."

This is untrue. I'm pretty sure I've just killed Adam Patterson. I can smell the mess he's made, his soul leaving his body through the back door.

But Paul must not realize what that smell means. He nods, takes the sock out of his pocket, and approaches the computer desk.

He pries Adam Patterson's mouth open, inserts the racquetball as far as it will go, then begins to tie the sock around the back of the man's head.

Paul is gagging a corpse, and he's doing a great job of it.

I'm proud of him.

I leave the room and join Harmony in the hallway.

I point to my ear, then tilt my head as if asking a question.

Harmony shakes her head: no, she's been standing here listening, no sounds from inside.

The bedroom door doesn't open as easily as the office door did. In fact, it sticks, makes a popping noise as I finally get it open, both Harmony and I wincing.

But nobody stirs. It's very dark in here, curtains blacking out the moonlight. Hobbes is still asleep. I don't need to be able to see her to know; I can scent the humid smell of sleep and sweat.

See me, I think.

Then I feel my way into the room, feet probing before I step, checking for anything I could trip over. I try to remember the pictures from her Instagram. Hashtag breakfast in bed. I find the edge of the bed in the dark, hover my hand over the bedspread, and can tell from the warmth which side Victoria Hobbes sleeps on.

Harmony follows me into the room, waits at the edge of the bed.

I crawl onto the bed, and Hobbes starts to wake as I straddle her over the comforter. But by then it's too late. I keep her in place by closing my knees.

The only thing I can see in the dark is the glint of her eyes.

I don't know why Victoria Hobbes is so afraid.

I thought she's had *plenty* of students like me.

Is this not an every-weekend occurrence?

I push one hand over her mouth, needing to feel my way up her chin a bit to make a good seal as she starts to scream.

"Don't make another sound," I say, speaking firmly and clearly. "Don't try to scream again or we'll kill your husband, then kill you."

I feel her jaw trying to work under my hand, and I tighten my grip, lay the hammer down onto the pillow beside her so I can have both hands free in case she's able to squirm out from under me.

"Say 'mm-hmm' if you understand me," I tell her.

It takes a moment. She seems to think over her options. But then, finally: a muffled *mm-hhhmm*.

Paul opens the bedroom door a little, computer light spilling in. He doesn't cross into the bedroom with us. This isn't his job. His job is to stay with Adam, keep an eye on the man.

I look down into the English teacher's face. Her muscles are tight under me. I can tell that she's making a lot of decisions with every twitch and jerk.

She's looking into my mask, and she's thinking, *I could get loose. I could pull him off me. He's not that big.*

I show her the gun, make sure to swing it side to side over her vision so the nickel-plating glows.

It must be terrifying. Seeing me like this, on top of her in a ski mask. Like every scary news story she's ever seen. From the small petty crimes gone wrong, a robbery that dumb-lucks its way into a homicide, to the biggest, most historical news stories, Munich in 1972.

Nothing good comes when there's someone in a ski mask standing over your bed.

I motion for Harmony to crawl onto the comforter with us. She doesn't need to be told twice. The homemade ball gag is out of her sweatshirt pocket. She also has the knife, copies my motions with the gun, showing the teacher that we're both armed.

The zip ties go on, the ball gag goes in, and we let Victoria Hobbes walk herself into the hallway under her own power.

She only tries screaming when she sees her husband. The racquetball absorbs most of the sound.

Paul has dumped Adam Patterson out of his rolling chair and has laid him in the hall in order to tie the rope around his legs and wrists.

I give Victoria her only warning. "That's your one. The one scream you get." I say to her, "I know this must be upsetting, but that's the only sound you get to make, okay?"

Even in this situation, you want people to feel seen. So I make sure to direct her eye contact to me, not her husband.

I want to say something to hint to her that it's me. I want to quote Shelley to her. I've been reading the book in my spare time. I could do it now. I could say something like "I will work at your destruction, nor finish until I desolate your heart so that you should curse the hour of your birth."

But that would be showboating. An unnecessary risk if tonight goes wrong.

So I don't.

I let Harmony walk in front of me, leading Ms. Hobbes with the knife. Harmony sticks her a time or two, causing small flesh wounds, before we're to the top of the stairs. And I don't think it's an accident, but I *do* worry that we're leaving blood droplets, so I tell her to be more careful, not to cut her.

I take Adam Patterson under one armpit, Paul takes the other, and together we're able to lift the body. The toes of his socks drag behind us. He's heavier than I thought he'd be. He's—no pun intended—dead weight as we carry him to the top of the stairs.

Here's another inflection point. If the Shanes waking up and calling the cops were our number one liability, getting Hobbes and her husband out of the house and into the van is a close second.

One of us could run ahead, pull the van to the front of the house. But I've driven this block in the daylight, taking notes, and I think that could leave us more exposed. There are more neighbors, someone could realize there's a strange van idling outside and take a description.

It's fine if someone gets a quick glimpse of the van, but we don't want them seeing *us* in it.

No. It sounds counterintuitive, but it's easier to walk the couple to the van than bring the van to them. Like me walking around at night with my hoodie, things are only suspicious if you make them look suspicious.

At any sort of distance, we're five teens walking down the block, one of them drunk enough he needs to be carried. But we're not loud. We won't cause a disturbance.

On the way back, we'll only pass two houses on this side of the street, and neither of them has one of those pesky video doorbells. I checked.

Once we've got the woods on the left side of us, we should be fine . . .

Unless we encounter someone taking their dog on a late-night walk or stepping out of their house for a smoke. Then we're . . .

I shake my doubts away.

No. We'll be fine.

I look ahead, watch Hobbes and Harmony cross the living room. Victoria Hobbes is following directions, not saying a word. Why, then, can I still hear her saying "You're not *that* smart"?

No. Don't listen to her. This is fine; you planned this well. There won't be dog walkers or anyone else.

It's a two-minute walk, two and a half to three while lugging Adam Patterson.

We'll be fine.

We're two steps down the stairs leading to the front door, Harmony and our hostage ahead of us, when the body starts to slip out of my grasp.

Fuck.

The stairs aren't wide enough to accommodate us three abreast.

I should have stepped down first. I should have been the one taking the majority of the weight.

"Get out of the way," I hiss at Harmony, who pushes the teacher in front of her.

Paul can't maneuver Adam Patterson by himself, so the body droops at the waist, then slides down the stairs, the back of the dead man's skull thudding against each step.

We've turned the body into a torpedo, taking Harmony's legs out as she tries to run out the doorway, a domino effect that sends Hobbes falling forward down the porch's two cement steps.

This is all so fucked up. How did I think—

No.

I have to listen.

Outside on the walkway, I can hear Hobbes whine through her gag.

Paul starts to whisper-yell at me that he's sorry that he dropped him, and I scramble down the stairs, ready to put the gun on Hobbes if she tries to run.

As I reach the threshold, I watch Hobbes wriggle on the walkway.

She's not even on her feet yet.

I'm so relieved.

Hobbes is—ostensibly—a smart woman, she should have realized that this was her best and only chance, that we'd screwed up and given her a window to escape. She should have stood and started running.

Maybe we both aren't *that* smart.

I can feel sweat beading and then wicking up into my mask as I crane my neck out the front door. I look beyond the two iron mailboxes, and, sure enough, as I watch, the Shanes' bedroom light clicks on.

Fuck. Fuck, fuck. Fuckfuckfuckfuckfuck.

But all's not lost.

Harmony's already guiding Hobbes away, is hurrying the teacher up by knifepoint. "This way," I hear Harmony say in the woman's ear. "We don't want to hurt you. Just get up."

"Help me," I hiss to Paul, and he descends the stairs to me as we drag Adam Patterson's body up, getting it between us.

I lean the body against Paul, make sure he can brace it against the side of the house if he needs to, then I close the door behind us. It's a risk, but I take an extra five seconds to wedge the screws and wood chips of the doorknob back into the ragged hole, then close the screen door. You'd only need to look through the screen to see that someone's broken in, but who knows, maybe we'll get lucky?

I rejoin Paul, take my armpit of the body, and we limp off, a three-legged race up the street, only slowing once the houses on our left side turn to woods.

It's not *all* a shitshow, though. Not everything goes wrong.

The Shanes don't come out to try to chase us down. We don't encounter any dog walkers, and I don't spot the cherries of any cigarettes as I scan the hedges and fences to our right.

No.

It's okay.

Yes, things went wrong. But nothing's gone wrong in any way that *matters*.

Nobody's seen us.

Every part of our plan worked. Sure, it was a little rough around the edges and we might have left more physical evidence than I wanted us to, but overall, as I get my emotions in check, I'm happy with how things turned out.

I don't *act* happy, though. I want Paul and Harmony, but especially Paul, to feel like I'm angry with them.

This is another conditioning tactic. Charlie used this one. All the greats did. You want your target to feel like they have to work harder for your love. That they have to apply themselves, give more of themselves, to get back on your good side.

We don't talk or remove our masks; I communicate that I'm disappointed through sighs and body language.

Before we start driving, I take two plastic bags from the backpack. They're from a local supermarket chain that none of our families shop at: King Kullen.

Harmony slips one bag over Adam Patterson's head, then I do the same for Hobbes.

As predicted, she begins to freak out.

"I'm not going to tie it," I tell her. "It'll be loose. You'll be able to breathe. You just can't see where we're going. Or our faces. It's to keep you safe."

I try to keep my voice calm and caring. I wonder if she's recognized me yet. I'm not using my New Aaron voice, exactly, but some variation of it.

Even with that bag on, I wonder if she can "see me."

She can't.

Hobbes whimpers, blows snot onto the inside of the bag as she tries to clear her nostrils since she can't breathe through her mouth.

I tap Paul on the shoulder, and he begins to drive.

Harmony rides in the space between the two second-row seats, keeping Adam Patterson propped against the window, his bag crinkling as his face rolls against the glass. There's no in-out of respiration. But it's fine. I don't think Harmony or Paul has realized he's dead.

I sit in the third row, beside Hobbes.

When we get where we're going, a fifteen-minute drive, no highways, Paul gets out first, then opens the side door to help everyone out.

We park on the far side of the lot, walk the rest of the way to our destination. We travel as the crow flies, avoiding footpaths that might have cameras or security lights.

It's not easy carrying Adam Patterson uphill through the tall grass and brush, sand under us shifting.

As we climb, I hear crickets and cicadas. We had insects in Arizona, but they sounded different than these.

Once we're on the other side of the man-made dunes, it's still, the water quiet, the air here on the beach a full ten degrees cooler than in the parking lot.

I carry the hammer in my free hand, crouch at the waterline, and help Paul set down Adam Patterson's body.

Then I take the gun from my pocket.

The bags over their heads aren't to stop Hobbes from seeing where we're going. Or even to minimize physical evidence inside the van, which they do help do a bit.

No, we've got the bags around their heads to help make Paul and Harmony feel more at ease.

It's the same thing the Taliban does when they're preparing to cut someone's head off on camera. Or that *we* do to the Taliban, in places like Abu Ghraib and any number of black sites around the globe. It dehumanizes the person behind the bag, makes things slightly easier for their interrogator or, in this case, executioner.

"We've got to go," I say to Paul. "That did *not* go smoothly. We've got no choice now."

I turn the gun around, hold the butt of the Colt out for him to take.

"What?" he says, the word making his mouth an O behind his mask. He looks down at the gun, moonlight on the tarnished silver muzzle.

"Shoot him," I say to Paul, nodding down at Adam Patterson.

"I . . . ," Paul says. "It's loaded? You said it wasn't loaded." Then he starts to make excuses. "I don't think . . . I think he's really hurt. I think—"

It's hard to concentrate on Paul's indecision, because behind him, kneeling beside Harmony, the knife against her throat, Hobbes starts making noise. The woman's given up trying to scream, but now she's keening, a high cry that carries out over the water. The sound oscillates, Hobbes biting down on the racquetball, giving her lips a little room to let her sobs escape the sock.

"Shut her up," I say to Harmony. Harmony pushes Hobbes back so that the woman's splashing in a few inches of water, then lays the knife against her throat.

Yes, this is about what I expected. That Harmony's the truest of true believers. If anything, Hobbes is easier than Madame Tabitha. Harmony loved that cat.

Paul's not like his friend. No matter the big game he talks when I get him revved up about his parents. No. His tipping point is different. He'll kill because we've pushed him far enough, involved him enough that he has to go along, not because it's in his nature.

I put the Colt's grip into Paul's hand, then cup his chin in my hand, like I have when we've kissed. I want him to see behind my mask that I'm growing more disappointed with him by the second.

"Don't just speak," I say.

"Act," he finishes, fingers curling to accept the gun.

Perfect. Even though he's against this idea, all of my love-bombing and repetition and conditioning has turned repeating the Speaker's mantra into muscle memory.

I let go of the gun.

"Toward the water," I say, watching him readjust his grip, finger against the trigger.

Here it is. That scary moment where he could turn the gun on me if I've somehow misjudged his convictions. If that were to happen, I doubt I could get my hammer up fast enough to defend myself.

"We're running out of time, Paul," I say.

Hobbes is crying again, ignoring the knife Harmony has at her throat.

"You just need to squeeze," I say.

"I . . . ," Paul says. He's kneeling, has the barrel of the weapon under the dead man's chin, pointing up toward the water.

He really doesn't know, hasn't realized that he's agonizing over shooting someone who's already dead.

"Just fucking do it," Harmony says, "so we can go—"

Paul fires. The gunshot blows a hole in the King Kullen bag, a sluggish runnel of blood leaking out the top of Adam Patterson's head.

Quickly, I take the gun back.

I give Paul no praise.

Then I offer the still-smoking weapon to Harmony.

I don't even need to say anything.

As Harmony climbs to her feet to meet me, she uses the knife to stab Hobbes in the side of her neck. I didn't tell her to do that, but I'm not mad about it.

She then takes the Colt.

Victoria Hobbes sits up, zip-tied hands at her neck, trying to hold her lifeblood in.

"Don't just speak—"

If Harmony says her part, I don't hear it; the word *act* is drowned out by the gunshot.

Ms. Hobbes falls back into the water, motionless save for the occasional finger twitch.

We all breathe. It's a similar quiet to lying in my bed that first night, the playlist having ended and the two of them huddled together for warmth.

A bridge crossed that cannot be uncrossed.

An exhilarating bridge that most people will never understand.

A taboo broken.

"Let's hurry," I say. "In case anyone heard the shots."

We weren't going to be digging any graves or walking our victims deep into the woods. The parks around here are too small, from what I can judge on Google Maps, and probably too well patrolled. But I learned a thing, researching Long Island: the beaches on the south shore face the Atlantic Ocean. Those beaches are all sand, because of the crush of the waves and more extreme tides. But the beaches facing the Long Island Sound are rocky. There are stones here, mixed in with the sand under our feet. Smooth stones ranging in size from a quarter to as big around as my fist.

I take more plastic bags out of my pockets, and we fill them with these stones, then tie six or seven bags to each body, then walk the bodies out into the Sound and let them sink.

Paul throws up twice, but we're in salt water, so what does it matter? There's plenty more physical evidence, but unless someone actually saw us, that kind of evidence takes forever to result in questioning or arrests.

There's the broken doorknob, the signs of the struggle in the house, the testimony of the Shanes—if they remember hearing an odd noise and made note of *when* they heard it—but none of that worries me.

Crimes like this. They're rarely solved. Or, I should say— statistically—they rarely get solved *quickly*. Especially with no bodies. And no motive.

All we need is a week.

Six days, actually.

Then we'll be at the terminus. The tipping point.

Nobody's going to stop me in six days.

Not before prom.

TWENTY

CRYSTAL

It's Monday morning, and I'm convinced I've been making things up again.

I'm not a spy. Or a detective.

My ability to pay attention is not a superpower.

I'm just a paranoid nerd, absorbing information and twisting it into a fucked-up story that some small, insecure part of me wants to hear.

There's no plot to get me because nobody thinks that much about me.

And that's fine. It's who I am, I think as I lie here, my phone alarm trying to rouse me. I have already snoozed the alarm.

But no.

What about what Gayle said? Did I somehow misinterpret *that* too? It seemed pretty clear.

Clearish.

She *said* she'd keep me safe, because . . . I don't know. And from what? I don't know.

But whatever I thought was going to happen on Saturday night, the Coates Murders Part Two, it clearly didn't. Because my family is alive, the house didn't bur—

I still have my eyes squeezed closed, but I know that buzz by feel . . .

It's a text.

I crack one eye open and read: Trevor Seye has shared his location.

Huh?

I open Messages, trying not to look at the top half of the screen, trying to block out the last text Trevor sent me.

But I read it anyway, and it still makes me flinch with embarrassment.

> By the way: I love my sister.

I click the link in his new text, and it opens the Maps app.

No, this text wasn't sent in error.

Trevor's down the block from my house.

He's closer than he usually is when he sends this text. And I'm still under the covers, sweating into my fleece pajamas.

I need to scramble.

I stand and start sniffing laundry, start trying to find the bookbag I haven't seen since Friday.

But I'm not fast enough. I hear the honk of the van's horn.

I pull on jeans, and I'm out my bedroom door by the second honk.

"If that boy's brakes are as worn out as that horn," my dad says, not looking up from his phone as I pass, "you shouldn't be getting in that van."

I ignore him, wave at Mom, and blow air-kisses at Ant, which probably looks suspicious because I never do that.

But I'm feeling weird right now, still not quite awake, and something about this dreamy half-space I'm in, it allows me to kindle a spark of hope in my chest.

What if I run out the front door and it's the carpool again? Like normal. What if, as I approach, I see Paul riding shotgun, and as I get closer, Gayle pulls open the back door and she's wearing her boots and her dark lipstick and Harmony is lying down in the third row, ready to ignore all of us on the drive to school, but she looks good doing it?

What if there never was a Speaker? What if my theories and monologues are still safely password protected? What if I dreamed that picture of the Coates family?

It's the good ending in the video game. When you finish without using any continues and do every side quest.

It's *The Wizard of Oz*, waking up with everyone you love standing over you after you just had the strangest dream.

I pull open the front door, look in the driveway, and . . .

Yeah. I figured.

Those endings don't happen in real life.

Trevor's hunched over the wheel, hand poised to honk a third time, but he stops as he sees me.

There's nobody in the seat next to him. Nobody behind him either, from what I can see.

Trevor doesn't say anything. He doesn't need to, because I buckle into the passenger seat before he can tell me to.

Then we sit in silence as he backs out.

It's brighter than it is most mornings. We're getting a later start to school than usual, but it's more than that. Are the seasons changing? It's the end of April. When does spring end and summer start? I don't think it's in May, but it feels like it should be, at least unofficially.

"It smells in here," I say.

I should have started with an apology. And I will try to backtrack to one. But it really does smell in here.

I don't mean like a normal smell. Like the day after Paul convinces Trevor to do Wendy's drive-through for the bunch of us, where it smells of ketchup-spotted wrappers and fryer oil. Like how the van smells like suntan lotion during the summer when we're all in our bathing suits, towels down on the seats after the public pool, me still wearing the T-shirt I swam in.

No, the van smells like bleach.

"I know," Trevor says. "It wasn't me."

Since I've last seen him, the sharp line dividing Trevor's sideburns from the fine stubble on his chin has blurred.

He hasn't shaved this morning. Possibly in multiple mornings.

It's such a subtle change, but the overall effect is striking. It's like the accuracy of Trevor Seye as a person, not just his haircut, has been dulled.

"Uh," I say, when it doesn't seem like he's going to elaborate. "Who was it?"

"They borrowed the van. And it came back smelling like this."

I don't know what he wants me to say. So I turn my head to look behind me.

Even from here, I can see that the windows look especially clean and that the dark upholstery of the second-row driver's side seat—*my* usual seat—looks like it's still got wet spots. Stains.

I think of what Gayle would say, try to channel her sense of humor:

"Did they," I say, unclear if I have the follow-through now that I've started, "*do* something in here? Like make a movie or something?"

"You trying to make a porno joke?"

I shrug.

Trevor stops watching me, puts his eyes back on the road just in time for the major intersection by the Dunkin'.

"I don't know. They actually might have." Trevor's not in a joking mood. "I kind of hope they did. But I . . ."

A horn sounds, and we both flinch.

The light's green, and the people in the car behind us have no patience.

Trevor wipes at his eyes, then accelerates through the intersection. This isn't like him. He's not driving the way he normally drives.

"I don't know why I let them take the keys," he says. "I've never seen him like this."

"Him?" I ask, for some reason thinking only of one him, the *him* who's been dominating my thoughts for weeks now, the *him* who's ruined my life. Aaron Fortin.

But, no, of course to Trevor, Aaron's not *the* him.

"Paul dropped off the van yesterday morning. He was weird. Spaced out, maybe a little angry. But also did things that . . . I think we might be getting back together? I don't know. It all feels different."

"I'm sorry?" I say. It's not the "I'm sorry" I got in this van wanting to say.

Trevor doesn't respond.

"Or that's exciting? That you're back together?" I try. And still nothing.

I change the subject.

"Thank you for the texts. I apologized to Gayle, like you said I should do. And I want to apologize to you, too. What I did was inex—"

"You saw her?" he asks.

"Yeah. At her house. It was—"

Weird, I was going to say, but he doesn't let me finish.

"How did she look?"

"Different," I say.

"Yeah. She *looks* different," Trevor says. "Acts different. Just like Paul. I see them in school, but they . . ." He swallows.

I try to make a face, like *Tell me more,* or maybe even *Dish!,* but I'm not used to conversations like this, so I don't know if I'm doing any of this right.

"After I texted you all that, at the party, I might have made a scene. I don't think they want me around anymore. Paul . . . I've only seen him a couple times outside school since. Then he came over this weekend, snuck in my bedroom window, if you can believe it."

I make a face that I think says *Oh, that's interesting* but is also probably a little bit *Please watch the road,* because Trevor does flick his drifting eyes back to the windshield.

"He's never done that before. Well." He smiles, maybe even goes a little flush. It makes him look different, more like the old Trevor for a second. "He's come in through the window, late, but he's never done it uninvited. And we talked for a bit. Really talked, like the old days. And maybe he was just fucking with my head, using me, but then he asked to borrow the van."

"Then it came back smelling like this," I say, after a pause.

"Yes, and we really did talk like we did before, our voices low so my parents wouldn't hear. The door locked and blocked with a chair. But then, after he had the keys, I tried to ask him about Aaron, and it went back to being like it's been."

"Spacey."

"Yeah. He took the keys and left."

Trevor's worried about Paul like I'm worried about Gayle. For a split second I feel bad for Harmony, that she's neither of our first priorities. That we haven't even mentioned her.

Now it's my turn to talk about my time with Gayle. But how do I explain it?

"Gayle doesn't just look different. It's not that she's"—I struggle to articulate it—"giving me bad vibes or anything. She warned me. Like actually warned me, with her words."

Then I think about it, try to remember exactly what was said. God, I was so tired, I should have written it all down so I didn't forget what and how she said what she said.

"Warned you?"

"Maybe not those exact words. But she said that she'd try and keep me safe. That he's planning something. What does that mean?"

Trevor goes silent. Turns to me, then back to the road.

"I don't think they shot a sex tape in here," I say.

It's not until the words are out that I realize that it's true.

"You know what?" Trevor says. "Me neither."

I could tell him about the Coates fire. I could show him what I've printed and three-hole punched.

But would it scare him off? Would it remind him of what I told the whole school about him, my speculation about his family?

"What do we do?" I ask.

He doesn't answer. And he doesn't look back toward me. If he's thinking he's going to do something, confront Paul, Harmony, or Aaron, then he's thinking about doing it himself. His jaw's set that way. Which is bad. Because whatever he's thinking, whatever dread I've passed to him through the osmosis of my paranoia . . . I don't think it's as extreme as I know it is. Bodies not burned, preserved in fiberglass insulation.

We drive for a few minutes, and we're in line in front of the school when I unzip my bag and find that I've got my green binder in there. I don't even remember putting it away after getting back from Gayle's place.

Finding it, it's less like I've lucked out, more like I've been offered a challenge.

I could take the binder out right now.

If I was strong enough.

Am I strong enough?

I am.

Trevor parks and we spend the next five minutes looking at headlines, pictures of the Coates family, Chuck's and Kelly's social-media posts. I share my thesis, just the gist, and then go quiet as I watch him.

He doesn't shake his head. Doesn't push me away. Tell me I'm crazy. That I'm making things up.

Trevor picks out sheets of printer paper, looks, reads, and nods. He's careful to return everything when he's done, reclips the three-ring clasps.

"Have a good day, Crystal" is all he says as he hands the binder back to me and steps out of the van.

He doesn't close the door, just looks at me for a second, standing in the parking lot.

Then he says, "Find another ride home. I've got to go straight to work this afternoon," and closes the door.

That's it? I think, but then, in a weird way, I'm grateful. He doesn't call me crazy. Doesn't tell me I'm making things up. And then there's that determined look, that set of his jaw.

It's almost like a weight's been taken from me. The contents of the binder are a burden that's no longer just mine, because I've transferred some of it to Trevor.

An Eagle Scout. Smart. Competent. Prepared. Someone better equipped to take care of this.

I get out of the passenger side, remembering to lock the door even though the back driver's side lock is still broken, can never be properly closed.

I look around the parking lot; nobody going to class looks back at me, and I don't see the Acura.

It's almost like I can pretend nothing's wrong.

When I get to the locker room before gym, Gayle is already there. She doesn't have her dark lipstick or eye makeup, but she *is* wearing her choker. She's in the process of taking it off and hanging it on the hook in the locker.

She looks more like herself after putting on her black sneakers, black shorts, and black gym shirt.

I smile at her. Remember that my apology was accepted. Or that she said the words, at least.

She doesn't smile back at me, and I find it hard to look at anyone while I'm changing, standing angled into my open locker door.

By the time I turn around Gayle's gone, and by the time I'm out onto the hardwood of the gymnasium floor, she's put on a yellow pinny and is standing on the opposing team.

That's fine. If she doesn't want to talk to me, that's fine.

I remember her words: *And I can't be your friend. Not for now.*

Maybe she'll talk with Trevor now that I've shared what I know. Maybe, however she's planning to keep me safe, they can team up.

✗

In English we have a sub.

Which isn't *that* odd. Maybe Ms. Hobbes decided to take a vacation. She's even said something to the class before, made jokes about how her vacation days are "use 'em or lose 'em."

Our substitute is Mr. Nyquist, who can't just teach Film. He's the school's floating sub. He's wearing his suit jacket with patches over the elbows. He doesn't wear the jacket in his own class. It's like his uniform when he's a sub.

"Crystal," he says, nodding at me, marking down my attendance.

He knows most of the grade by name, since he's been watching our classes since we were freshmen, and he clicks off the next two students who walk in behind me.

But Aaron Fortin stumps him.

"Fortin," Aaron says, before Mr. Nyquist can even ask. "I'm new."

Mr. Nyquist nods. "Nice to meet you."

I want to turn my head, look toward the back of the class to keep an eye on Aaron, but I don't.

"Okay," Mr. Nyquist says. "So I wasn't left any work."

Not really odd, but it does make me think Ms. Hobbes is actually sick, not just taking a day off, since when she's absent, she usually leaves a handout to complete in groups for class credit.

"Does anyone want to tell me what you're reading?" Mr. Nyquist asks, "Maybe we can have a discussion?"

Nobody answers him. We all just stare straight ahead, the boys sinking low in their desks.

"Cool, that's what I thought," Mr. Nyquist says.

He uses the projector to play us an episode of *The Twilight Zone*, which is one of his go-to tricks when substituting. Ekon Smith and the rest of Tommy Burke's former crew boo the screen, because it's old, but eventually they stop talking to each other and are quiet, watching or asleep.

I've seen this episode before. It's the one where there's a fuzzy monster on the wing of a plane, and only one neurotic guy in a window seat sees it, but nobody believes him that the monster's out there.

Somehow the show hits different today.

Lunch is the same as it ever is, looking over at a conversation I can't hear, am not a part of, doing my best to interpret.

Paul stares at the ceiling, Aaron's hand across the back of his chair. *Spaced out*, I think.

With Paul not looking, Harmony grabs a mozzarella stick off his tray, eats it while she keeps talking to Gayle. And talking and talking. Harmony's in a good mood. All smiles. Gayle's nodding along to whatever she's saying.

Does Trevor sit a little different in his seat? Does he look like he's talking more than usual?

If he is, I can't tell.

Back at my own table, Grant and Tim seem to be in a fight. They don't talk to each other. Tim doesn't eat his lunch, just puts his head down on the tabletop. I think he's crying.

In US History, Paul and Harmony don't spend the whole class on their phones like they usually do. But they don't talk to me or even look over at me either. Both sit, shoulders up, taking notes. It's a review day; we're going over the first section of the final we'll be taking in a few weeks, and I'm pretty sure Ms. Beckett is reading directly from the test, giving answers to the students who know enough to listen and write down the answers.

Up close, Paul looks tired. Harmony looks the same as she ever has. Maybe even cuter than usual.

Film is a lecture day, a slideshow that Mr. Nyquist yawns through. This means that half the lights are on in class, and we sit in rows, not in a circle. For the first time in a week, Gayle takes her normal spot, sitting beside me, not off in the corner where she's been.

She's still not dressed like herself . . . but the choker remains. It reminds me of middle school when she'd just started down her goth path. I try to think back to earlier this month, back when things were normal. Was she wearing her choker then? I can't remember.

"Hey," she says, looking over to see me looking. Her eyes seem weird, too black. Not her makeup, but her eyes themselves, her pupils.

Looking closer, I can see that there's a thin sheen of sweat across her face. If she's worn makeup, it's been wiped away as she has perspired. I can see her freckles.

Then she takes something from the small purse on her desk and passes it to me.

It's a small neon-blue envelope, like an invitation to a kid's birthday party might be inside.

The envelope's unsealed, the flap folded over and tucked. It might be a note or a letter. Maybe it's even an explanation of why she felt the need to get me so worried on Saturday.

"What's this?" I ask.

I must say it louder than I want to, because Mr. Nyquist stops lecturing, puts his hands on his hips, and stares at me.

While he's looking at us, Gayle presses a palm to her temple, asks if she can be excused to go to the nurse. If she's acting, it's a really good performance.

She's up and out of the room before Mr. Nyquist can write her a pass.

Once she's gone, Mr. Nyquist goes back to teaching about Hollywood breaking from the Hays Code, putting sex and violence back in movies. How, after the code, stories didn't require that the villains pay for their crimes.

But I can't concentrate on taking notes.

I open the envelope.

There's eighty dollars inside. I look down at the four twenty-dollar bills. The most cash I've held since my last birthday when my uncle Luis gave me a hundred-dollar bill and my mom yelled at him about it for the rest of the day.

I squeeze the envelope open to see that there's a Post-it note stuck to the outer bill.

On the note, only two words are written:

For prom.

What? What for prom? A ticket? Doesn't she know I've already got one?

Then, I can't help it, I start building a story again.

No. She knows I have a ticket, and she's trying to buy it back from me.

Trying to make it so I haven't wasted my money if I don't attend.

I close the envelope and put it into the smallest inner pouch of my backpack.

I'm so confused.

TWENTY-ONE

AARON

Am I being impatient?

Were the murders too much, too fast?

I don't think so.

No, I think they were a crucial team-building exercise.

Years from now, some author—or *podcaster*—may look at this period and say "rapid escalation" or "he lost control" or "berserker mode."

But that's only if this Friday doesn't work.

I think it's going to work.

And look at the numbers. The numbers don't lie. My follower counts keep climbing.

That's without a stream this week, too. I'm saving that for Thursday. Is tomorrow Thursday already? God, how time is flying.

Even if things go wrong, I die a legend. And these anonymous masses who've joined in this last week, because the content is good and their friends are bounding down the rabbit hole ahead of them, *they* will spread that legend. Yes, these thousands and thousands of Jill- and Johnny-come-latelies will say they were there, that they suspected, even if they had no idea, couldn't grasp the enormity of what I've been weaving, not a scintilla of it beyond the "vibes" they catch from my posts.

There's so much prep work to finish.

Like this, what I'm listening to on my phone while I have a dozen or so browser windows open.

No. Not a podcast. Not a recording of any kind.

This is live.

"I know," Paul says. "I'm worried too."

Paul's the trickiest of the three. Because his control is the most complex. It's not sex, like you may have guessed, but love.

And he doesn't love me.

He loves the Speaker, as a fan.

But he also loves Trevor Seye in the true, romantic sense.

And I can use that. But it's also dangerous. I have to monitor their communication. I can't let Paul be talked out of anything. Or into anything. Or into divulging anything. Not when he's talking with his true love.

Harmony, her control is power. And I gave that power to her late Saturday night, the power of life and death. Her dad got to choose when he tied that ragged knot he called a noose. But he only got to choose that one time. Harmony's going to get to choose over and over. And she's going to choose death every time.

Gayle's control, it's not me becoming her pharmacist. Her style, her goth look, is what was keeping the wheels on. Those boots, that skirt, those stockings—they weren't concealing anything. They *were* her. And I get that, I sympathize, because I put on my mask and act all emo and poetic, but I do that to build a brand. Gayle's clothes and makeup:

they're a way of life. Something she found power in, fully embraced after her unfortunate encounter with that boy, Tommy Burke, and his friends.

Yes. I've pieced it together, about Burke and his friends. If we had more time, I could even offer to help Gayle take bloody revenge. But I'm not some kind of charity worker.

The clothes and makeup helped Gayle to cope. She's spent her life enjoying the macabre, and it took something terrible to make her realize that life was too short, that she wanted to externalize those interests. That she could only be her *true* self when she dresses in black, drinks goat's blood or whatever.

So, to wrest control from her, I needed to take all that away. I needed to get Gayle back in sundresses. I needed her in a tasteful pink lip with a touch of blush. And, with the pills and a little help from Harmony, I was able to do that in a few days' time. A total makeover.

And now, listening in on this phone call, I'm working on Paul while he's, in turn, helping me.

"Worried about what? Specifically," Trevor says, on the phone. "Tell me what's going on."

Paul is in the van with Trevor, I can hear the indicator light clicking as Trevor signals to make a turn.

I had Paul call me and put his phone on speaker mode.

I've muted my own side of the call and am listening the best I can as I moderate comments and respond to DMs on my desktop.

Multitasking. There's not much I can do to change the outcome of how Paul handles this talk anyway. But it's a test, like how, before we even returned the van, I told Paul and Harmony that there was no going back now, asked them both if they thought we could trust Gayle and Trevor. Not that I'm going to take their word for it. Or that I have any other use for Trevor than as a patsy. But I wanted to see what each would say. Their answers were what I expected. I turn my attention back to the present.

"I don't really know what's going on," Paul says. "But I think Harmony and Gayle are spending too much time with him."

That's it, Paul. Distance yourself from me. Gain his trust.

Paul Witkowski III is not a great actor. But I think he'll hold it together well enough. He's rebounded remarkably well from the murder. A few days with bags under his eyes and a faraway look that's started to sharpen back to normal. His orders tonight are to seduce Trevor, get it so that they fall back into each other's arms, and while he does, he's supposed to gauge Trevor's threat level. What Trevor knows or what he suspects.

It's not like I'm oblivious to Trevor's suspicions. I've changed his friends. I've remade them. Trevor's no dummy. He's going to want answers as to *why*.

"Crystal's convinced you're going to do something . . . violent," Trevor says, the car slowing, gravel crackling and making the speaker-phone connection echo.

"Violent?" Paul says. "Come on now."

Ha. Now, that's acting! Well, at least his voice didn't crack.

Paul's supposed to stop at my house, no matter how late the night goes or how far he has to walk on foot after he slinks away from the shaggin' wagon.

Trevor's been outed at school, but it's been over a week and the gossip hasn't worked back to his parents. At this point Trevor's thinking that maybe it never will, since high school's nearly over, he'll be going away to Northwestern in the fall, his sister's homeschooled, and both of his parents speak English as a second language.

But *I* have that nuclear option if I need Trevor to do something for us in the next two days. Before the end of it all. And I have more than Crystal's say-so as evidence, as blackmail . . . I have all the private pictures and videos I've taken from Paul's phone.

"Trevor, can we stop talking about him now?" Paul says. "We're together. We haven't been in so long, and . . ."

Fabric rustles over the phone's mic, and the next few seconds are garbled. I almost think I hear the word *Arizona*, and my ears prick up.

No. I'm being paranoid. The rustling fabric stops, and the van's cab is quiet.

Then there's the soft, wet sound of clumsy kisses delivered while leaning over a van's bulky center console.

They must have parked.

Then there's . . . music? And the radio, though it drowns out their whispers, must mean that things are moving in the right direction.

I look up at my second monitor.

I see something that causes me to hang up the phone.

News 12, the Long Island local television news, has just posted this headline on their website: "Police Seek Couple Abducted from Home."

Wow. I'm surprised that it's taken this long. It's been four days. I click through, curious how the story's evolved from zero news coverage to putting the word *abducted* in the headline.

It's a worrisome word.

An accurate word.

I read, then I watch the two-minute on-air news package embedded in the article.

From what I can tell, it wasn't the Shanes who investigated and found the broken doorknob, but the mailman, trying to stow a package behind the storm door to keep it off the stoop. He opened the door and found splinters and a shattered doorknob.

Which makes sense; the Shanes must have been incurious about the sounds they heard last weekend. That's how we've made it all the way to Wednesday night without news coverage.

I open a fresh tab and begin an advanced search, limiting the window to the last few hours.

No. None of the national news wires have picked up the story.

Good. That's good.

I bet that it'll take a few hours, maybe even until tomorrow, for news to trickle down to Victoria Hobbes's students.

And when that happens, I'll be ready.

I spend the rest of the night reading comments, tracking who publicly shares the News 12 article through their Facebook page.

Eventually, some concerned mothers post it on the official East Bay High page's wall, are demanding a statement from the principal and superintendent. But that still doesn't mean that the students know.

What high-school student spends time on Facebook?

I keep clicking around, lurking in the comments, until Paul texts me that he's upstairs.

I let him in, both my parents long asleep.

Yes.

He did it.

He has the trophy I've asked for. Something to prove his loyalty. Something we can use.

He's brought me Trevor's knife.

I kiss Paul. Then tell him to go into the bathroom and wash his face.

When he comes back, I have my Moleskine notebook open on the desk, and I wave him over.

"Come here," I say. "I want to show you something."

He's done good, I tell him, and now I want to share something with him that I've never shared with anyone, do something with him that I've never done with anyone else.

I want him to help me write tomorrow's poem.

It's almost like I can hear my hold on Paul lock into place.

He's made his final choice between his two loves.

He's chosen the Speaker.

TWENTY-TWO

CRYSTAL

"So it's," Mr. Nyquist says, glancing at a wristwatch he's not wearing, "third period. By now I'm sure you've heard why I've been covering this class this week."

There's a small intake of breath from several students, the class quiet for the first time all week.

"He knew?" someone behind me asks.

Mr. Nyquist must have heard her, too.

"No," he says. Maybe too quickly. "I wasn't keeping anything from you. I learned about this last night, first from Facebook, then in an email. We're all on the same page here, okay, guys? Foundation of trust. And you're going to get a free period, and I'll write passes to the counselor for anyone who needs it, but first I want to say a few things about the news."

There are groans around me, classmates upset that Mr. Nyquist is trying to turn this into some kind of teachable moment.

"Not just because this might be a difficult time for some of you," he continues, "but because, well, this is an English class, and media literacy is an important part of the curriculum."

The hairs on the back of my neck are pinpoints. I want to turn around and see what Aaron Fortin is doing, who he's looking at, but I won't. I won't give him the satisfaction.

"For those of you that haven't heard, Ms. Hobbes and her husband are currently missing." He pauses for a reaction, but he doesn't get one. He's right. Everyone's heard.

"What we know now is that the police are involved. That is it. That is *all* we know," he says. "Everything else you've read online, the interviews with Ms. Hobbes's neighbors, the inferences made by the news media themselves, and especially whatever rumors you hear in school— *all* of that is speculation. What we know is what the police have chosen to release. That is it."

"Um," someone says. I don't look to see who it is, because I don't want to mistakenly lock eyes with Aaron. If I look at him, I will lose it.

If I look at him, he'll know that I know.

"But, Mr. N, I watched the news." It's Ashely Nu. Who's not usually one to raise her hand, to complicate a situation like this. She's not someone who argues with substitutes. "The cop I saw interviewed said they'd found blood."

"Yeah! Blood upstairs and outside," a boy says, backing her up.

"Well," Mr. Nyquist says, "sure. Yes. I guess we know *that*. But not much more than that. We shouldn't speculate. We should keep the faith. We shouldn't . . ."

But it's too late.

Yes, we know Mr. Nyquist's name, but he's still a sub. He's not any better at controlling a classroom than the nameless men and women called in from outside the school to watch classes, the ones who my class-mates have been breaking, making cry since middle school.

Everyone talks among themselves, over each other, and Mr. Nyquist, defeated, goes back to the desk and starts clicking around on Ms. Hobbes's computer.

"Ms. Hobbes was married?" Donna Collins asks. For a second, I think she's asking me, since we sit next to each other, but then someone else answers.

"Oh please, she flashed that ring around like it was some kind of achievement, like it was going to impress us," Alexus Esposito says. "Fucking Zales."

I listen to the conversations, but I don't participate. I keep my eyes forward, looking at the front of the class, and when that gets too dif-ficult, I take out my English binder and flip through pages of old notes.

I want to cry.

But I can't now.

Not because Donna or Alexus or anyone else will see; I'm past car-ing if I'm invisible or not, but I . . . I can't give *him* the satisfaction.

Can I really feel Aaron's eyes on me? Or is that just something that people say? Is it the same as when you feel someone is in the room with you, and it turns out you're right?

"My man's in Florida right now," Ekon Smith says.

"Oh, so you think the husband did it?" one of his buddies asks. Blake or Nick, I can never tell those two apart. With Tommy Burke no longer attending class, Ekon's risen from second-in-command dirtbag to chief executive officer of dirtbag affairs.

"All my mom watches are *Dateline* and *20/20*," Ekon says. "Sounds cliché, but it really is always the husband. The first few commercial breaks, they toss these weird clues and suspects at you, but that's just to pad. Stall for time and keep you watching. Last half of the show? Nine out of ten times, that's the show explaining how the husband killed the wife. And the husband usually confesses too, the first or second interview with the cops. It's always some shithead who never watches *Dateline* and doesn't know to ask for his lawyer."

"Not always," Blake or Nick says. "Remember that girl who lived in the van? The YouTuber? Sometimes the guy shoots himself instead of confessing. And he wasn't a husband, he was her boyfriend."

"Same difference," Ekon shrugs.

I look down at the paper in front of me, and I've been writing over my old notes, transcribing the words that I'm overhearing without realizing I've done it.

On a review sheet for *Beloved* by Toni Morrison, I've written some words and letters in bold where they've overlapped. The words:

Florida.
Husband.
Van.
Shoots himself.

I look to my right, the only direction I can turn and know I won't see Aaron in my peripheral vision, and notice that Donna Collins is watching me, looking down at what I'm writing.

Our eyes meet, and she sneers, her top lip getting caught on her braces. It's a look of total disgust that reminds me of that first day when this all started, how Aaron had looked at Ms. Hobbes, how he was offended not only that she was talking to him, belittling his ideas, but that she even existed at all. Had that been the moment? When he'd decided to turn away from killing families, like mine, to making married couples disappear?

But Donna's expression doesn't change. She doesn't try to hide that she thinks I'm weird; she just turns back to the conversation she was having with Alexus.

I close my binder and stare at my hands.

And, sitting like that, I remember the *other* binder I have in my backpack.

I have to stop worrying what people will think of me, and I have to try to tell someone that I know who is responsible for Ms. Hobbes's disappearance. That I'm worried that something even worse is going to happen.

For prom. I think of the two words written on the Post-it note. An envelope stuffed with eighty dollars. I think of the smell in the van.

I could leave now, try to look like I'm going to the bathroom. But Aaron would see me go.

I don't think I've ever spoken to our principal, Ms. Davis, one-on-one, but I've been to assemblies. I've heard her speak. I've walked past her in the halls and shared a warm smile and nod. She wears pantsuits with slight padding in the shoulders. And for more formal events she wears the kind of stockings that have a line running up the back.

I can trust her.

If I can get to her.

But why do that? Why not go to the police? Who should I call? 9-1-1? No, this is a school affair. And school *affairs* . . .

Images of blood on concrete, cable news chyrons, thoughts and prayers fill my head, make it feel like I'm going to pass out.

School *affairs* can get the police's attention better than I ever could alone.

For prom, the note said.

He's planning something.

For prom.

Yes.

I will lay it all out to Ms. Davis, and she can call the police in from there.

Eventually, I've stared at my hands long enough, imagined the conversation I'll have with Ms. Davis enough times, that the bell rings.

I walk the halls, start to descend the stairwell to the first floor, and that's when I see him. Aaron Fortin is right behind me.

Shit.

But it's not like he's following me. There's a press of students, all of us headed the same way down this side of the staircase, going to lunch. My backpack feels heavy and hot against my spine, the skin there starting to sweat.

If I peel off from the crowd, begin walking *against* the flow of lunchroom traffic, then he'll see me and get suspicious.

No. I *have* to go to lunch. Otherwise, Aaron and the rest of them will be able to see that I'm not at my table, not sitting with Grant and Tim.

I can't let him think that something's wrong.

I'm choosing to act. I've gathered evidence. I can share everything I know about the Speaker, the dots I've connected in his coded messages, every parallel to Arizona. I know at least Trevor and Gayle will back me up.

I just need to be patient.

I need to wait forty more minutes.

So I eat my lunch like normal, every bite of square pizza giving me reflux, like I'm going to burp it all up in one dry, mealy clod no matter how much diet ice tea I drink to try and make it go down.

Grant and Tim seem to have drifted closer to my seat today. Grant's even on my side of the table, beyond the break where the two rectangles of tabletop can be folded together so the custodians can wheel them away and sweep.

Yesterday Grant had stopped wearing his wrist brace, and now I watch as he scratches at the large bandage on his palm, loosening the glue around the edges.

He peels the bandage free while Tim eats. And then things get worse. Grant tweezes together his long fingernails, pulling at the small black knots of the stitches that run across his palm, testing them, then releasing each.

"That's gross," Tim says, his mouth full, but he laughs as he says it, which makes Grant move down the line of stitches, keep tugging at them.

"Doctor says they'll fall out on their own," Grant says, picking at the scabby sutures, a fresh purple scar running up his hand. "That they'll dis-in-te-grate. But I want to see if I can help 'em along."

I feel the pizza lump creep back up my esophagus.

"Stop that," I say to Grant.

He looks up at me. So does Tim.

They look surprised to hear my voice.

I've gotten the feeling, the whole time I've been sitting here, that both have wanted to talk to me. That they're secretly happy that a girl—any girl—has chosen to sit at the connecting half of their table.

"Fuck off, YouTube girl," Grant says.

Well. Maybe my feelings were incorrect.

✖

"Hello," I say to the woman at the front desk. I can feel myself sweating again, and I switch my backpack to the other shoulder to air out. I'm not used to this kind of interaction. "I'd like to speak to Ms. Davis, please. If possible."

"She's in a meeting, darling. You can't," the woman says. I like that she's called me darling, but she doesn't look up from what she's doing. I watch as she feeds calendar pages into a lamination machine. Usually, there are more people in here when I walk past in the morning and look through the glass and blinds, but I guess I've never been to the front office in the middle of the day.

"Oh," I say.

"Mr. Boselli's in. You want him?" she asks.

"I'd . . . I'd rather Ms. Davis." I hit the *Ms.* extra hard. But this isn't a gendered thing. I don't want the assistant principal, the guy whose whole job is to deal in discipline. Mr. Boselli's intimidating, stalks around the hallways swinging his keys on a lanyard, readjusting his belt.

I don't want Aaron suspended or expelled. I want him arrested.

I want to talk to the person in charge.

"Please," I say. "It's important. Can I wait for her meeting to be over?"

I want to add something along the lines of "It's a matter of school safety," but should I? Is that like saying the words *bomb* or *box cutter* passing through airport security? Does even saying those words trigger a whole cascade of procedures and protocols? Does it end up getting *me* in trouble? Would it give Aaron a moment to escape?

The woman looks up at me for the first time. I don't know what she sees, but I think the sweat on my scalp is starting to bead, so maybe she sees that. Maybe she sees the seriousness in my eyes. And maybe she combines that with the fact that she's never seen me in this office. Maybe because I'm not a regular, that makes her take me more seriously.

She sighs.

"Take a seat. What class are you in? Do you need a pass?" She picks up a pink pad of passes, starts searching in the jar beside her laminator for a pen.

"Study hall," I say, then add: "I'm a senior." She drops the pen and puts the stack of passes down, then waves me over to one of the three seats next to Principal Davis's office.

Nobody cares about a senior cutting study hall. Especially not at this point in the year.

"Should be fifteen minutes," the woman says, then goes back to her laminating.

Fifteen minutes.

It's a small wait compared to how I've waited through English, then lunch, as a precaution to ensure he's not warned about what's coming.

I set my backpack at my feet and take a seat.

The chair's upholstery is scratchy. I wonder if that's on purpose, by design. Uncomfortable chairs as an intimidation tactic to keep students who've been called down to see the principal uneasy while they wait.

It's working.

I unzip my backpack a few inches, suddenly worried that my green binder might have been lost or stolen. The last time I can remember holding it, I was taking it out in Trevor's van to show him. And that was Monday.

I spread the zipper apart, roll one flap down, and see that the binder's there, sandwiched between its color-coded friends. Red for Calc and black for English.

Then I sniff the air.

I smell something.

I smell someone.

Harmony is sitting next to me, leaning over in her seat and peeking down into my partially open backpack.

Hers is a smell I used to love.

And it still gives me goose bumps.

But the goose bumps are different now.

I sit up straight, the scratchy upholstery at my back suddenly not an issue.

"What are you doing, Cris?" Harmony asks.

I look over to the desk. From this angle, the lip of the desk too high, I can't make eye contact with the woman who helped me, but I can hear her there, still laminating calendars.

"I asked you a question, Crystal," Harmony says.

I still haven't looked at her, but then I do. I have to.

This close, she smells the same as always, but there's a sheen to her hair and skin, like she's skipped a few showers. The pores on her nose, usually invisible and powder soft, are wide. It's like zooming in too far on a picture, beginning to lose fidelity, the most attractive person in the world rendered unattractive if you look at them in a certain way.

"I'm . . . ," I say, then find my strength. "I'm waiting for Ms. Davis."

"To tell her what?"

"About . . ." I don't know how brave I want to be right now, how brave I *can* be.

She's just appeared here.

I didn't hear the office door open. I didn't see a shadow or hear a creak in the chair beside me as she sat down.

I feel like I'm losing my mind.

"You know, I kind of wondered why you never got called down here. How you never got in trouble when all those videos went up with you talking shit," Harmony says. Her voice is somehow meaner than I've ever heard it. And over the last six years, I've heard Harmony Phillips be *very* mean.

"Maybe it's because we all reported you to YouTube for harassment and got the channel taken down so fast."

I feel tears begin to well up in my eyes.

"Maybe it's because the statements you made were really hurtful, the rumors and 'theories' you spread about our lives." She hits the word *theories* hard, like she's pulled it straight from my brain. "Maybe Gayle doesn't want to have to answer questions about her history. Maybe Trevor's ashamed.

"Not that I was going to blow the whistle. I mean, everyone already knows about my dad. I hear them sometimes, reminding each other. It's probably part of why you *love* me. Because I want everyone looking, want them saying I'm hot if it keeps them from bringing him up."

I hear a teardrop hit the canvas of my backpack.

"But, no, I don't think any of that's it. I think you never got in trouble because you. Don't. Matter."

"Stop it," I say.

The laminating pauses, but only for a moment. When it resumes, Harmony keeps going:

"Crystal. Even if you go in there, even if you could somehow stammer out some ridiculous story well enough to get a high-school principal to believe you, you're fat and slow. So slow that we'll be at your brother's school and your dad's shitty truck lot faster than anyone could get to us."

Us.

Who's "us"?

Her and Aaron? And Paul too? And who else? The conversation I had with Gayle, the one I had on the drive with Trevor—what were those? Lies? Am I being toyed with?

No. They're my friends. I know them. I would know.

Right?

Harmony must see the tremble of my chin as I clench my jaw, trying to get the strength to speak, because she puts a finger up to shush me.

"Your mom's probably safe," she says. "At least until she gets out of work. We're not going to, like, walk into a bank or anything."

"I hate you," I say. And I mean it.

"Sure, but you still think I'm sexy." She puts up a second finger to the one she's still got up to shush me, then spreads them apart in a V. "Now pick up your bag. We've got US History next. I need to borrow your notes."

She puts her hand on my arm, guides me up, and we're out of the office, the woman who checked me in not looking up from her laminating.

I feel weak, but Harmony holds me up as we walk the halls.

Nobody, in any of my classes or on the bus ride home, asks me why I'm crying.

It's like I'm invisible.

TWENTY-THREE

AARON

How did I do it? How did I know she was on her way to snitch? That she'd gone to the principal's office to tattle, like I called her a bad name, a move as pathetic as it was predictable?

Because I could have guessed that was what she'd do upon hearing that Ms. Hobbes has gone missing. Based on what Gayle's told me when she debriefs in the mornings, before I dispense her pills.

Over the week, without Gayle noticing, I've slowly weaned her to the absolute minimum dose of Halcion. And yesterday, because I felt like her heart's not in it, that she's trying to keep something from me, I picked two pills out of the drawer at random. Not much of a punishment, but I doubt whatever I gave her helped with her anxiety or her growing withdrawal symptoms. I don't even think it was the same class of drugs.

And today, Thursday, the penultimate day, I tell Gayle that, so sorry, I forgot the pills at home. I've got nothing on me to give her.

Fuck her. It'll just make her twice as eager, will mean she'll gulp down whatever when we see each other tomorrow night.

But, oh yes, we were talking about how I knew that Crystal was headed to the principal's office.

Because I'm tracking her.

As long as she's carrying her backpack—which she seems to carry everywhere, she even had it on her when she stood outside my house—I can track every step she takes.

No, this isn't more hacker shit. I didn't *clone* her shitty poverty-row iPhone. Nothing that elaborate.

Last week I ordered a few GPS trackers on Amazon, free two-day shipping with Prime, and put them on all my new friends. It was surprisingly cheap, for a pack of five. They aren't Apple AirTags; those have too many privacy restrictions. Apple's aware that they're a stalker's dream tool, so they're programmed to emit a sound whenever they're near a stranger's iPhone for too long. There are workarounds, ways to disable the chime, but it's simpler to order a bag of generic tags from a Chinese company. You're meant to put the dongles on your keys, your dog's collar, your laptop bag. Takes a few seconds to link with an app that tells you the location, with a margin of error of about five feet. You can even separately sync each of the tags as pins in the Maps app, watch them move around in real time.

My tags tell me that, right now, Crystal's sitting in her room, probably in the dark, thinking about the threats I had Harmony deliver.

People like Crystal, they put too much faith in systems. Which they fool themselves into thinking isn't the same as putting faith in authority. Because I bet that Crystal likes to *think* of herself as being distrustful of authority figures. But she's not, because she still has faith in systems, and those authority figures *are* that system.

She thought the safest way to stop me would be asking to speak to the principal, telling her what had happened, disclosing everything she has in her little green binder—yes, I know about the binder too, thanks to Gayle—and that the principal would then be on the phone to the police, then the FBI, then patched through to the president of the United States, if the case needed to be escalated that high.

And, no, we're not going to break into her house. No. Crystal Giordano does not get the privilege of being on Larissa Coates's level. She has a part to play in this plan, but it's a less sympathetic one. Larissa got to die. Crystal has to live and watch.

Or at least stay alive as long as any of them.

At this point, for me, that's where a good chunk of the satisfaction is coming from, watching Crystal deal with—

"You're lucky," the man says. He's holding a garment bag as he exits the back room, coming to a stop where he left me in front of the dressing-room mirrors. "Or I guess we shouldn't say that until you try it on," he says. "Still gotta make sure it fits."

I take the bag from him and enter the changing room. I can hear the man hover by the door. I get the impression that he'd come into the dressing room, work my zipper for me, if I asked.

The tuxedo jacket is a little long, but maybe that adds to the appeal. Makes it look kind of retro, something James Bond would wear.

I square my shoulders, take in the silhouette, clip open the rental cuff links.

It works.

I thought, before coming here, that I might go for something a little weirder than a white tux. Maybe one of those salmon monstrosities, with the frills down the front and the satin lapels and cummerbund.

Or not that flashy, but at least baby blue for the jacket, a slight nod to the suits Bundy wore in court.

But I'm not Bundy. I'm not Dahmer. Or Gacy. Depraved cranks, all of them. And—not that I don't look like a young Christian Bale in this tux—I'm not any of the fictional killers either, even though they can be sexier.

And I'm none of those heavy-metal-brained losers who we don't seem to count when true-crime discussion turns to who it isn't *okay* to be a "fan" of. I won't be wearing a Harris and Klebold trench coat. No flak jacket, like any of the anonymous manifesto-writing cucks who think they're playing Call of Duty.

My vision? Expansive. And my leadership qualities? Unsurpassed. Which means I'm not Manson. I'm not Jones. Or Applewhite. Or Koresh. Thin-skinned egomaniacs with no exit strategies.

Also, not to reduce things to a numbers game, but . . . the spree killers and the serial murderers, even the cultists and the fanatics: How many *followers* did they have?

Yes. That's right. I have more.

I look at myself in the mirror, adjusting the clip-on bow tie.

This tuxedo may be a rental, but it does better than "works."

It looks exactly right.

Not too outré, but bright enough to make a statement.

This is the kind of tux that the New Aaron would wear to the prom. And one the Speaker's not ashamed of, at least.

"I'll take it," I say, stepping out of the changing room.

"You said last minute, but when's the big day, my dude?" the salesman asks me as he looks over the information I've filled out for the rental.

The date's right there in front of him. Can he read?

"Tomorrow," I say, smiling my big New Aaron smile. "Like you said, I'm very lucky you had my size."

"Ah. Prom. Best night of my life. You're going to have a great time, son," he says.

"I will," I say.

And I mean it.

TWENTY-FOUR

CRYSTAL

Why did I come to school Friday, the half day before prom? What did I expect?

Well, I *hoped* to see Gayle or Trevor. Maybe I could catch Trevor between classes, walking the halls, or see Gayle in the twenty minutes we have for Film. But they're not in school today. Neither is Aaron. And it's not just them. Ninety percent of the senior class has skipped, because we're allowed to, and the kids that are here: they're either the Grants and Tims of the world or they're girls on the prom planning committee, set up in the nice bathrooms on the second floor with flat irons and hair dryers, doing each other's makeup.

I could try texting Gayle or Trevor. But without *seeing* them . . .

No. I can't text. There'd be no way to know if they're alone. That there's not someone peeking at their screens.

But it's more than that. I need to see them, look them in the eyes, to know they're *with me*, that they *want* to stop this.

In class, if I'm acknowledged by teachers at all, they are surprised to see me. In my two mixed periods, the juniors seem depressed by my presence, like they can't fully enjoy when the teacher puts a movie on the Smartboard, with that one lame senior around.

I go the entire three-and-a-half-hour day without speaking to anyone.

The bus home is all lowerclassmen. Dad offered to drive me to school and pick me up, but I told him no. If I have to spend time with him, I don't trust that he won't be able to get me to tell him what's wrong. Or at part of what's wrong.

That's been the dance for weeks now, actually, but it was especially bad yesterday. And not because my parents have been *asking* me what's wrong, but because I want to *tell* them.

But, like Harmony said . . . fat and slow.

Too slow to protect them.

The thought makes me do something I haven't done since the principal's office, because I've been too scared to, I guess . . . I check Instagram.

What I see is not what I expect.

The Speaker's got a new post. But that's not the odd thing. He's posted every day for the last week and a half. Two nights ago, he broke the Reddit threads by posting a poem that was not in his handwriting, not entirely.

Every line one word's written in the Speaker's regular, angular penmanship, but the rest of the poem is . . . Paul's handwriting. People were complaining that they couldn't read it, Paul's left-handed smudges blurring the ink, but those complaints were quickly replaced by speculation about what the poem might *mean.*

And today Aaron's switched up his style again.

Today's post, the first thing I see when I open the app, uploaded just minutes ago. The picture's in color.

And outside. An exterior shot.

And . . .

Happy? The picture looks happy?

The subject of the photo is Trevor's van. Ugly, mahogany, and wood-paneled, as always, but also decorated with strings of gold Christmas garland secured around the roof racks and up the antenna, the words *Prom 2024* written across the wood stripe in shaving cream.

It looks like the album cover for an indie rock band. It *doesn't* look like a post from the Speaker.

There's a slice of blue sky in the photo. I look up from my phone and out the window of the school bus to see if the color matches, and it does, though clouds are starting to roll in.

The top comment is simply "wtf," lowercase, with a string of fifteen more comments under it either agreeing or calling the original commenter an asshole, defending the Speaker's right to post whatever he wants.

The next comment down is "Enjoy!" with several more exclamation marks and two champagne-bottle emojis.

I scroll up, look at the image again. The picture is sunnier, but no less meticulously composed than the Speaker's other content. He's made sure that the van's license plate is obscured. Not only that, but he has the background so out of focus that house numbers or street signs beyond the van are unreadable.

No geotag either. Something he stopped doing on that first day. When I called him on his lies.

But I don't need a geotag to tell me where the picture's been taken. That's Paul's house; the van's parked in Paul's driveway, not Trevor's. I can tell through the blur at the edge of the frame that the garage door is open, but I can't see anyone inside.

I think back to the beginning of the week, Trevor picking me up on Monday, saying what he said about Paul borrowing the van, the smell inside, and then how I haven't heard from Trevor since sharing the binder with him.

I leave Instagram, open my messages, then look out the window, try and figure out how close we are to my bus stop.

Shit. I missed it. Have to walk home from six streets over. As I walk, I type my message to Trevor.

I type, then delete everything. No. I have to think of the worst-case scenario, what would happen if Aaron, Harmony, or Paul saw that text, either by chance or because I've misjudged Trevor and he shows it to them.

I redraft, delete again.

No. Too frantic.

What I finally settle on is:

> Going to prom? Have fun, be safe.

It only takes a few minutes to get a reply, and by that point I'm walking up the grass toward home.

> Stay away. We're handling it.

We're handling it?

I think of what Gayle said, that she'd try and keep me safe.

And I think of them, without me, not paralyzed by fear but instead working together to "handle it."

Like I have been for years, I'm amazed by them, my friends, awe-struck by these two in particular. But my love and respect for them makes me feel even worse, even more like a loser who's done irreparable damage to our relationships and can't even get it together to intervene when people are in danger. When lives are on the line.

They're doing something, and I'm doing nothing.

I arrive home. Dad's truck is in the driveway. He and Ant are home, but Mom's still at the bank.

They've left the front door unlocked. But neither of them is in the living room as I push open the door.

There, hanging on the floor lamp beside the couch, is a dress I've never seen before.

It's wrapped in plastic, the hem floating an inch above the carpet.

"Hey," Dad says from the kitchen, startling me. He's making sand-wiches for himself and Ant. I can smell the tuna from here. "Lunch?" he asks.

Ant walks out from the kitchen. He has my Switch, which he's got-ten from my room, but I don't care. Let him play whatever he wants, let him delete all my save files too. What does it matter?

"What is this?" I ask, pointing to the dress.

The dress is dark blue, nearly black in the low light of our living room, with sequins and plastic jewels sewn into the hem that are a little lighter, azure. I never went dress shopping. At the beginning of April, I imagined that'd be how I celebrate getting accepted to an out-of-state school, with enough of a scholarship and work study. That's all hap-pened. And my mom's asked a few times if she can take me to get fitted. But over the last few weeks . . . I haven't felt like it.

"That . . . ," Dad says, plating a sandwich, "looks like a dress."

303

He enters the living room, offering me half of Ant's crustless tuna-and-white-bread sandwich. I shake my head no, then touch the thin, clear plastic dress bag. There's a crinkle as I probe at one of the jewels, let it catch in the light. At the top of the hanger, skewered at one corner like a dry-cleaning receipt, is my prom ticket.

I feel like I'm going to cry.

"You got me this?" I ask.

He blushes. But not quite with pride. Instead, he looks . . . embarrassed.

"I want to say yes," Dad says, "because I love you, darling. But I think this was all your mom. Funny. She left right after me this morning. Didn't even tell me she was doing it. Must have had it in a closet or something."

He looks a little wistful as he says that last part, like Mom's done this nice gesture but hasn't let him in on it.

Did she really do this?

It seems silly, with what's going on, with blood found in Ms. Hobbes's bedroom, that I should care that I'm going to break my mom's heart by not going to prom.

But I do care.

I unhook the hanger, the metal warm from where it's been resting against the cheap plastic shade of the lamp. I fold the dress under my arm, start to leave the living room, then think better of it, walk back in, take the half a sandwich from my dad, and kiss him on the cheek.

It's all the normalcy and sweetness I can perform right now. I take a bite of the sandwich, which I didn't think I was going to eat, but my appetite returns, and I finish it in two more mouthfuls.

I pull my comforter over my top sheet, then lay the dress down on the bed. I don't remove the plastic, worried I'm going to muss it somehow, but I do push the edges of the fabric so there's enough room for me to crawl into bed beside the dress.

It's still early in the day. Where the skies were blue and clear in the Speaker's picture, clouds have appeared, and the light from my window is glowing that green bloom it does as the bushes outside are hit by the afternoon sun.

I close my eyes for what feels like a long blink.

I want to say it's the crush of exhaustion, but my last thought before I lose consciousness is a selfish one: *I hope I fall asleep and when I wake up, whatever is going to happen has already happened.*

I wake up in darkness.

In my sleep I've rolled over, drifted toward the center of the bed, and as I try to sit up my hands slip on the plastic of the dress. I breathe in, the plastic in my mouth, the polyester smell of the dress filling my nostrils.

As I get my bearings, I realize it's not total darkness. There's still faint light behind my window, no longer green, but the dark amber of dusk.

I look at my phone. It's not even 7:30.

I haven't slept. I've only napped.

No new messages. No update from Trevor.

But just as I tilt the screen away, it flashes.

It's from Trevor:

> Put on the dress. There's still time for you to make it to the dance.

I read the message again.

How does Trevor know about the dress? I look around the dark room, eyes settling on my laptop, the webcam there glistening like a gem.

But, no, that doesn't make any sense.

I type a message. I don't censor myself like I did before, don't write and then rewrite:

> Trevor, where are you? Is Gayle there? Are they there too?

I watch the three dots bounce.

I feel the pause, suspense, but it doesn't take long at all for the reply to come:

> Who said this is Trevor?

> Put on the fucking dress and get yourself to prom or you'll end up like your friends.

TWENTY-FIVE

AARON

Trevor's not really drinking.

He's bringing the cup to his mouth, letting the Diet Coke touch his lips, then putting it down.

He thinks I'm going to poison him.

I'm flattered. That in his mind I'm able to somehow poison a drink from half a room away, a drink he poured himself.

No, Trevor, that's not how it's going to go.

But at least he's playing the game, isn't walking blindly toward his grim fate.

I can respect that.

I'm curious. I know the broad strokes of his plan, a plan that's not going to work, but I have no idea when he's going to begin.

My guess is that he'll excuse himself to the bathroom, call the cops, and then, because he's a tough guy and because, like Crystal, he has too much faith in systems, he'll probably confront me, figuring that backup is on the way.

Ticktock, Trevor.

The van is leaving soon. You're not driving. But the van is leaving.

Everything's going as planned. I surprised myself, those first few days in East Bay, with how quickly inspiration struck.

Most of it just that first week, as soon as I met these four, saw when prom is.

The first weekend in May sounded a little early to hold a prom. But after a quick search, checking with different school districts first in New York, then expanding to the Midwest, and ending in California, I find that it's a pretty common time to hold the dance. Either the Friday or the Saturday.

There were wrinkles added to the plan later, of course, details that needed to be revised, but the broad strokes were all there from the beginning, the last piece clicking into place once I'd watched some of Crystal's videos.

It will look like Trevor's done it. That Crystal's videos, spreading through the school, were the beginning of his violent spiral.

And in these crimes the repressed radical had the strangest of bedfellows: a popular, well-liked girl with a troubled, tragic past. Can you believe it? The two of them driven to go on a rampage that includes killing their own friends *and* Trevor's lover.

Far-fetched? Maybe, but it's what the eyewitnesses will corroborate and what the security footage will confirm. Tonight, Paul will stand—ski-masked—beside Harmony, doubling for Trevor.

And if all that's not enough, Trevor's own digital footprint will betray him.

Not that Trevor's aware, but over the last few weeks, he's become quite a fan of the Speaker. All of those socials that he's left on Paul's phone for safe keeping so his conservative parents don't find out? I've been using them to follow and comment on *every one* of the Speaker's posts. Trevor's even sent the Speaker a few deranged DMs.

Not that the Speaker deigns to respond.

But, no, that's not true. The Speaker's not *that* unreachable. He's been in contact with a lot of people over the last month, using a few different accounts.

He's been talking with a girl in Des Moines who's part of her prom committee, who's in charge of refreshments. The punch is going to be spiked in central Iowa, all right. With rat poison.

In Saugus, outside of Boston, during the final slow song of the night, a tragically disturbed youth is going to climb up into the assembly hall rafters and toss buckets of homemade napalm onto his classmates.

The Speaker sent him the recipe, told him how he could produce the chemical with gasoline and Styrofoam.

Outside of Sacramento, at a private-school prom held outdoors under large tents, a follower of the Speaker is going to wrap barbed wire across the grill of his mom's Cadillac Escalade and run down as many of his classmates as he can.

Those attacks and *dozens* more.

Of course, there will be a few among my followers who aren't true believers. A few that chicken out. But I estimate that more than half of them will go through with what they've planned.

All in the name of an internet personality who will disappear into the ether as I delete it all, deactivate my VPNs, and become Aaron Fortin once more.

And it all happens tonight.

My followers are eager, waiting for the signal, which they've been told will come around nine or ten o'clock, Eastern Standard Time.

But that's not for a few hours.

We've still got a pre-prom party to enjoy here at Paul's house, the sound of rain pattering on the windows.

Paul's parents are long gone. They're staying at a hotel tonight—a hotel with a casino. This lines up with everything else I've learned about Paul's parents and their parenting style, what we've commiserated over. That they think they're helping Paul by being the *cool* house, where the pre-prom party is no adults allowed and the after-party is no rules at all. In reality, what Paul really craves is a mom and dad who embarrass him, who try to get pictures of him with his date, who give him unsolicited advice regarding proper corsage placement.

"Beer's in the garage fridge" is the last thing Paul's dad said to us, before pointing to Trevor and telling him: "Drive safe."

Paul's dad is savvy enough to realize Trevor is his son's date. But he's wrong about who our designated driver is tonight.

Tonight Paul's driving. I watch Paul, who's taking very large sips of his own drink. Yes, we've got a slightly tipsy designated driver. He's had about two full beers during the drinking games and now has a Corona in his hand after a shot of tequila before that. But that's over a three-hour span. He's fine.

If I see him reach for another, I'll cut him off.

But I don't think Paul's drinking is a sign of indecision. Merely a smoothing of nerves.

And who'm I to judge? I've had a beer and a half myself.

And my drinking? I'm just thirsty. It's an act. Me trying to disarm Trevor with my normality. Make him second-guess whatever he's going to try to do.

Harmony is taking pictures, moving around the carpeted room, trying to find the best light. I had considered inviting some other East Bay kids to make the party feel a little realer, a little fuller, but why give up the control that I have here?

Paul is leaning against the kitchenette's small counter, doing his best to calm Trevor, using one hand to massage the other boy's neck and shoulder, finishing his third beer with the other.

I stand in the middle of the space, where I can watch both the combination kitchen/dining room and the living room.

We all look our best. My jacket's folded over a dining-room chair, close enough I can get to it in two big paces, but the other boys have kept their jackets on, apparently unaware they should be keeping them crisp. Paul is in a houndstooth jacket, while Trevor's in black and white, a traditional rented tux. They'll swap on the ride.

Gayle's wearing Count Dracula red, a dress chosen before she calmed her style, and Harmony's wearing a dress similar to the one we bought Crystal, two sizes smaller, looking good in it.

Harmony looks over to me, then flicks her eyes to Gayle, who's on the couch scrolling her phone.

I see what Harmony's trying to alert me to.

Gayle's eyelids are getting heavy, and her head bobs down, nodding off.

Today's pill, administered later than usual, is finally kicking in. I've watched Gayle sleep. I know how prone to drooling she is. I hope she doesn't get any on her nice dress.

Paul has been tasked with watching Trevor, and Harmony watches Gayle. They know their roles. Know to monitor Gayle's and Trevor's phone use.

But I don't like how stiff and serious everyone looks.

It's still a party.

This gathering is New Aaron's last chance to pretend to be a normal high schooler. We decorated the van. We played a game of flip cup. Everyone but Gayle made out a bit. These final few hours were meant to put everyone at ease. They're a snapshot of what it means to be a teen in America. Doing things that are both against the rules and a little boring.

Everything's in place. All the messages I need to send have been sent. Well, except the one.

I check my phone to make sure Crystal hasn't moved, and, predictably, she hasn't. Neither the tracking tag in the backpack nor the one sewn into the dress has changed locations.

There was a chance, a small chance, that she might try coming here. And while it might have made things a little cleaner, there would have been a certain element of "herding cats" if I had her distracting Paul and me from watching Trevor. But the option was there. It's why I posted the van on Instagram. To see if I could lure her over.

Yes, I agree with the comments section. The van is unexciting. Tonight's *real* post is in my drafts folder, picture and caption ready. I can't send it too early, though. I don't want any of my followers to get . . . overexcited. There can be no window for error.

I'll post the final photo once my prom ticket is torn, once I've walked through the doors of the gymnasium, danced to a few songs, then notice that something's wrong. That there are masked figures here, and oh god, they're armed and—

"Okay," I say aloud, clapping my hands together. On the couch, Gayle startles awake, bobbles her phone. "Should we go? It's after seven. We're already fashionably late."

I look at Paul. He should take over from here. It's his house.

But he doesn't, he just keeps rubbing circles on Trevor's back like he didn't hear me.

We should assemble at the door. The five of us should take a final, normal-looking photo, so everyone can see how, no, not everyone in this room knew what was going to happen. How could they? Those psychos kept even their best friends in the dark.

"Actually," I say, placing my mostly full beer can on the dining-room table, no coaster. The sound causes Paul to jump, gets his attention. "I've got to pee."

I keep eye contact with Paul, try to mentally ask him, *We good?* And he gets the message, gives me a tiny nod.

We're good.

But then I think about what I've just said. It was an ad-lib, but there's a kernel of truth in it.

I really *do* have to piss.

A beer and a half. I'm not good at flip cup.

I walk the carpeted hallways to the bathroom, and as I do, I draft a text to Paul:

> Get it together. If he tries to call anyone, break his fingers.

Now *would* be the time he'd act. Me giving Trevor this window. I almost want it to happen while I'm not in the room. So whatever Trevor's plan is it can be Harmony and Paul's problem.

I'd love that, actually. If it ended up being Paul who stopped Trevor.

The betrayal of that.

The bathroom is clean except for a circle of black-spotted tooth-paste scum around the sink drain. Somebody doesn't rinse properly after spitting.

I take my time unzipping, make sure I completely clear my underwear before I start my stream.

Heh. Stream.

But really. I'm serious. If I get a few drips of pee down the front of my cotton boxer briefs, I'll be uncomfortable all night and I—

There's a sound, down the hallway, headed this way. Quick footsteps on carpet.

I turn my head. Ready to make a joke, ready to say "Occupied" or something similar.

And then I hear hinges groan as the bathroom door is pulled tight in its frame.

See the shadows of two feet darken the half inch of space at the bottom of the door.

Fuck.

I don't zip, barely stop pissing as I lunge at the door, pulling at a knob that won't turn.

Fuck.

The door holds fast. Bathroom doors open inward, and the lock's on my side, so it's not like the door is locked.

Trevor is just *that* strong.

He's holding on to the knob with one hand, probably opening his phone and dialing with the other.

"Okay, open up," I say.

I'm ignored.

"Gayle, you good?" Trevor calls down the hallway behind him, into the living room.

Nobody answers him.

Then I hear more feet on carpet.

"Trevor, what are you doing? Stop," Paul says.

"Stay over there," Trevor says to him. "Don't. Don't come any closer."

"Trevor," Paul says. "What. That's stupid, don't be stupid. Let him out and we can . . ."

Paul's not handling this well. He's too timid.

It's possible I've put too much faith in, given too much responsibility to Paul Witkowski III.

"Paul?" I ask. I don't want to say too much. I don't like not being able to see. But this is okay. This is cool. Even if Trevor *does* call the cops, he's got no evidence of any wrongdoing, right? Just a boy locked in a bathroom. And if I've misjudged? It's incredibly unlikely, but if I've somehow overlooked some tiny detail that could tie me to a crime? Then we've got a contingency for something like that. Rapid escalation.

"Paul," I say again. "Paul, I can't get the door open. This is all you now. Don't just spe—"

"Shut the fuck up," Trevor says from behind the door, interrupting me. "Gayle." He calls again. "Gayle, did you get through? Are you on the phone with them?"

Hmmm. *That* might be a problem. If Gayle and Trevor are working together. Was she only pretending to fall asleep? Did she cheek her pills? Throw them up?

But before I can think back on whether I *really* saw Gayle swallow, the two boys are joined in the hallway by another voice.

"Open the door or I'll cut her fucking head off."

Finally. Someone with some balls has joined the party.

I picture Harmony, the blade of a kitchen knife or meat cleaver pressed tight against the Gayle's throat.

"Paul, listen to me," I plead through the door. "You need to fix this. There's been some kind of misunderstanding. Someone's going to get hurt."

This is chaos. And not the good kind.

"Trevor," Paul says, then clears his throat, his breathing getting closer to the door. Closer to Trevor.

"S-stay where you are," Trevor says.

"Trevor, please."

Closer.

"Please open the door. Put that down and open the door." Put what down? Does Trevor have a phone, or does he have something else? A weapon of some kind?

"Trevor, you have to trust me," Paul says.

Closer.

I think I know what Paul's doing, but I can't be sure. A pang of doubt and sudden panic surges through me. I wonder if Paul's somehow switched allegiances, if maybe I was wrong and—

"Please don't," Trevor finally says in a whisper.

And then, on the other side of the thin bathroom door, there's the sweetest sound I've ever heard.

The slip of a knife removed from its sheath and quickly buried into flesh.

"Paul?" Trevor says in disbelief. Disbelief tinged with hopelessness. And he hasn't even felt *real* pain yet.

"Don't kill him!" I yell to Paul as the door opens, hinges squeaking as I pull and Trevor falls into the bathroom with me.

I step back, allowing him to catch himself. He gets a hand on the sink, leaves a streak of blood against the porcelain.

Able to steady himself, Trevor grimaces at me, his phone falling out of his hand and onto the tile.

Trevor's own knife is sticking out of Trevor's stomach, an inch or two below his first rib.

The hilt bobs there for a second.

And I look down at it, smiling to see the violence.

And when I look back up to Trevor's face, there's no time to dodge the fist.

Far from dead, Trevor Seye punches me full in the face.

My nose mashes. I fall back, trying to catch myself on a towel rack, anything, but all I'm able to do is pull the shower curtain off its rings.

I hit the floor, one ear colliding with the cool tile.

"Shit!" I yell. And it's not the pain. Really, it's not.

It's the surprise is all, that even stabbed, Trevor had that kind of fight in him.

In the doorway, Paul's crying, trying not to hyperventilate.

"Gayle," Trevor yells, his voice distorted by pain, his knees buckling as he slumps forward, coming to rest between the sink and the toilet tank.

"She's fucking dead," Harmony tells him. "Like you, she's fucking . . ."

"Don't!" I yell to Harmony. My two front teeth throb, like they might have been knocked loose, are going to fall out in a day or two. But I have to push through the pain and shock. I have to stop Harmony from scuttling all of this. "Don't kill anyone!" I say again, my own voice sounding strange over the throbbing of blood in my ears.

And then Harmony starts to scream: "Ow, ow, ow, she's fucking biting me!"

Okay, good. If Gayle's biting her, it means she's not dead.

"Tell her to stop," Paul says to Trevor, entering the bathroom with us.

I'm able to get to a sitting position in time to see Paul take hold of the knife in Trevor's stomach.

"Tell Gayle to stop fighting us," Paul says, then sniffles. His face is tear streaked, but I don't see any *new* tears. He's in the zone. I've trained him well.

Trevor blinks in Paul's face. Looks like he doesn't understand. Like none of this computes.

Then, to show Trevor what's happening, Paul twists the knife. Not far, just enough so that Trevor screams.

There. That's real pain.

Then there's the sound of something heavy being thrown against a wall, down the hallway.

"Okay. I got her," Harmony says.

Somewhere in the house, Gayle moans. I hope nothing's broken.

I take a closer look at where Paul's placed the knife. Good. We've talked about this. The blade's gone into Trevor's shirt, not the jacket. There's seepage, of course, but the blood's not showing up on the black fabric of the tux.

"Harmony, get me my jacket," I call out the door as I sit up. And I hear quick, obedient footsteps leave the hallway and enter the dining room/kitchenette.

"His phone, Paul," I say.

Paul takes his hand from the knife, leaving it where it is, then searches in the shag of the circular rug outside the shower for Trevor's phone.

Trevor blinks up at him. I hope he doesn't die. Not yet. We could do everything we have planned with him dead. But the timing would be weird. The forensics would be off if anyone looked closely enough.

"Did you call anyone?" Paul asks, his hands shaking as he tries to unlock Trevor's phone.

"Paul," Trevor says, takes a long blink, sweat beginning to break out on his face. "Paul, I love you. Why are you . . ."

Paul needs to hurry up. If Trevor called the cops, even if he disconnected before an operator could answer, then everything's changed. Because now there's a lot of evidence leaking out of Trevor, smeared on the tile and dripping into the rug.

If he called the cops, we don't have time for all this. We need to be in the van.

But, no, panicking won't solve anything.

I stand, pinching the bridge of my nose with one hand, tipping my chin back to slow the bleeding. I step over the both of them, cross to the doorway.

"Also need your keys, Trevor," Paul says. "Please."

Trevor starts to dig in his pants pocket, but then he hisses at the pain, the knife handle trembling, and Paul has to bend to help, to go into Trevor's pockets himself.

"Did he call anyone?" I ask from the doorway.

"I think we're good," Paul says, checking the phone, now unlocked. He doesn't even realize that he's opened himself up for attack. His trust in Trevor, that the Eagle Scout would never do anything to hurt him, runs so deep.

I take my jacket from Harmony and make it over to them in time to avert calamity as Trevor hisses in pain again.

I take the gun from my breast pocket and push the barrel behind Trevor's ear.

"Don't," I say.

Trevor has the knife out of himself, is ready to plunge it into Paul's neck or back as the other boy scrolls his phone.

Trevor nods at me, acknowledges that he's been bested, and lets the knife drop through his fingers.

With me kneeling, the three of us are so close that we're all sharing the same exhalation, hunched on the floor of the bathroom, the air humid with blood. It reminds me of my time with Paul and Harmony, the intimacy of it.

Paul hands me the phone, then puts the keys in his own pocket.

I look to the end of the hallway, toward the rest of the house. Harmony's got Gayle lifted to her feet, a clump of the shorter girl's hair balled in her fist. Well controlled.

"Her phone?" I ask. "She call anyone?"

"Please," Harmony says, holding Gayle's phone, screen out. She's offended by the question. "I was watching her the whole time."

I inspect Trevor's wound. It's deep, but at least his breath doesn't hitch or burble, nothing that would suggest a punctured lung.

He'll live. I think. Or at the very least, he'll live for a short time longer.

We'll have to change the narrative around a bit to accommodate the timeline of the stab wound, but . . .

Nothing's fucked up.

This isn't like it was with Chuck and Kelly, dead in the wrong place at the wrong time.

No, I tell myself. My nose and teeth hurt, but this doesn't change anything.

But time is short. We've got to get on the road.

I look down at my shirt. The three bloody fingerprints where I've touched my jacket.

"Paul," I ask, "do you know if there's a Tide pen anywhere?"

I take care of the stains, explain to Paul how to best mop up the bathroom, while Harmony force-feeds Gayle some pills. With gusto.

She might have been pocketing her pills earlier, but there's no trickery from Gayle this time. Harmony shovels a powdery mash into the girl's face, and Gayle swallows enough pharmaceuticals that in a few hours her body will forget how to breathe.

We limp to the van slowly. It's begun to rain harder. Nobody will be outside to take notice of five beat-up teens marching to a van decorated for prom.

Harmony goes ahead, opening the doors for us. I stay closer to Trevor than Gayle, feeling ready to shoot him in the head and be done with it, my nose hurts so much.

But that would *really* mess with the forensics.

I climb into the van first, taking the third-row bench seat, then Trevor falls in, takes the second-row driver's side seat, where Adam Patterson's body had bled into the headrest. That's good. The mingling of their blood will confuse things.

Harmony loads Gayle, already fading, into the second-row passenger side. I move the Colt between them, more for Trevor's benefit than for Gayle's, since she seems so out of it. Just letting him know that it's not only his own life he's gambling if he tries anything.

Paul takes the bags from the garage and puts them into the back, the goodies I've secreted out of my father's collection over the last few days, the mask and elbow-length gloves Paul will wear once he switches jackets with Trevor.

Paul then gets in the driver's seat. Harmony rides shotgun.

"Buckle up," Trevor says to Gayle.

I'm surprised he's able to speak.

Then, with obvious effort, he grabs for his own seat belt and clips the buckle.

Gayle struggles with her strap, so Paul needs to reach back and help her. Trevor nods, like he's thankful, even though less than fifteen minutes ago Paul's stabbed him.

We sit, taking a moment to listen to the rain against the windshield as everyone calms down. Paul and Harmony use fast-food napkins to pat their hair dry. Then, when they're done, Paul hands Trevor's phone to Harmony, who then tosses it, underhand, onto the bench seat beside me.

Yes. In all the excitement I almost forgot.

There's one last person we need at the dance.

I open Trevor's phone with my free hand, not even needing to think about his passcode, and text Crystal Giordano.

TWENTY-SIX

CRYSTAL

The dress is too tight.

But I'm able to get it on.

The sequined fabric cutting into my sides is a final confirmation that, no, my mother did not buy this dress for me.

It was left here, in our living room, while I was at school.

They were in my house, I think, and shiver.

I don't have shoes that go with this dress, but the text message didn't say anything about shoes, so I keep my socks and sneakers on.

The message didn't say a lot of things. And I don't know that I believe what it does say, but . . .

Or you'll end up like your friends.

I can't risk bringing violence here, to my family.

I step over and listen to the rest of the house through my bedroom door. While I've been asleep, my mom's come home, dinner's been cooked, and I can hear the faucet over the sink going. It's already time to do the dishes.

They've eaten without me. They've left me alone.

I wonder how long my mom and dad are planning to be this patient.

Until I'm out of the house and moved into a dorm? Probably not.

I could try walking past them, a sweatshirt on to hide the top half of the dress but . . . no, I'll never make it out the front door without them asking questions.

There's no time to lie. No time for pre-prom pictures, even if they believed the lie, let me drive myself to the event.

I look at my window.

I've never snuck out of the house before. With the greenery that covers most of the window, I'm not even sure if it's possible.

But I don't have time to think of an alternative.

I grab the spare car key from the front pouch of my backpack. I have my license. I could drive my mom's car anytime I want. I just choose not to.

Then I take a hoodie from the floor, put it on.

Then I open the window, paint cracking and dust coating my fingers. The window makes more noise than I thought it would, and as I listen, the kitchen the faucet stops.

Have my parents heard me? Are they about to investigate the strange noise coming from their daughter's bedroom? The daughter who's been acting increasingly erratic?

I sure hope not.

The screen is a bigger problem than the window itself. The metal clasps have rusted and fused, and I can't pry them apart. But then, as I'm pressing, my hand slips and a small tear at the bottom of the screen rips open into a hole large enough to put my knee through.

I keep pulling at the screen, the tear opening around the frame, sounding like a zipper.

I've got one leg out the window, my butt on the sill, branches and leaves cracking under me, cold and wet, when the twin shadows of feet appear under my bedroom door.

"Are you up in there?" my mom asks.

"Kind of," I say, wincing as I'm poked in the leg right above where my sock stops protecting me. Does this bush have thorns? How have I never noticed that?

"Well, we have Hamburger Helper and yesterday's cinnabread," she says. "I haven't put it in the fridge yet."

She starts to walk away, then adds, "And your family would like to see you. If only as proof of life."

"I'm alive," I say, feeling like I'm going to fall out the window, stomach crunched and straining to hold me in place so I don't make any more noise, don't pop the screen out of its frame or any of the other alarming noises that would cause her to push into the room.

I should have gotten up and locked the door.

"Good," my mom says. "It's the first and last time I'll say it, I promise, but if you want your dad or I to drive you to prom, we will."

"I'm okay. Really not feeling it."

"Well, I was just talking to Layla on the phone and—"

"No!" I say, then get myself under control. "Really. I'm okay not going."

I watch the crack under the door, the perspiration under my arms slicking the sequins that have already begun to chafe. And, finally, the shadows of my mom's feet step back.

"Okay, love you," she says.

"Love you too." I lower my other leg out the window, sneakers sinking into the mud puddles where our gutters have overflowed against the house.

My forearms are scraped, but my legs are more exposed and get it much worse. There are small pinpricks of blood where I'm stuck with thorns, and finally I fall forward, pushing through the space between the two bushes.

Clear of the brambles, I look out at the driveway.

Oh, come on!

My dad's truck is blocking my mom's car in, not leaving an inch of space behind her bumper. How did they even do that? With how the cars had been when I'd gotten home? Probably something to do with their work schedules tomorrow, since my dad's at the dealership on most Saturdays.

Shit!

I need my dad's keys.

I'll have to drive the truck. Which I hate, which I actually have anxiety dreams about sometimes. Dreams where I need to drive the truck, and I feel like the seat's too high and my legs are too short and I can't work the pedals properly.

I rub my knees, widening the cuts there to wake myself up and start thinking straight.

I've just crawled out my bedroom window.

I've decided to act, and I'm going to follow through, goddammit.

I'm going to save my friends.

I have my license. I know how to drive.

All I need are those keys.

I tiptoe to the front door, muddy sneakers sloshing. The sky's misting, but judging from the color of the clouds, the depth of the puddles, and the way everything around me drips, this is just a lull in the storm.

I hope my mom hasn't locked the door, otherwise I'm going to have to make more noise using my key.

I reach out and . . . the knob turns. I wince as I push the door open a crack, worried that my parents are going to be right there, staring at me as I paw for the key dish.

But they're not.

I open the door five or six inches, hoping they're in the kitchen and won't see. Then I reach my hand inside to the key dish.

I grope for a second, blind, almost sure I'm about to hear my dad say something snarky, a "Can I help you?" as he opens the door from the other side.

But that doesn't happen.

I hook a finger through the loop on my dad's key ring, watch the keys begin to rise out of the dish and . . .

Ant's face fills the crack of doorway.

I freeze as he looks up at me.

He starts to say something but must see me wince, because he doesn't.

I purse my lips together and whisper, "Shhhhh."

Anthony's never *once* done a thing I've asked him to do. He's not a bad little brother, per se, but the way he is, it means that being quiet isn't his thing.

But Ant must see something in my eyes, in the dampness of my skin, the mud and blood on my shins and socks.

Because my little brother nods, then steps back into the house and doesn't say anything as I lift the keys out and shut the door as quietly as I can.

Thank you, Ant.

I climb up into the cab of the truck and get a kind of vertigo, even though I'm not *that* high off the ground.

It's fine, I tell myself. Then I turn over the engine, stumble for a moment figuring out the headlights, which are different—way brighter—than the ones on my mom's car and am out of the driveway.

I check the rearview mirror before the house disappears, half expecting to see my dad running out in his pajama pants, yelling that someone's stealing his truck, but he doesn't.

I accelerate and feel the truck pulling forward beneath me, the steel cases in the truck bed rattling, my dad's tools shaking inside. Like the truck itself, the tools are something management at the dealership asks him to keep back there. They think it appeals to their market, men who think they'll do it themselves, even if they aren't construction professionals.

I'm speeding until I reach Trevor's favorite intersection to complain about, where I know enough about the commute that I stop on a yellow light.

The rain's gotten worse.

I check my phone; there are no new messages.

Who's sent those texts? Has to be Aaron, right? And what's he done to Trevor? To Gayle?

For the first time since stepping out my bedroom window, I realize that I'm doing what I'm told. I think I'm *acting*, I think I'm on my way to the rescue. But I'm really just following directions. I'm driving, quickly, toward the person who's ruined my life, who—I think—has killed close to ten people.

I'm driving into a trap.

But what other choice do I have?

The rain comes down in sheets, so heavy now the windshield wipers struggle to keep up.

I'm not used to this drive in the dark, against the glare of my own headlights. I should have thought to put on navigation so I don't have to squint out the window at street signs.

The night has gotten so much darker since I've been behind the wheel. And it gets darker still as I pull onto the road to school, the arboretum on one side of the road, no light pollution of any kind.

In the distance, I think I see a spotlight play against a cloud. The prom.

I know there are two directions to approach the school from and that the carpool and I are used to taking the "back way," but I would have imagined there'd be more cars here, any cars at all, with the dance tonight.

But prom started nearly an hour ago, I tell myself, so maybe that's why.

Without stop signs or intersections, I put my foot down until I see the flash of brake lights appear in the slight turn of the road ahead of me.

No, not brake lights; I see my own headlights glinting off the chrome ladder and bubbled back windows of a van . . . a van with an out-of-date paint job, wood paneling, and soaking-wet streamers of tinsel flapping against the wind.

I've caught up with them.

They aren't at prom yet.

Whatever they're planning to do at the school, there's still time for me to stop them.

I weigh my options, very quickly, and, looking at the glint of the van's bumper in the night, I rev the truck's engine and hope that I'm doing something Aaron won't expect.

"The bigger the car," I say, repeating my dad's sales line, "the safer you are."

The last thought I have, before chrome touches bumper, is to wonder who Aaron meant by "my friends" when he warned me that I'll end up like them.

Does he mean Trevor? The best of us?

Does he mean Harmony and Paul? As much as they've begun to look like Charles Lang and Kelly Closterman, to me, they're still my friends.

Does he mean Gayle? Has he done something to Gayle? Has he killed her?

I can barely stand the thought. It makes me so sad and angry.

I hit the van harder than I thought I would.

Taillights crunch, and I watch the ladder bend against the press of the truck's fender.

But the van doesn't slow and pull to the side of the road.

No, it speeds up.

And this is it. This is me acting. I'm no longer sitting quiet and listening. No longer curled up, invisible in the passenger seat, fooling myself into thinking I'm active because I'm *paying attention.*

The truck's engine revs, and I move to overtake the van.

Because, no, I can't walk into a trap. I won't do what I'm told. I have to do something that Aaron Fortin can't be expecting, something the Speaker didn't plan.

And my dad's right. Trevor's van is a piece of shit.

Please be buckled up, I think as I prepare to nudge the van again.

The gunshot sounds like thunder at first, or the pop of a tire blow-out. But then I look over and see the quarter-sized blast in the driver's-side window, the spiderweb cracks already spreading against the raindrops.

Fuck.

He's shooting at me.

And the realization causes me to hook the wheel, the front of the truck colliding with the van.

The van bobbles, skidding, hydroplaning, but I keep my foot down as metal groans and the window beside me cracks and shatters, either from flying shrapnel or the spreading cracks from the bullet.

I press into the van again, the twisted metal holding us together for a moment as there's a terrible grinding sound.

I only let my foot off the gas when I hear the sound of a second gunshot.

No, I think. *We're going too fast.*

I lift my foot from the accelerator, but by then it's too late to stop what's happening.

TWENTY-SEVEN

AARON

Across the country, there are hundreds of schools having their proms tonight. Tens of thousands of teenagers on the East Coast, right now, filling belt-buckle flasks, posing behind their dates in front of tacky backdrops, crying with their best girlfriends at every sentimental song the DJ plays. And it's late enough that the central and Pacific time zones are arriving to get their own parties started.

Thousands of the Speaker's followers have their proms tonight . . .

"Hey, wake up," Harmony says. She's turned around in her seat, is waving a hand in front of Gayle's face, then snapping her fingers.

"Leave her alone," Trevor says, but there's no fight in him now. His fight's leaking all over, soaking the waistband of his boxers.

Harmony sneers at him but *does* turn back around to face front.

Trevor looks back at me, his voice weak. "Is she going to die?"

I inspect Gayle, her eyes moving under her eyelids, like she's dreaming.

"She looks fine to me, peaceful," I say. I'm holding the gun, and I have my phone on the seat to my left, and Trevor's phone on my right in case I need to text Crystal again.

"Fuck you," Trevor says.

I ignore him. I don't have time to exchange patter with a dying patsy. I can see that Harmony's doing something in the front seat.

"Harmony," I say. I'm sweating into my jacket. I hope I'm not leaving noticeable stains. "How does my nose look?"

Back at the house, I had her apply a thick layer of makeup, but—

Harmony turns toward me, and I can see that she's taken Trevor's knife from the center console where Paul placed it.

I smile at her, and she must take that as some kind of signal, an endorsement of whatever she's thinking of doing, because I watch her turn the blade to make the light catch.

We wiped the knife down in the house. None of us are supposed to be touching it, and I think Harmony knows that. She's being a bad girl.

"Trevor's got a knife!" she yells, which causes Paul to swerve a bit, he's so startled by her voice.

Harmony giggles, pointing the knife at Trevor, who tries to sit straighter in his seat but can't.

"Jesus," Paul says. "I thought you were serious." He gets the van back under control. He's hunched over, his seat moved up so he can be closer to the windshield, his view obscured by the rain, the gears of the van's wipers straining to keep up.

"Harm," Trevor says, the word a breath, eyes on the knife. "What are you doing? What are *any* of you doing right now?"

Harmony's completely turned around on the passenger seat, has her knees under her. Trevor puts a weak hand up as she waves the knife in front of him.

Then, in a fake-out so quick it surprises even me, Harmony lunges forward with the tip of the knife, not at Trevor, but over into the seat behind her, into Gayle's stomach.

Gayle's eyes shoot open as she screams.

"I said wake up," Harmony says, wiggling the tip of the knife, only about an inch of the blade, into the cut she's made in Gayle's dress, the blood matching the color of the fabric.

"Harmony," I say, "that's enough."

But maybe I went too paternalistic with my tone of voice, because Harmony looks up at me. Then, to show she's purposefully disobeying me, she smiles as she stabs Gayle again, her arm extending all the way as she leans over her seat.

"What?" Harmony says, jiggling the blade, Gayle screaming. "I'm not going deep."

It's suddenly easier to see in the van, and Harmony lets go of her headrest to shade her eyes.

There's cool blue light streaming in through the tinted back window.

"Fuck. Shit." The words come from Paul. "Can you just fucking listen and sit down, Harm?"

Paul's frazzled. This is too much for him. I can see it in his eyes, wide and frantic in the rearview mirror. I've pushed him too far.

Harmony scowls at Paul, looking like she might take a stab at him, just because.

He takes a hand off the wheel, holds it up to her, palm out.

"I'm sorry. The stupid fucker behind us has his brights on and I can't—"

The van lurches forward. I hear the steel of the ladder behind my seat crimp, the bags of weapons under me jostle.

"He hit us. The bastard hit us!" Paul's eyes bounce frantically between the rearview mirror and the road.

He, I think. *Why does he assume it's a* he?

I raise my phone, swipe it open as the lights flash again and the truck pulls alongside us.

No, that's not a he. I watch as the blue dot of the tracker I've placed on Crystal Giordano's dress overlaps with our own dot.

Beside us the truck engine revs for another hit.

I point the Colt out the window. Out at the rain-streaked truck. I imagine that I've perfectly sighted Crystal's mottled, forgettable face—a face, in truth, that I can't see—and fire.

I turn back to the van just in time to see Trevor disengage his seat belt and lunge at me.

Besides him, Gayle roars, her hands clamping down to keep Harmony's arm in place as the girl tries to swipe at Trevor with the knife.

Trevor's on me before I can get my gun hand turned, the nickel plating of the Colt disappearing in his black tuxedo jacket.

Crystal collides with us again, ramming the truck into us. The van spins, makes a rattling sound like the engine is about to fall out.

This was . . . not at all what I planned for. I try and think of how this can be staged now that I've introduced a gun.

But, no, I don't think I can fix this. Not easily.

Trevor claws at my face, cutting my lip as I try to bite him. He can't get any leverage to punch me, his elbow is knocking against the back of Gayle's seat.

He's getting more blood on me. More stains.

That and me firing the gun in the car.

The ballistics are fucked.

He's ruining everything.

They both are ruining everything.

All three of them are, as Gayle keeps struggling with the knife, her eyes impossibly wide from the drugs she's taken.

I decide I have to do it, that there's no wrestling back control of this situation if I don't kill him.

I level the gun at Trevor's stomach.

And fire.

But then the powerslide the van's been locked in stops abruptly and everything's moving.

Instead of Trevor's punctured and perforated body falling limp against me, I see a splotch of spotlighted blood fan out across the inside of the windshield.

Oh no.

I've missed.

I've shot Paul.

The van goes airborne, and gravity seems to pause for a moment, then resume, slamming all of us to one side.

Jewels of glass bounce off my eyelids as I press them closed. I have time to think one short word:

Fuck.

And then the van rolls and rolls and rolls.

TWENTY-EIGHT

CRYSTAL

What have I done?

The feeling of regret is so deep, hits me so fast, that I think it's possible I might pass out, still speeding along even as I apply the brakes, tires stripping as the rain pours down.

I turn into the skid, not on purpose but because I need to keep a death grip on the wheel to press my weight down on the brake, the rubber of my sneaker slippery with rainwater and mud.

The centrifugal force must be more than the latches on my dad's toolboxes can stand, because I hear tools clatter around in the truck bed, some flying over the gate onto the asphalt and into the ditch where Trevor's van has just rolled.

But the truck doesn't flip.

It skids to a stop, perpendicular to the road.

I'm jostled side-to-side as the truck rocks on its suspension, the front two wheels across the double yellow line and into the other lane.

I breathe, my fingers numb from gripping the wheel.

If I didn't have nightmares about driving my dad's truck *before*, I definitely will after tonight.

There's no time. I have to get them out. I have to call 9-1-1 and get an ambulance.

I grab for my phone, dial, and open the door.

I don't take the keys, but I do remember to put the truck in park as I hop down.

"9-1-1, what is your emerg—"

I don't wait to hear the rest.

"Hello, I'm on, uh, I don't know the name of the road." Stupid, stupid. "I'm near East Bay High School. The road in that . . ." Why can't I think of the words? "By the park," I sputter, rain in my mouth, rain soaking the ruching on the dress, weighing me down. "By the woods! There's been a car crash. People are hurt. Please hurry."

The operator tries to calm me down, but I can't pay attention to what they're saying. I hang up and put my phone back in my hoodie pocket.

Shivering, I look back toward the truck. No headlights approach in either direction. Hopefully, with the big silver truck parked like that, the first carload of kids coming from or going to the prom will stop and investigate. But right now there's nobody. No one to help me.

I can smell burning rubber, but I can't see where the van has gone over the asphalt, into the ditch and the woods beyond.

I kick something, nearly lose my footing, and see that there's a wrench at my feet. It must have been thrown from the truck.

I look down at the wrench.

I remember the gunshot. That someone in the van has fired a gun.

I've never struck anyone in my life, but . . . I've never run a van load of my friends off the road either.

My legs and lower back burn, but I bend and collect the tool.

Then, carrying the wrench, I run back toward where I saw the broken taillights start to corkscrew. I stay on the edge of the blacktop, my eyes scanning the trees and tall grass, looking for smoke or lights or something . . .

And then I see it, the van's interior lights flickering, hard to distinguish in the rain and darkness, through the tinted side windows.

The van is upside down, front wheels still spinning.

I step off the edge of the asphalt into the gravel of the ditch, and then my feet slip out from under me as I hit the first grass clods, the earth underneath spongy and soaked through, torn up by the top or side of the van as it rolled. I crab walk the rest of the way down the ditch on my hands and butt, keeping a hold on the heavy wrench.

"Gayle! Trevor!"

The other two, I don't yell their names.

And the fifth name.

I don't want to yell for *him*.

I hope the second gunshot was for Aaron. I'm pretty sure it wasn't.

The van has skidded to a stop against a fence post, signage nailed to the fence about how this land is a protected nature preserve.

I bend down. I can't see. Everything is so much darker here under the harsh shadows of the tree line that starts a little before the fence.

Already I'm disheartened.

Have I killed them all?

Was there anyone innocent to kill?

Where is he and what has he done to my friends?

I don't hear crying or moans, just the sound of the front tires still spinning in slow circles.

I pull my phone out; it feels hot, and it may be well on its way to overheating and switching off, if it hasn't already. I despair a little bit more. The screen doesn't respond to my touch at first, but my fingers are wet from climbing down here, and I'm finally able to get them dry enough to pull up flashlight mode.

I approach the van's passenger side, and once I can see what's left of the windshield, I can tell that the van didn't skid to a stop at the fence post. The fence post *stopped* the skid, ejecting whoever was sitting in that front passenger seat out into the woods like a missile.

Please don't be Gayle, please don't be Gayle, I think as I direct the phone's weak beam out into the woods, try and see if I can tell where the body came to a stop. But there's nothing and no one out there in the darkness. Not that I can see.

I keep walking closer to the van. I can't hear *human* movement inside, but I hear metal groan and water sizzle as it drips onto the undercarriage. As I get closer, I worry that the van's going to roll over and squish me. But I need to keep going. I need to see if I can help.

I crouch lower and see that whoever was driving is still behind the wheel. I direct the flashlight over and catch a glimpse of coppery hair.

Paul.

Paul. Not Trevor.

Paul's been driving the van.

He looks like he's sleeping, belted in, his nose bleeding in reverse, going up his forehead into his hair, but then I see the bullet wound, like a large beauty mark under one eye.

The gummy spatter across the steering wheel and dash.

I gag.

I'm too late to save Paul. Paul's brain is coating what remains of the windshield.

But . . .

Gayle.

Trevor.

I think their names, not enough strength in me to call out.

Then I reach a shaky hand to the passenger-side rear door.

The metal of the door's so twisted and crimped I wonder if I'll even be able to glide the door open a few inches, but as I depress the button on the handle, I'm surprised to see that I can . . .

And that Gayle's there, belted in, her stomach black in the dim light's glare, her red dress darker across her abdomen, a mess of blood.

Under and behind her, between the headrests, a pale white hand.

Aaron, crushed under the seat.

He's motionless. I can't even see the rise and fall of breath. But it couldn't have been that easy, he must still be alive, he might still—

Then Gayle speaks:

"Hey," she says, then the corner of her mouth, upside down, begins to twinge upward in a smile.

She's hurt. She's hurt really bad, but she's alive. She's alive and I—

Then Gayle vomits. It comes out white and chalky, and then she starts to sputter and choke.

"Oh god, I'll get you out of there," I say.

But Gayle keeps smiling through the next round of vomit. "It's okay. I—" But she doesn't get to finish what she's going to say, because her eyes go wide as she sees something behind me, and she screams, "Look out!"

I smell what hits me before I see it.

Harmony collides with me, arms spinning, her scent like it always is, but more intense tonight—because it's prom, so why wouldn't it be?—and we tumble to the ground.

If it weren't for the smell, I'd barely be able to tell the figure on top of me is Harmony at all. Her face is studded with glass. She has a gash that splits her features down the middle, and as she lashes out at me with the knife, the wedge of the blade is mirrored by part of her face, the part where I can see her skull, where the rain's washed the flap of skin carved away from her cheek and rinsed the bone clean.

As much of a ruin as she is, Harmony's still able-bodied, still mobile. Still a threat.

I can see it in her eyes. The hurt and hate aren't slowing her down. No. Instead the hurt and hate keep her going.

I try and bring the wrench up, but it's too heavy, and Harmony's kneeling on that arm. Why didn't I pick something lighter to try and protect myself with?

Harmony reels back with the knife, aiming for my neck and face. But I'm able to twist. She may be on top, but I'm still bigger than her.

Her thrust misses her intended target, but she's still able to stab me in the shoulder.

The night flashes yellow and for a moment I think it's lightning, or the flashing lights of police and ambulances. But it's just the shock of the pain messing with my vision.

"Why do you always fuck erryting shup!" Harmony screams. She's crying now, and her lips are so ruined that the end of her sentence gets slurred.

She's coming back down with the blade when Gayle screams at her. I look over at the last second to see that she's on her way. Gayle seems sluggish and dazed getting to her feet, but she pushes off the side of the van to close the distance quickly, with enough force to knock Harmony off me.

Now Harmony's on Gayle.

Gayle has switched places with me. And she didn't hesitate, just did it.

I watch in the dimness as the knife glints, Harmony bearing down, Gayle resisting but not having the strength or leverage.

I stand, the wrench so heavy it pulls me down on one side.

The blade begins to press itself flat against Gayle's chin.

Gayle. No. Please not her.

Not my best friend.

I don't have much time to aim, but I try and make up for what might be a glancing blow by swinging as hard as I can.

I bring the wrench across my body, hitting Harmony on the bridge of her nose.

The crack is soft, like when my mom prepares a whole chicken, cracking the sternum down with a meat tenderizer, crushing the bird flat to season and cook evenly.

And though I know I had to, that it was self-defense, that I've saved Gayle, I immediately regret the swing. I know that I'll be able to hear the sound of Harmony's face breaking for as long as I live. That some nights, in unrelated dreams, I'll hear that same soft cracking sound and the dreams will turn into night terrors.

Gayle falls away from the blade, getting out from under it, breathing heavy.

Harmony lies there, doesn't move.

After a moment of watching the body, I snap out of my stupor. I turn, thinking that the night's not done. I have to find Aaron, to check if he's breathing. In my imagination, my dread, we return to the van, and he's dislodged himself from under the seat. He's escaped into the night. In that imagined scenario he'll come for us. It might be days, weeks, years from now, but he'll get his revenge.

But then a familiar voice calls out. It's not Aaron. And the voice needs help.

Gayle and I lean on each other, limping back to the crash.

TWENTY-NINE

AARON

Blood dribbles out of the side of my face.

The Tide pen won't fix this.

I think I've lost a tooth. Maybe more than one tooth. And, worse than that, I think I've swallowed some of them. I can feel the jagged shattered enamel stuck in my throat like popcorn kernels or a pill that has gone down sideways.

I cough and the pain brings me back to fully conscious.

But all I can think about is how it wasn't supposed to be like this.

Be sure to sign up on my page for notifications so you don't miss Friday's special upload.

No.

They haven't stopped a fucking thing.

There's going to be a national day of mourning named after all this.

I'm supposed to be living free and clear to see it.

They're supposed to die, and I'm supposed to go to college, dammit.

Look at this fucking mess. Dead bodies, pulverized automotive glass, and bullet holes. Two bags of firearms under the seat, for the first officers on the scene to find. The cops are probably on their way here already . . .

Crystal Giordano in a truck has taken it all away from us.

All because I thought it'd be cute to let her live to see how it all ended.

No.

It's not true.

Can't be. I won't let it be.

She hasn't taken anything from me, from us, the Speaker and me.

I can still have an impact. I can still energize my followers. I can still be loved, speak to the loveless. I can still be worshipped.

All I need to do is find my phone.

I need to go into my drafts. I need to give the signal.

I can hear rain entering the van through the floor and windows, but I can't tell if the wetness all over me is blood, gas, or rainwater.

My nose is no longer bruised, it's broken, permanently stuck to one side, and I can't smell anything through my congestion.

I raise my head, but it takes significant effort. I can only see what's directly in front of me, what I can make out in the cracked and tilted rearview mirror.

My white jacket is copper with my own blood.

I'm lying in the middle of the van, between the two seats of the second row, one headrest against my side when I try and push myself up, pinning my waist in place.

The seats of the second row are empty.

Where are they? Where's Gayle? How far have they gotten? Is Trevor's corpse behind me, still on the bench seat?

Outside, through the broken windshield and the open door, I can hear voices, a struggle.

I look around. Where is my phone?

Where's the gun?

No, fuck the gun. The phone's more important at this point.

Where's the phone?

I need to post before I black out again. I need to—

Then I see it, by moving my head as much as I can, with great effort and pain. The phone's under me. It's pressed against my shoulder and the crook of my arm.

My best chance is my left hand . . . if I can get it out from under me.

I scream. I don't have *a* broken bone, I have many, and the nerves at the end of each break sizzle and grate against each other.

For one horrible moment I consider that this might not be *my* phone. Neither of us use a case, and this could be Trevor's phone trapped under me.

I grunt one last time, flex and undulate the muscles of my stomach to try and let the pressure off my hand. Through the pain I'm able to sweep the phone to where I can better see it.

My mashed nose drips on the surface of the phone. The screen's cracked, but the warm touch of my blood's enough to wake the device.

And, with my one good eye, I can see that it's *my* lock screen! It's my phone!

I'm doing it.

Face ID doesn't recognize me, but that's not surprising.

Something shifts in the van behind me, but I can't check to see what it is. I need to finish this. I can't have done all this work for nothing.

I bring my broken hand up, decide that the thumb's my best chance to work the screen.

I begin to type in my passcode, get an error message, an angry buzz, and then try again.

Then there's that shifting sound again behind me, in the third row. Then a groan.

Trevor. How is this fucking guy still alive? He must—

All thought is blotted out as an immense pressure lays against my ribs and kidneys.

I look up, can see enough in the rearview mirror to know that Trevor's got his knee on my back.

This fucking guy. This Boy Scout. This patsy. This human pawn for me to move around the board.

He's kneeling on one of my broken ribs, and it's hard to breathe.

I see the glint of nickel plating in his hand.

No, it can't end like this.

I press my thumb down on the screen, waking the phone and trying the passcode again, leaving smeary, bloody thumbprints across the screen.

"Stop," Trevor says.

I don't listen to him.

I almost have it. One more number.

The phone unlocks, shows me the Maps app, shows me all the dots I'm tracking, that they're all here in this one spot of green: the John Campbell Arboretum.

I swipe up; the app I need is two open apps back. I just need to scroll—

"Stop what you're doing or I'm going to shoot you," Trevor says, louder, gaining strength.

Trevor's not going to shoot me.

He's got strength but not conviction.

I hear him pull the hammer back. Must be something he's seen in movies, because you don't need to do that every time, not with this model of revolver.

I scroll over. I open the app.

He won't shoot me for posting to my social media.

The blood on the screen has gone tacky. The touch doesn't respond as I tap the drafts button.

Trevor presses the barrel of the Colt against the base of my neck, starts guiding the gun down. But I might have a broken neck, because at a certain point I can't feel the metal anymore. I'm numb.

I get the drafts folder open, and all I have to do is post when . . .

A wrench swings down and pulverizes both my hand and my phone.

I look up. Crystal is standing there, her short nothing of a friend leaning against her, puke and blood smearing both of them.

No. I yell.

I look up at them and I yell.

No, no, no, no.

Or at least I *think* I yell the word.

Neither seems to react.

I look down at the destroyed phone.

My destroyed hand.

Is it my hand?

Don't just speak, act.

The New Aaron's hand.

Don't just speak, act.

The Old Aaron's hand.

Don't just speak, act.

The Speaker's hand.

Don't just speak, act.

I can see all these words typed out in my vision, flickering like the world's a cracked phone screen.

The van is flashing white and red.

Voices are calling and people are crying.

And none of them say my name.

None of them know who I am because I've done nothing.

I am no one.

EPILOGUE
CRYSTAL

If the sound of Harmony's face breaking will haunt me for the rest of my life, then the crunch of Aaron's phone will stay with me as well.

It's an incredibly satisfying sound.

I will try to think about it whenever I start to shudder in the night. Likewise, I will try and focus on the friends and strangers I saved and not the ones I let die.

My parents and counselors gently push back on that idea whenever I say something to that effect, whenever I linger on my indecision, on what could have been.

Trevor doesn't walk up toward the road with us as we limp away from the wrecked van and the first ambulances start to arrive.

He's too weak, he says. He's lost too much blood. So he stays back, tells us to send a stretcher.

But when the stretcher arrives, they find that he's pulled Paul's body clear of the wreckage. They have to gently untangle the two boys as Trevor kisses Paul's wounds and whispers things that he'll never get to hear.

Gayle's heavy against me as we walk up the ditch, her steps unsure. At first I think she has a concussion, but then she tells me not to worry, that she's actually feeling better with every step. That she wants a Gatorade.

We step into the headlights; there are both ambulances and carloads of East Bay High kids stopped. From the side of the road, they all look down at us, and my vision wavers for a moment. It looks like the paramedics are also wearing tuxedos and prom dresses.

"How do I look?" I ask Gayle, angling my face to the light like I used to do when she'd check my makeup for me in the mornings.

"Gorgeous. Spectacular. A goddess. Would take a knife for you."

I don't see Gayle much, these days.

We're at different schools, studying different things, but occasionally she'll text. Both in the thread we share with Trevor and in the one that's just us.

As for Aaron . . .

We don't ever talk about him, but I imagine we all think about him.

I know enough about how he lives now, in his little room, to know that he's broken and alone.

I also know that, where he is, they don't allow phones or the internet, and I take some measure of comfort in that.

But I also know that some nights, when the insomnia I experienced in high school flares up, I search his name.

I thumb through the stubs of Wikipedia. The news items published when we were still in high school. The articles about the two fans on the other side of the country—one in Tacoma and one in Bakersfield—who didn't wait for the signal and went ahead with their attacks anyway.

The Speaker's social pages have been taken down. And the archived streams are no longer on YouTube. But if you dig deep enough, if you hunt through the comments sections, you can see that it's small, but it's there: his tiny cult following.

"Whatever happened to the Speaker?"

"Yeah. Used to love his stuff."

"The Speaker, that's my childhood."

"Still have all his poems at this link here."

"Fucking losers. Lot of dead kids, though, so cool."

"His streams! Those eyes! Have some Speakerfic here, if anyone's interested. [Fire emoji]."

"Anyone know if he can get mail? In prison?"

"Yes, address here."

"Cool. Thanks. Aaron Fortin did nothing wrong."

"Speeeeeaker for life."

"So proud of Aaron."

"Sorry, no spam, but if you like the Speaker, starting my own channel here."

"Nice."

"I'll check it out."

"Me too."

"Anyone know how he made his mask?"

"Pattern here."

"Don't just speak, act."

"Don't just speak, act."

That's usually when I log off and try to go back to sleep.

ACKNOWLEDGMENTS

East Bay, NY, is not a real town on Long Island. But it's not quite Kettle Springs, MO, from the Clown in a Cornfield books either.

Like the horror and violence in *Influencer*, East Bay's a little realer than fake and a little faker than real.

I grew up in a town just like it.

To try and reproduce where I went to high school felt natural because I have a lot in common with the characters. Don't worry. I'm a lot more Crystal than I am Aaron.

The book's suburban landscape wouldn't have been the same without growing up on Long Island, but *Influencer* itself wouldn't exist at all if not for the faith, help, and expertise of dozens of professionals.

So let's thank some of them.

First, Pete Harris at Temple Hill, a steadfast and encouraging creative partner. Boy did he have to hear a lot about serial killers and cults on this one. Also at Temple Hill big thanks to John Fischer, Alli Dyer, Marty Bowen and Wyck Godfrey.

Next Jessica Almon Galland at Audible who believed in this story enough to turn it into a big, splashy Audible Original, complete with knockout narration and a couple of well-placed gunshot sound effects. Thanks to Isabela Merced, Christopher Briney, and Brittany Pressley for their wonderful performances.

The edition you hold in your hands is slightly different than that original recording, expanded, fuller, more book-y, and that's thanks to editor Ardyce Alspach. Ardyce wanted this story to really *live* as a novel, just as much as I did, and I'm so grateful for her patience, insight, and guidance. Additional thanks to the team at Union Square including Tracey Keevan, Lisa Forde, Liam Donnelly, Renee Yewdaev, Alison Skrabek, and Marinda Valenti.

A book's first impression is its cover, and Tomasz Majewski's art reaches out from the shelf to deliver a stranglehold . . . for which I'm incredibly grateful.

Stephen Graham Jones, Darcy Coates, and Jonathan Maberry: it's a huge ask, an investment of time, expertise, and good will, to blurb a book. I am so thankful for your kindness, each of you are inspirations to me and it's an honor.

Big thanks to the unflappable Alec Shane, who's never annoyed because I send him too many texts and emails. Also to Adam Goldworm at Aperture Entertainment.

Love and gratitude to my family who, yes, have read the opening chapter of this book and still talk to me.

And last, but most important: thank *you*. I pinch myself every day, amazed I'm able to make a living telling these kinds of stories. And that's all because folks have been kind enough to support the books, tell their friends about them, and review them online. To the communities on BookTok, Bookstagram, and Facebook (looking at you, Books of Horror), THANK YOU. But even if you don't belong to a wider reader community, you can help spread the word about the book. Please take a moment to review on your retailer website of choice. It helps out so much.

Love and appreciation,
Adam Cesare

ABOUT THE AUTHOR

Adam Cesare is the author of the Bram Stoker Award–winning Clown in a Cornfield series, the graphic novel *Dead Mall*, and several other novels and novellas, including the cult hits *Video Night* and *The Con Season*. An avid fan of horror cinema, you can watch him talk about movies on YouTube, TikTok, X (formerly Twitter), and the rest of his socials.

If you or someone you know is struggling with bullying, abuse, self-harm, or emotional distress, call, text, or chat 988 to reach the Suicide and Crisis Lifeline 24 hours a day, 7 days a week. For more information, visit their website at 988lifeline.org.